The Man on a Donkey, Part 1
A Chronicle

H. F. M. PRESCOTT

Introduction by Jim Campbell

LOYOLA CLASSICS

CHICAGO

LOYOLAPRESS.
A JESUIT MINISTRY
3441 N. ASHLAND AVENUE
CHICAGO, ILLINOIS 60657
(800) 621-1008
WWW.LOYOLAPRESS.ORG

Originally published in 1952 by Eyre & Spottiswoode, London. The first U.S.
edition was published in 1952 by the Macmillan Company, New York.

*Picture credit: The Forty Martyrs of England and Wales (colour litho), Pollen (nee
Baring), Daphne (1904-86) (after) / His Grace The Duke of Norfolk, Arundel Castle, /
The Bridgeman Art Library*
Series art direction: Adam Moroschan
Series design: Adam Moroschan and Erin VanWerden
Cover design: Maggie Hong
Interior design: Erin VanWerden

Library of Congress Cataloging-in-Publication Data
Prescott, H. F. M. (Hilda Frances Margaret), 1896–1972.
The man on a donkey : a chronicle / H. F. M. Prescott.
    p. cm. — (Loyola classics)
  Originally published: New York : Macmillan, 1952. With new introd. and study
questions.
  ISBN-13: 978-0-8294-2639-7
  ISBN-10: 0-8294-2639-6
  ISBN-13: 978-0-8294-2731-8
  ISBN-10: 0-8294-2731-7
  1. Aske, Robert, d. 1537—Fiction. 2. Great Britain—History—Henry VIII,
1509-1547—Fiction. 3. Yorkshire (England)—Fiction. 4. Catholics—Fiction.
5. Christian fiction. I. Title.
  PR6031.R38M36 2008
  823'.912—dc22

                                                        2008006548

Printed in the United States of America
08 09 10 11 12 13 Bang 10 9 8 7 6 5 4 3 2 1

The Man on a Donkey, Part 1

Books in the Loyola Classics Series

Catholics by Brian Moore

Cosmas or the Love of God by Pierre de Calan

Dear James by Jon Hassler

The Devil's Advocate by Morris West

Do Black Patent Leather Shoes Really Reflect Up?
by John R. Powers

The Edge of Sadness by Edwin O'Connor

Five for Sorrow, Ten for Joy by Rumer Godden

Helena by Evelyn Waugh

In This House of Brede by Rumer Godden

The Keys of the Kingdom by A. J. Cronin

The Last Catholic in America by John R. Powers

The Man on a Donkey, Part 1 by H. F. M. Prescott

The Man on a Donkey, Part 2 by H. F. M. Prescott

Mr. Blue by Myles Connolly

North of Hope by Jon Hassler

Saint Francis by Nikos Kazantzakis

The Silver Chalice by Thomas Costain

Son of Dust by H. F. M. Prescott

Things As They Are by Paul Horgan

The Unoriginal Sinner and the Ice-Cream God
by John R. Powers

Vipers' Tangle by François Mauriac

Contents

Introduction by Jim Campbell   vii

Author's Note   4
The Beginning and the End   5
Christabel Cowper, Prioress   13
Now the Chronicle Begins   30
Now the Chronicle Is Broken to Speak of:
    Thomas, Lord Darcy   64
    Julian Savage, Gentlewoman   108
    Robert Aske, Squire   140
    Gilbert Dawe, Priest   203

Plan of Marrick Priory   504
Historical Note   506
Questions for Reflection and Discussion   510
About the Author   516

Introduction

Jim Campbell

We have an ongoing fascination with the story of the Tudor dynasty (1485–1603). The reign of Henry VIII (1509–1547) is filled with spectacle, intrigue, and tensions that led to the separation of the Church of England from Rome. Elizabeth I (1558–1603) faced down her enemies internally and externally, most spectacularly the Spanish Armada in 1588. During the reign of the Tudors, England began to move onto the world stage, setting the foundations that would lead to English dominance at sea for over two hundred years.

In the twentieth century, there were some fifty-five movie and television productions dealing with the coming to power of the Tudor dynasty and their colorful careers. Most productions dealt with the reigns of Henry VIII and his daughter Elizabeth I. The larger-than-life character of King Henry VIII has been played by actors of the caliber of Charles Laughton, Richard Burton, Keith Michell, and Robert Shaw. As we moved into the twenty-first century, the fascination continued with a ten-part cable production of the history of the escapades of Henry VIII and a major movie about his relationship with Anne Boleyn. The colorful life of Henry VIII—his six wives, his spectacular divorces, his break with the Catholic Church—naturally attracts attention. Henry VIII's reign includes the confrontations with Thomas More and Bishop John Fisher, who in conscience could not follow Henry's plans for the future of the Church and lost their heads as a result.

Who Were the Tudors?

The Tudor dynasty came into power at the Battle of Bosworth Field in 1485. This was the culmination of the Wars of the Roses, the fratricidal conflict between the noble Houses of York (the white rose) and Lancaster (the red rose). Richard III, the last York king, was killed on the battlefield, leaving Henry Tudor, the last living man representing the Lancaster claim to the throne, the "last man standing." Henry was crowned as Henry VII. To heal the breach between the Lancaster family and that of York, Henry married Richard III's niece, Elizabeth of York. She was the daughter of King Edward IV of York (1461–1470, 1471–1483). As far as we can tell, the marriage was a happy one. Henry and Elizabeth had seven children, four of whom survived childhood. Their oldest son, Arthur, the unhealthy heir apparent, was married to Katherine of Aragon, the young daughter of Ferdinand and Isabella of Spain, in 1501. About six months later, in April 1502, Arthur died, possibly of tuberculosis or "sweating sickness."

Not wanting to lose the enormous dowry that came with Katherine, Henry VII proposed that Katherine marry his second son, Henry. Before the marriage could take place, an impediment in the Church's canon law had to be dealt with. This impediment was based on two verses in the Book of Leviticus. ("You shall not have intercourse with your brother's wife, for that would be a disgrace to your brother." [18:16] "If a man marries his brother's wife and thus disgraces his brother, they shall be childless because of this incest." [20:21]) Based on these verses, canon law at the time declared that Henry was forbidden to marry his brother's widow. Katherine maintained that since Arthur was so ill their marriage was never consummated. A dispensation was petitioned for and received from Rome allowing the marriage to go forward. After the death of Henry VII, the seventeen-year-old Henry VIII married Katherine, who was five years older than he, in 1509.

At first the marriage between Henry and Katherine seemed to go well. Their first child, a daughter, was stillborn. The second child, a boy named Henry, was born in 1511 and died two months after birth. In the following years, Katherine suffered at least two more failed pregnancies. Only Mary, a daughter born in 1516, survived. Though Henry's personal hold on the throne was strong, he knew that without a strong male heir to follow him the country could plunge back into civil war. By 1526, Katherine was in her forties, and it was apparent that she would not produce a male heir. Henry petitioned Rome for an annulment of his marriage to Katherine so he could marry a younger woman who could give him a son.

Cardinal Wolsey, Archbishop of York and Henry's Lord Chancellor, negotiated with Rome in seeking an annulment.

When Pope Clement VII ultimately refused Henry's request, Henry had Cardinal Wolsey arrested for treason in October 1529. Wolsey was stripped of his wealth. Henry noticed that much of Wolsey's wealth came from twenty-eight small monasteries Wolsey had shut down. Wolsey had used some of the profits to establish schools, but he had also kept a great deal of the wealth for his personal use.

By 1533, Anne Boleyn, Henry's mistress at that time, had become pregnant. This forced Henry to act. He secretly married Anne Boleyn in January 1533 without the annulment that he now believed he did not need. In May 1533, Archbishop of Canterbury Thomas Cranmer declared Henry's marriage to Katherine of Aragon invalid. In June 1533, the English Parliament declared papal authority in England no longer existed. Anne of Boleyn, much to her chagrin, gave birth to a daughter who would eventually become Queen Elizabeth I. She did not bear the son that Henry so desperately wanted.

In 1534, the English Parliament passed a number of acts including the Act of Supremacy, declaring that the king was "the only supreme head of the Church of England," and the Treasons Act, which made it high treason, punishable by death, to refuse to acknowledge the king as such. Because of their refusal to acknowledge Henry VIII as supreme head of the Church of England and recognize Anne Boleyn as rightful Queen of England, Thomas More and Bishop John Fisher lost their heads in 1535. In 1536, Katherine of Aragon, exiled by Henry from any contact with the court, died.

The Man on a Donkey: Part 1

The lives and fortunes under Henry's rule are the subjects of H. F. M. Prescott's *The Man on a Donkey*. Prescott covers the years between 1495–1537, not only telling the story of Henry and his personal and social ambitions but also providing a well-rounded picture of the society he changed. She tells the story of the uprising in Northern England known as the Pilgrimage of Grace. The Pilgrimage of Grace was in response to Henry's decision to close the monasteries and religious houses in England and loot them of their accumulated wealth.

As in the original edition of the novel, the story of *The Man on a Donkey* is told in two volumes in this Loyola Classics edition. In the first volume, Prescott slowly introduces us to this world of the Tudors. She does so by means of a chronicle centering on the lives of five people who are shaken by the events of the time.

Christabel Cowper is prioress of Marrick Priory, a small Benedictine nunnery. We are introduced to Christabel at the beginning of the book as she is leaving the priory. Henry VIII has dissolved the priory and pensioned off the nuns. Christabel is bitter, believing she has been betrayed by God in losing her priory. Much of the first volume tells her story from novice to prioress and her efficient management of the priory.

Note: Marrick Priory was an actual nunnery where Christabel Cowper was prioress. Upon closure of the priory, she received a pension of 100 shillings a year which was paid until 1562, the year she probably died.

Thomas, Lord Darcy, is an elderly Lord who has a high position in Henry's court. From his perspective, we see the changes taking place in Henry's attitude towards Katherine of Aragon and the movement toward annulment. Lord Darcy is uncomfortable with these changes. The centralization of power in the person of the king especially makes him nervous. In a conversation with his son George, Darcy is upset because his son seems to be living in a different world than the one he grew up in.

> "Now by God's Death, George," Darcy interrupted him, "I wonder sometimes that you are son of mine. My father taught me as I have taught you, that a man that is a lord stands by his friends and his men through flood and fire."
>
> "And not by his Prince?"
>
> Darcy turned and looked at him, and answered after a while in a different voice, thoughtfully.
>
> "You and some others have a new idea of a Prince. You think he must have his way, whatsoever it be, with the law or maugre [in spite of] the law. That was not the way of it in England when I was a lad."
>
> "And a right merry England you made of it with wars and bickerings, and making and unmaking of kings." George got up and went over to the door and wrenched it open.
>
> "Give you good night, Sir," said he, and went out.

Julian Savage, gentlewoman, is the plain sister of a beautiful woman. She and her sister Margaret are the illegitimate daughters of the Duke of Buckingham. After the death of the duke, they are shuffled about by his family. Margaret, with her beauty and captivating ways, moves more easily in the world of men. Julian tags along having no other place to go. She is a pious girl whose life is improved when by chance she is found by Robert Aske, a young lawyer, who is the first person to treat her decently. As a result of his kindness, Julian falls deeply in love with Robert. Robert does not return her affection but continues to treat her with sympathetic kindness. Julian is finally sent to Marrick Priory as a novice. Julian has difficulty with the spirituality of the age, especially in the graphic descriptions of Jesus' suffering for us. How could a God who is merciful let his own Son suffer so?

Robert Aske, squire, is a young lawyer who is making his way in London. He befriends Julian Savage with an act of kindness, and supports her as she tries to find her way. Robert is busy learning the law, but is troubled by the direction the king is taking the Church and Christian life. In 1534, adult men are required to take the oath to uphold the king's daughter Elizabeth as his lawful heir, born of a lawful marriage. This means that Henry's first marriage was no marriage at all, and the pope's dispensation for marriage was nothing. Robert Aske takes the oath as required, but is troubled. After a long discussion of the issue with a friend, Robert Aske brings the discussion to an end.

> He was silent for a minute and then said, as if he were in a hurry to have it spoken before they stepped into the wherry [rowboat], "Sir Thomas More and the Bishop of Rochester lie this day in the Tower. Yet is their conscience clean."

Robert Aske's troubled conscience will lead him to fateful decisions in response to Henry's move to shutter the monasteries and priories, as will be seen in Part 2.

Gilbert Dawe is a seriously troubled priest who is assigned to be chaplain at Marrick Priory. He has broken his vow of celibacy in a long-term relationship with a local woman. This relationship has resulted in the birth of four children. The first three died, as did their mother. The affair troubles Gilbert because of his inability to keep his vow of chastity. Gilbert is attracted to the new ideas bubbling up during this time of Reformation. Reading the Bible in English and questioning the mores of the Church and the validity of the sacraments makes him even more uncomfortable in his duties.

When Gilbert learns that his son is not living in good circumstances, he brings the boy to Marrick to live with him. His actions bring him little joy, as the boy, who is mute, is a daily reminder of Gilbert's failings.

The boy, Wat, becomes the only real friend to Malle, a woman who was brought to Marrick and survives by doing menial tasks for the Priory. Malle is a visionary sharing what she sees with Wat. In her visions we see the inner meaning of the historical events beginning to emerge.

In *The Man on a Donkey, Part 1*, the stage is set for the great happenings in *Part 2*. Henry has his wish: by 1536 he is permanently relieved of Katherine. Anne Boleyn discovers the cost of her ambition. Now the head of the Church of England, Henry will bring to bear the power of the state to squeeze the Church for all that it is worth.

James Campbell is a veteran religious educator and author. He is the coauthor of the Finding God *religious education program, published by Loyola Press, and the general editor of the Harper's New American Bible Study Program. He has three post-graduate degrees, including master's degrees in theology and history, and a doctorate in Ministry in Christian Education from the Aquinas Institute of Theology, St. Louis. He is the staff theologian at Loyola Press.*

The Man on a Donkey, Part 1

A Chronicle

To Dorothy Mack
because it is her book

Author's Note

The book is cast in the form of a chronicle. This form, which requires space to develop itself, has been used in an attempt to introduce the reader into a world, rather than at first to present him with a narrative. In that world he must for a while move like a stranger, as in real life picking up, from seemingly trifling episodes, understanding of those about him, and learning to know them without knowing that he learns. Only later, when the characters should by this means have become familiar, does the theme of the whole book emerge, as the different stories which it contains run together and are swallowed up in the tragic history of the Pilgrimage of Grace. And throughout, over against the world of sixteenth-century England, is set that other world, whose light is focused, as through a burning glass, in the half-crazy mind of Malle, the serving woman, and in the three cycles of her visions is brought to bear successively upon the stories of the chief characters of the chronicle.

The Beginning and the End

Sir John Uvedale had business at Coverham Abbey in Wensleydale, lately suppressed, so he sent his people on before him to Marrick, to make ready for him, and to take over possession of the Priory of St. Andrew from the nuns, who should all be gone by noon or thereabouts. Sir John's steward had been there for a week already, making sure that the ladies carried away nothing but what was their own, and having the best of the silver and gold ornaments of the church packed up in canvas, then in barrels, ready to be sent to the King. The lesser stuff was pushed, all anyhow, into big wicker baskets; since it would be melted down, scratches and dints did not matter.

Sir John's people left Coverham before it was daylight, because the November days were short. They had reached the top and were going down toward Marrick when the sun looked over the edge of the fells in a flare of wintry white gold. It was about ten o'clock in the morning that they came down into Swaledale and through the meadows toward Marrick stepping-stones; the priory stood opposite them across the river, at the top of a pleasant sloping meadow whose lower edge thrust away the quick running Swale in a great sickle-shaped curve. The cluster of buildings and the tall tower of the church took the sunshine of a morning mild and sweet as spring. Behind the priory, with hardly more than the width of a cart way between, the dale side went up steeply, covered for the most part with ash, beech, and oak; the mossed trunks of the trees showed sharply green in the open sunlit woods. There was one piece of hillside just behind the priory where there were no trees, but only turf nibbled close by the nuns' neat black-stockinged Swaledale sheep; in the summertime the ladies had used sometimes to sit here with their spinning and embroidery, and here in spring the priory washing was always spread out; now, on this winter morning, the slope was empty.

They crossed the stream, climbed the meadow by the cart track, and turned the corner of the long priory wall. Sir John's steward stood in the sunshine that struck through the gatehouse arch; he swung a big key from his finger—the key of the priory gate, which the prioress herself had a moment ago put into his hand.

And now he watched the prioress and the last two of the ladies who went with her, and a couple of servants, as they rode alongside the churchyard on their way to Richmond and into the world. Of the three middle-aged women, one, plump and plain, was crying helplessly and without concealment; she kept her face turned to look back on the priory, for all that her tears drowned the sight of it. Another, a handsome woman yet, who had flashed her dark eyes at the steward, glanced once over her shoulder; her mouth shook, but she tossed her head and rode on.

The prioress herself did not look back, nor was her face in any way discomposed. Down at the core of her heart she was angry, though not with the King for turning away all the monks and nuns in England and taking the abbeys into his hand—surely he had a right to them if any had. She was not indeed angry with any man at all, but with God, who had tricked her into thirty years of a nun's life, had suffered her to be prioress, and to rule, and now had struck power out of her hand.

But that anger lay beneath, so that she did not even know it was there. Her mind was set on the future as she considered and tried to estimate what her position would be in the house of her married sister. She would have her pension—but suppose it were not paid regularly—? On what foothold could she stand so as to make her will felt? Her thoughts were so closely engaged that she did not notice when they crossed the muddy lane which was the boundary of the priory lands, and so left Marrick quite behind.

The steward stood where he was until the ladies were out of sight. Now, for the first time for close on four hundred years, there were no nuns at Marrick. But he was not thinking of that as he turned back into the gate. Before Sir John arrived there was much to be done; he gave his orders curtly, and even before dinner was ready the servants were all about the place, sweeping up stale rushes, scrubbing, unpacking trussing beds and coffers that they had brought on the baggage animals, shaking out hangings, lighting fires.

Most of Sir John's men were of the new persuasion, and glad to see the houses of religion pulled down. One or two of them opened the aumbry in the cloister, and there came upon a few books which the ladies had left behind. They found great cause for satisfaction, as for laughter, in tearing out the pages of these books and scattering them in the cloister garth; one of the books was very old and beautiful, gay with colors and sumptuous with plumped-up burnished gold; another had initial letters of a dusky red like drying blood; when the pages were strewn about the garth it looked as if flowers were blooming in November.

Two only, out of those who had come this morning from Coverham, took no part at all in this business of setting the house to rights for its new owner. One of these was Sir John's old priest, the other was the woman Malle, who was the priest's servant now, and had therefore, with him, so strangely come back to Marrick.

The old man sat down on the horse-block for some time in the sun, then wandered out and down to the river, to pace the level bank there just below the stepping-stones, telling his beads, and letting the unceasing hushing of the water fill his mind with peace. There was nothing for him to do but wait. His stuff was among the rest that had been unloaded in the great court of the priory, but he knew that the steward would have no time to think of sending it to the parsonage till all was ready for Sir John's coming.

Even before he came down to the river, Malle left him, to drift about looking here and there, more as if she were searching for something or someone than merely revisiting places that had once been familiar. After going to the edge of the woods and staring up over the little wooden gate at the foot of the nuns' steps, she came back into the kitchen, then into the great court and climbed the outside stair that led up to the door of what had been the prioress's chamber. It was quite empty now; all the goods of Christabel Cowper, last prioress of Marrick, had been taken away; there were no rushes on the floor nor wainscot on the walls; only cobwebs, and the marks where the wainscot had been. Over the hearth the old painted letters, which had been hidden by a small but specially fine piece of arras, showed once more—I.H.S. Malle could not read but she knew that the symbols meant, somehow, God, so she curtseyed and crossed herself.

From the prioress's chamber she wandered over to the guest-house and stood inside the door of the upper chamber, just where she had stood when my Lord Darcy had sat on the bed, with his hands on the cross of his walking staff, questioning about her visions. She did not remember him nor his questions because something in her that had been a restlessness was strengthening into belief; she began to know that if now she sought, she would find.

So she went quickly once more across the great court and into the cloister. The crumpled pages of the books were sidling about the grass, the flower beds, and the cloister walks as a light fresh wind shifted them. She stooped to pick up some that moved just before her, because they were pretty to look at; from between two of the red-lettered pages a pressed flower fell, the bell of a wild foxglove, pale purple, frail, and half transparent; she did not know that Julian Savage had put it there one day, because Robert Aske had worn it on his finger, like the finger-tip of a glove, while he talked to her. She had put it there for a charm to shield him from hurt.

Two men coming down the day-stairs shouted at Malle; they knew that she was at least three parts fool, and they laughed loudly as she bolted out of the cloister and into the great court again. She had meant to go into the church, but, since she did not dare until the two men had gone away again, she began peeping into the stables on the opposite side of the great court. In them some of the beasts stood, patient and idle, only their mouths working; there were empty stalls too, for some had been led out to the fields; this morning the priory servants had each done as seemed best to himself now the bailiff was gone already, and the prioress to go by noon.

After the stables she looked into the dove house; the sleepy crooning there had a summer sound, which made it seem that time had turned back. She went next into the guesthouse stable. Leaning in one corner among some pea-sticks was the fishing rod that Master Aske had put there on the afternoon when Malle had sat here peeling rushes for lights, while the rain poured down outside. She did not now think of Master Aske, nor of that day, nor of any time since, because all the sorrows of the world were clean washed from her mind by the shining certainty that was growing in it.

So she would wait no longer for the men, but went back, hurrying, into the cloister, and so into the nuns' church.

But he was not in the nuns' church. The door in the wall that separated the nuns from the parish church was open today; so she went through. Here Gilbert Dawe had told her that he was dead, and now lived, and was alive forevermore. But he was not in the parish church either.

She did not know where else to look, and it was without thought or intention that she came to the frater and opened the door; there was no supposing that he would have come to that room. No one ever used it except at great feasts like Christmas, since for a long time the nuns had eaten by messes, each mess in its own chamber.

Yet today the frater had been used. Today, instead of eating in their chambers, all stripped of furnishing, the ladies had breakfasted together, according to the ancient Rule of their order, but hastily and in confusion of mind. The disarray of that hurried meal lay upon the table, and the sun, shining through the painted glass of the windows in the south wall, spilled faint flakes of color, rose, green, gold, upon the white board-cloth.

There were eleven wooden trenchers set on the table, with crumbled bread and bits of eggshell on them. There were eleven horn drinking pots too, and several big platters, all empty, except that there was upon one a piece of broiled fish, and on the other half a honeycomb.

The chronicle is mainly of five: of Christabel Cowper, prioress; Thomas, Lord Darcy; Julian Savage, gentlewoman; Robert Aske, squire; Gilbert Dawe, priest.

There are besides, the King and three who were his Queens, and many others, men and women, gentle and simple, good and bad, false and true, who served God or their own ends, who made prosperous voyage or came to shipwreck.

There is also Malle, the serving woman.

Elevaverunt Flumina Fluctos Suos: A Vocibus Aquarum Multarum. Mirabiles Elationes Maris: Mirabilis in Altis Dominus.

> *The floods arise, O Lord: The floods lift up their noise,*
> *The floods lift up their waves.*
> *The waves of the sea are mighty and rage horribly: but yet*
> *The Lord that dwelleth on high is mightier.*

Christabel Cowper, Prioress

She was born in 1495 at Richmond in Yorkshire. Her father's house stood looking up at the barbican, and at the proud head of the great keep above the barbican, across the wide and steep square. Her father's father had built the house of stone, very solid: very small as his son came to think it. But the warehouse behind where the wool was kept, was large; for that, to Christabel's grandfather's mind, was far more important than the place where he ate and slept.

Christabel's father, Andrew Cowper, was not so good a man of business as old Andrew; but then, he had a better start, for when the old man died there was gold money, mostly in coin of Flanders and Spain, in leather bags, hidden in the recess behind the red and white curtains of the great bed. Only Christabel's father, as well as old Andrew, knew the secret of that hiding place, and he was not told of it till he was a grown man of twenty-five, married, and with four children of his own.

As well as the hidden gold there were silver gilt cups on the livery cupboard in the great chamber downstairs, and in the chest at the foot of the old man's bed there were six bags of silver, and a standing cup made of a polished coker-nut enclosed in roped bands of silver gilt, which he drank out of during all the Christmas feast, and at Easter, Whitsun, and upon St. Andrew's Day. The name of the great cup was Edward.

When old Andrew knew that he was dying he sent for one of the Grey Friars, an old man too. They had birds'-nested and played at marbles together in the old days, and snowballed in the square below the window that very day that the snowy field of Towton was dabbled red with blood.

Andrew Cowper told Brother William that he wanted him to make a will, so the other old man sat down by the fire, and taking on his knee one of the square scrubbed chopping boards from the kitchen, spread his parchment on it and wrote down what he was told.

It took long to do, for it was a stormy day in November and the wind brought the smoke swirling out from the chimney till it filled the room and the air was blue; the smoke caught old Andrew's chest, and sent him off into long fits of coughing that left him panting and speechless.

The beginning of the will was all in Latin, for it was about the money that was to be spent on the old man's obit, and on a mass every year on St. Andrew's Day, and on wax candles for the rood-loft in the friars' church, and on a cow to give milk to the poor of Richmond; and besides the money for these pious purposes old Cowper's best velvet gown was to be given to the friars to make a cope.

After these things they came to the rest of the old man's clothes, and the beds, and kitchen pots and pans, the hangings, a golden chain, silver spoons, and all the household stuff that was to go to son Andrew and his two brothers and sisters, and to son Andrew's sons and daughters. Here Brother William gave up the Latin, fetched a deep sigh, relaxed his toes which had been crimped upward with the effort—for his Latin was rusty—and wrote the rest in English.

Andrew got most, which was natural, for he was to be a merchant and freeman of Richmond as his father had been. But the other two sons had money, or a bit of land here and there which old Cowper had bought, and the daughters had money too, though much less than the men, and enough to buy themselves a mourning gown each. Andrew's sons came off almost as well as their uncles, but his daughters, grown women now except for Christabel, had no more than a silver spoon of the apostles each. Except, again, for Christabel; to her the old man left his great cup Edward—the cup made out of a nut.

There was a great quarrel over that when the old man was dead and buried. But Christabel got the cup and held it, while the quarrel raged, and her two married sisters, and the one not yet married, and her brothers all said what they thought of a bequest so outrageous. They had known, they said, that Christabel was the favorite of their grandfather, but their father, or their mother, or the old friar should not have permitted him to do anything so foolish and unfair. The eldest married sister, who was of an excitable disposition, was even heard to murmur something about sorcery, though when pressed she only mumbled, "Well, how could he have done it else? No, I don't say it was—but—" They all agreed however that it was as absurd as it was wrong of the old man, knowing quite well that Christabel was to be a nun, to leave her the cup. What did nuns want with a coker-nut cup which had come from Flanders, and was a rarity, and very costly, and his favorite cup into the bargain?

Christabel was twelve at the time, a square-built, solemn girl. She sat clutching the cup, pressing it into her lap, really afraid sometimes that they would try to wrench it out of her hands. If they had she would have struggled with them, but they kept to words, and with words she met them. It was hers by will, she told them, and why should not a nun have a cup, and the old man had always promised it to her (which was not true, for the gift had surprised her very much), and she could not see that being the youngest made her any worse than the rest of them, and—going back again to the beginning—it was hers by her grandfather's will.

She was only a child, but while they lost their tempers she kept hers and in the long run she kept the cup. What was more, being puffed up by her success, she asked to have it to drink out of the very next Sunday, being the Feast of St. Andrew, as her grandfather had done. Her mother refused, and was so put out by the request that she beat Christabel handsomely, and recommended her to learn to be of a meek stomach or she'd come to ill someday.

Her father, however, only laughed when he heard of it, and said she'd be prioress at Marrick before she'd done. He was a very easygoing man, little like his father except in his size and big bones. He dressed always like a gentleman, everything not only very trim and good but also gay. Quite a lot of the gold from behind the tester bed was spent on a gold belt buckle, and a brooch for his cap which had a naked woman in a circle of leaves, holding a pearl in her hand. Perhaps it was right that he should dress so much more fine than his father, seeing that his wife's mother was a second cousin of my Lord of Westmorland. Certainly Christabel thought it was right; she liked to watch him amongst the other merchants of Richmond; he looked well, he made a good show, though she knew inwardly even at this early age that he was not the man his father had been, and worried herself sometimes lest he should make some disastrous mistake that would lose money, and besides that make them all look fools before the more provident merchants of Richmond. She tried once to tell her mother of her anxiety, but only got her ears boxed for speaking so undutifully of her father.

As time went on Christabel thought less of her father, who was kind and careless, with now and again a fit of temper when he had drunk too much. And at the same time she grew into a feeling of kinship with her mother. Christabel believed that though her mother had boxed her ears, yet she also watched Andrew Cowper with anxiety and irritation. Christabel's eyes would go from one to another at table, reading or guessing by the signs in her mother's hard, pale face, at the hidden but embittered disagreement between them when Andrew came in with a new jewel or talked large before friends of the arras he would buy for the ball. Christabel approved of her mother, though she got no tenderness, and indeed, barely kindness, from her. Only one thing she must disapprove of—"If I'd come of such a house," she decided when she was not quite thirteen years old, "I'd not have married so low." She felt, because she had her mother's blood in her, that she could despise her father. And always a thought rankled—"He has no right to waste that which my grandfather had laid up, which is for us."

Christabel had not been able to despise her grandfather, in spite of his plain merchant blood, even when she began to grow up and count these things as important. When very small she had been his pet, to be carried round Richmond, tossed up on his shoulder, and fed with cakes, wafers, or strawberries. When she was a little bigger than that she would trail after him, stumping along on sturdy fat legs, hanging on to the long metal-studded tongue of his belt, or tugging at his gown as she grew tired, to ask him for a pick-a-back.

But as she grew older Andrew had occasion more than once to box her ears for impudence, and once he took his stick to her and beat her. She never forgot that, and always would behave herself very meekly while he was in the house, but she never loved him after, nor went willingly near him; and when they told her that he had left her his great cup Edward, privately, deep down in her own mind, she thought the less of him, as if it had been a weakness in him not to know that she did not love him.

It was when she was eleven that her elders told her that she was to be a nun, and Christabel, having been taken a little while before by her mother to her eldest sister's second lying-in, decided that it was on the whole better to be a nun than a married woman, even though the clothes nuns wore were not near so fine as her sister's gray velvet nightgown with the white fur.

However, she had noticed that the prioress of Nun-Appleton, who was the sister of Christabel's sister's husband, and who came to the christening, wore a silk, and not a linen, veil, and that her girdle was of silk too, and that the skirt of her habit opened up at the front over a damask petticoat which, though black, was very rich. As she rode home pillion behind her mother, with her cheek jolting against Elizabeth Cowper's shoulder blades, she announced that when she was a nun she would wear a silk veil, and a silk girdle, and a gold pin; she threw that in as an extra flourish. Her mother, who had been too busy to notice what the lady prioress wore, and who was now running over in her mind all the things which she would send from Richmond for the new baby, only said: "That you will not. For nuns must not wear such things."

"I shall. I shall. I shall," Christabel whispered, and because she could not stamp her foot she thumped Gray Hodson's flank with one heel. Her mother did not hear; Gray Hodson was old and too staid to show resentment; and reflecting afterward Christabel came to the conclusion that it was well her declaration had gone unnoticed. "I shall not tell them what I shall do," she thought. "But when they have made me a nun I shall do it. *And* I shall drink from the coker-nut cup whenever I please."

A year after old Andrew Cowper's death Christabel's father and mother took her to Marrick, where she was to be a nun. It was more than ten miles up the dale, and to reach it you had to leave Swaleside and go up and over the fells. That, since they would take a mule laden with all Christabel's stuff, meant a whole day's ride, and an early start.

The night before they set out Christabel was sent to bed specially early, and not to her own bed in the little attic but to her parents' bed in the great chamber. Her mother came and fussed about the room a bit while Christabel undressed, and even when she had slipped into bed and lay, naked as a fish, between the sheets. It was as if Mistress Elizabeth Cowper felt that she had forgotten something, or left something undone—"and yet that," thought Christabel, listening to her movements, "is not possible." She knew that her mother was a most methodical person and that everything was sure to be completely ready for tomorrow.

Dame Elizabeth stood for a moment at the door, looking across the thin slit of light that came between the shutters, to the blank curtains of the bed in the dusky corner of the room. Not a sound nor stir of movement came from the child behind them.

"Go to sleep."

"Yes, madame."

"We shall start at sunrise."

"Yes, madame."

Mistress Elizabeth lifted the latch, and Christabel held her breath, waiting for the sound of the door closing which would tell her that she was alone. But her mother still lingered.

"You must be a good girl and heed what you're told."

"Yes, madame."

She heard her mother sigh sharply, as if with exasperation.

"Well," said Elizabeth Cowper rather loudly, but more to herself than to Christabel. "Well. It's the best for you. I've done what I can for you all. Go to sleep." The door shut sharply even before Christabel had time to reply "Yes, madame."

So she waited a little, listening to her mother's deliberate, heavy tread. A stair creaked, that was the sixth one down; another creaked with quite a different note, that was the last but one; then she heard the parlor door shut. She waited till she had counted over her fingers twice, then she pulled her feet from under the sheet and the green counterpane, and slid out of bed. But still she stood listening.

There was no sound in the house. From the yard outside came a steady burr, which she knew for the noise of Marget's wheel. Old Marget always sat out in the yard spinning on warm evenings, following the sun from the edge of the wall to the mounting block, then to the hayloft steps, and last of all, when the sunshine was no more than a narrow wedge, to the corner by the pigsties.

Christabel slunk across the room meaning to ease up the latch of the shutters and look down on Marget, but thought better of it, because Marget might look up. A knife blade of sunshine still slit through the dusk from the joint in the shutters. She turned about in it, like a joint on a spit, twitching her shoulders, and enjoying the delicate warmth on her naked back. Then, with a sudden skip, she made for the bundles that lay alongside the wall at the far side of the room. Her purpose in stealing out of bed had not been any thought of taking a last look at the yard, the wool-store, or Marget, but to feel and finger and prod the bundles.

The biggest of them was bulgy and soft, and swelled up between the cords that bound it; that was the feather bed and the fustian blankets, and the two pairs of sheets. The second was not so billowy, but it was heavier and had a hard core to it, for in between the bolster and pillow there was a little square chest of ashwood that held, wrapped up in a tester of painted cloth for the bed, a silver spoon and two candlesticks, two pewter plates, and a little brass pot. The two other bundles were quite small. In one was a pair of tongs, a frying pan, and a skillet. In the other, which was the smallest of all, were her three new shifts, two pairs of shoes, and the habit of a novice of the Order of St. Benedict—white woolen gown, white linen coif and veil, with enough woolen cloth to make hosen for the next two years, and the great cup Edward—all these things packed up in a coverlet of striped say, red, white, and green.

Christabel hung over the bundles, wriggling her fingers into the folds in the hope of touching what was inside, poking them, thumping them gently with her fist, feeling them softly all over. She did not envy her eldest sister, even though she had married a knight, and he was just now building a new house which would have glass in all the windows of the hall, and of the summer and winter parlors—and carved wainscot too. If Christabel could have had the house without the husband it would have been different. But as that couldn't be, she thought, "This is better. He tore Meg's best sheets tumbling into bed drunk with his boots on. No one can tear my sheets. They're mine."

She punched the big bundle again, possessively and defiantly, and then, hearing a door open downstairs, scuttled across the room and dived between the curtains of the bed.

Next morning the dale was still full of mist when they turned up the road which led to the fells, but here the sun was warm on their backs, the larks were up, and the sky blue without a cloud. Their shadows, jerking along the road before them, were absurd pointed shapes; the two big bundles corded on the mule's pack-saddle showed in the dust like shadows of another and huger pair of ears. Christabel, riding pillion behind her mother, kept looking back—not to see the shadows, nor to see the last of Richmond, where the smoke was going up as the mist cleared, thin and steady and blue as hyacinths, against the woods beyond the town; but to see her goods coming safely after her.

There were, as well as the mule laden with her gear, two others going light. On the way home all three would be almost hidden below the great sarplers of wool, for Christabel's father would be buying wool up and down the dale—wool from the manor and priory at Marrick, wool from the little house of Cistercian nuns a mile down the river, and from the manor at Grinton and the manor at Marske. The two seven-pound leaden wool-weights, bearing the King's leopards and lilies and joined by a strap like a stirrup leather, hung down on either side of his horse in front of the saddle.

They stopped about noon to dine, and sat down on a bank beside the road. The turf was short, crisp, and wiry, and med-dled with bright pink thyme and yellow crow's-foot. A shepherd came near as they sat eating, and crossed the road, his flock going before him. They were fresh from the shearing, very trim in their black and white, small black faces, neat black stockings, and some spotted with black; when the sun shone through their ears it made them rose-red. On the wool of every sheep the shear marks showed like ripple marks.

The shepherd knew Master Cowper quite well, and stopped to talk. The woolman gave him a pull of ale out of the leather bottle, and a bit of brawn between two tranches of white bread; when the shepherd saw the white bread the look came into his eyes that a dog has when it is begging, rapt and exalted. While he ate, with his crooked staff leaning on his shoulder, Master Cowper talked to him about wool, and the condition of the dale sheep, and the good weather they had had—praise the saints— for washing and shearing. And the shepherd, his mouth very full, nodded or shook his head in answer, and only when necessary tucked as much of the victuals as he could into his cheek, and spoke indistinctly through the crumbs.

Christabel watched first the shepherd and then her father, for once approving of him. Master Cowper looked well, with his long legs stuck out before him in leathern riding hosen, and his doublet of fine holly green Flanders cloth. He sat leaning back on his hands, very much at ease, and his beard jigged as he talked.

"The shepherd thinks my father to be some very great man," Christabel decided to herself, forgetting that the shepherd knew every woolman who went up the dale.

He moved on at last over the fell top, into the great silence of blue air above green turf, and even the sound of his piping died—for he had laid his pipe to his lips when he parted. In the noon heat Andrew Cowper and his wife and the servant drowsed; Christabel sat looking along the road, where it dipped and rose again and vanished over the long lift of the fells, going toward Marrick.

They reached Marrick Manor in the early evening, and the bailiff came out, a great fat pleasant man who shouted for ale and cakes, and a dish of strawberries. So they all sat down on the benches inside the hall, and Andrew Cowper talked again of wool. When Christabel had drunk dry her cup of wine and water, and shaken the crumbs from her lap, and licked as much of the pink of the strawberries from her fingers as she could, she stole out and stood on the steps looking about her. Across the dale there were woods; below her were woods; looking back toward Richmond there were woods too, with crags of stone sometimes breaking through, steep as the walls of the castle at Richmond. Only behind the manor, in the direction from which they had come, there were the open fells, while farther up the dale a great crouching hill, spined like a beast, and dark with heather, split the wide dale into two narrow valleys; beyond that hill were fells and more fells, higher and higher, melting now into colorless disembodied shapes as the sun stood low over them.

When her parents were ready they all left the manor; the bailiff kissed Christabel, and pinched her ear, which she resented silently, and called her his pretty little sweetheart, which pleased her. Perkin, with the laden mule, was to go down by the longer way, but the others by the steps. So, when they had gone through some little stone-walled closes, they came to a flagged walk of stone that ran down the steep slope, dived into the woods, became steeper, and turned into great slabbed steps of stone. Christabel went bouncing down them at a run, bunching up her skirts with both hands. Sometimes she would stop, and look back at her parents, but mostly she looked forward, peering through the trees for a sight of the church and the priory. The trees however were too close, and the slope too steep; only now and then she caught a glimpse of the spined, sleeping hill at the head of the dale, or far down on the left, the quick, shallow Swale, running clear brown, and flashing white sparkles of light from its ripples.

Then, quite suddenly, they were out of the woods, and upon a steep slope of clean turf, and there, just below, was the priory; you could have thrown a stone down into its court. The chief thing among the buildings was, of course, the church, with its tall bell tower, but all round that there were stone-slatted roofs, and lower and smaller roofs of thatch. Christabel, searching the buildings with her eyes, saw an orchard, and there were ladies in it, walking about in twos and threes under the trees. They were every one in black and white. One of them stopped and pointed upward and spoke, and they all stood looking toward Christabel; she heard an exclamation go up from them, and, though she could distinguish no words, she said to herself, "They were watching for me to come," and she felt important. She did not know how little important a thing need be, and yet the ladies would be watching for it.

When the parents had sat talking a little while with the prioress they said good-bye to Christabel, refusing an invitation to supper but accepting one to dine tomorrow at the priory. They bade Christabel be a good girl, and serve God truly, and learn what she was taught, and do what she was told. She was to be sure and mind her manners, and not wipe her fingers, if they were greasy, on the tablecloth, and certainly not on the hangings—that from her father—and to keep her clothes neatly mended, "not cobbled, mind you"—this from her mother.

Then they both kissed her, and her father put her hand into that of the prioress. The prioress's hand was hot and damp, as was natural with such a large fat woman on a warm evening, but Christabel did not like it, so she wriggled her hand free, and then waved it to her parents as though that was why she had wanted to get it away.

She stood beside the prioress on the top step of the outside stairway of stone that led up to the prioress's chamber, where they had all been sitting. Her father and mother went along the court below, turned at the gateway and waved their hands to her; then they were gone.

"Oh!" cried Christabel sharply.

"There! There!" the prioress comforted her. "Thy mother will be here again tomorrow."

Christabel said, "Yes, madame." The dog which had certainly intended to make a convenience of one of her two bundles, dumped down by Perkin in the court, had changed its mind and preferred the leg of a wheelbarrow. But she hoped the bundles would not long be left where they were.

"I will show you the cloister," said the prioress, and they went down, Christabel alongside the sweeping bulk of the lady, through the narrow great court, where hens followed hopefully, and an old gray pony looked out kindly at them from over a half-door. They turned under an arch just beyond the bell tower, and found themselves in the cloister, which, after the open court, seemed very dark. It was very small too, small and somehow countrified; mustard was laid out to dry upon a trestle table along one wall, and there was a bunch of teasels hanging from a nail beside the door into the church.

At the far end of the west walk, in which Christabel and the prioress stood, there were two children, a boy a couple of years or so younger than Christabel, in a brown coat and with brown curls, and a girl who looked to be about her age. The boy was whipping a top and took no notice of them; the girl jumped off the low wall, between the cloister arches crying—

"Look, John! She's come."

John said, "I care not," and gave a great slash at his top, but so unskillfully that it scuttered across the stone flags on its side, bounced off the wall, and lay still.

"Come, John! Come, Margery!" the prioress called them, and they came, staring all the time at Christabel.

The prioress told Christabel that Margery Conyers was a novice; this Christabel could see for herself, since Margery wore a white woolen gown just like the one in Christabel's own pack. "And John is her cousin." Christabel would not have known that, for Margery was a thin child with a large nose and a little proud mouth, whereas John's face was round, snub-nosed, and merry.

"Lout down, knave, lout down!" said the prioress, tapping him on the shoulder, so that he bowed to Christabel. He did it awkwardly and looked at her with a pouting face, but then smiled at her suddenly, a bright, sunshiny smile.

Behind and above them the bell in the tower began to ring, and several of the ladies came into the cloisters from one side and another, arranging their veils and pulling up their black hoods which had lain on their shoulders.

"After Compline," the prioress said, moving toward the church door, "you shall have supper."

"Yes, madame."

It was a strange thing, but till that minute Christabel had never thought that, of course, nuns were nuns in order to go to church over and over during the day and night. She looked back over her shoulder and was sorry to see that John had returned to his top, though Margery was coming after them into the church.

"You shall lay off these tomorrow," the prioress said, touching Christabel's blue hood as they curtseyed before the rood.

"I have my habit in my packs, madame," Christabel answered sedately, and she thought, "There is supper to look forward to."

Now the Chronicle Begins

1509

July 20

The last loads of the hay harvest were bumping and bouncing along the rough track homeward to the priory. The sun, low down over Mount Calva, filled all the dale with gold, and shot long shadows before them. Those of the nuns who had come out to help stood while the wain moved off, flapping their hot faces with the big straw hats they had tied on over close coifs; no one wore veils in the hayfield. Some of them had taken off their black gowns and worked with the white woolen undergown—more yellow than white from repeated washings—tucked up over their girdles.

"Where," said one of them, "are those children?" and they turned to look back across Applecote Ing, where the mown grass was all rough from the scythes, and smudged with small gray strewings of hay which the rakes had missed. The ing, which had been so full all day with horses and wains, and men and women raking and pitching the hay, was empty now.

Margery Conyers said, looking at her feet, that "they two had gone up toward Briary Bank," so the ladies stood staring up and calling "John! Christie!" and telling each other to shout louder.

But they must have cried loud enough, for now they heard John's shrill hail, and down the slope the two young things came pelting, hand in hand.

"Truly," said one of the younger nuns, "it's as well that that boy's going away."

An elder, smiling to see the two, told her, "Lord, there's no harm. Christie's a little mother with him. I love to watch them."

They came near and stood panting.

"John made me this garland." Christabel pointed at the honeysuckle garland aslant on her hair. She shot a quick glance at Margery Conyers, who stood in the background, and gave her a triumphing smile; then she looked at John, and smiled very differently.

He said, "It's all awry with running down the bank," and he straightened it for her. The two young faces were grave and happy, and close together, for John, though he was nearly three years younger than Christabel, was grown so tall that they stood the same height.

"Go along with you, go along," the ladies told him, and, "Go you with them, Margery." So Margery went on alongside the others, but as they were hand in hand again she walked a little apart.

By the time the hay had been tossed up on the new rick the sun had set; only the top of the bell tower was still bright, and when the pigeons, which had been disturbed by the shouting and stir, floated down again, wings raised and spread, they dropped out of the sunshine into shadowed air.

But if the great court was in shadow the cloisters seemed almost dark; and more than dark, for after the long day in the sunny, sweltering field, the familiar, small sheltered house suddenly seemed strange. It was as though, while they had gone from it, it had also slipped away from them; as though, empty since dawn, it had been engaged upon some business of its own, and was not quite the same, and never would be quite the same again.

It was the children who felt it most, though they only stood still, looking round with quick, searching glances, and then looked at one another.

One of the older nuns said, "How strange—yet it's only this morning we went out."

Then all of them went toward the laver beside the frater door, where there were twelve little wainscot cupboards—one for each of the nuns to keep her towel in.

Someone turned on the water-cock, and the water tumbled out in a shining glassy curve; even the sound of it seemed cooling, and the older nuns were already splashing their hot faces, and bathing hands and wrists with exclamations of satisfaction.

John, to while away the time, kicked the end of a bench, then, lifting up his brown paw began to sniff at it. The palm smelt of all sorts of things; of the horses' sticky, dusty coats; of hay, of earth, of dirt. The back smelt different, and rather pleasant; he did not know what the smell was, and then realized that it was the smell of John. He put his tongue to it, and it tasted slightly of salt.

Margery Conyers was standing near.

"Smell my hand," he said, shoving it under her nose. She struck it away.

"It's not foul. Not the back." He was angry, and punched her with his fist before he turned away to find Christabel.

"Smell my hand, Christie," said he. She smelt it and then her own, and then he must smell hers, holding it in both of his, while Margery watched them.

Christabel slept in the very last room of what had once been the open dorter, but had for a long time now been divided up into a series of little chambers. This one, which they called the Richmond Chamber because of the blue and yellow checkers painted on the ceiling, was shared by three of the nuns and Christabel. Here they slept and ate, as all the other ladies, three or four to a mess and each mess in its own particular chamber, fetching its food away from the kitchen. So the old frater on the cloister was hardly ever used, except at the great feasts.

It was just on midnight, but not dark because of the full moon that shone through the two little windows. The ladies had gone down to the church for Matins and Lauds, but Christabel had not wakened either at the candlelight or the shuffling about in the room as they pulled on hosen and shifts and gowns, or at their sleepy, yawning conversation. She only woke when John laid a hand on her.

"Christie! Christie!"

She woke up then with a start.

"Oh! John!" She put out a hand and felt his—yawned, stretched, and whispered, "How did you come?" She made room for him on the bed, and he curled up by her inside the curtains.

"Up the pear tree."

"And through the sacrist's chamber? Did Margery hear you?"

"No—she was snoring." He began to fumble in his shirt, and then put something into her hand in the dark.

"It's cherries and some comfits."

"Oh, knave!" Christabel said, putting a comfit into her mouth.

"I'm not. Maudlin gave them me," he said, and they ate them together merrily.

But when they were finished he sighed.

"I came to tell you something. When I was in the kitchen with Maudlin, the Lady"—that was what they called the prioress—"the Lady went by in the great court, and I heard her say that she had writ to my father that I must go from here, now that I am so big." He put his arm round her neck and said, "Oh, Christie!" and kissed her. She kissed him as readily, and put her arms about him.

"But you'll come back to see me, John."

"It won't be the same. I can't come often. Christie, come with me."

"You silly boy," she said, "how can I?" She felt much older than he; he was only a child.

He pulled himself away from her. "You don't love me."

She said again, "How can I?" because, though she knew it was silly, yet she was setting two things up against each other. The one was life at Marrick—it was made up of solid, sensible things—meals, lessons, her own gear in this little room. The other was nothing to be seen or touched—it was loving John.

"Oh!" she cried, "I do. I do love you." It was true, and she had never loved anyone before, except her grandfather, long ago, before he had beaten her. But John was so easy to love. John was her little boy, and her lover, and the child she played with, all in one. Being yet children they could have it so, without even knowing that it was so.

She took a deep breath. She couldn't go away with him; she was old enough to know that. But at that moment for Christabel foolishness was wiser than wisdom, and things that are not, brought to naught things that are. She caught him again in her arms. She must do something to show him that she loved him; she must somehow break and hurt the things that are, for the sake of the things that are not.

"I know. I shall give you my great cup Edward."

"Oh! Christie!" he said, in such a voice that she felt warmth and light all through her, and glad to be giving away the great cup Edward. Tears came into her eyes, and were running down her cheeks when he kissed her, and when Dame Anne Ladyman, stepping softly, suddenly twitched the curtains of the bed open, and stood looking in, shining a candle upon the two of them.

"Jesu!" said Dame Anne, "it's as well I slugged abed and did not rise to Matins."

Margery Conyers crept away, quiet as a mouse. She had seen them, but they had not seen her. Yet she had done right to waken Dame Anne. John had no business to be out of his bed at this time of night, a little boy like that. And he was her cousin,

not Christie's. He should have loved and followed her. She hated
Christie.

1511

March 11

The bishop had arrived last night and lay in the guesthouse;
Christabel's father and mother, her eldest brother, the sister
who had married a knight, and her husband too, were all staying at Master Christopher Thornaby's up at Marrick village;
and any time now, for it had been light for a couple of hours,
Margery Conyers's father and mother might ride in from
Marske. None of Bess Dalton's people would be coming; her
nearest kinsman was a cousin, a cross-grained, ill-conditioned
fellow, who was only too ready to be rid of the girl, but who
did not mean to spend any more on the settling of her than
he need.

For at chapter Mass the three of them, Christabel, Margery,
and Bess, were to be made nuns by the bishop, and afterward
the Conyers and the Cowpers would feast the new nuns and all
the rest of the house. It would be a great dinner, served in the
old frater, which had been scrubbed, and cleaned, and strawed
fresh with rushes, and with whatever little tufts of greenery the
young year provided.

Christabel and Margery were at it now, scattering the pansy
leaves they had gathered, which would smell sweet, though
faint, of violets. As was fitting they spread them thickest at the

table set crosswise at the dais end, for there the bishop, the prioress, and the guests would sit.

"My ring," said Christabel, because she knew that Margery's father and mother would sit above her own at the board—"my ring has a ruby in it." She knew also that Margery Conyers's ring was of plain gold. Margery had said that nuns should not have precious stones set in their espousal rings, but that was only to make the best of it.

"My cousin John, who is page to my lord my uncle, is coming to the feast," said Margery.

Christabel had not known this before and wondered if it were true. She said nothing for a minute, scrabbling in the basket for the last of the leaves, and dropping them carefully where they would best show.

"My sister's husband, who is a knight," she said, "has offered a gold piece to St. Andrew. And my father has brought a whole bolt of cloth for gowns for the house, and last night he sent a servant down from Marrick with pounds and pounds of spices to the kitchen here."

"My father has sent a heron and two cranes, and partridges, I know not how many."

"Huh! Those cost nothing." Christabel tossed the last of the pansy leaves disdainfully out on the rushes.

"Last time I went home," Margery said, "I saw my cousin John, and I asked him if he would be sorry that you should be a nun, Christabel. But he said he cared not, whether or no, and when I said that you would be fain to see him at the feast he pulled an ugly face and made a scream like a peacock."

"Little boys," said Christabel, "that lack the rod, grow up unmannerly."

But Margery Conyers, in order to have the last word, had gone out into the cloister, leaving the door open. The snowdrops in the garth were almost over, and here and there the daffodils had pushed up a green mace among the leaves. A delicate sunshine, shining through thin cloud, made the cloister light, but threw no shadows. The big pear tree, up which John had climbed, was covered with large buds; they had been caught and blackened at the tips by the late frosts, and every day now, since the weather had become warm, one of the nuns would wonder if the frost had really spoiled the blossom. Across the other side of the cloister Bess Dalton stood, looking up into the air. On an ordinary day the ladies would have been sitting there, sewing and reading in the sun, but today they were far too busy preparing for the feast, or entertaining the bishop, to have time to sit in the cloister, and Bess should not have had time either, to stand there, only staring.

She began to throw handfuls of corn out into the cloister garth, and down came the pigeons. Bess watched them, and then saw Christabel and came round the Cloister to her. She was a fat, cheerful, stupid girl, never out of temper. Today she looked happier than usual.

"They should have their feast too," she said, tipping her head back toward the birds.

Christabel answered, thinking of the good corn: "The cellaress will be angry."

"Oh! Not today."

"Your cousin," said Christabel, not looking at Bess, but fiddling with the empty basket on her arm—"your cousin—hath he sent aught toward our feast?"

Bess laughed. "Perdy! Not he! He's a mean old snudge. But there's plenty. Oh! it will be a rare feast!" She went off quite happy, though everyone knew that her cousin had paid no more than her bare dower, and that what household stuff she had brought with her was poor and old.

Christabel was thinking about this when she found that Bess Dalton had come back, and all, so it turned out, to tell Christabel that she was so happy she could jump out of her skin, because today she was to be made a nun at Marrick, where all the ladies were so good and kind, every one of them. And if her cousin had not paid her dower, and she had had to leave Marrick, "I should have broken my heart, Christie, for I love them all here, they are so kind to me."

When she had gone away, crying a little and smiling, and wiping the tears off with the back of her hand, Christabel went again into the frater. She had been pleased this morning at the thought that she would be made a nun today, but what Margery Conyers had said seemed to have overcast the pleasure. And there was Bess Dalton, so happy about nothing. Christabel thought, "The ladies are not so bad." If Margery Conyers were gone, and Dame Eleanor Maxwell who was so deaf, yet always wanted to be talked to, and Dame Anne Ladyman—"then I would like them well enough." It was Dame Anne who had found John and her together in the middle of the night, so it was Dame Anne who was responsible for the beating that Christie got, and the days on bread and water, locked up in the closet beyond the prioress's room. John had been beaten too, and sent off the very next day. Christabel had not seen him since, and did not want to see him now. Loving John had been pleasant and sweet. But they had made her smart for it, and had made her ashamed of it, so that now it was an offense to her.

The serving-woman came in from the kitchen and began to set out the wooden platters on the nuns' table, with here and there a small silver cup. They brought them from the latticed aumbries beside the cloister door. Christabel cheered up at this, and watched them now in pleased anticipation. Yes. There it was. One of the women took off the shelf a tall handsome cup, the bowl made of a coker-nut, cunningly borne in worked bands of silver gilt. It was Christabel's great cup, Edward. She watched the woman set it on the table, right down at the lower end of the frater. But none of the ladies had one fit to match with it, not even the prioress. The bishop today would drink from the prioress's best, which was an old small silver cup. Christabel would drink from Edward.

She sidled up to the table and began to run her fingers about the rim. "Supposing," she thought, "I had given John the cup, and he had gone away with it." She felt that she had been spared a great loss. Now she would always be pleased when she used the great cup. It was unlikely anyone at Marrick would ever have one so fine. She felt secure again, and content. If she could only avoid having to speak to John today, she could enjoy these solid, real, dependable things—her great cup, the new coverlet her mother had brought for her, the gold pin her father sent her last New Year, the ring with the ruby which the bishop would put on her finger today. And in the future there would be other things to look forward to, and to scheme for.

As it turned out she did not have to speak to John. She did not see him in the church until the very last of the long Mass. She and the other novices had laid their new habits at the foot of the altar, and the gowns had been blessed and sprinkled with holy water, and taken up again. They had put them on in the vestry, and come in with their lit candles, and knelt before the bishop, received the veils, and had been espoused to Christ by the rings—wet and difficult to get on because they too had been sprinkled. At the very end of the office, with Bess Dalton crying happily, Margery shivering with excitement, and Christabel very proud and demure, they had come once more to the bishop, their hands covered in a linen cloth, bearing the bread and wine with which he should communicate them. As Christabel knelt she heard a scuffling noise behind. She turned and saw John: he and another page boy were trying to stamp on each other's feet. Then a tall man behind cuffed them each soundly, and they were still, with crimson faces. Christabel turned back and received the bread.

She saw John serve, of course, at the feast, but he served only at the table where the bishop sat. When her own folk had taken leave and ridden away she saw him again. She was going along the cloister toward the door leading up to the Richmond Chamber. There was a shout and a scuttering of feet, and three boys, John the smallest of them, came out from the parlor, and went by her at the rate of a hunt. She had to jump out of the way, and they raised loud and jeering shouts as they passed her; she thought they jeered at her, and went on up to the Richmond Chamber with her cheeks burning. But they were jeering at the cook's man, whom they had braved, stealing wafers from the kitchen.

By evening they were gone, and now she sat at table with the other nuns, and the great cup Edward was before her, and nothing would take it from her, nor uproot her from the comfortable security of her possessions in this house at Marrick.

1515

December 3

On a fine and bright winter morning the ladies at Marrick were always pleased to be able to walk for a while in the orchard. They grew very tired of the cloister during the winter and, "Really," said Dame Anne Ladyman, holding up her bare palm to feel the sunshine on it, "it's as warm today as if it were spring."

Today there was news to listen to, and talk over, for Dame Anne and Dame Bess Dalton had been away at Dame Anne's sister's house at Topcliffe on Swale, for the christening of a first child. Just a year ago they had been given leave by the prioress to go there for the wedding, so the ladies knew about the house, and the family, almost as much as could be known by those who had never seen any of the places and people. That made this second visit all the more interesting in the hearing. There were younger sisters of last year's bride, who might by now have had marriages arranged for them. And last year half the bees at

Topcliffe had died of disease; how had they sped this year? And had Dame Anne's sister finished the embroidery for the chair that she was working last year? And did the parlor chimney still smoke? And the babe? He, of course, was new, and as a subject of conversation, inexhaustible.

Last year Bess Dalton and Dame Anne had talked so fast, prompting, and correcting, and supplementing each other, that hardly a question had to be asked; but this time Bess seemed heavy and dumpish, and Dame Anne would stop in her talk, when she was speaking of the guests, or the games they played, or songs that were sung, and purse her lips, looking sly and saying, "Well! Well! least said soonest mended," or, "Lord! you must ask Bess to tell you who sang the sweetest." The nuns, knowing Dame Anne, and seeing Bess's crimson cheeks, could guess what all that meant, but little Margaret Lovechild, the youngest of the novices, who walked hanging on with both hands to Bess Dalton's arm, was too simple to guess.

"And the babe," said Bess, brightening up a little at a question from one of the older nuns who wished to stop Dame Anne's tongue—"the babe is the prettiest little gentleman, with the bluest eyes."

"Ah!" Dame Anne cried, "but there was a prettier little gentleman yet, whose eyes were brown."

"Were there twins?" piped little Margaret, and Dame Anne let out a squeak of laughter.

Bess grew crimson, tried to answer Margaret, stammered, and burst into tears. When she had gone away, hurrying off with her head bent, Margaret began to cry too.

The others stood silent. The air here was never perfectly quiet, for always there was the sound of the rushing Swale below, and almost as constant as that the sleepy meditation of the wood pigeons in the bare bright woods high above the priory.

"Run away, child!" Dame Anne bade Margaret, and she went, with a scowl at Dame Anne, because she loved Bess Dalton dearly. Dame Anne tittered again.

"Now I can tell you all about poor Bess and her—"

"No one wants to hear it," the old cellaress interrupted heavily, and pushed past her. Most of the others followed, so Dame Anne had not much of an audience.

Christabel was in the Richmond Chamber when Bess came in; but Bess did not see her, and flopped down on her bed and sobbed aloud.

"Jesus!" said Christabel. "What's amiss?"

Bess cried for awhile and then told her. The priest at Topcliffe was a young man, comely and gentle. "So gentle and so good," Bess said, lifting a hot, wet face for a moment. "Anyone must see it who but looks at him." Bess had seen him at the wedding a year ago. "He lives in the house, for he's chaplain to Sir Wat, in a little bare room. I looked within once—only from the door, Christie; there was but a bed and a crucifix and some books. And such a torn coverlet upon the bed. A blue coverlet."

Christabel had to wait till Bess had snuffled a little before she could go on.

"He said my eyes were like a dove's. And he said— But then— No, Christie, I can't tell you what he said, for it is sacred. But I know that he will go wretched all his days for want of me—as I for want of him." At that she broke down again, and wept desolately.

Christabel laid a hand on her shoulder and shook her.

"Fiddlesticks!" she said, and again, loudly and clearly, "Fiddlesticks!"

"What's fiddlesticks?" Bess sniffed.

"That either of you'll be wretched all your life long. In a twelvemonth he'll have forgot, and you too."

"I'll not," cried Bess.

"You'll see you will."

Bess gave a great sob. "I must try to forget. It's sin to love him."

"You'll forget sooner if you don't try," Christabel told her, with greater wisdom than her years.

Bess only shook her head, and drooped in silence for a while. Then she started up—"A twelvemonth! I can't endure not to see him for a twelvemonth. Oh! Jesu-Mary! I can't stay here."

"You!" said Christabel bluntly. "You, that was glad that always you should live at Marrick."

"It's different now. You can't understand."

"Tush!" said Christabel.

1516

March 19

The first of the peddlers to come up the dale every year was a lean, leather-faced, elderly man with a gray donkey, which he called Paul of Derby. The peddler's name was Jake, but the ladies always called him "The Lent Peddler," because of the season of his visits.

There were other peddlers with better wares, for this man bought only in Richmond, to sell up the dales, whereas some others went to York and even farther. But Jake was one of the most popular because he came after the long winter, and brought news of the world from which the ladies had been cut off perhaps for months when the snow blocked the road over the fells.

This year there had been snow lying from Christmas to Carle Sunday only ten days ago. But since then the spring had come with a rush, and from the dale the snow had vanished almost overnight. The Marrick Manor shepherd was reported to have said that the road was clear to Richmond, but they could not be sure of that till Jake actually came into the gatehouse late one afternoon.

Then, when the prioress had had him up to her chamber, to choose, with the sacrist, a length of fine linen for a new alb for the church; and the cellaress had had him into her office to buy whipcord, and cheesecloth for the summer ewes-milk cheeses, he was allowed to come into the cloister, where the dusk was falling, and spread out the pack that contained more frivolous things: pins for veils, carved wooden combs, purses and girdles of leather or of silk. The ladies came round him, fingering and turning things over, and he doled out his news little by little, knowing pretty well how much they could be persuaded to buy, and never parting with his last titbits of information till he had given up hope of any more sales.

So tonight, it was not till Dame Elizabeth Close had at last made up her mind to lay out a shilling upon two bobbins of red and green silk that he sat back on his heels, rubbed his hands together, and said:

"Marry, if I bain't a fool not to tell your ladyships the biggest bit of news of all."

"What, Jake? What is it?"

"Why none else but that the Queen was brought to bed of a fair child."

"Knave or girl?"

"Girl."

"Will she be our queen? What is her name?" Bess Dalton had bought nothing, for she never had money to spend. Yet she could not help watching and wishing—not cheerfully in these days, as she had used to watch, but with a long face. However, now that the buying was over she could join in the talking.

"Silly!" said Christabel Cowper, "it's a prince we want to be our king."

"Aye. There'll be a knave child soon. King Harry's a lusty gentleman. They say he—" Jake gave a bit of high-spiced gossip, which embarrassed some of the ladies, amused others, and interested all.

"What is her name called?" Bess Dalton asked again.

"The little lady is the Princess Mary."

"Queen Mary," Bess said, trying the name. "I should like it well if there were a queen."

"There never hath been a queen to rule in England," Christabel maintained, and none of them knew enough to contradict her.

At the King's palace of Greenwich that same day was sweet and mild. The gardens, bare of flowers and leaf but for primroses, and here and there a company of daffodils, were almost as full of ladies and gentlemen, strolling or sitting, as they would have been on any summer day. And all, except perhaps the oldest, felt the exquisite exhilaration of the spring, so that a waft of scent, a snatch of a blackbird's song, or only the warmth of the sun on the cheek, brought longing, promise, and rapture, all in one. Below the garden the river ran, glittering, and beyond the river lay the green Essex shore.

Someone had spread a tawny velvet cloak on one of the benches under the south wall where the sun was warmest, and the King sat on it, a young man in green and white satin, with a complexion like a rose, a small, soft mouth, but a nose fine-boned and imperial. A crowd of gentlemen stood about him, some close enough to join in the talk, others only listening and looking.

What those said who were talking with the King none but themselves could have understood anything more than the bare words, for their jokes and their teasings were those of men who know each other well, and who play and drink and hunt together. So such a remark as, "Mass, *he* would. Trust him. We all know about his stirrup irons," or, "And where was your lute string that time?" or, "Not the points of his hosen! Oh, Mass! Not again," provoked long gusts of laughter, though it was not so much the shared jokes that made them laugh, as their own well-being, and the sweet white wine of the day.

"Look," cried one, "a bee!" and pointed to the flower bed below the wall where, above the soft fresh turned earth, and the small leaves of plants just pushing up toward the light, a worker bee was hovering uncertainly.

"I'll have him!" cried the King, and snatching off his velvet cap with its jeweled brooch, flung it toward the passaging glitter of tiny wings and golden brown velvet. "I have him. No, Tray! Tray!"

Others now, laughing and shouting, flung their caps till the flower bed was gay as summer with scarlet, green, blue, and carnation color; then the bee, finding no flowers for its rifling, rose in the air, and went away into the shining blue while they cried after him, "Hue! Hue!"

As they were laughing and picking up their caps, someone said: "The Queen's Grace," and the outer parts of the group about the King—those who merely watched and listened—opened a way, by which came into the midst the Queen and her ladies.

Queen Katherine was five years older than her husband, and today, six weeks after the pains of childbirth, she looked older even than her years. So, when she came and stood beside the King and asked, "What do you? I heard laughter even within," it was more as if an indulgent mother had spoken the question than a wife.

But when the King told her, "Hunting of a bee," and proclaimed it a new sport that he would, one day, write a book on, so that every young gentleman should know the courteous terms of that quarry, she laughed as merrily as any of them, and laughed again, softly, looking down into the King's face as he looked up at her, with the sun making the red gold of his fine, closely curling hair glitter as if it burned. "And his teeth," she thought to herself with a weakening pang of delight, "are like a little boy's."

The King put up his hands and pushed her, gently but masterfully, so that she stood between him and the sun, and then, lowering his eyes, which had been dazzled by the glare, he began to play with the long gold lace of her girdle from which hung an enamel of Paris and his three goddesses.

"But what," said he, and dropped the pretty jewel, "what's this?" and he pulled at the end of a ribbon that strayed from beneath the parted skirts of her crimson velvet gown, and trailed across the gold brocaded petticoat. Quite a lot more came out as he pulled, and he began to laugh, while the Queen snatched at his hand and tucked the ribbon away in a painful embarrassment.

"Oh, madame!" cried the King, still laughing. "Fie on your women!"

"No. It was my fault. They had no time to make me ready for Mass, because I slept so long."

"So long? I know how long you lie abed, sweetheart. Charles!" He looked up at the big, good-humored Duke of Suffolk who stood close by, his fine legs in their white hosen straddled wide. "Charles, what should you do with a wife that steals from her lord's bed before it's light, to hear Masses?"

Suffolk laughed, and made no other answer, not being one of the quickest witted, but Katherine cried out:

"Sir, sir, I pray you! These gentlemen—"

But the King interrupted.

"No, madame, these gentlemen are all on my side. So I shall kiss you now, this once, for all the kisses I've lost when you go gadding after holiness betimes in the morning."

He had her by the wrist and pulled her to him, though she put her hands first upon his, to pull them away, and then upon his breast.

"No, no, my dear!" she cried. "No, sir!"

"Why not? A' God's Name, whom but thou should I kiss this fair morning, and whom but me shouldst thou?"

She muttered, "No—for it is uncomely behavior."

"What?" said he, catching her now by the arms, and drawing her down toward him. "To kiss? Or for a king to kiss? Or to kiss openly in the sunshine? There!"

But she had turned her face away so that he could only kiss her cheek.

"It is not so done in Spain," she whispered, at which he cried "Fie on her!" for she was a Spanish woman no longer.

"No," she said. He had loosed her, but now she seemed unwilling to move away. She touched his cheek with the back of her hand, and withdrew it sharply; it was the advance and retreat of a young girl, unpracticed and shamefaced. "No. I am English now. But in Spain I was bred, and what a child learns early, that she cannot forget."

He was looking up at her, but, because of the brightness of the sky behind her head, he could not see the tenderness of her look as she added in lower tones, "So it will be with our little maid." But because he himself was fascinated and amused by the smallness and perfectness of that ridiculous puppet their daughter, a new human being, a microcosm, like a mirror to catch and reflect the universe and the Maker of the universe; and because besides he was a man who loved scholars and loved learning, he answered eagerly—

"It is true. And I have been thinking—" and, drawing her down beside him on the bench, began to talk of how the child should be taught—first letters, then music and the ancient tongues, then French and Italian.

"Already!" she teased him, "at six weeks old!" But soon she became as absorbed as he. Some of the gentlemen who stood about gave their opinions on this and that, and the group about the King shifted and settled into a different arrangement, as Suffolk and those of the younger men who cared more for the tiltyard than the study fell back, and others took their place.

On the outskirts of the little crowd Suffolk found himself beside one of the Queen's ladies—a very young lady, gawky and self-conscious, "yet," he thought, "she has the skin of a peach," and so he began to be pleasant with her, but found it heavy going. Growing nettled he rebuked her. "My child, you're a fool if you take a lesson from your good mistress in how to deal with men. For if a woman wears always her virtue about her, like the boards of her stays, it wearies a husband, and—there are other women more conformable to a man's liking."

He left her then, nodding to her in a friendly way, for he was rarely put out for long. But the girl stood, twisting her hands together and hating the things he had said, both those about herself and about the Queen.

"She is too good," she said to herself, and wished that she
had been in time to say it to him—"she is too good to think of
such things."

That would not have disconcerted Suffolk, being exactly
what he himself thought; but, for the Queen's sake, he considered that it was a pity.

1519

July 15

Chapter began in the murk and hush that goes with thunder
weather. All week a storm had threatened, and had not broken,
but today, by all the signs, it must break. When the prioress came
to the lectern, to read the daily chapter of the Rule, it was so dark
that she had to send Christabel to the kitchen for a taper, and
while she went there was silence, without wind, without stir, in
the small chapter house, so that if someone moved her feet upon
the hassock of sedges, or if someone's inside gurgled, all heard.
Christabel came back from the kitchen with a burning taper.
She lit the two fat candles of the lectern, blew out the taper, and
went back to her seat. The prioress opened the book and at that
movement the spiry flames of the two candles, which had just
steadied and lengthened, flinched aside, and flared out, so that
the embossed golden letters and the blue and green and scarlet
decorations seemed to crawl and quiver. The prioress found her
place and began to read, following along the lines with her finger.
No one listened to the Rule. They knew it too well; and today,

irritated by the heat and oppression of thunder, most of the ladies were thinking rather of those sins of omission and commission in their fellows, which it was their solemn duty to bring to light, when the time came for confession and accusation.

The prioress finished reading, went back to her chair, and murmured the words which would set tongues free. There was hardly a pause long enough to give any penitent the chance to confess her own faults before the cellaress coughed behind her fingers, stood up, and accused the chambress of having more fried eggs from the kitchen, last evening at suppertime, than she and the other ladies of her mess should have had—more eggs by three, the cook had said.

That brought in not only the chambress but the other two ladies of her mess. The chambress grew shrill in her indignation, the cellaress's voice was as loud as it was deep, and old Dame Joan, who was one of the chambress's mess, though she could hardly make her thin piping heard, did what she could to add to the din by clattering the iron end of her stick upon the stone floor. Even Dame Elizabeth Close grew ruffled, and no wonder, for the chambress, losing her head and striking a sidelong blow at one of her own side, hinted that if too many eggs had been eaten last night it was Dame Elizabeth who had eaten them. This, however, was only a glance at Dame Elizabeth's known reputation as a trencher woman, and did not, in the eyes of the affronted mess, mean that they for one moment admitted the charge, either corporately or singly.

The chambress, who had just denied having ever asked for more than the just share of three devout and hungry women, was soon hard pressed by the cellaress. For the cook had said—

("God be his judge," cried the chambress)—that he could not help it if some went short when others would not be content with their portion. Dame Elizabeth, whose anger never lasted long, threw in a suggestion that perhaps the eggs were double-yolked. The chambress would have no such appeasement, and retaliated upon the cellaress by a general condemnation of her management of the priory hens. How could such poor starved bags of bones lay anything but eggs that would shame a sparrow. And where hens were poor scrags what wonder if the nuns pined. Christabel Cowper looked from the soft bulk of the chambress to the hard bulk of the cellaress, and put her hand over her mouth so that she could smile.

"And," concluded the chambress, "did the cellaress think that the priory would take their frumenty this Founder's Day without a word gainsaying? If so, she was mistook."

That sudden diversion, from eggs to frumenty, was too sudden for the ladies. They needed a moment to work from eggs to hens, from hens to corn, from corn to the cellaress's known unwillingness to feed corn to hens in the winter, and from that small meanness to the moldy corn in the frumenty last year.

In the short silence which resulted from this preoccupation Dame Anne Ladyman stood up, and accused the cellaress of talking for a long time—a very long time—through the kitchen window to the miller's wife of Grinton.

The cellaress, turning on her like an angry bull, retorted by a long account of the burdens which lay upon the bowed but faithful shoulders of any hard-driven cellaress. From that, somehow, the dispute broadened out so as to include the character of the miller's wife, thence to the honesty of the miller, and so to that of other millers scattered throughout Yorkshire and known to the nuns before they came to Marrick. In this stage the argument dwindled, since not one of these other millers was known to any but the lady who happened to cite him as an example of depravity or rectitude.

Christabel Cowper waited for a pause, and when it came stood up. It was the first time that she had made an accusation, and they all turned and looked at her. More than one face could be seen to fall when she said that she spoke not in accusation, but for the good of the house.

"For there are," she went on, looking down at her clasped hands, "moths in the vestment press."

"Moths!" cried one or two in shocked tones.

"No. Never!" cried Dame Anne Ladyman who was the sacrist.

Those whose faces had fallen brightened again. If this was not an accusation it was as like one as pea to pea in the pod.

Christabel said, with her eyes on the worried, sagging face of the old prioress, "I fear it is so, madame; I found one yesterday."

"Found a moth! Found a night-moppet . . ." Dame Anne scoffed—and so on. "There's lavender laid in every fold," and more to this effect. "Do you think I know naught of embroidery?" They did not think so. All knew that the sacrist was the best embroidress that had been in the priory for long enough.

When she paused Christabel spoke again, and this time she looked Dame Anne in the eyes: "Madame," she said, "I saw moths yesterday. I killed one and one flew away."

All this time the prioress had said nothing. These days she would rarely speak in chapter except to mumble the well-known forms, to read, or, when she was forced, to give a decision. Now, as so often, she sat, pressing her white plump hands together, never lifting her head lest she should catch the glances thrown at her, and read in them the reproach that she was past her work.

The cellaress heaved up her great bulk.

"I think we should look," she declared.

They all rose, the prioress too, as if the cellaress had pulled them up from their seats, and went out into the cloister. The novices there, whose heads had been very close together, drew them quickly apart, and bent them studiously over their books.

The church was darker even than the chapter house or cloister, for the painted windows made the dull light outside little better than twilight, even though the ladies left both doors standing open.

The sacrist had lifted up the lid of the big press, and was ferreting among gold fringes and silk fringes.

"Moths!" she says. "Show me the moths!"

As though all had expected moths to rise in clouds when once the press was opened, the ladies stood dumb till Christabel Cowper said that the vestments should be lifted out, one by one.

Someone murmured then, "If they have got at the great white cope!"

Even that faintly whispered suggestion was enough to harden the determination of the ladies, for the cope, though very old—some said it was as old as the priory itself—was the loveliest thing they had. It was of white velvet which had changed with age, as ivory changes and deepens in color, but the wheat ears which were worked all over it were still of a rich, lustrous gold.

"We must look," said the cellaress, and laid hold of one end of the topmost vestment—it was of blue velvet sprinkled with white stars, and had been given to the priory two hundred years ago by one of the Askes. The sacrist took the other end and they lifted it out. The chambress puffed with her breath to clear the dust from the top of an old alms chest, and they spread it out over that.

Under the blue velvet there was a dun and green silk, worked with true lovers' knots, and under that a crimson banner powdered with harts and butterflies, and then a very old black sarcenet cope with roses and stars on it. And as they lifted it out the cellaress dropped the edge she held, and began to clap her hands together in the air.

"Oh!" cried the ladies. The cellaress opened her hands and showed them on her palm a little smear of dulled silver-gold dust, and shattered wings. "Oh!" they cried again.

In the silence that followed, while they watched the sacrist's face grow red and begin to work, there came suddenly from outside the church a sound as though someone had breathed a long, harsh sigh, and the rain began.

That evening when everything lay drenched and still, except that the gutters still ran and eaves dripped, Christabel was walking with Bess Dalton in the little garden.

Bess said that the prioress's cushion was nigh done now, and very fine.

"If I were the prioress . . ." Christabel began.

They were just passing the parlor door as she said it, and a shrill laugh came from within, which they knew for Dame Anne Layman's, and next minute she came to the door with her embroidery frame in her hand, and the white damask trailing, which she was embroidering for a new banner.

"Ah!" said she, "it's Dame Christabel who is to be prioress, is it? God-a-mercy! and which of us does she think will want to make her so. D'you hear that?" she cried to someone behind her in the room, and turned back. As the two girls passed on they heard her begin to retail the story, and heard Margery Conyers laugh.

Christabel had grown red, but not so red as poor Bess.

"Oh, Christie!" Bess could not speak till they had reached the first of the beehives along the west wall. "That she should say such a thing! You did not mean that at all."

"No. I was going to say that if I were the prioress I should have worked the buck's horns in gold."

"How absurd to say you think to be prioress."

"I do not think of it. I shall not be old enough when the Lady dies, for anyone can see she will last but a year or two longer."

"Oh, no!" cried Bess.

"Unless the cellaress—but no. I do not think of it."

1520

June 30

Sir William Aske came rarely to the little manor house at Marrick, partly because it was so little a house, and partly because he was so old a man. He had survived his only son Sir Roger, and when he died there would be two little girls to inherit all the lands that belonged to Askes of Aske.

But now, at the end of June, word had come to the bailiff at Marrick to set all things ready for Sir William's coming, and there had been a great business of scouring and cleaning and strawing, and fetching in of beasts and cheeses, of flour and spices from York: there had also been much to-ing and fro-ing between the priory and the manor, for the bailiff, being taken by surprise, had borrowed soap and scrubbing brushes and goose wings for dusting, and the prioress, who remembered Sir William when he was a young man and she a little girl, sent up her best coverlet—the one with the white hart standing on a green hill between lilies—and two great candlesticks. She knew that Sir William would bring all necessary household stuff with him, but these would help to furbish up the old, deserted house for an old and lonely man.

Tonight Sir William had to come down to sup with the prioress, and, as it was Christabel Cowper's week to eat and sleep in the prioress's lodging, she came to supper with them. The prioress had tried to hint that perhaps it would be fitting for the cellaress or another of the older ladies to sup with Sir William instead of Christabel, but Christabel had not taken the hint.

Old Sir William, very lean and bent, sat in the prioress's own chair, and his big knotty hands were laid upon the arms of the chair which ended each in the carved head of an angel. The heads were worn smooth as silk and pale as straw by the hands of prioress after prioress, since the chair had been carved very long ago in the third King Henry's time.

The Lady's servant came in with a dish of veal, served in a sauce of mulberry juice and eggs and spices. She set it down on the table, and stood back a moment looking proudly at it, because it was a special dish at the priory; no one else round about knew how to make it, and it was only made on very great occasions. It was called "Red Murrey" or sometimes "King's Murrey," because thirty years ago or so a cook of King Richard's kitchen had told the nuns' cook of those days how to make it. The King's cook was all for King Richard, though it was that Richard who was nicknamed Crouchback and had such an evil reputation. But when the old man who had been his cook had drunk too much ale he would tell tales to show what a good master Crouchback had been, and call him Duke Dick, because he had been in his household long before Richard murdered his nephews and made himself king. Duke Dick had once given the cook a ring for making this very same "Red Murrey"; he showed it to the nun's cook—a dark ground sapphire set loose in gold claws, so loose that you could turn it about, but safe as the world hung in the midst of all the turning stars; it was, the cook said, a ring that had been made in Italy.

So the Lady's servant set down the dish and looked at it proudly. She was very hot with helping in the kitchen, and she wiped her face with the loose end of the kerchief that covered her head, bobbed her curtsey, and began to serve forth.

Christabel sat eating, and taking no part in the talk, which was all of old days, and old people, of whom she had heard sometimes barely the names and sometimes nothing at all. She was so discreetly silent that they seemed to forget her, and Sir William spoke of his dead son Roger, and the prioress cried a little, and then the old man spoke of his own death—"which won't be long," said he—and of Masses to be sung for him in the Founder's Chapel in the church, and wax for lights on the rood-loft. The Founder's Chapel, or the Aske Chapel, was part of the parish church, which lay to the east of the nuns' church, all under one roof, but separated by a wall taller than a man, and, above the wall, a wrought-iron grille twined in curves like a briar. There was one door only in the wall, and the prioress had the key of it, and the priest.

All this did not interest Christabel much, but when Sir William said he'd found a husband for little Nan she pricked up her ears, because she knew that little Nan was Mistress Anne Aske, his grandchild, and, with her sister Elizabeth, heir to all the Aske lands. "It's Nan," said Sir William, "shall have Marrick and all that goes with it. Oh—a good enough match," he told the prioress, who asked who was to be the groom, "Rafe Bulmer, Will Bulmer's second son." The prioress only knew the Bulmers by name—a family with lands in Cleveland and farther north in Durham. What age was Sir Rafe? Sir William told her and then went on to tell her of the bargain he had struck with Rafe's father. "Oh, yes, a towardly young gentleman enough," he said, when she pressed him for more. But he clearly cared little what sort of man the young man was, and soon went back to the question of his own death, and how he would provide at Aske for a chantry priest. "My Lord Darcy," he said, "showed me a while ago the book of his foundation. He had builded a hospital and free school, where Masses shall be sung forever for him."

"But," the prioress objected, wrinkling up her face, "he is not old." The prioress's mother had been a Tempest of the dale, so she was connected with Lord Darcy, though distantly, through his first wife. Besides, there was little she did not know about the great families of Yorkshire.

Sir William agreed with her that Tom Darcy was not old. Indeed to him to be fifty-five years old seemed to be young. "But you know that rupture he got at Thérouanne; it is for that reason he thinks of his soul." He stopped and sighed heavily, for it was of the same disease that his son Roger had died, suddenly and in great pain. "I told him that he need not fear to die, since many live long ruptured. He said he did not fear it, but would have all in order. So the hospital and chapel are built already, and his friends send to him singing men and boys from all the North Country. I cannot do so much, but what I can I will, for Roger's soul and for my own."

He sighed again and they sank into silence. The candles had been lit, and now the sky darkened outside the windows, and grew gloriously blue.

❋ *Now the chronicle is broken to speak of Thomas, Lord Darcy.*

Thomas, Lord Darcy

This Lord Darcy, though, as Sir William said, a devout man, was also a great fighter, and as well used to courts as to camps; a man too with as many friends as enemies, because, while he could use on occasion guile or violence, he stood by his given word, and by his friends and his men in all things.

Nine years ago he had gone to Spain as a Crusader. The thought to do so had come to him when he was, by chance, in company with a Venetian merchant at the table of the King's chaplain, Master Thomas Wolsey. After supper talk turned somehow upon doctors, and the Venetian said that the Saracens were the best doctors he knew, and began to tell how, at the place where the Saracens bathed, there were those who would so stroke, rub, yea, and strongly pummel a man that he would get up cured. "I have seen," said he, "how they would wrench a man's neck, till I thought he was dead; but dead he was not, and when he rose up, from being bent and in pain, he could instead go strongly and at ease."

"You have seen this?" Darcy leaned to him across the man that sat between them. The Venetian nodded.

"In Jerusalem."

"You have been to the holy places?"

"It was when I was a lad. But I remember that Saracen, and how great a crack the man's neck made."

"Tell me," said Darcy, "of the holy sepulchre."

But the Venetian could not tell much, though by now those around were listening. Ten days only he had been in the Holy Land, for the galleys that brought the pilgrims from Italy would not stay longer for them than that. "So we ran from place to place," he said, and blew out his cheeks and fanned his face with his hand. "Oh! I was weary!"

"But you saw Jerusalem? Bethlehem?"

"Jerusalem. But Bethlehem, no. For to Bethlehem we went by night, when it was dark, and all I remember of it was the hard-boiled eggs and bread we ate sitting on some steps. But as for the holy sepulchre,"—he pulled a ring off his finger—"my father laid that ring upon the holy sepulchre."

They stared at it. When Master Wolsey, from farther along the table, asked what it was, Lord Darcy answered him, but without taking his eyes off the ring where it lay between the paring of a red-skinned apple and some crumbled bread.

"A precious ring indeed," said Master Wolsey, and reached out his hand as if he expected that someone would take up the ring and give it to him. When no one did that he turned back to the French ambassador who sat on the farther side, and went on talking about the King of Spain.

Those near the Venetian asked him questions, and he told them quite a lot about the oranges and grapes that the pilgrims had of the peddlers in the Church of Calvary, and how fine the two galleys were which brought them all from Venice, with their painted banners, and the trumpets, drums, and fifes which played every time they set out from any port. Darcy listened but he spoke no more; only when the Venetian reached out his hand and took the ring again, he gave a start and a sigh, as if something had been taken away from him.

That night in bed beside his wife, Lord Darcy told her of the Italian: how fine a dark sanguine silk his coat had been, and of the silver spoon and prongs of silver which he brought out from a little leather case, the color of raspberries, which he carried at his belt; he had used those things at supper and afterward had wiped them and put them back. And he talked about the way Italian faces seem to have been made with greater care and skill than English faces. By that time she began to snore, and he had told her nothing about the ring.

He spoke about it to no one else till next Christmastime, and then only to the priest who houseled him. It was in the chapel in his house at Templehurst, and beyond the shut door they could hear voices, footsteps, and laughter, and sometimes the scratch and hiss of the boughs the servants were bringing in to deck the house for the feast.

"And," said the priest, "you will go on pilgrimage to the holy places?"

"No. On Crusade. Against the infidels in Spain. King Ferdinand has asked for fifteen hundred English archers, and will need some nobleman, besides captains, to lead them."

The priest sat silent, and Lord Darcy let his eyes rest upon the crucifix in his hands. It was a little thing of bone, old and smooth.

"Since," he said, "there is peace in the realm in these days, and peace with the French—" But he stopped there, because though there was restlessness in his mind, it was not that which was at the root of it. At last he pointed with his finger at the little bone crucifix. "Because I am a worldly man and a sinner I would be glad to strike a blow for God who was killed for me, and if he will have it, to be killed for him."

The priest blessed him then, and after they had talked a little about how my lord would raise men to go to Spain, Darcy went out. As he crossed the court he looked up at the blue sky, for it was a day like spring, and then about at the roofs of the house where the pigeons were sidling up and down. It was a great house, Templehurst, great and fair, and now he knew that it was most dear to him, and that it would be hard to leave it, if that meant that he must never come back. He was glad it was so, that Templehurst was a thing worthy to give to God, and his own life precious to him. That afternoon he wrote a letter to the King.

Lord Darcy, and the gentlemen who were captains under him, and the English archers, landed at Cades on the first day of June in the next year. All that blazing afternoon they were at it, bringing ashore their gear and finding lodgings: the dust lay thick, and blinding white, and there were flies everywhere. It was difficult to make anyone understand them when they spoke, but by the time that the sun was setting in a golden pomp beyond the infinite extent of the sea the archers were housed in the town, and my lord and his captains in an abbey outside the walls.

When Vespers were over Darcy and the others sat drinking the abbot's wine in a vine arbor in the monastery garden. The garden was quiet, and cool in the failing light, but the town, where the archers were drinking, was not quiet at all.

"There'll be heads broken before night," said Sir Robert Constable, and laughed. He, like most of the other captains, was a Yorkshireman, a dozen years younger than Darcy, short, broad, red-haired, and with green eyes.

The others laughed, and began to brag how the English archers would come off the best. Darcy thought so too, for he was proud of the men, but he took no part in the talk. Instead he drew back, drinking and saying nothing, but feeling to his very bones the strangeness of this strange country, where bread, wine, people, smells, and even the very sun itself seemed new. That strangeness had worked so strongly as to make these friends of his, and the big, ruddy, upstanding archers strange also; he could see them now as he had never seen them before, set over against the dark Spaniards; he saw Templehurst too, as clearly as if he were there, and yet as he had never seen it before, because he saw it from this warm, shadowed garden, where the dark trees stood up, straight as spears. When he tried to realize the purpose with which he had come here, it seemed to have become as unfamiliar as the rest, as if God had been left behind in England, or lost overboard upon the seas. He sighed sharply, and then straightened his shoulders. Thank God he need not think now, or only of the things about which a soldier must think in the way of his trade. But this time, when he fought, he would fight for God, so that it did not matter that his mind was like a boat drifted from its moorings; thoughts did not matter now, since it was by acts that he would serve God.

Three days later, in the hottest of the afternoon, he came to where his captains, sick of doing nothing, had rigged up some butts, and were shooting with the bow. They had a couple of the archers with them—"For to shoot against 'em will keep us up to the mark," said one of the gentlemen. So it did, but the two big silent men, who seemed to draw the six-foot bow as easily as if it were a willow withy, and loose off the clothyard shaft with hardly a pause to take aim, were on the mark itself every time, and the gentlemen could not match them.

"Death of God!" Sir Robert Constable stamped his foot. "Again!" His shaft had scudded off to the left.

"It was prettily shot, sir," said one of the archers soothingly, "well knocked and well loosed. But you feared to draw the shaft through the bow, and so you looked at the shaft and not at the mark."

Sir Robert groaned. The archer glanced at him with a twinkle, "We've a saying, sir—'Shoot like a gentleman, fair and far off.'"

They saw my lord then, coming to them, and the archers drew away, and moved off toward the butts, while the captains went to meet Darcy. He came quickly, with a very red face, but they saw at once that he was not only hot but very angry.

"This King!" said he—and wished a pox on him, and on all Spaniards. He did it so loud that any might have heard; the archers must have heard, but that did not matter since they were English, and at this hour of the day there were no Spaniards about and awake except a few ragged children watching the shooting.

It was a little time before they got from him, so angry was he, the cause of his anger. When they had it they were angry too, for the news that the Duke of Alva had brought from King Ferdinand was that he had made peace with the infidels, so that having come they might now go away again.

Lord Darcy was thinking of that day, and the time that followed it, as he lay in his bed at Templehurst, ill and in pain, more than two years later, while the October gale swept the rain past the windows with the last of the leaves. He was angry still; if it had not been for King Ferdinand's yea and nay ways this rupture that he had got fighting at Thérouanne last summer against Christian Frenchmen might have come on him in war against the infidel. Then, if he had died of it, God would have looked gently on his sins; and if he had lived, as he was now likely to live, it would have been easier to endure a life crippled by a hurt taken in God's service. He turned over in bed carefully, and groaned, not for the pain, but because he would have to live and move with care.

This morning Sir Robert Constable and two other gentlemen had been with him; in fact they had not been long gone. Sir Robert had grumbled fiercely at the rain. "It'll beat in our faces the whole way," he said, and to Darcy, when they left, "Lie you snug there, my lord, and think of us as wet as drowned rats." Darcy thought of them now, but he was not glad to be snug.

"I must," he said to himself, "learn how to live as an old man," and he knew that it would be hard to do so, although he was now past fifty.

Yet even an old man, if he have a stout heart and a busy, working head, may play a part, and next summer Lord Darcy was again captain of Berwick, and going about the ramparts of the castle with Tom Strangways, the master porter, or walking along the river strand to see what the catch of salmon had been, though now, wherever he went it was with a cross-handled stick to lean on. He must not ride, except at a soft pace, and for a little while, but must go in a litter; yet that did not mean that he had forgotten how to pick a good man-at-arms when he saw him, nor how to command the men whom he had chosen. And when Parliament was called, in the late autumn, my lord went to it, traveling by easy stages, and took the same house at Stepney that he had hired before, and sat with his peers to give counsel to the King.

In these days Master Thomas Wolsey, who had been the King's chaplain when Darcy first knew him, then dean of Windsor, then bishop of Lincoln, then this, then that, was become more things than a man could easily remember, and cardinal into the bargain. Six years after Darcy had got his rupture, that is, in July 1518, the papal legate landed at Sandwich, and came by way of Canterbury to London. My lord was with the other lords in the great cloth of gold pavilion that was pitched in a meadow beside the road from Blackheath, to welcome the legate. Though July, it was a chilly, gusty morning, and the cloth of gold flapped and bellied out in the wind, and by the time the legate arrived, the lords, in their efforts to keep out the cold, had well drunken of the wine that was to regale him. So when the cry rose that he was coming there was some scurrying to have the gilt cups swilled out and set again on the rere-table in the pavilion, and some covert laughter among the lords, though the welcome they gave him was as stately as it should be.

With the rest my Lord Darcy came into London at the head of the great procession, and by that time the sun was out and the day fair, so that the gold and silver crosses of the clergy, friars, and monks, who welcomed them beyond London Bridge, and the copes of cloth of gold that they wore, made a most brave show.

That afternoon he was among those who waited upon Thomas Wolsey, cardinal of York, to announce the legate's arrival, and wait they did indeed. He and some other lords sat in a window, and played cards for an hour and more before the door of the chamber was opened and they were bidden through seven other rooms, each one hung with tapestry of arras, to the chamber where Wolsey was. And even then they had little of his attention, for he was busy with the choirmaster of his chapel, choosing the music that should be sung at next morning's solemn Mass.

So they went away more than a little chafed, and in a mood to carp at everything. One of them said, as they looked across the street from the cardinal's gate, "All this mighty show, but look you there at that!" and he pointed at where a handful of hay hung out over the door of a house; they all knew what that meant—the sweating sickness, and most likely death, were in the house that showed that sign, and they crossed themselves and held up a lap of their coats before their mouths, and went on quickly.

"And what," said another, "of this Crusade?" The legate had come to get the King's promise for a great Crusade against the Turk.

"Mass!" said Darcy, in a loud reckless voice. "I think the Soldan must laugh to hear of it. For the cardinal will spend on painted pictures from Flanders, and clocks—such as are most cunningly and artificially made—and tapestries, so that they may hang a fresh set every week in every one of those great chambers of his. And the King will spend on jousts and revels. But if they will spend money on men-at-arms, and shipping for them to go against the Turk, then . . . then I'll . . . I'll eat my hat!"

"Say you'll eat my lord cardinal's," one of the others cried; and they all laughed, thinking of the great scarlet hat with its hanging cords and tassels.

"Aye, so I will, and his scarlet satin gown, and his tippet of sables," Darcy declared. At one time he and Thomas Wolsey, the King's chaplain, had been familiar together, when they shared a room and a bed in the palace of Westminster; but now the cardinal of York only gave my Lord Darcy his ring to kiss; so my lord was free to make game of him with his fellows if he chose.

1520

July 2

On this morning Thomas, Lord Darcy, prepared himself to accompany the gentlemen who were the French King's envoys on a visit to Princess Mary, King Harry's only heir, four and a half years old this month, and betrothed since last year to the little French Dauphin. She was at Richmond just now, and they would go there by river after they had dined—early because of the tide—with the lord mayor.

My Lord Darcy was in his bedchamber at the house at Stepney; one of the young gentlemen of his household was with him, and a servant, and the servant's head was inside a great standing press where my lord's best gowns hung on perches. He was searching for a black silk doublet with cloth of gold sleeves, while my lord stood in the middle of the room in his shirt, breeches, and hosen. The young gentleman knelt beside him, tying up the points that held his hosen to his short breeches.

My lord looked every bit of his fifty-five years, but he looked, too, a remarkably handsome man. Very tall, very lean, he had curling hair which might have been as easily silver as gold. With that hair went a fair complexion, and blue eyes that had a keen, or laughing or blazing look in them, but which were never dull.

"Then," said he, "if it's not there, Will, give me the cloth of silver!" He laughed. "It'll do no harm if it makes the Frenchmen think that all is as loving between their master and King Harry as it was when I wore it at Guisnes!"

At Guisnes the two kings had met in the great splendor which had got that little valley and small decayed town the name of "The Field of the Cloth of Gold."

Darcy, wandering over to the window while the servant ferreted still in the press, thought of that day four weeks, when he and all the King's company had ridden from Calais to Guisnes, reaching there just before sunset. Guisnes castle and town took the low light, but it was not that half-ruinous keep, nor the moat, grown thick with weeds, at which they stared and marveled.

Beyond the moat, upon the castle green, a palace had been built of carpenter's work, larger than the King's great house at Eltham. When Darcy and the other nobles passed inside the embattled gate of this mushroom palace there were fresh marvels, for the roofs of the galleries under which they went were covered with white silk, fluted and adorned with gold, and all the hangings were tapestry of silk or gold, while the red Tudor rose was set on every ceiling upon a ground of fine gold.

"Come on, Will, come on," he said, without turning, "give me the cloth of silver."

"My lord, let me try the trussing coffer," said Will; so Darcy shrugged. He was not eager to show these Frenchmen more courtesy than was needful. He did not think he was meant to do so, though it was hard even for a clever man to read the purposes of the King and the cardinal.

His thoughts ran on to a night in his tent outside Guisnes, when the flaps were tied up to let in the cool air, which was refreshing after the long heat of the day. He and the Duke of Buckingham had sat together there, with candles lit, talking over their wine; laughing talk mostly of the day's jousting. His Grace of Buckingham was a great talker, and a great mimic. He had aped one by one the knights that rode that day, French as well as English, and then he aped another whose name he did not mention, but Darcy knew well enough it was the French King himself, by the habit he had of tossing up his head sideways like a fidgety horse. He and Buckingham laughed, and heard the gentlemen, sitting a little apart from them in the tent, laugh too, and whisper together.

And then the duke leaned toward Darcy; a little man, he was as quick and graceful in his movements as a fish, and he murmured in Darcy's ear—

"But we'll taste the wines of Spain again after these light French wines, and I think we'll be content thereof, every man of us."

Darcy, who was older than the duke, and wiser, only nodded. He knew well enough what was meant. After all this show of friendship between France and England there was to be a meeting between King Harry and the sober young Emperor at Gravelines, and that meeting, though less splendid, might make a truer story than this fairy tale of gilded palaces, and jeweled doublets, and burning cardboard dragons drawn through the air for a wonder and a show.

"Perdy! and here it is!" Will cried, and Darcy turned back into the room.

Will drew out the black and gold doublet and held it up. The young gentleman took it from him, and put it on my lord, while Will laid back the rest of the clothes that he had taken out of the coffer, and shut the lid, and set on it again the silver basin still full of warm soapy water from my lord's shaving.

After dinner the French gentlemen, and Lord Darcy and Lord Berners who were to conduct them to the Princess, went down to the mayor's barge, and so by river to Richmond. It was a gray afternoon, so that the silk awning of the barge was not needed, but as it was warm the motion and the air were pleasant. The gentlemen sat together under the awning, and if there was little conversation between them there was sufficient for courtesy, especially after so plentiful a dinner and on so warm an afternoon. The country people were cutting and carrying their hay in the meadows on either side of the river, so there was plenty to watch, and merry sounds to hear of shouting and laughter, or of some old man piping a tune to cheer on the workers. If, for a space, the wide reaches of the river were solitary, with no laden barges going up or down, and no one in sight in the meadows, there were always the long glassy ripples to watch, which the barge pushed out before it, spreading smoothly till they were caught by the churned water the oars tossed up, which, spreading in the wake, became smooth again and only lapped softly at the pale mud of the banks, just stirring the drooping comfrey and water-mints and small forget-me-nots there. The French gentlemen were so content that they shut their eyes, and one of them even made a little snoring noise through his nose.

In the presence chamber at Richmond they were all wide awake again. The Countess of Salisbury was there, and the Duke of Norfolk's daughters. And then the gentleman usher opened the door and the Princess came in, very solemn and flushed in cloth of gold with pearls in her hair. She stood while the French gentlemen and English lords knelt and bent down to kiss her little perfect dimpled hands. She said that they were "very welcome," and then looked at the countess.

"Ask for the Dauphin's Grace that is to be your husband."

"How does my husband?" said the little girl.

One of the Frenchmen, who had little girls of his own at home, told her that His Grace was well, "and playing merrily at ball when I saw him last."

"Is he as big as me?" the Princess wished to know, and quite a lot of other things. When the countess suggested that my Lady's Grace should play upon the virginals, so that the gentlemen could tell the Dauphin how good and clever a girl she was, the Princess was not at all shy. One of the ladies set a cushion on the stool and lifted her up on it, and she played, very earnest, and biting the tip of her tongue over the trills and runs.

After that the servants brought in a big silver-gilt platter of honey wafers and strawberries, and poured wine for all. The pages carried these round, and the Princess kept on calling to the page with the platter of strawberries to bring her more, until the countess forbade it, "for we shall have you all out in spots if you do eat more."

Lord Berners laughed aloud at that, and at the way the Princess pouted, though she obeyed. But Lord Darcy turned to the French gentlemen and said now they had seen Her Grace— "not only how fitly taught in music and deportment, but how meek of spirit, as a maid should be to make a good wife."

"*Sang de Dieu!*" they cried, "she will be a very worthy lady, worthy both for her noble parentage and for her own excellencies. Well may we pray that such a lady shall be Queen of France."

"And Queen of England too," said Darcy, a trifle acid.

That, they said, was not to the matter in hand. They had heard their master say that if King Harry had ten children and

all sons but this lady, King Francis would rather have her for his
son's wife than any other—"Yea, than the Princess of Portugal
with all the spices that her father hath," they said.

That remark had a shrewd point, for it was pretty well
known to all there, except the little girl, that the Emperor was
even now hesitating whether to ask for her hand, or for that of
the Portuguese Princess. Darcy got up and went to the open
window which looked out toward the river. When he came
back he said that the tide had turned and was fair for their
departure.

December 6

The tawny velvet gown that Sir William Aske had left to make
a vestment to the priory, when he died last August, had all
been unpicked, and now lay spread out, yards and yards of it,
on one of the long tables in the old frater. Several of the ladies
had come in to look and talk about it, and advise Dame Anne
Ladyman, the sacrist, how best it should be cut up into a cope.
The seamstress with the shears stood respectfully waiting for
their decision.

Dame Anne had asked them to come. She wanted advice;
she had been scheming and planning, turning the stuff this way
and that. There was so much of it, surely it would make more
than one cope. Yet there were places in it worn and rubbed, and
try as she would she could not devise how to avoid these, unless
she cut wastefully and were content that it should make one
cope and no more.

So she had asked the cellaress to come, and the chambress, because they were the two ladies most used to dealing with such practical matters. But she regretted that she had asked anyone when she saw Dame Christabel Cowper come in with the others. She remembered then what she ought to have remembered before—that the old cellaress leaned much on Dame Christabel in these days.

However, it was too late now to do anything more than put up her eyebrows in surprise when she caught Christabel's glance.

The cellaress saw the lifted eyebrows, and she explained Christabel. "I brought her because she's the best head for contriving of all of us." That did not improve matters, nor did the account the cellaress gave, after she had sunk heavily down in the bench, of how Christabel had detected the trickery of the miller. They had all heard it before anyway; Dame Anne barely let the cellaress finish before she began explaining to them the difficulty about the tawny velvet. While she did so she managed to edge in between Christabel and the others, and then, quite naturally, and as it might have been unconsciously, turning her face toward the older women she was able fairly to turn her back on Christabel.

Christabel smiled, and made no effort to regain a place in the conclave. She put out her hand and stroked the smooth bloom of the velvet. What had been the lower edges of the gown and of the huge hanging sleeves was most cunningly dagged into a pattern of leaves in the fashion of half a generation ago.

She stooped and sniffed at the stuff. The faintest scent still clung to it; a scent of musk; a rich, worldly, seductive scent, though now dwindled to a ghostly fragrance. She thought, "It's known some brave doings at court," and she was right, for Sir William had worn it the year the dead Prince Arthur was born, this King Harry's elder brother, and it had seen pageants and water parties and maskings, much gaiety and some gallantry.

The sacrist explained her problem, more than once. She asked each one, except Christabel, what her advice would be, and got nothing very clear from them. The chambress hesitated. The cellaress weighed one advantage against the other.

"What do you think?" said the cellaress, craning her big dark face round Dame Anne, so that she could speak to Christabel.

"Why"—Christabel was always prompt and always confident—"it's a fair piece of stuff. Let's have one cope that'll be fine and seemly and rich. Not two that are worn in patches like a scabbed sheep."

She knew directly she had said it that the matter was decided. The sacrist would cut her velvet as thriftily as she knew how, and the rubbed parts would be an eyesore to all who liked things trim and neat, for many years to come.

When the unpleasantness which followed had been somehow smoothed over by the chambress, the ladies went away leaving Dame Anne and the seamstress standing over the velvet with the shears.

"A cope and a chasuble," Dame Anne said, before they had gone out of hearing.

1521

May 11

The primroses in the woods above Marrick Priory were almost over, and the bluebells well begun, but the skies were heavy, and a bitter wind blew off the fells. The young leaves shivered in it and cuckoo was dumb. "Miserere!" said the nuns, as they splashed their hands in the cold water of the laver, "Christmas was more kindly than this."

The prioress and the new cellaress had gone up the hill to Marrick Manor, because Sir Rafe Bulmer and his bride, who had been Anne Aske, were come home there. The prioress rode the little mule because it had the easiest pace; the nuns called it Francis. The new cellaress walked, and of the two servants one led the mule and the other carried the priory gifts—an embroidered cushion, cut from what had been left over from Sir William Aske's gown, after the tawny velvet cope and chasuble had been made, and, in a little pannier, a pot of the ladies' rose-leaf conserve.

It was much colder in the village, for here there was no shelter from the wind. The prioress was very glad when they got inside the manor house; she always had a bad cough in wintertime, and this winter weather had brought it on again.

But the parlor was gratefully warm, and from the fireside old Dame Felicia Aske, Sir William's widow, got up to welcome her. They knew each other from a great many years back, and were soon deep in recollections and inquiry, while the cellaress stood with one foot on the edge of the raised hearth, listening for the approach of Sir Rafe and his wife.

"For," said the old lady, "there they are, both of them, outside in the stable, as though she were no gentlewoman but a lad. Alas! I know not what's come to the girls of this day. Ever since she could walk it hath been horses, horses—nothing but horses."

The two came in just then, both of them windblown, Sir Rafe with muddy boots, and the girl with mud round the hem of her draggled gown, and wispy, light-brown hair blown out from under her hood. Sir Rafe was a big man, like all the Bulmers, but thinner than most of them, with a big craggy nose. Dame Nan's face was still childishly round and soft, for she was only fifteen, but she had bones in it that would make her handsome when puppy thinned out to hound.

They stayed just long enough for courtesy, and then went back to the stable yard, for Sir Rafe was buying a horse, sired by the Jervaulx breed, which is the best in the North Country. The new cellaress went with them; she did not ask leave of the prioress, but simply went. The two old ladies were pleased to be left alone; the waiting gentlewoman who sat apart did not count as company unless the mistress chose.

Dame Felicia asked after Clemence; Clemence had been the name of the old cellaress.

"Ah!" cried the prioress, '*Deus misereatur anima sua.*' She died at Christmastide, suddenly, like an elm bough falling. I thought always it should have been I to go first." She wiped her pale eyes, and her lips shook a little. Dame Felicia murmured something of sympathy, and then asked who was now cellaress at the priory.

"That gentlewoman." The prioress nodded toward the door by which Christabel had gone out.

"She's young."

"It's a gray head though the shoulders be green. And for the last two years she did much for Clemence. Clemence needed help; she must have been ill and we knew it not, for when she died Christabel found out how the bailiff had wronged us at Downholm, and at Topcliffe too, taking our rents— Oh! I can't tell you what we lost by him."

"What is her name?"

"Christabel Cowper," said the prioress. "And her father's a worthy woolman of Richmond. At least—" She began to tell Dame Felicia something of the gossip about Andrew Cowper's doings that had filtered through from Richmond.

May 19

My Lord Darcy sat in the little closet beyond the chequer chamber at Templehurst. It was here that were kept all his evidences, the old, butter-yellow parchments, sealed by kings long dead, which had granted lands or offices, rights of warren or fishing or wood, to Darcy's forefathers; and there were other writings, newer, larger, and more floridly written in the present style of the chancery, for lands and offices which had been granted to himself.

He sat wrapped in a long, fur-lined gown, for there was no fire in the room, making up a list of stuff that his steward should buy in London and have sent up here. He had put down already—

"Three bonnets. One choice butt of Malmsey of the best that can be chosen. Sixty of the greatest Spanish onions, the whitest and greatest that can be found."

He stopped to nibble at the end of the quill, and stare out through the little barred window. Then he looked down again at the list, and added, "John Trumpet and Roye my brewer's wife can help therein."

He stopped again, drew inky patterns on the table and wiped them out with his thumb.

"And 2s. in nutmegs," he scrawled, "and 12d. in citron."

He stopped there and called out "Come in!" because someone had knocked at the door.

A man came in whose face was pinched by cold and weariness. He had on Darcy's green livery with the Buck's Head, and his leather hosen were splashed with mud. He shut the door, and stood against it.

"Well?" Darcy said, and when the man made no answer, "It is done?"

"I saw it done."

Darcy looked harder at him, because of something in the tone of the man's voice.

"You mean you saw him tried?"

"No. I saw the execution of the sentence."

"God's Death!" Darcy muttered, and crossed himself. "What was the sentence?"

"He died by the axe."

After a silence Darcy said, "Well, go away and get them to give you to eat and drink. You shall tell me more after."

When the man had gone he sat there thinking of the Duke of Buckingham whose head had fallen by the axe. "This," said Darcy to himself, "is because he was of the blood royal." He himself had half expected it, since he had heard that the duke was brought to trial, yet it was strange to him to think of so great a nobleman, and so confident and imperious a man, thus quickly and easily brought down.

"This House of Tudor," he thought to himself, "will be masters, by guile or by plain force. They will be kings indeed." He was not too sure if this new way pleased him. Here in the North many men had liked their Lancastrian kings, between whom and the nobility a hard bargain had been struck, and who had been sworn to rule by law.

Well! The duke was dead. The King lived, and the cardinal. Not that Darcy was of those who believed that the King went hither and thither as the cardinal's hand guided him.

He returned to the papers before him, and wrote down instructions as to how the stuff should be sent—"by an honest sure carrier, and the wine with an honest man by sea."

But as he wrote it the thought of the duke hung over his mind. He remembered a bastard daughter. "I'll wager Thomas Fitzgerald will never wed her now." But that was nothing to him. He only remembered the girl—her name was Margaret— because she was very well favored, a lovely young creature.

September 30

The cellaress, Christabel Cowper (and now she was treasuress too), sat in her office, which looked out on the great court, and, across the great court and the stone-slatted roofs of the stables and dove house, to Calva, the hill that was like a great beast crouching, red russet now in the morning light, with heath and bracken turning for the autumn.

She sat on the bench-stool with carved ends, on which her predecessors had sat for the past fifty years, and the account roll of the priory was laid out upon the desk which they had used. In the corner of the room by the door there was another bench, heavier, larger, and plainer. On it the priory tenants sat when they waited to pay their rents. The only other furniture in the little low room was a great iron-bound chest with three locks; the prioress, the cellaress, and the chambress had the keys for these locks, and inside the chest were all the evidences of the priory, from the foundation charter, a strip of parchment yellow now as honey and with a dark green seal dangling, to the injunctions which the bishop had written to the house after the last visitation.

The cellaress had her eyes on the priory roll; but when she heard the door shut she knew that Jake Cowton had gone out. She looked up and found that the bailiff was still in front of her; he was an elderly man with a watery eye and thin gray hair; his pursed lips made him look a fool, but the cellaress knew that he was no fool.

"The man can't pay more," he said, "and he's a good tenant. He's held that yardland for twenty years."

"He'll have to pay more if he wants to hold it again. All landlords are taking bigger gressums when the leases fall in."

"We'll lose him. He'll go elsewhere. And maybe we'll get worse in his room." He waited between each remark for the cellaress to answer but she listened in a silence which disconcerted him. "We all know Jake's a good tenant," he said.

"We all know he's your cousin." The cellaress let the roll run itself up with a rattling sound. She tied it with the little strip of parchment. The bailiff realized that she had said the last word.

"I'll speak again with Jake," he said.

"He must make up his mind quick. He's had three months to think of it; and now it's past Michaelmas."

The bailiff went out. The cellaress tossed the big sheepskin roll onto the top of the chest, and went out after him, locking the door behind her.

1522

March 24

From the Round Tower to the Piper and Gascoigne Towers, thence by the stables, bakehouse, kitchens, and hall, with its cellars, then on by Queen's Tower, King's Tower, and so, back by the gatetowers to the great Round Tower again—that was how my Lord Darcy went about Pomfret Castle, taking view of the defenses, and of munitions and stores, as the King's constable for the castle and honor.

He stopped quite a while on top of the Queen's Tower so that the two sergeants who went with him could count the quilted leather jacks and the pikes stored in the room below, while the clerk, who followed after, wrote all down in his roll. As Darcy waited, with the fresh wind whipping the long skirts of his gown and the clouds racing by overhead, he looked about him, estimating, with a satisfied eye, the great strength of this castle of the King's Grace. From the Piper Tower round to the King's Tower (that is a full half-circle from west to east through north) walls and towers were built on the crest of a deep and steep fall, naked rock in places and perpendicular as the walls themselves, in other places a sharp slope of broken sandstone jutting out of the tough clay. To the south where the slope was gentler a barbican guarded the gate, and on the west, below the huge Round Tower which was the old keep, the Norman builders had carved out a deep and wide moat. Not that the Round Tower looked to need much strengthening, because the sandstone bluff on which the castle was built rose highest here, and if part of the keep were built of ashlar, part was the rock itself.

"Blood of God!" Darcy muttered to himself, thinking of the builders of such a hold. "They found a right place for their castle." For though the western windows of the Round Tower looked up a long wide street to Pomfret town high above it, yet the castle stood apart, secure and orgulous, upon that huge isolated outcrop of rock.

"Fifty, fifty-one, fifty-two—no, the shaft's sprung—fifty-one; cast it aside, Sim." The elder sergeant was counting the pikes; the shafts rattled together and the blades clashed. Lord Darcy stamped his feet because the morning was early let, and chill. Far below, on low ground, through which a brook went rambling, stood the Abbey of St. John. As he looked the bell in the tower of the monks' church began to ring, and he could see how from the outbuildings and orchard, from garden and from offices, the brothers came, like hens at feeding time, all making for the cloister and the church door. For a moment the knowledge that they would soon be singing Mass made a quiet in his mind.

"One hundred and thirty-four," said the sergeant in the room just below.

"The full tally?" asked the clerk.

"Aye, the full tally."

Darcy turned and went down the stairs. "Bows and arrow sheaves in King's Tower, you said?"

"Aye, my lord."

They went on toward the King's Tower.

October 30

Dame Christabel, the cellaress, was making a new little garden where before there had been only a tangle of rosebushes, no one knew how old. The best of them she kept, and in the spring they would be cut back and trimmed. But when the others had been grubbed up there was room to plant the gooseberry bushes that Sir Rafe Bulmer had given her, and raspberry canes from her brother at Richmond. She stood watching the gardener now. It was a perfect day for setting, for the rain fell, steady, mild, and gentle, steeping air and earth. The gardener's leather coat was dark with wet, and, as he stooped over the gooseberry bush that he was planting, heavy drops fell from the edge of the hood above his eyes. Christabel went near to him.

"Leave space enough between for the strawberries."

"Aye, Lady." He did not look up, but went on treading in the wet soft earth round about the roots.

"And send out one of the lads tomorrow to dig up roots from the wood. I saw plenty beside the steps where we felled that beech last year."

"Them's no use." He had filled in the hole and made all fair and smooth, and now he turned away and picked up his spade. "The best always grow among thorns. I'll get 'em myself. A lad don't know how to choose and pick them."

"And see that you dung them well," said Christabel, and went out of the garden and through the nuns' court, thinking of her rows of raspberries, gooseberries, and strawberries, all in bearing next summer, and of the neat rows of pottles on the shelves of the stillroom, when the conserves were all made and ranged in order.

"Tell me to dung 'em well!" said the gardener to the haft of his spade.

November 20

A month and a day ago Andrew Cowper had died; everyone at the priory knew that it was drinking had killed him, but his month's mind had been celebrated yesterday with great solemnity, so too had his burial been, for by his will he had been buried in the Church of St. Andrew of Marrick. The nuns, and Christabel, passed the slab of stone under which he lay every time they went into the church. There was to be a fine brass upon it later, bearing the figure of a merchant in a long furred gown, with a dagger hanging from one side of his belt, and a laced pouch at the other, and his children kneeling in two rows below, girls to the left, boys to the right. There was room upon the stone for a brass of his wife.

Today those things which he had left by will to the church, and to Christabel, had come up the dale by the packhorse carrier. There was one small pannier for the church, and a much bigger bundle for Christabel.

She had opened both, the little one in the presence of the prioress and sacrist and as many ladies as could find excuses for not being in the cloister at that moment. The pannier contained a pair of silver-gilt candlesticks—"Not the best pair," Christabel said, preferring that the ladies should think Andrew deficient in piety rather than in goods; then there was a yard or so of lace of gold of Venice, set with pearls. The Ladies said "Lord!" and "Jesu! Mercy!" at the sight of such a pretty gaud. The last thing in the pannier was a tiny silver flagon; Christabel remembered it well; she took out the stopper and sniffed, and remembered a dozen other things, and happenings, and feelings, that she had forgotten; or rather she did not remember them but they were present with her again at the faint scent of rose water that still lingered in the little flagon.

Altogether, she thought, she need not feel ashamed of her father's gifts to St. Andrew. He might have nigh ruined the fine inheritance of trade that his father had left him, but these relics of his extravagance were respectable enough. "And," thought Christabel, "Will will soon have the trade again." Will, even when she was a child at home, had been a close and saving young man, and very industrious.

The big bundle Christabel unpacked in the room which she shared with two others. She found that the great bulk of it consisted in a roll of hangings of painted cloth. As she spread them out they brought back as many memories as the scent of the rose water, for these had hung around the parlor when she was a child. For the last two years, so her eldest sister had told her, there had been fine hangings of arras in their place, but she had not seen them, and as she opened the roll she was back in the parlor at home. The dusty, dry, yet oily smell of the stuff was the same, and there was the place where a fool of a serving woman had scorched it; the scorched part had worn into a hole and been mended, so that a winged child standing by a fountain of water in a garden had no feet, but stood up to his ankles in a patch of green say. Besides the hangings there were Andrew's mother's beads of white jasper, and two pewter pots.

Christabel was standing in the midst of the room looking down at the painted cloth and the pewter pots at her feet, and swinging the beads from her hand when Dame Elizabeth Close came in. She and Dame Bess Dalton were the other two ladies of Christabel's mess. Dame Elizabeth looked down at the floor, and then at Christabel. She was excited to see the hangings—they would make the chamber look very well; but she felt it would be as unbecoming to rejoice as to allow it to appear that the death of Andrew Cowper was anything but a sad loss to his family.

Christabel looked round at her, and murmured that these things used to be in the parlor when she was a little girl.

"Ah!" said Dame Elizabeth, feeling sure that sympathetic regret was her cue. "To see things you remember brings old time again."

"Yes," Christabel answered her vaguely. "Yes, it is so." Her mind was concentrated on the problem as to whether her brother could possibly have held back anything which was due to her by her father's will. "If he did," she thought, "Mother would stand by him. But there are the others. He couldn't be sure that they wouldn't tell me."

She decided with relief, and at the same time with a feeling of disappointment, that it would have been too risky a thing for him to try. Then a new idea struck her. Supposing Andrew's will had said only, "the hangings of my parlor." Would Will have substituted these old hangings for new fine arras cloth ones? Did he think that she did not know of the others?

She said to Dame Elizabeth, "There are new hangings in the parlor now."

"Ah! But your father knew it was the old that you would best like to have."

"I wonder," said Christabel. It was not a reply to Dame Elizabeth, but the expression of her own thoughts.

❄

Last evening, under a glum sky that brought the dusk early, Lord Darcy and his household had come to Temple Newsam. Templehurst, which was the house he liked best, would be empty for a month or so, of any but servants and a steward to see that they scrubbed and swept the house, cleansed the privies and made all ready for my lord to return and keep his Christmas there.

This morning, because it was a saint's day, and he at leisure, and his thoughts turning that way, he went to Mass as soon as he got up. There was a little old chapel, dark and rather damp, so that the painted frescoes had stains on them and in some places the plaster had flaked away. But the vessels on the altar were of gold, and the candles lit sparkles in the jewels of the great cross, and the priest wore a magnificent cope of blood-red damask; blood red because this was the Feast of St. Edmund, the King whom the heathen Danes had made a martyr.

"A brave man," Lord Darcy thought, as the priest moved here and there, "and now in bliss." He thought, "I'd die for the faith!" It was true; he had been ready to die for it in Spain. And yet he thought again, "I'm a worldly man. To die would not make me a saint," and he began to feel shame and to wonder, "What would God have of us then?" but his eye caught sight of a painted hawk sitting on the fist of one of the three Kings, upon the wall, and his thoughts went off to his falconer here at Temple Newsam, and though he kept calling them back he missed the meaning of most of the rest of the Office.

1523

July 15

Four of the ladies and the singing man from Richmond were in the orchard; the ladies sat on cushions on the grass with the music spread upon their knees; the singing man stood in the midst beating time and sometimes singing with them. When he did so the deep voice that came so strangely from such a thin shrimp of a man made beautiful and solemn harmony with the fluting notes of the women.

They were singing antiphons and responses, practicing them over and over with great earnestness. The idea that they should do so, and the more daring idea that they should have a teacher, had been Dame Christabel's. The prioress had not been difficult to persuade; it was an attractive prospect—to have such singing in choir that St. Bernard's ladies down the river, White Nuns, neighbors, and therefore perpetual rivals, should fall into the sin of envy at the thought of it. The idea that the lesson should take place in the orchard and not in the church was Christabel's too, but she did not take that to the prioress; she thought it enough to persuade away the faint objections of Bess Dalton, Margaret Lovechild, and Bessy Singleton.

And then, when they had perfected their chants, it was Dame Christabel who asked the singing man, "What songs are they singing nowadays?" So he sang a song about the mutability of fortune—very moral, and with a most cunning melody; and then he paused, and looked at them and cleared his throat, and gave them two pretty merry love songs. When he had done Dame Christabel cried, "O! those we must learn! Jesu! what sweet airs."

So they did learn them, taking no notice of the expression of disapproval on the faces of two of the older nuns who looked out of the window of one of the upper rooms. The bell for Compline began to ring before they had fully mastered both songs. They went on till after it had finished, and only then, with a good deal of smothered laughter, smuggled the singing man through the cloister into the kitchen, and afterward, composing their faces, tiptoed to their places in church.

"We'll hear of this in chapter," Dame Christabel whispered behind her hand to Bess Dalton. Bess looked startled and apprehensive at that, as though she regretted what they had done; but Christabel met Dame Anne Ladyman's accusing eye across the choir with a faint but sufficient hint of a smile.

November 3

Lord Darcy and his eldest son, Sir George, came out of the parlor on their way to the stables, and found one of the old women servants and Mistress Bess Constable—Bess Darcy before her marriage, and my lord's only child by his second wife—kneeling in front of an open coffer, out of which trailed old gowns, and testers, and hangings, and unmade lengths of stuff: purple velvet, tawny velvet, crimson damask, black satin.

Bess was holding up a gown of yellow velvet; it was old-fashioned, but for that reason easier to cut up into a gown such as ladies were wearing at present. Bess waved it at her father. "See what I've found."

Lord Darcy did not take it from her, but he laid his hand on the soft, crushed pile, and looked at it, and not at Bess, and she saw that his face was serious. Then he smiled.

"Well, if fine feathers'll make a fine bird—" he said, and brushed her cheek with the back of his hand and then went on with Sir George.

They had gone down the steps before either of them spoke.

"It was my mother's gown," said Sir George.

"I know," Darcy turned and looked at him, but saw only George's severely handsome profile, and thin mouth as always set hard. "You remember it?"

"My lady my mother wore it one Christmas—the year the Lord of Misrule got his coat set on fire."

Darcy smiled. "By the rood! Yes. How he skipped. And they put him out with the ale they were drinking." He looked at George again sharply, but again could learn nothing from his face.

"Your mother," he said, with some hesitation. "Do you think on her often?"

"I paid for 'de Profundis' daily for a year. And every year ten gallons of oil for the lamps before our Lady." Sir George faced his father for the first time. "But I do not see, sir, why Bess should help herself to what she will of my mother's gowns. There is Doll too." Doll was his wife.

1524

April 12

The cellaress came down from the prioress's chamber with her lips pursed up and her cheeks pink. She hurried into the cloister, shut the door behind her, and began to laugh. All the ladies sitting there in the pleasant sunshine looked up. "What is it?" they cried. "Tell us what it is."

She told them. "Here's the sacrist from St. Cross"—that was the little priory of St. Bernard's ladies down the river—"and she says they have a precious relic, the girdle of St. Maura. They found it in the church—just like the holy lance, she says. For that fat old thing their cellaress dreamt of it, and then they found it."

"But what is it?" The ladies were querulous. They did not want the nuns of St. Bernard to have a holy relic, and if they all disbelieved in it perhaps it would work no miracles. But if someone had dreamt of it and then it had been found! Things looked bad. Could it be that it was indeed the girdle of St. Maura? "What is it? It can't be," they cried again.

"A bit of old horse harness!" Christabel began to laugh again. "The buckle's on it still."

They all began to giggle then, relieved of their anxiety, and enjoying the gullibility of the nuns of St. Bernard.

"What will they do with it?" they asked her.

"There is a girdle of the holy St. Maura at Paris, and another at Worms. And the sacrist says that both these are a most sovereign help to all women in childbirth."

"And how useful that will be then to the ladies of St. Bernard!" cried someone shrilly, and they all laughed again till their sides ached.

September 28

The cellaress was getting ready to ride to Richmond. It was yet early, and the morning sharply cold since the sun had not yet risen above the top of the fells.

She came down into the cloister holding tight the fringed purse in which was money for those things which she must buy. The list was in it too, written on a scrap of paper torn from the bottom of a letter:

A rundle for the roller towel.
Wooden spoons.
A new meal shovel.
Two dozen hoops for the swans' necks—Spanish latten if it
    may be had.

She and Dame Margery Conyers, who was to ride with her, drank each a pot of mulled ale, standing in the cloister, and chatting with Dame Bess Dalton. "Oh! that I were coming too!" said Bess, who now found many things to wish for that she did not have. The lack of them was pulling down the corners of her mouth which had used to turn up in a pleasant silliness. Dame Margery made some effort to comfort her, but Christabel's head was too busy with the thought of what she must see to in Richmond that day, and what she would not be able to see to in Marrick. Presently the bell began to ring for Terce. Bess said, "That bell!" and went away from them. Christabel swilled the dregs of her ale about the bottom of the pot as she watched the ladies go into church. She was glad not to be going in with them.

Outside in the great court a servant was holding the horses, and another sat already in the saddle. As they rode out of the gate behind the two men, they heard the sound of singing from the church, and a great squawking as someone chased a hen out of the dairy.

November 19

The court was at Greenwich, and Lord Darcy went there two days after he had come to London. He landed at the steps and stood with Sir Robert Constable waiting for their people to get ashore. A little farther along half a dozen men were heaving and straining to lift into a barge a great erection of beams and painted cloths, battlemented, and with towers, made to represent a castle. Already the effigy of a unicorn stood in the barge, its brown paper side torn in places and fluttering in the wind, a forlorn sight, except that its painted horn was still gay and fresh. The staging and properties for the last jousts were being taken back to the wardrobe in London.

They found the King coming away from dinner, and when they had kissed his hand they followed him to the Queen's apartments. There, not being noticed anymore by His Grace, they withdrew to a window, and watched the group by the fire, where the King stood, his feet wide apart, swinging a big jewel which hung by a gold lace round his neck, and talking and laughing with a cluster of gentlemen and ladies.

"His Grace," Darcy murmured in Constable's ear, "is thickening," and Constable, looking at the round bulge of the King's jowl above the fine shirt collar worked in gold with a pattern of roses and pomegranates, nodded his head.

"Yet he rides, hunts, and plays at tennis."

Darcy's eyes had left the group at the fire, and looked beyond Constable's head. He said, "Yea. Yea," but not as though he heard what was being said to him.

Constable gave a little laugh under his breath, "And His Grace's father was as lean and little as a smoked herring."

Darcy said, in a voice as low but with no laughter in it, "I can remember His Grace's grandfather, King Edward. His Grace is a man much like to him."

"What are you looking at?" said Constable, and turned, craning his neck to see what it was.

Darcy told him, "Nothing. Nothing," and brought his eyes back to the group round the King. But he had been looking to the place where the Queen stood, pleasant and smiling, and with people about her. And yet he thought that she seemed ill at ease, as if she would have come where the King was, and yet, again, would not.

"And the why she would not," thought Darcy to himself, "is that young maid in sanguine red," and he took a good look at the girl who stood up, slim and glowing in her velvet gown, with black hair falling loose over her shoulders. He could see that she had a marvelous pretty throat and neck, and thought that she knew it too, and, young though she was, knew how to show it, for she would let her head droop, now this way, now that, and then she would lift her chin till all the whiteness of her throat was displayed, and then would dip her head again, as graceful as a swan.

Yet she was no languishing beauty who trusted only in her looks to bring down the game. When she turned herself about Darcy saw that her dark eyes were alive and alight with mockery, and her voice as well as her laughter sounded often and merrily. By and by indeed it was her voice and the King's which answered each other, while the rest of those about spoke less and less, as though they found it more absorbingly interesting to listen.

So now Darcy and Constable could catch most of what was being said by the fire. Just what it was about they could not tell, but the girl was certainly asking His Grace for something, now imperious, now wheedling, now saucily feigning a timorous humility.

"Well, then," said the King at last, "you shall have it. And if wives are more importunate than maids, God help me!"

"Oh! Sir, Your Grace is the noblest Prince in Christendom. I humbly thank Your Grace," and she gave him a very low curtsey, and caught his hand and kissed it; Darcy was not the only one who could see how the King seemed to wish to prevent her lips touching his hand. "And when?" said she, standing before him again, palm laid to palm under her chin—"And when?"

The King swore then, by God's Blood, that she was the most insolent beggar of them all, and when she only laughed at him, he swore again, and walked a few paces from her, but came back, and stood close to her. "Someday," he said, "someday."

"Lord!" she cried, "what a promise! As they say in France—'Faictes moi une chandelle quand je suis morte.' For I fear the fashion may have changed by then."

His Grace still stood very close to her, looking down at her laughing face. But he was not laughing.

"Someday. And it may not be as long time hence as you think."

He turned from her then and went away down the room. The group at the fire broke up, and several passed close to the window where Darcy and Constable stood. Darcy called to one of them, "Sir Thomas! Sir Thomas Wyatt!"

The tall bearded man would have gone by if Darcy had not caught him by the arm. He paused then unwillingly, while his eyes followed the girl in the blood-red gown. Only when he saw her join those about the Queen he shrugged his shoulders, and seemed content to linger.

They talked for a while about the Duke of Suffolk, and last year's campaign in France, and Sir Thomas was very caustically witty at the duke's expense. Then Darcy asked him—"Who was that merry, free-spoken maiden?"

Wyatt looked at him sharply. "She that was asking the King to give her a husband?"

"A husband?" said Darcy with his eyebrows up, and Sir Robert Constable muttered something about a whipping.

"Yes. Mistress Anne's a mad lass. She says she wants to have one of those billements of pearls, those new things that women are wearing. And since maids must wear their hair loose, so that without a husband she cannot have a billement, she says forsooth that she will have both."

Sir Thomas Wyatt shook his head smiling indulgently, and Darcy had to remind him that he had not told them who the young gentlewoman was.

"Why!" said he, "she is Mistress Anne Boleyn."

Darcy whistled. "Sister to her that is now Lady Carew and that was the King's minion a year or two—"

Wyatt interrupted him. "You North-country men talk too free."

"Well," said Darcy, very much the nobleman, yet with a spice of mockery in his voice, "perhaps you'll give me leave to say, Sir Thomas, that the King seems to like well that family. But how is your good lady and your bairns?"

Sir Thomas seemed to care for that subject as little as the other. He muttered a hasty answer and moved away. The two watched him pushing through the crowd till he stood beside Mistress Anne Boleyn.

"That manner lass," said Constable, "is born to make trouble among men."

Darcy agreed, and suggested that such should be drowned, like kittens, when young.

It was dusk when Lord Darcy parted from Sir Robert Constable near St. Laurence Pountney, and went on toward the Pope's Head Tavern where he was staying. His way took him past the long wall of the house which had been the Duke of Buckingham's and was called the Red Rose. The gates were shut now, and no smoke rose from the chimneys behind the mean tenements that bordered the road on either side of the gate-house. But though the great house was deserted the tenements swarmed. Men were sitting on the doorsteps, and within, by the light of the fires, women were cooking supper. Children ran out and in and screamed and laughed at their play in the road.

Just as he came abreast of the gate itself it opened a little and carefully. A man in a sober plain gown of good cloth came out, and after him an old woman in a red kerchief, and a very lovely young girl. She was so lovely that Darcy could not but stare at her. Between them squeezed out also a little maid of perhaps four years old, who stumped across the road and began to ferret about among the rubbish that lay there.

"Tomorrow, then," said the man to the elder of the two children. "And now a kiss, sweetheart."

He had his arm half about her but she drew back with a twist as strong and graceful as the motion of a fish turning about in a running river. He looked angry and muttered to her: "You wait till tomorrow."

"And so do you," said she, and dipped him a curtsey that did not accord with her company. Then she went back into the gates. The man went on just in front of Darcy; the old woman picked the child up from the kennel, and carried her, kicking, and clutching to her a trampled cabbage leaf, back into the great house.

It was not till Darcy had passed the garden of the Red Rose that he remembered who the elder of the two young girls must be. She was, he was sure, that bastard daughter of the Duke of

Buckingham, who, had her father lived, would have been the wife of young Fitzgerald. And now, Darcy supposed, she was to marry the man who had wanted a kiss from her, a comfortable worthy London merchant by his look.

Her beauty was such a rare thing, in tint so delicate, in contour so rich, and in spirit so quick and keen, that Darcy was still thinking of her when he reached the Pope's Head. He wondered how she came to be living still in the great deserted house. To the other little girl he did not give a thought, supposing her to be some neighbor's child.

❋ *The chronicle is broken to speak of Julian Savage, gentlewoman.*

Julian Savage, Gentlewoman

Yet little Julian was, as well as Margaret, the bastard daughter of the duke, by Agnes Savage, the priest's niece at Southampton, whom Edward Stafford had first seen one evening in the summer of the year young King Harry became King—that is, in 1509. She was down by the sea, shrimping at low water, when he and some others came riding back from trying their horses, one against the other, along the shore. She had on a coarse gown of soiled white woolen, and it was kilted up about her legs, as she stood almost to her thighs in the water. The sun, which was low and golden, lit her white and her gold to a lovely rose, and Edward Stafford knew that he had never seen so beautiful a creature. He rode on with the others, and as soon as he could rode wildly back to the shore again, and caught her up, pulling his horse back on its haunches with a long slither that cast the sand up all about like gouts of water. Then he sat, looking down into her face, and at the wet gown where it clung to her.

The sun had dropped below the horizon, but all the sky toward the west was warm, and in the east a half moon hung. The tide ran whispering in, with only the laziest small tumbling waves at the edges, that broke and spread forward, and then lapsed back. She stood quite still, meeting his eyes, until slowly, for in everything she did she was slow, she flushed as rosy as when the sunset light had painted her with rose. He took the wet sack of shrimps out of her hands, and rode back beside her, through the dunes, not even knowing that the salt water from the shrimps was soaking his hosen and spoiling his long green riding boots of Spanish leather.

He had her to Thornbury that autumn, caring nothing for what his wife said or thought about it, and Margaret was born almost a year to the day after that on which Edward Stafford first saw her mother. Then the duke married her to the miller of Rendecombe, giving her a good portion, a gown of green sarcenet and some fine shifts, and a chain of gold for little Margaret when she grew up; the Stafford knot set with garnets and pearls hung from the chain.

He did not see her again for nine years, and then only by one of those seemingly casual decisions which can bring life or death as their consequences. He was in the West Country, and, in the summer of 1519, found himself one day alone in a great wood, having lost the rest of the hunt. He followed a track that brought him to the fall of the hillside and thence, through the treetops, he saw far below a valley, a river, and a mill. A hind passing up into the wood with an axe on his shoulder told him that it was Rendecombe. When the hind had gone by, the duke sat looking down at the quiet and sheltered place. But for some red and white cows in the closes down by the river it seemed deserted. And then he saw a thin feather of smoke, blue as wood bluebells, go up from the chimney of the mill.

Between him and that distant quiet place the woods were dressed in all the colors of autumn's arrogant, mortal beauty, but the valley seemed still to be green with an unfading summer. He put his horse to the downward track with something of the impatience and the despair that had made him separate himself from the rest of the hunt. He was come, early in his years, to that time in his life when a man asks himself what he has been seeking? Whether he has found it? Whether it has been worth finding?

He said to himself that he was a fool to turn out of his way to see her, that by now she would have grown fat; and once he pulled up and half swung the horse round. Yet he went on.

He found her standing in the hazy autumn sunshine among the beehives, spinning. If she had been lovely before, now she was glorious.

Yet it was not her beauty which this time gave him happiness, because now what he needed, and what she brought him, was security, quiet, and rest. She chose, and he would in nothing gainsay her, to go back to the old priest at Southampton. "Then," he said speaking lightly, but clinging to her hands as if she were saving him from drowning, "then I shall come to you whenever the King goes to war with France." She said, "I shall be there."

She went back, and at Southampton, during the next summer, when the duke was in France with the King, she bore him another female child, and died. He learned it when he came again to find her, and found only the priest, a wailing infant, and Margaret, a little girl in a ragged gown and barefoot, but already beautiful.

So she and the baby, Julian, came up to London with the duke, and with a countrywoman whom he had hired to suckle the baby, and Julian had swaddling bands of the finest, and a little cap worked with gold, and a fine carved cradle, for the duke was unmeasured in his desire to care for Agnes's children; and in the autumn of the year he betrothed Margaret to young Fitzgerald, of whom he had the wardship.

But before Agnes had been dead a year the duke himself had gone the same way, by the axe, and for a week the two little bastards remained in a strangely quiet house, whose ordinary inhabitants were almost all gone, being replaced by men in the King's or the cardinal's livery, who went round into every room, making lists of all that was there, even of the cradle in which Julian Savage lay.

Soon after that the two were fetched away by the late duke's brother, Henry Stafford, Earl of Wiltshire. The little caps stitched with gold, which Julian had worn, were now replaced, when she had outgrown them, by plain ones of linen, and Margaret was no longer the betrothed of young Fitzgerald, but one of the serving gentlewomen to Earl Henry's countess; that was a change of fortune which grieved only Margaret, since the little one cared nothing for gold upon her caps, so long as she was wrapped warmly and had her posset regular.

And as she grew, and began to blunder about the house, the earl took note of her, because of the almost absurd and increasing likeness that there was between them. Unless she changed very much Julian would be no beauty, like her sister, for the earl, who was a thin man and lightly built as his brother the duke had been, lacked his fine features; Henry Stafford's jaw was so heavy as to make him almost seem undershot; his coloring was indeterminate and sandy, and the little lass was a small copy of him.

Afterward, when she was a grown girl, Julian could not remember her uncle's face, but only the jeweled buttons of his doublet, and a great pearl with some emeralds round it that he sometimes wore, and, clearer than all these, the velvet or damask pouches that hung at his belt and out of which came comfits, or money to buy them, or sometimes a gift of greater value, such as a ring for her finger, or a brooch to pin her gown. She remembered too the roughness of his cheek and chin as he kissed her; a salutation which she much disliked; and apart from these tangible things he remained in her mind as a person who was always kind. Not everyone in that house, which was the first place she remembered, was kind, but he was, and another man, an old priest who never kissed her but once, because he saw how she turned her baby face away, but who would let her climb over him, and make her cat's cradles, or show her the painted pictures in his books when her hands were clean.

But he died before her uncle, when she was not three years old, and Julian took good care not to remember him, except sometimes when she was going to sleep, and then would waken screaming, because she remembered something else (unless it was a nightmare) which made her stop her ears and dive under the bedclothes. There had been a dog that ran about slavering, and people had screamed and shouted. The old priest had tried to catch hold of the dog; some of the men had come running out with bows and shot it, but not before it had bitten the old man. And afterward—he—he—had died. For long after when the memory stirred, Julian, cowering in bed, would drive her thumbs into her ears, saying to herself: "It did not happen. I am awake. It is not true."

Two years after his brother, the earl died, and after that Julian got no more kisses and no more comfits. But though she did not know it, her uncle had set a charge upon his manor of Shute in Devon to give her a marriage portion, or, if she went into religion, a dower. It was no great thing, but more than Margaret got, for she got nothing. That, to Henry Stafford's mind, was fair enough; Margaret had her beauty; Julian had nothing but her likeness to himself, and it was right she should profit by it.

As for Margaret, her beauty was unfolding like the young leaves in spring, as fresh, as vivid, and as delicate. Once, after the earl died, Julian let out to the countess that Master John Bulmer had kissed her sister, a lot of times, behind the screens in the hall. She never was so indiscreet again, whether it were Master John who kissed, or any other, for Margaret was well beaten, and from the beating came away, without a tear on her cheeks, but flushed and disheveled, and beat Julian, telling her not to be such a little silly, not ever again. Julian never was; whatever she saw, she kept to herself.

One noon in November, a year after the earl's death, Julian was playing by herself inside the well house with some colored pebbles which she had collected. She was cold, but she blew on her fingers and spat once more on the pebbles to brighten their colors. Margaret came in wearing her cloak and hood. She said

nothing but, "Hush! Quiet!" and when the horns blew for dinner, would not let Julian go in, but after waiting a little took her
hand and led her, by way of the stables and privies, to the little
gate of the house that let out on Gracechurch Street. A bundle
and a very small trussing coffer lay on the ground by the gate.
Margaret picked them up, bade Julian, "Keep hold of my gown,
and don't let go or the Blackamoors'll get you," and then they
both went out into the street.

The house they came to Julian did not at all remember,
though Meg said that they had lived there with their father,
and it frightened her because it was so empty and so quiet.
Only an old woman and her husband lived there now in one
small room beside the gate. But Margaret insisted on going
about, opening doors upon empty echoing chambers where
rats scuttled away, and great clogged spiders' webs hung
across every corner. Julian began to cry, and hung back, but
Margaret would have her come on, and up the narrow turning
staircase—"For," said she, "you shall see the great chamber
where my lord duke slept." And when they came into a long
room, lighted dimly now by three windows in which the colored glass was all thickly clouded with dirt, she said: "Here my
father slept. He was your father too," she added, but rather as
though he had been so only in some indirect, secondary way.
Then she told Julian where the bed had stood, and told her of
the sparver and tester, damask cloth of gold with the Stafford
arms, and here a great painted chest, and just here a little coffer of ivory, very precious. "And all round the walls there were
hangings of arras. One was of the tale of King Arthur, and it

was woven with gold in the woof." The walls were bare now, and only the pegs for the hangings showed below the carved timbers of the ceiling.

Julian was glad to come back to the fire and the untidy huddle of the little room by the gate, though she was not glad to find Master William Cheyne there. Margaret did not seem to welcome him either. "Well, sir," she cried, "did you give him my message; and will he or no?" She looked at him with her chin up, very haughty but lovely as a thorny rose.

Master Cheyne looked away from her, and at the fire.

"He will, in a manner."

Margaret gave Julian a push from her, and went to the hearth, moving with her light step, that was almost dancing even when she walked. "What manner?" she asked, and Julian, knowing by her voice that she was angry, got herself away into a corner.

Master Cheyne was a pale young man with a pink and white complexion, fair hair, and a thin face with full lips; he had a sidelong glance that seemed to wait its opportunity for a stabbing look when others should be off their guard. Now his eyes came no higher than Margaret's knee.

"He says he cannot put away his wife."

"He told me he would."

"She has borne him five children, he says."

"Not since this day fortnight."

Master Cheyne looked as though he felt himself to blame. He rubbed his chin and mumbled something about it being best that Margaret should go back to her kinswoman.

"She's none of mine." And Margaret, forgetting for a moment the matter in hand, told Master Cheyne of all she had suffered at the hands of her uncle's widow, the countess. "And now she would have had me married to that creature with a hump on his back, and no more than a merchant; not one drop of gentle blood, let alone noble, in all his miserable body." As she ran on, Cheyne continued to shake his head and to murmur what might have been sympathy or advice.

"She would have been glad to disparage me by such a marriage," cried Margaret at last, "but she shall not."

Cheyne became audible then. He said that bastards could suffer no disparagement.

Margaret looked at him as if he were a sheep that had roared like a lion.

"I'm a Stafford," she said, after a minute, and he let that go by with a shake of his head. But he had managed to remind her that though not noble, and in trade, he was true- and not base-born, and also of a gentle house. She spoke to him now in a different tone, quick and broken, almost as if she asked his help—

"I cannot go back."

He looked at her then with one of his sharp looks, and she dropped her eyes. "You said that in a manner he would . . ." she muttered, turning her face from him.

"Why surely," Master Cheyne laughed. "Any man would, and most gladly."

Margaret was, as her father had been, a creature of swift movement. She sprang at him, struck his face with her open palm, and was away again. "I'll be no man's drab," she cried at him, and then broke into an astonishing storm of tears.

He watched her, and after a little went near her and took one of her hands. She turned to him then, suddenly childish, for she was still in years a child. "Oh! what shall I do? What shall I do?" she cried, and clung to him.

"Be my wife," he told her, so quiet and almost casual about it that she did not take it in at first.

When she did she drew away from him. "No. No."

But just then the old woman came back followed by her husband. She carried a pie, and he a big pot of ale. "Come now," they cried, full of good humor, "Fall to! Fall to!" and when Cheyne turned to the old woman, telling her what had passed, and bidding her counsel her lady, the old woman made no bones about it, but was all for a wedding.

Margaret looked from one to another, and then at Julian, who watched, and listened, from her corner. "Well," said she at last, "let's eat," so they all went to table.

At the end of it, and it was not a merry meal, Margaret spoke to Cheyne, as if they two were alone.

"I cannot stay here. I will not go back. How quick can it be done?"

He answered her, in the same curt tone, that it could be done as soon as she pleased. "And soonest will please me," he added, but she took no notice of that.

"Without they cry it at the church door," she objected, "it will not be lawful."

"Trust me. It shall be lawful," he said; but she took him up.

"I'll trust you if I see cause."

Yet she did not really distrust him, and did not guess for some time after—not until he told her indeed—that he had never taken her message to John Bulmer, but had come there that evening determined to have her himself if he might.

When it grew dusk they took him to the gate, and she refused him a kiss, and so laid up trouble for herself. Next day, very early in the morning they were married at St. Martin's, Vintry, for Master Cheyne was a vintner and lived in the parish. Afterward there was a feast, not a great affair, but there was plenty of wine to drink, and they kept it up, both friends and servants, long after the bride had been put to bed.

Nobody remembered about Julian, so she slept on some cushions in a window, cold, unhappy, and frightened at all the strange people.

1525

February 20

The cellaress was coming back from Grinton where she had been buying winnowing fans at the market. Dame Elizabeth Close was with her, and after them a Grinton man carrying the big wicker fans.

It was a pleasant walk back along the riverside, for though the sun did not shine the clouds were high and thin, dove-colored, except where a gleam of blue deepened them. It was dirty underfoot, but that did not matter for the two ladies were country shod. Dame Christabel was gay as she swung along, humming a tune, and feeling pleasure in everything, in the fair soft day, the business well accomplished at Grinton market, and in herself.

She stopped for a moment to look down at a pair of swans, softly oaring their way up the river, with silken ripples rising before them and streaming out, traced with fine lines like waving hair. One of the birds paused, turning her head to stroke the plumage of her side with a stretched snakelike head; with her knobbed brow she ruffled, and with her bill she smoothed the soft feathers. Her wings, slightly lifted, made a heart-shaped, shadowed hollow among the lovely white of her plumage.

The fellow from Grinton caught the two ladies up, and stood beside the cellaress as they watched the birds, which now sailed on past them.

"Good eating they be," says he, watching them wistfully. "I tasted their meat once. It was at Sir Rafe's marriage, and some was left, and came out to us that were eating in the great garner."

"Tcha!" said the cellaress, and moved sharply away from him. "These fellows think of nothing but their bellies. And how he stinks of garlic and I don't know what else!" She fanned the air under her nose, and walked quickly on. Dame Elizabeth agreed breathlessly; she found it difficult to keep up with the cellaress.

Behind them, at a good distance, trailed the man from Grinton. He was indeed a dirty creature, with foul teeth and a look of a hungry stable cat. But then he had eight children and a thriftless wife. That also was perhaps his own fault.

February 28

Lord Hussey had just gone away from the house which my Lord Darcy had hired at Stepney, when Lady Elizabeth came to her husband in the upper privy chamber, beyond the great chamber, where the two lords had been alone together. She looked about it, and could see no one, but, "Bet! Bet!" Lord Darcy called to her, and she found that he was standing in the deep window, looking down at the road, where in the early twilight the last of Hussey's gentlemen was turning the corner beyond the orchard wall. She said nothing for a minute, and, after the first quick glance, did not look at him. But that had been enough to tell her that my lord was angry.

She said at last, not beating about the bush as many wives might, but going to the heart of the matter because she was a great lady and her husband's trusted friend, "Tell me, sir, what my lord has said."

Darcy turned to her. "That fellow Banks will have a writ against us."

He was silent again, and, because she dreaded his silent anger, knowing him, old man as he was, capable of some wild doing if he brooded on a wrong, she prompted him. "It is this business of my Lord Monteagle's will?"

He told her "Yea," and she thought he would say no more, but suddenly he began to talk and to stride up and down the room, whacking at the table and the cupboards with his staff. "Was not Monteagle my friend? Did he not leave his son in my charge? Am I a man to waste the boy's heritage as this villain says?" She heard him grind his teeth as he came near her. "And he says—this Banks—that Hussey and I crept into poor

Monteagle's friendship when he was ill, by feigned talk of holy things. Am I such a man? Am I, Bet?"

He came and stood staring down at her. She shook her head.

"But he will have a writ against us, and hath procured a fellow in the cardinal's house to be his friend."

"But who? But what can he do?"

"You won't know him. Thomas Cromwell is his name. An apt servant of his master, and, they say, hath his master's ear. And much justice I'm like to get from that same cardinal who voided me from my office at Berwick, as if I were. . . ." Lady Elizabeth had heard it all before, and heard it patiently again. "But," she tried to soothe him when he had finished. "He cannot prevail so manifestly against justice."

"Who? Banks? The cardinal can. There's nothing in England he cannot."

She watched him as he stared out of the window. She was very well content with this second marriage of hers, and now she suddenly slipped her hand through his arm and pressed it, meaning to show him that she was angry with them that could believe such a charge against him. By all she knew of him he was not one to cheat the son of a friend who was dead, and that son left in his charge.

He took her hand and smiled at her, but stared out of the window again, and she saw him gnaw his lower lip, and the pressure of his fingers grew hard so that she was sure he had forgotten her.

He said: "His servants' servants will bear rule over us nobles soon," and after he had brooded a while she heard him mutter,

"If fair won't serve, then must foul. But some means we shall find to tumble him down."

"Ah! Sir!" she cried out, because it seemed so hopeless a thing, and dangerous, to work against the cardinal. He turned on her angrily.

"You don't understand, being a woman. No man can meddle in things of governance and keep his hands quite clean. If the honest men should try always to deal honestly, then they would leave the field to the knaves, and they should rule all."

She saw that they were at cross-purposes, and let it be so. After a silence she said:

"That fur on the sleeve of your gown is worn quite away. You must use your red say for a while and the wenches and I will see to this. There's a marten fur on an old gown of mine that will . . ."

"Mass!" he cried impatiently, interrupting her, but then he laughed. "Never, you tyrant, will you suffer me to wear the old stuff that I like. What does it matter if the budge is rubbed?"

She told him, as she had told him fifty times before, why such a thing should matter.

March 19

Master Cheyne came into the solar where Margaret was sitting by the fire with a heap of his shirts on the floor beside her, and a lute on her knee.

He looked at the shirts and at the lute, and then turned away and threw down in the window the birch that he had been using. He said that if that brat didn't learn her manners he'd not keep her. He did not say it blusteringly but rather in a flat, casual way, as if he had said that it would rain before night. But Margaret had learned to know him well enough to fear that tone more than she would have feared another man's bawling. She put down the lute, though she knew that it was too late, and picked up a shirt. As she stooped over it she was deciding that if he turned July out, she would go too. It was not that she had any tenderness for the little plain sister. Yet it would be worse than ever to be alone here. And they two were Staffords, she and July. He should not—she felt the heartening glow of pride rise—he should not wrong that blood.

"I'd be loath we should lose the profit of her marriage." She did not look up, but she knew that she had his attention. "My lord our uncle left her a portion for her marriage, or to dower her in religion."

He came then and sat beside her and began to question her closely. When she had told him all she knew he was silent, rubbing his chin. She knew that he was angry, both because she herself had no portion, and because Julian's was so small a thing. But she did not think that he would now send Julian away.

August 14

"But she will live?" said Sir Rafe Bulmer.

Dame Christabel, holding the veil under her chin to keep the wind from flapping it across her face, answered that, thank God, the Lady would live, and soon after that Sir Rafe Bulmer and his wife rode away from the priory.

As they passed the East Close on the way home, Sir Rafe heard Nan give a little giggle, and turned, and cocked an eyebrow at her.

"So there won't be a new prioress yet," she said, and he laughed out loud, though he told her not to be a ribald. "And cannot she be content," he said, "to be cellaress, and treasuress also?"

"All the same," she told him, "I like Dame Christabel."

"I like a woman to be gentle and meek spoken . . . womanlike," he argued, forgetting how little the young wild thing riding by him in a shabby green gown, stained with the cast of her hawks, was like the women he thought he approved of. "And," he said, speaking almost to himself, "if Dame Christabel were prioress we should never get those closes up at Owlands from the nuns."

Dame Nan knew all about those few closes of good grazing up among the sheep walks of Owlands; they had been granted to the nuns by her ancestor, that Roger Aske who had founded the priory, and every Aske after him had wished them back in the manor. Sir Rafe, though no Aske, wished for them most vehemently, and meant to get them if he might.

They turned up the hill and the track grew very steep; she, riding featherlight on her big horse, took the lead. Halfway up she turned to say over her shoulder:

"I think we might get them from her."

"Never," he said, and then, because he greatly respected this girl's shrewdness, "How?" and he drove his horse up alongside hers to hear the better.

But Nan shook her head and was vague. She was thinking, she told him, that if ever there came a time of great need at the priory, then, "She wouldn't be afraid to sell them, if there were need. The others would be afraid."

He admitted the truth of that. "But what sort of great need?" She could not tell him.

September 18

Lord Darcy sat in the closet that led off from the council chamber in the Castle of Pomfret. It was chilly there, so they had set a brazier of coals near his chair, and, since the day was gloomy, candles burnt on the table among the scatter of papers that he and the steward, Tom Grice, were busy with.

They had talked of Darcy's Manor of Torkesey in Lincolnshire, looking through old parchments, and a copy of the Lincoln Doomsday to trace out my lord's rights, and had come now to the matter of the prioress of Fosse, whose predecessor had cut down thirteen oak saplings in the waste of my lord's manor there, claiming that they grew in her freehold. But she had lost her case, and now this new prioress must pay to my lord 117*s.*

"They were but little saplings," said Tom Grice, biting on his knuckles, and looking at his master under his big rough eyebrows.

"Well?" Darcy's tone was not encouraging.

"The bishop of Lincoln thinks the fine very grievous."

"I've no doubt." Darcy was stiff. It was clear that Tom Grice agreed with the bishop.

"Look you, Tom," said Darcy, with that sudden comradely tone that made men love him, "you think that because these ladies are in religion I should deal softly with them. But I'll not. If it is a grievous fine, yet they shall pay it. They have land and rents of their own, and for what? To serve God?" He gave an angry laugh. "Snug in their beds perhaps. Oh! no, it's not only of the nuns of Fosse I'm thinking. It may be a well-ordered house. But all these religious live easy and lie soft. I tell you, Tom, there's no estate of the realm so meet to be reformed as the religious, and the clergy."

He shifted his papers about on the table impatiently, and said: "Now, what of the woods in Knaith Park? How much can we fell?"

Tom Grice, having in mind Lord Darcy's debts, understood that he must choose between the prioress of Fosse and the woods of Knaith Park. My lord would not, and could not, spare both. Tom abandoned the prioress. "It were pity to fell at Knaith," he said; and they began to argue that out.

November 20

Julian wakened up at a sound, but too late to know what it was that had wakened her, so she was frightened, and her heart was pounding before she was fairly awake. And then the light from the torches, carried before the merry party of gentlemen just going by, cut like a knife through the shutters, and began to slide, silent and furtive, across the unceiled timbers of the floor above, rippling over the big crossbeams like a snake. Last of all it ran down the wall in a long pencil of brightness, and then was eaten by the dark. Julian began to scream, and then buried herself in the bed lest Master Cheyne had heard her.

1526

July 8

The cellaress and Dame Bess Dalton came slowly along the side of the wood from the home of the parish priest.

"Poor soul!" said Bess, and sighed.

"He can blame none but himself," Christabel told her. "For years he has soaked himself in ale."

They had been to visit the old priest in the parsonage which was just beyond East Close. He lay sick in bed, with his face still twisted, but had now got again both his speech and the use of his hands, and, so far as Christabel could see, was likely to live.

They stood for a moment at the gate of Kid Close before going out into the heat of the open field.

Christabel thought—"How these old people live on!" The prioress was in her mind, as well as the priest, and down at the bottom of her mind, in a place nearly dark, even to herself, was the thought that it would be well if there were a way by which they could be made to yield place to others, younger, more able.

October 3

Although there was a moon outside the window, inside the curtains of the bed it was quite dark. Lord Darcy, wide awake, and restless because of the unseasonable warmth of the night, shifted uneasily, and, because he had a troubled mind, he sighed.

"Sir?" his wife whispered, and, "Tom?"

"Go to sleep, sweet."

"What's amiss, Tom?"

"It's too hot for October," he told her, but the obvious truth did not put her off. He felt her hand grope for his, and when she had found him she said again, "What's amiss?"

He broke out, and it was with a great sigh—"By God's Death! I think all the world's amiss."

"Is it," she asked, "this great battle in the East that the infidels have won?" It was only a little more than a month since the King of Hungary and most of his chivalry had fallen at Mohacz, and the Turk was pouring into the eastern parts of Europe.

He told her it was that, but she asked, "And what else?"

He said nothing for a moment, and she felt him move in the darkness, and knew that he had shaken his head.

"If you were not a woman who is as secret as any man," said Darcy, "I could not tell you. Come near that I can speak low."

When her head was close to his mouth he told her, in a whisper.

At first she could not believe him.

"The King put away his wife? Divorce the Queen? After all these years? How many? Fifteen or more. He cannot. Why should he wish?"

She was silent, and then murmured, "How do you know this thing?"

"Never mind how, but I know. There's the bishop of Bath in Rome treating with the Holy Father of it."

"Shame on him then—the bishop I mean."

"Oh! He likes it as little as any. '*Istud benedictum divorcium*,' they say is what he calls it."

She took him up. "'As little as any?' You like it little?"

He moved restlessly. "God knows—" he began again. "If it's the King's will—"

"Fie on you, Tom," she cried, "it can't be God's."

He stiffened at her rebuke. "The King needs an heir."

"The Princess Mary."

"She's a girl."

"She's lawful. But there's the bastard boy as well."

"Hush!" he told her, but she said she was not afraid to speak the truth, and Henry Fitzroy might be Duke of Richmond but certainly he was a bastard.

"And why else," she persisted scornfully, "does the King wish it? There was great talk about that niece of Norfolk's, the Boleyn girl. Ah!" She read his silence. "It's that, is it?"

After a long time she turned suddenly toward him.

"Tom, why will you suffer this as if it would be well?"

He told her, hesitating, at first, but then in a hard tone—"For an heir for one thing. And for another because, in so great a business as this will be, we may find means to pull down the cardinal."

She drew away from him, but he could hear what she muttered to herself. "God forgive you men!" she said.

November 1

When Julian heard one of Master Cheyne's men say that he was going down to Asselyn's Wharf to find the master of a ship unloading there, she waited till he had gone out of the house, and then ran after him, and asked if she might go too.

He looked a little doubtful, but made no trouble. She could come if she would, but she must be a good lass, and hold on to his coat, and not go roving off nowhere alone. So she went with him, one hand clutching the skirts of his brown coat, and the other pressed tight to her thin, flat chest to keep the precious scraps of silken stuff from slipping down inside, out of reach.

Those precious bits she had found in the yard a week ago, and swept up in her hand, and hidden, meaning to keep them for always. They were bits thrown aside from the making of a gown for Meg, of a scarlet silk so brilliant, rich, and lustrous, that the stuff seemed to hold in it a light and life of its own.

But just after she had found and hidden the pieces, she had seen, when at Billingsgate with one of the women who had gone to buy fish, the ship. The ship had been quite a long way off down the river, but near enough for Julian to see great yellow and green sails, and pennons of all colors straining out upon the wind. Among all the shouting and stir of the fishermen and the housewives and the servants on the wharf, the voice of the ship's trumpets had come across the water, sharp, eager, and confident, as she moved off down the river toward the sea. The ship was a lovely thing, and more, she was free and was going away.

All the way home Julian had tried to find out where the ship was going, but the woman could not tell her. However, it did not matter very much. That night in bed Julian suddenly saw a way of following the ship, a way of belonging to the ship, or else of possessing the ship; she was not sure which.

So, today, when Master Cheyne's man was talking to the little wizened master of the *Trinity* of Calais, which was to

Julian's eyes a small and wretched craft, she let go his coat, and slunk off to the edge of the wharf, till she was looking down into the restless green water that sidled by, slapping at the wooden piers of the wharf, and then dipping past, sleek and shining.

Julian took out the little bundle from inside her gown, clutched it once as hard as her hand could close, so as to say it good-bye, and threw it down into the water. It spread out, a brilliant spatter of scarlet, for one instant, then darkened sadly as the water soaked through it. That shocked Julian so that she cried out, for she had thought of it sailing on after the ship in all its bravery. But still, it did begin to sail. She followed it with her eyes, leaning over till she began to be dizzy, and then went stumbling backward just as Master Cheyne's servant found and snatched her. He took her home, holding her not very gently by the arm the whole way, and all the way Julian wept for the lovely silk which she had thrown from her.

December 31

The cellaress had gone into the kitchen to make wafers for the New Year feast. She would trust no one else to make them. She guessed that if she left it to the cook much of the cream and some of the rose water would go into dainties that would never come to the nuns' tables.

The cook was very busy today preparing for tomorrow's dinner that all the priory servants would eat. There was a big cauldron of souse steaming over the fire, and on the table a row of pots where the brawn was just setting in a rich jelly, and five great pies. Two women were plucking poultry and in the yard outside one of the men was singeing off the bristles of the pig that had been killed. He passed the flame over the carcass, shielding his eyes from the smoke as well as he could, while some of the carter's brats watched him, absorbed. Now and again he would flourish the burning straw toward them to make them jump back, and then the sparks dripped, and the flame curled back on itself like a horse's tail in the wind.

The cook went by the cellaress toward the big bake oven. He paused a moment, leaning on the long wooden shovel for lifting out the loaves.

"They'll have a rare feast and right good cheer," said he, wagging his head about at all the food. The cellaress was just breaking her eggs. She tipped the oozy yolk of one backward and forward from one half of the shell to another, and let the white drain sluggishly down. She tossed the yolk into the bowl of finest white wheat flour, before she answered.

"Give 'em good cheer, and they'll work the better. I'll not grudge it them, nuts and apples, carols and all."

The cook went on and opened the bake oven, letting out a tide of warmth, and an exquisite sweet smell of bread. When he had got out the loaves he shoveled them onto a wooden tray, and carried them out on his shoulder. The cellaress glanced at them as they passed her, and stopped sprinkling cinnamon into her batter. "What are those?" she asked him sharply.

"Loaves," he told her, a little saucily, but dropped his eyes when she looked at him.

"Of wheat flour? I thought you had baked enough for the ladies' tables, and for the servants."

"These," he said, "are for the poor men's dole," and he went on with them, hurrying, as if they were too heavy to linger with. She did not speak again till he came back, and then she told him that the poor did not have wheaten bread, but maslin, "and see that you put in a fit amount of rye, not just a handful to say it's maslin."

If it had not been Christmastime, and he had not already drunk a good pot of mulled ale, he might not have tried to argue. But now he said, "It's Christmas. The poor's fed for Christ his sake—"

"Not on white wheat flour," she told him. "Poor man means idle man. If they'll eat let them work. If you kindle more faggots in the oven at once you can bake the maslin after the pies."

He went off mumbling inaudibly, while she continued to beat the creaming batter in which the long, sluggish bubbles were rising.

1527

February 13

Margaret Cheyne kept the door of the solar open long enough for her husband and all the company drinking there to hear her mocking laughter. Then she slammed it and went off, still laughing, down the stairs and into the kitchen. Yet she was afraid. "But—No!" she told herself, pausing outside the door of the kitchen, and hearing the din inside there. "I'll not fear him," and she tossed up her chin. She was beginning to learn that she could, almost, make William Cheyne fear her. But to do that she must be herself reckless and fearless. She thought, loitering in the darkness, and thinking of his anger, "I must goad him, and goad him, until—" But she did not know whether it would be until he was goaded into a killing cruelty, or into fear of nothing more substantial than her spirit. "I'm a Stafford!" she cried out to that spirit, to hearten it. "He shall smart for all."

She opened the door of the kitchen, and stood still. At the sight of her the babel died down, and it was not because she was the mistress, but because even the most fuddled of the men drinking there saw her beauty in that moment glowing like a blade before the smith seethes it.

"Where is my sister?" she asked them, looking about for July.

She was not there, but one said this, and another that, and then one of the men said he'd seen her at the stable door. Margaret knew now where she would be, and left them to drink.

But though she knew Julian's bolt-holes she had much trouble in laying her hands on the child in the darkness of the hayloft, and before she succeeded she caught her foot in her new gown and heard the damask rip. So when she had Julian by the arm she twisted it with even more intent to hurt than she would have meant otherwise, and Julian kicked and screamed, and so got a crueler wrench yet.

"You're not to lie, you hear, you little jade," Margaret cried, shaking the child.

Julian screamed at her. "You lie. You do. You said that chain was your own that Sir John Bulmer gave—Ow! Stop it! Don't!"

"Hold your tongue then. It was my own since it was given me. And if you tell him that Sir John . . ."

"I'll not. I'll not. Oh! Meg, do stop."

"Very well. But you're not to tell lies."

Julian, dropping on the hay, mumbled that she had to tell lies.

"Then don't tell such as he must know are lies. Saying it was one of the cats that ate the marchpane off that subtlety, and then being sick of it all over the place when he beat you."

"I wasn't sick of it till he beat me."

"Well," said Meg, "if he beats you I shall twist your arm, because when he's beaten you he's as likely as not to beat me."

May 6

The King, passing through the gallery that looked onto the orchard at Greenwich Palace, stopped to speak to this one or that. When he came to where Lord Darcy and the Marquess of Exeter leaned beside a window, sunning themselves, he stayed quite a long time talking and was very gracious. Darcy had been speaking to the marquess of the hospital and free school that he had been building, and the King asked questions about it, and spoke nobly and gravely of the value of such foundations, "so many in old time, and so few, alas, in ours," said he. And then he must give Darcy something for the chapel of the hospital; "Go to the keeper of the Great Wardrobe. Ask him for something of the chapel stuff he has: a Mass book or a cope, or what you will. Here—I'll write an order." He called, then blew on a little golden whistle that hung on a chain round his neck, and when someone had fetched a clerk an order was written, and Darcy put it in his pouch.

But while the clerk wrote, and while Darcy was speaking his thanks, the King began to fidget, and to glance toward the open window beyond Darcy's shoulder, and at last he pushed past him, put Exeter by with his hand, and leaned out of the window. A girl's voice was singing down below in the orchard while someone thrummed on a lute. Darcy caught the eye of the marquess, and each looked to the ground. They knew what it was that the King wished to see, for they had been watching before he came a group of young men and women sitting together on the grass, the women all gabbling like ducks. Mistress Anne Boleyn was among them, and she it was who was singing.

The King turned at last from the window. He had a look as of a man who has opened a box to feed his eyes on the sight of a very rare jewel; now he had closed the box, but the glow and softness of delight were still on his face and a little private smile that faded quickly. He went away, and they saw the crowd open for him, and in the empty space he met the cardinal, and the French ambassadors.

When the King and these others had gone, many people left the gallery, but the marquess and Darcy stayed at the window. The young things below had begun to play Hoodman Blind, and had scattered among the trees, with laughter, screams, and shouting.

The marquess turned his long, serious, irresolute face to Darcy, and he was frowning.

"My Lord of Norfolk," said he, "swears that niece of his to be a very virtuous and chaste lady. But—"

Darcy could have laughed to see this great nobleman blushing for a girl who had, Darcy thought, forgotten how to blush before she was well out of the schoolroom.

"They say her sister—" he began, but the marquess did not let him finish, muttering hastily, "Nay, my lord, nay. Let be!"

Darcy let it be, and asked what else Norfolk had said.

"It was all in praise of Mistress Anne. How she would leave the court and away to Hever, though her father was angry."

"He would be," said Darcy. "Some fathers would be sorry that a daughter should be a minion, even if it were a King's, but not Sir Thomas Boleyn."

The marquess shook his head, though not in disagreement, for he cared as little for the Boleyns as Darcy did.

"And who," Darcy persisted, "are this virtuous, chaste lady's friends? Sir William Compton that's an open adulterer; Bryan—Bryan. By the rood! he's made the name enough common in the stews. And, if it comes to a point, who is my Lord of Norfolk to talk of virtue, who keeps that drab Bess Holland in the same house as—"

Exeter hushed him again. "And," says he, "surely a wench is virtuous that will resist a king's desires. Grant her that."

"Or grant her a clever, scheming jade that dares to play for a high stake."

"What can she win? God's Body, my lord, not that! She cannot think to be Queen." He had whispered the word, but still he looked back into the almost empty room behind them.

Darcy raised his eyebrows and shrugged his shoulders. "If it is that she aims at, she plays well. Three years ago His Grace began to affect her, and now he looks at her as if he were a boy in love."

The marquess, remembering the King's face as he turned from the window, fell into a very troubled silence.

Meg had let Julian come out with her when she went to buy a pair of gloves, a sugar loaf, and some saffron. Meg walked ahead, leading a black and white dog on a leash of green ribbon, and Julian came behind with old Cecily who was to carry home in her basket the sugar loaf and the saffron.

In Lombard Street they came on Sir John Bulmer. He was talking to another young man, or rather, the other was talking to him, very merrily, in a voice that had in it a ringing note like that of a finely cast bell, and with a broad North Country touch in his speech like Sir John's own.

Sir John saw Meg, and said something hastily to the other, and left him to come to her.

"Who was that?" Meg asked, looking after the young man who had waved his hand to Sir John and gone off down the street; as he went they could see him turn his head this way and that, alert and quick.

"He looks a merry gentleman," Meg persisted, knowing that Sir John, if he could, would have emptied the streets of men when she came out. "And comely too, though it's a pity he hath not another foot to his height."

"And another eye to his face!" Sir John cried derisively.

"God 'a mercy! Hath he but one eye? How did he lose the other?"

"How do I know? I never asked him."

"But tell me his name."

Sir John told her very crossly that his name was Aske—Robin Aske. "And I don't know why you care to know," said he.

"I don't care. But I like to see you chafe." She looked up at him sidelong, laughing, and then became serious and drew near to him as they walked. By the time they reached the glover's shop he was in a very good humor, and bought Meg two pairs of Louvain gloves.

❋ *The chronicle is broken to speak of Robert Aske, squire.*

Robert Aske, Squire

The Askes, the younger branch of the Askes of Aske, had been at Aughton for about a hundred years—since the time when an Aske had married an heiress of the de la Hayes. For much more than a hundred years the old castle on the mound above the fen had been deserted and left to crumble; cows and goats had browsed over it, and down to the low-lying ings beside the river, for longer than anyone could remember to have heard tell, even by the oldest grandfathers. Instead, the lords of the Manor of Aughton, de la Hayes first, and Askes after them, had lived in the moated house a little to the southeast of the castle mound, and exactly east of the chancel of the parish church, so that they went to Mass through the orchard, and across a little bridge over the moat, and so into the churchyard.

Mound and church and moated house all stood at the tip of a tongue of land jutting out from a sort of low, flat-topped island in the fen; east of them on the same island was Aughton village, and to the north Ellerton, where the Gilbertine Canons were; but between Aughton church and the Derwent was nothing in summer but the green ings where the cattle grazed and grew fat, and pools and twisting channels where the rushes whispered, and marshy land with tussocks of reed; in the winter, when Derwent was in flood, the river came up, filling all the pools and waterways, drowning the reed beds and black quaking paths which only a man born in Aughton would dare to use, so that the feet of the churchyard wall were in the flood, and the squat Norman tower looked out, west and south, over nothing but water.

The house, at first cramped up within its moat, had now straggled over it toward the village, letting the ditch on this side silt up with farm refuse, so that when you came to the manor from the village you passed first all the huddle of barns and stables, the stack-yard, the carpenter's shop, and the long thatched shippens. Only after these you came to the corner of the old dairy where the moat began again, and so to the little gatehouse, stone below, and timber and daub above, for stone was scarce in these parts.

Inside the gatehouse lay the courtyard: the new dairy to the right, the brewhouse to the left, and opposite you the hall, its roof as high as the upper stories of the rest. Partly to please his wife, and partly because so many were doing it in these days, Sir Robert Aske had pulled down the old buildings at the farther end of the hall from the screens, and built a fine winter parlor there looking out on the stack-yard, and also southward over the fen; above it were two new bedchambers, in one of which all the younger children, from Robin downward, had been born. That older chamber, at the other end of the hall, above the kitchen, in which Sir Robert himself had been born, and in which his father had died, was now divided into several smaller rooms where the older children slept, joined every now and then by the newest and youngest, just promoted from the cradle to share a bed with an elder sister or brother.

Dame Elizabeth Aske was proud of her winter parlor when it was new, and spent much of her spare time embroidering cushions and stitching at hangings for it; but Sir Robert never took to it. He would go there if she asked him, for he was a good-tempered man, though not an easy one, and was, besides, fond almost to weakness of his wife. But habit kept him to the hall, and he would, if not prompted, potter about in the big bay just inside the screens which had been built out on the foundation of what had once been a tower, where the bows stood in their racks, and his favorite hawk sat humped on her perch.

And so, except sometimes when there were guests of great honor, the family never ate in the parlor, but had their meals in the old manner in the hall, and Sir Robert would carry on conversations with the plowman, or the stockman, down half the length of the room, and then turn to tease Dame Elizabeth in a boyish way that never left him, or to cuff the lads for quarreling or for bad manners at table.

Of these lads John did not quarrel with Kit, for John, though the eldest son, was always a gentle child, and a delicate, reserved youth. Nor did Richard, for he died when he was five, and was, for two years before that, a poor little shrimp, more often ill in bed than running about; but as soon as Robin was old enough to quarrel with anyone he and Kit were rarely at peace. Kit was five years old when Robin was born, and even from the first he resented the fuss that his elder sisters, Julian and Bet, made of the new baby. For they, being only too delighted to have such a creature to pet, certainly spoilt him outrageously, the more because Robin was a towardly child, sturdy and merry, and adorably ticklish; at any moment, just by feeling for his well-covered ribs, they could draw from him shrieks and gurgles of laughter. Kit therefore conceived it his duty to supply some discipline to counterpoise their petting.

This, being five years the elder, he could at first do easily, either by tongue or hand, and even in those early days Kit's tongue had a sting in it, and ran nimbly. As for physical correction, Kit supplied that too, when the elders were not looking, and Robin got many a buffet, at which, if he could not dodge it, he would howl lustily, till one day Jack told him that no man of worship would cry like that for a blow, but only cowards and those of villain blood. After this Robin did his best to behave like a man of worship, or at least to cry quietly and in secret.

But by the time that he was eight, and Kit thirteen, he did not try to dodge Kit's fist, nor passively to endure, but instead gave blow for blow. The difference in their ages did not count for so much now, and was to count for less as time went on, for Robin, always a stout and healthy child, was now a big boy for his age, not slim and graceful as both Kit and Jack had been, but stocky and sturdy, resembling in this, as in much else, his father, Sir Robert. Kit, on the other hand, Kit, with his mouth already twisted and tightly compressed by the habit of enduring the intermittent pain in his back, went always lame of one leg—nothing very much, but enough to make him slow on his feet in a fight. Because of that slowness, and the lameness, and the pain, of all of which he was miserably ashamed and which he concealed as much as he could, Kit set out to make sure of a foothold for his pride. If he could not run, then he would ride; if he could not fight on foot because of his dragging leg, then at least he would shoot with the bow so that none could match him. He heard his father one day telling Tom Portington, who was to marry Kit's sister Julian, how Kit had ridden the bay stallion, and jumped Hogman's Pool—the mad knave. "Of course I beat him for it, for he might have killed the beast and himself in that black bit of bog down there. I've known a horse go under there in five minutes, and no one would have seen him, for we were all the other way, busy with the barley." Sir Robert laughed. "Mass! I beat him soundly, but I liked him for it. I think he fears nothing, and he's got a good horseman's seat, and hands you couldn't better. Robin's nothing to him." Young Portington said that Robin would come on when he was a bit older, perhaps, and Sir Robert agreed, but Kit had slunk away by then without them knowing that he had been there. He had heard enough to warm his heart for him, and he went off to the stable and petted the bay stallion; he even shed some tears on the smooth, warm, and shining coat, because he was so glad. He took care, too, not to come away till there was one of the stable boys there to see him, walking out of the bay's stall, with the beast nuzzling his ear. He knew that most people, even Sir Robert himself, were chary of going too near the stallion's hoofs and teeth.

But, though Kit might be happy at such praise for a while, he was always too conscious that Robin was coming on hard at his heels ever to be really content. Robin was never tired, never ill, never, except when he fought with Kit, out of temper; and even the fighting he seemed to enjoy, and only to wish to knock Kit down for the fun of it. If he missed the mark with his arrow, he laughed; if he hit in the midst, he laughed. It was not that he was contented to do a thing badly; when he failed he would go on trying always harder, but cheerfully, and without any shame of his failure. Kit knew very well, that soon, though Robin would never equal him as a horseman, in everything else his younger brother would pass him, and the knowledge was bitter.

Things were always happening which made it clear how quickly Kit was being overhauled by the youngster. Though Kit was a very pretty bowman he had not the plain strength for a man's bow till he was close on seventeen. Then he got his first bow of full force, a lovely one with a fine long grain from one end to the other. He was immensely proud of it, though it was as much, even now, as he could manage, and for a while his shooting fell off, and Robin beat him at every match. All Kit could do was to mock the boy unmercifully for the way he had, when he had loosed, of standing on one foot and curling the other round his leg till he saw the arrow strike.

But as he came into his new bow Kit began to go ahead again. They were at the butts one still evening in summer, just after hay harvest. The light was beginning to fail a little, and Sir Robert, who had been shooting with them, had gone in. Their mother had left the place long ago to see that the little girls had been put to bed, so only the Aske boys and some village lads were there. Jack said it was time to go in; what use in shooting when you could not see, and to hit was all luck. But Kit, who was shooting beautifully, would not give up, nor would Robin, simply because he knew that when they went into the house it would be supper and then bed.

So, at last, it was Kit and Robin shooting against each other, the one from the men's distance, and the other from farther forward, because children's bows, being cut from the branch and not the bole, are weaker in their cast.

Then Robin, drawing strongly, snapped his bow; the arrow went wreathing aside, with everyone yelling "Fast! Fast!" to warn each other out of the way. But it lit, with no harm done, in a patch of thistles.

"You little fool!" cried Kit, "you might do hurt to anyone that way."

"How could I help it? It's that bow. It's all knotty and weak." Robin slipped the string out of the notch, chucked away the splintered pieces of the bow, and went off to get his arrow. He was not put out, being used to Kit's tongue, and being indeed rather pleased with himself for breaking his bow. When he came back he said, again, "It was all knotty and weak. I'll ask if I can have a man's bow."

"You!" cried Kit, but Robin had gone to Jack and was crouching down by him. "Lend me yours, Jack," he said. "Let me try how I can shoot with it."

"No!" Kit shouted, in such a strange voice that Jack turned and stared at him.

"I pray you, do," Robin wheedled, and Jack pushed the bow into his hands.

Kit got up and went away as quickly as he could, but not quickly enough. He did not hear the thrum of the string as Robin loosed, but heard him shout, "Ouch!" as the shaft flew wide and everyone laughed; Kit caught the sound of Robin's laughter among the rest. Then Robin must have loosed again, for he cried, with triumph in his voice, "There! That was better. I like this bow. I like the way he pulls so strong against the hand."

It was Robin who brought Kit's bow up from the butts where he had left it. He found Kit reading in the tower corner in the hall. Kit only glanced up from the book, and then held out his hand for the bow, without a word.

"Shall I wax him for you?" Robin asked, and stooping over the bow he rubbed his cheek on the wood, as if he loved it.

"No." Kit wrenched it out of his hand, and Robin went away whistling, to snatch as he passed at a dish of pasties that one of the women was carrying in for supper. She let out a blow at him, and he dodged it, laughing, his mouth full, and spluttering crumbs. Kit thought him insufferable.

Next morning, which was the morning before Jack's wedding day, he and Kit got up as soon as it was light, and dressed quietly. But Robin woke as Kit was getting into his hosen. "Where are you going?" he asked, and without waiting for an answer, bounced out of bed.

Jack told him, "A-fishing," and Kit said, "We don't want you," but he cried, "Ah! Let me come," and Jack, too weak, thought Kit, allowed it. It had been Kit's idea to have Jack to himself this time. Now Robin had spoiled it.

The sun was not yet up as they went out from under the gatehouse, but the sky was delicately and serenely blue. Some of the men were just going by from the village to mow their own hay, now that the Askes' hay was cut and carried. One of them hailed, "Master Robin! Master Robin!" and Robin ran off to him, and came back waving a pipe in his hand, such as shepherds play on. "See what Mat has made for me. Thank you, Mat," he yelled shrilly after the men; Mat's red hood jerked in acknowledgement.

They went down past the churchyard, across the ings, and on among the pools; the waters seemed as still as the air above them; they were bright with the sky, though a thin mist steamed up from them. The mist would be gone before noon, to gather again toward evening.

"It's as still as glass," said Kit, looking down into one of the pools and speaking low because of the silence and stillness of the unsullied day.

"No," said Robin, pointing at the shadows of the alders on the far side; "look how the leaves shiver in it." It was true that the reflection trembled ceaselessly in the water, perfect and unbroken, while the trees themselves were still. But, "God's Blood!" Kit muttered crossly, and went on after Jack with his rod jigging over his shoulder. Robin came behind; he began to tootle on the pipe; then he ran forward and said that he was the minstrels from York, playing before Jack at his wedding, and so preceded them, posturing and blowing on his pipe. Even Jack was angry with him and Kit hated him. When they came to the place where they meant to fish they turned their backs on him and told him to go to the devil.

He did not go, and soon, one way or another, he tried Kit beyond endurance. Kit struck him, and the blow sent Robin off into one of his brief rages. He skipped back, and fishing out a big handful of weed from the water's edge he slung it at Kit's face, yelling with triumph when he saw how lucky his aim had been. Kit, half blinded by the dripping, stinking stuff, ran at him, the long rod held like a lance.

And then Robin gave one scream, and went backward; for a moment he wriggled about on the dewy grass as wildly as if he had been a fish they had landed, but he got up again to his knees, and knelt bowed and with his hands over his face.

They both ran to him, Jack scared, and Kit scared and angry, crying, "What's the matter? What's the matter?"

He did not answer, and Kit wrenched at one of his hands and managed to drag it away. He let it go very quickly.

"His eye!" he said. "His eye!"

Because Kit was no good at running, it was Jack who went back to the house, and burst into his father's and mother's bed-chamber, shuttered and dark still, to tell them what had happened. Kit came after, leading Robin, who stumbled along with his hands over his face, and blood running down his chin on the right side, and blood sopping the breast of his shirt.

Kit wanted to be the one to ride to York for the surgeon, but Sir Robert sent off one of the men with a led horse. There was nothing for Kit to do but to go down to the river bank and bring back his fishing rod, and Jack's; he found Robin's pipe there, and brought that too.

This happened in July, and it was early September before Robin was out again. He had grown while he was in bed; he was pale now, instead of brown as a nut; and, for a while at least, he was rather quiet. Kit, whose heart had been wrung by fear, shame, and compassion, was uncommonly gentle to him, and for a few months there was peace between them.

By this time Jack's young wife was getting used to her new estate. Nell was fifteen, a little fair thing, with a finished prettiness which time might harden and sharpen. After being very meek at first, she was now beginning to show off. Sir Robert laughed at and petted her, Dame Elizabeth was too gentle to give her more than a mild rebuke. It was Robin only who infuriated her with his teasing. In return she would jeer at him for lacking an eye, and then he would threaten to lift the empty eyelid, and would chase her about the house on that threat. They were never good friends, and it was still worse between them when, in the New Year after Robin lost his eye, Dame Elizabeth died. Robin stopped teasing Nell; that had been done not out of unfriendliness, but because, being a boy, tease he must. Now he left her alone, except to scowl at her under his heavy brows, and sometimes to go out of his way to cross her. But Kit came on him one day, hammering at a bent arrow barb on the anvil in the workshop as if it were a thing he meant to kill, and with tears running down his face.

He smudged them away with a dirty hand when he saw Kit, and said, "I hate her. She is glad that our mother is dead."

Kit had seen that too. They talked about Nell, then about their mother for a time, and afterward for a while Kit was quite warm toward Robin.

By the time spring came, and Robin had passed his thirteenth birthday, he was strong again, but he had found out that there were things that could not be well done by someone who was short of an eye. He could not now aim surely with the bow, nor play at quarterstaff. At first he tried, harder and harder, then suddenly gave it up, and after that would sit watching the others, calling out now and again, "Oh! well shot!" or "Well laid on!" At home he would keep his bow most carefully waxed, so that it glittered like gold—it was a good bow, full strength, which Sir Robert had brought from York while he was in bed—but he rarely took it out, except sometimes to go fowling among the pools by himself.

One blustering evening that April, the young men were again at the butts. Kit was shooting most cunningly, so that the shifty wind hardly balked him at all. Robin sat watching among the rest, but when the groups broke and reformed, as one after another went to take his turn at the mark, he was left alone. And now he did not watch. Kit, glancing that way more than once, saw him digging his hands into the new grass, tugging at it, and frowning. After a while he got up and went away; Kit noticed that too, and grew angry, knowing whose doing it was that Robin did not now take his turn with the rest. Their brief accord was over. Kit could not forget what he had done to his brother, and besides that, since Robin had been ill he seemed to have grown up in his mind; whereas before he had fought Kit with his fists, now it was with his tongue, and he was as resolute, and was becoming as quick in argument, as he had been in the other kind of fighting.

Robin set off to go to Ellerton, through the great open Mill Field, in which two plows were still at work, breaking up the fallow for next autumn's wheat. He walked with his head down, kicking at the clods that lay loose on the trodden path. Before him Ellerton was half buried in pear blossom and the bright-budded apple trees, but he did not glance about, nor, hardly, at the men trudging back from the fields or the women at their doors when they gave him good evening. The gate of the monastery was open; he did not trouble to knock, but went in, and straight to the kitchen. When he came near he could hear the sound of scrubbing. He looked in and saw Dom Henry stand in the midst; one of the lay brothers was scrubbing wooden bowls; he had those that were already done set out in a long row at the window to dry in the evening sun; another, with his gown hitched up, kneeled on a folded sack and swabbed the floor from a wooden pail.

Dom Henry turned, saw Robin and said, "It is nearly done." To the lay brother with the scrubbing brush he said, "Are all the towels dry in the press?" and to another monk who came in beside Robin, "There. All's ready for your week's serving. And I have come to the end of mine, and today shall eat my meat with a conscience as clean as a well-scoured bowl." Then he laid his hand on Robin's shoulder, gave him a push and bade him, "Get out of this. I'm weary of cooking pots and sauce ladles. I would the brethren might live holily on manna, as Moses."

"Beginning today?" asked Robin saucily, and the monk chuckled and said no—beginning last Saturday night, and ending today. He reached down two horn cups from a shelf, went out of the kitchen and came back with them full of ale. "My brewing," he told Robin, giving him one, and together they went outside, walking with care so as not to spill the ale. The horse-block in the outer courts still had the sun, and was sheltered from the wind, so they sat down there, Robin on the top step and the monk below him.

Dom Henry raised the horn cup. "Ah!" he said, after a silence, "That's better."

He glanced up at the boy. Robin was twisting his cup about; a little of the ale slopped over onto his hosen; he shifted his leg and struck the drops off with his hand, but he did it absently. Dom Henry had taught all the Aske boys, and knew them as well as any man did, but he knew that Robin was changing, and he did not know what he would change into. "Not so sharp and eager a wit as Kit's," he thought to himself, "but it grips, and there may be more than wit in him."

"Well?" he said at last; but Robin, who was generally very ready, gave him no answer for a long time.

"If you'll not drink that ale, give it to me," Dom Henry prompted him.

Robin shook his head, and began to drink, then he put the cup down on the stone beside him, and said, "Sir, if I tell my father that I would be a monk, will you stand by me?"

Afterward, thinking it over, Dom Henry wondered why he had received the suggestion so unfavorably, pouring scorn on it as if it must be only a boyish notion. "All because you can't hit the middle of a painted mark with your arrow!"

Robin said, stiffly and angrily, that that was not all, and when the monk asked what else, he would not say, only he looked both resentful and unhappy. In the end Dom Henry made him promise to do nothing in the matter for a year. "And you shall say no word of it to anyone."

"Why should I? But why should I not?" Robin asked shrewdly.

"Because if you have told it to any, you're of that stubborn humor that you may hold yourself to it for very pride. And an unfit monk is a misery to himself, and a hair shirt upon the backs of his brethren. I know."

Robin flung off the horse-block then and went home. He told himself that he had been a fool to speak of it to Dom Henry, worldly and witty, who read more in Plautus than in any of the Fathers, even if he were a distant kinsman, and his schoolmaster.

Dom Henry, mechanically singing the responses which he knew so well, was able to reflect upon the conversation throughout Compline. He understood, better than the boy himself, he thought, why Robin, halting between longing and dread, had come to him, and not to the prior, who would have rehearsed for him all the old arguments why it was good for every man to be a monk, arguments so old that all the truth seemed to have been worn off them, like the pile on the old velvet copes. "Robin knows," Dom Henry thought, "that he'll get the truth from me, as I think it." That it was not the whole, nor the only truth, the monk was well aware. Men became monks for many reasons; leisure and comfort were his own. But if Robin were to be a monk, it would not be for these, but because for him the prior's old worn reasons were still harsh and fiery with truth.

He shut the Office book with a clap. Compline was over. As they went out into the windy chill of the cloister he thought, "In the old days—yes, perhaps. But not now. Monks should be quiet men." He was sure of one thing, that Robin Aske, either in the world or in the cloister, would not be a quiet man, contented, easy, amused, and comfortable. And he did not want his own quiet disturbed with something that would be too like shame to be pleasant. He went into the little room beside the chapter house where the books were kept. For a moment he hesitated over Origen. Origen had a piercing subtle wit that Henry could relish, but though he drew half out the big book in its yellowing sheepskin binding, he drove it back again with his fist, and took to read instead the companionable Horatius Flaccus. "Man," he thought, "isn't all soul." He did not confess to himself that he could have wished to be entirely without that troublesome and hungry flame.

Before Dom Henry's stipulated year was out Kit had gone to Skipton, to be one of the gentlemen in the household of the Askes' Clifford kinsman, the Earl of Cumberland, and Robin to the household of the Earl of Northumberland. When his father had first told him that he was to go there he had come, rather shamefaced, to Dom Henry, asking, "What shall I do?"

But the monk, who was in the grip of one of his great and sore winter colds, had little patience for him this time.

"Do? Go," he answered.

"But—"

"Do you suppose that you cannot as well choose to become a monk, if you do so choose, at Wressel as at Aughton?"

"No," said Robin with an obstinate look, and went home.

When he came to say good-bye Dom Henry was kinder. He kissed Robin, blessed him, clapped him on the back, told him not to forget his latinity, and gave him a little gold brooch with a crucifix upon it. He was really sorry to part, but having always made a semblance of finding boys even more ridiculous creatures than men, he could not well show it.

So Robin set off to Wressel Castle with his father, in a new doublet of the Percy colors, crimson and black, and crimson hosen under his long riding boots. Will Wall, who was to be his servant, rode behind with the two men who would go back to Aughton with Sir Robert. Will was fifteen, but saucy enough to teach monkeys, the two men said, as they were riding home again. Sir Robert replied that to live in so great a household would teach him sense and a meekness proper to his age and station. He did not say that it should do the same for Robin, who, though not exactly saucy, was in his opinion too positive and pragmatical a lad; but that was what he was thinking when he rode under the gatehouse at Aughton, and the three little girls, Nan, Moll, and Doll, ran out to welcome him. Mistress Nell, Jack's wife, came out more slowly, and rebuked them, telling Nan to pick up the spindle she had dropped, before everyone had caught their feet in the wool and fouled it. Nell was seventeen now, and very pleased to rule the household and the little girls.

But that same evening Sir Robert found Nan and Moll, the two who came after Robin in age, sitting together on the top step of the stairs going up to their bedroom. Nan was sniffing and gulping after tears, and Moll was helping her to wipe them from her face with the hanging lappet of her coif. Nan said that she was crying because Robin had gone away.

"Silly little goose!" Sir Robert told her, but not unkindly, "Look at Moll. She does not cry."

Moll answered for Nan that though she did not cry, yet she was sad for it. "But," said she, "it is Nan loves him best," and then she screwed up her face and began to whimper too.

Sir Robert, thinking of the way that Robin teased and tyrannized over the girls, more than either of his elder brothers had ever done, hoped that there was something good in the lad that made them now cry for his going.

He did not come home for close on three years, and by then he was for his sisters a young man, and a stranger, with already a dark shaven chin, and lips that pricked when he kissed them.

Yet to Dom Henry it seemed at first that the young man held out a hand, as it were, to the very young Robin, the careless, good-humored boy, over the head of that lad who had begun to appear before he went away. Dom Henry was down near the river among the fish ponds when Robin came to him. It was a day in late October with a steady wind, and the sky looming blue through gray cloud. Some of the willows had already turned yellow, while others kept their gray-green, but all had been thinned out by last night's storm. Now the wind, flowing through their branches as strongly as the swollen Derwent in his course, streaked all the tiny sharp leaves one way.

Dom Henry had been in a mood of chilly melancholy, but he brightened up when he saw Robin. He was pleased that Robin had sought him out, and at the new grace with which he went down on his knee for a blessing; he had not grown much taller, but had broadened, and wore his livery well—a thought carelessly, as a gentleman should. They walked together toward the priory gate. At first the young man seemed to think that the last two months which he had spent with his master, young Henry Percy, in the household of the cardinal of York, qualified him to correct Dom Henry when they spoke of a book by Erasmus of Rotterdam which the monk had read and he had not. It did not take his old schoolmaster long to put him right on that point, and then he became just an eager boy, talking of all the strange things and people that were to be seen in London; ships from Spain, Italy, the Levant; Venetian merchants in silks that noblemen envied them; French gentlemen that came and went with the ambassador, all chattering like monkeys; the wonderful things, gold plate, clocks, pictures to be seen in the cardinal's house.

"By St. James!" said Dom Henry, "though Kit has his books—did you know that he is copying a great book on hunting with his own hand?—and Jack his wife and those three stout knave children of his, I think you have better than either."

Robin made no answer for a minute. His face was lifted and he seemed to be intent upon a couple of wild duck flying fast down the wind; his blind eye was toward Dom Henry, but the monk could see the new hard line of the jaw where before had been a boyish softness.

Then Robin said, "If he—if my master were another manner man! But he's sick, and he's silly. Oh! you know not how many hours we kick our heels, waiting on him, while he's slugging abed, or biting at his nails in his chair. If I could but have some work to set my hand to now I am a man—some good work."

He stopped, then muttered, "for Christendom," and turned his face full on Dom Henry, looking at him with an eye that was hard and ready to be angry.

But Dom Henry did not wish to laugh at the great solemnity of the young. He was thinking that the other Robin was there, and had just looked out; Jack had sweetness, and Kit was clever, but here was strength. He was silent, and by his side Robin soon rattled on again with one tale after another.

"Well," says Dom Henry at last, stopping and looking at him with his odd quirk of a smile, "they haven't cured you of talking, nor you've not grown out of it for yourself."

The lad stopped, flushed, then laughed.

"They say I could talk the hind leg off my lord cardinal's mule, did I set my mind to it."

This was in the autumn. After Christmas Day Henry caught one of his colds; it went to his lungs, and, being a man of a full habit of body and no longer young, his heart could not stand it,

and he died on Twelfth Night in the year 1519, so that he and
Robin did not see each other again.

1527

May 12

Master Robert Aske sat on a stool in a small room in the lodgings
of Sir Henry Percy, son of the Earl of Northumberland, in the
village of Westminster. It was a small room, dark even on this
bright day, and the hangings were old and faded. Aske sat with
his legs stuck stiffly out in front of him, staring under his heavy
brows at the woven picture of a woman in a gown of the fashion
of eighty years ago. She knelt and put a black shoe on the foot of
a man sitting on a flowery mount in the garden. Aske turned his
head and looked round at the other walls of the room.

"What's it all about?" he muttered. "There's a man kneeling
on his cap and sticking a duck's bill into the ground. Why? And
look at that king in his crown, taking up the harvest man by his
middle. Why? There's no sense in it, that I can see."

Another young man, tall, slim, and pale, who perched on a
trestle table dangling his legs, asked, in the same low voice, what
did it matter whether there were sense in it or not.

"I like to know," said Aske; and he got up and began to rove
softly round the room staring at the hangings, his tongue running on, bidding look here, at this king crowning another king,
and this woman with a banner and a helmet. "Well," said he at
last, "either the folk of old time were mad as geese or the servants

have got these pieces all mixed up like Christmas pie," and he came back to his stool, and sat down. Then they both looked over their shoulders to where, in a deep window, a third young man sat lumping on cushions. His back was against the wall, his chin on his chest, and he snored gently from time to time. Henry Percy slept after his dinner. He was not dressed with any greater show than either of the other two, and indeed they were all three a little shabby, but upon Henry Percy's slack hand a great emerald caught the sunlight and sent up a fuzz of light.

The young man on the table said, speaking quietly, "When the earl, his father, dies, what'll *he* do?" and he jerked his head toward the sleeper.

"Do?" Aske grinned. "What he's doing now. Unless the cardinal chivvies him up North again to the border."

"Would you be glad of that?"

Aske did not answer at once. Then he said, "Whether he goes or no, I'll not be there."

"Mass," the other cried, then slapped himself across the mouth, looked anxiously at Henry Percy, and whispered, "You'll leave his household? For my Lord of Cumberland?"

Aske pulled down the corners of his mouth and shook his head.

"You could. For your mother was a Clifford."

Aske thanked him politely. "But have me excused," said he. "My brother Kit's with the earl. One household isn't big enough for Kit and me. We always fall out. Kit thinks I'm too cocket."

The other turned his face away to smile because that was so exactly what others thought of Robert Aske. "Well," he concluded, "I suppose I shall stay with this Earl Henry when Henry the Magnificent is dead."

"That, my good fellow," Aske told him, "is what you will not do."

"Won't?"

"Won't. The cardinal will see to it."

"God's Death! But the cardinal has nothing to do with it. He can't turn off Lord Henry's gentlemen, more especially when he's earl."

"Can and will—all of them but one or two and a groom or so. The old earl's deep in debt. I know. And the cardinal will see that till his debts are paid this earl shan't have two groats in his pouch to jingle together."

The tall young man rubbed his chin. "Mass!" he murmured, "are you sure?" He knew that Aske always was sure, but remembered with some dismay that he was often, though not always, right. Besides, as comptroller of the young lord's household he must see better than the others what was going on. His long pale face was dismal as he asked, "What'll I do?" Then he brightened a little. "What'll you do?"

"Take to the law," Aske told him promptly.

"God's Soul! But how old are you? Four and twenty? And you've learned none."

"But I can learn. I'm not a fool."

The other threw his head back to laugh, then, remembering the sleeping man, clapped his hand again over his mouth. Henry Percy stirred but did not wake, so he said, "No, Robin, no one would take you for that."

Aske, who had begun to frown, laughed softly instead. The other slid off the table.

"Get your bow," said he, "and I'll take you on at the butts."

"But you always beat me."

"I do. Of course we all know that you'd beat me if you had your two eyes. But pride's a deadly sin, so I'll beat you soundly to save you from damnation."

Aske got up. "Forward then to the good work," he said and both went out laughing quietly, and stepping gingerly so as not to wake their master.

May 30

Darcy was just leaving the chamber of presence at Greenwich Palace when he found the Duke of Norfolk at his elbow—not the old duke, who had died three years ago, but his son Thomas Howard, who had been Earl of Surrey and got himself much honor at the Battle of Flodden. Darcy had never liked him, and liked him no more now that he was duke, and high treasurer of England, but Norfolk greeted him with particular courtesy, walked on with him and after a minute or two edged him away into a little closet of painted wainscot. Darcy thought he looked very pleased over something.

"Sit, my lord, sit," said Norfolk. "I saw you lean heavily on your stick while we waited for the King." There was only a stool and a pair of virginals in the closet, but the duke would have Darcy sit on the stool, while he tucked his own backside onto the virginals, jangling all the keys once in painful discord. Then he inquired with great kindness about my lord's old disease.

But after a little of this he was silent, and pulled a comical face and laughed.

"Indeed we can see that it is Maytime; yea, even in London and at court," he said.

Darcy did not pretend to misunderstand him.

"How long will it last? May's but thirty-one days, and then?"

Norfolk shook his head, still smiling, then he narrowed his eyes and looked crafty.

"My niece is a most virtuous and chaste lady. You know the King—how set he is to have his will. Yet here he can have it not. I promise you I could weep for him, to read the letters he writes to her when she has crossed him, or runs away home from court to be done with the importunities of his suit. 'H.R.' he will sign himself at the foot, and *'Aultre ne cherche'* between the letters, and right in the midst of all a heart drawn, and inscribed with A. B."

"Very pretty," said Darcy sourly. "But if she will have none of him, and he will not tire, what will be the end of it?"

"Ah!" Norfolk leaned closer. "She will none of him except lawfully. Yet—if the Queen should become a nun—!" He broke off there as if he had said too much. "A little while ago," he went on, "she sent him a jewel, representing in diamonds a maid solitary in a ship, and the posy *'Aut illic aut nullibi.'* To which he replied somewhat to this end, for she showed me the letter— 'My heart is dedicated to you alone, wishing that my body were so too, as God can make it if it pleases him.'"

"Ah!" Darcy remarked, not without malice, "God?"

The duke got up and the strings of the virginals whined. "My lord, I can see God's hand here, if you cannot. The realm lacks an heir. The Princess? Pooh! We lack a Prince. And one other we have with us that we could well lack." He came close to Darcy and whispered, "You and I think alike of the King's prepotent subject, my lord cardinal. We should be friends."

Darcy considered that for a minute, and with it the rest of what the duke had told him. Then he said:

"You tell me that the King means marriage with your niece?"

Norfolk was looking at the floor. He did not raise his eyes but rustled the strawing with one foot and answered softly that he believed no less.

Darcy also looked down at the duke's foot, and at a faded head of clover that Norfolk was shifting this way and that; it was as if neither wished to meet the other's eyes. The duke moved away again, but paused at the virginals, and leaning one hand that held his blue velvet cap upon the painted case of the instrument, with the fingers of the other picked out a shivering sweet chord or two. Then he looked round at Darcy.

"And your niece, Mistress Anne, is of the same mind as yourself, my lord, toward the cardinal?" Darcy inquired.

"I promise you," Norfolk chuckled. "Sometimes I think a woman can outdo any man when it comes to pure, piercing hatred."

When the duke had gone Darcy sat a while alone, turning over what he had heard. Then he shrugged his shoulders and got up. He did not think it likely, on the one hand, that

Mistress Anne's virtue would prove as impregnable as Norfolk rated it; nor, on the other, if it did, that even that lively bold slip of a girl was an adversary whom the great cardinal should fear. She might dance like a dark flame through the maskings at court in her cloth of gold and with rubies about her neck which Darcy was sure her father had never given her, but the King must go from masking to the council table, and there the cardinal would rule.

June 4

Master Robert Aske pushed his hair behind his ears, stuffed his thumbs into them, and bent over the law book again. But Will Wall's snores could not be kept out. He shut the book at last, got up, and stretched himself, for he was stiff with long sitting, having been at work from four in the morning. This business of learning the law needed time, and he had, he felt, lost several years in Henry Percy's household. It was useless to try to waken Will; he was more than usually sodden with drink. "Miserable swillbowl!" Aske called him as he passed him, sprawling on the straw pallet, and gave him a gentle kick. It was the second time this week that Will had come home drunk as ten tailors.

Hunting in the cupboard for something to eat Aske found a piece of mutton pie at which he sniffed suspiciously, and then tipped out of the window. Besides that there was only a heel of cheese, the flabby remains of a salad, and half a loaf. Well, he must make do, for he had sworn to himself that he would read so much in Bracton every day, and that left no time for going out to taverns to dine. "But what," he asked himself angrily, "do

I keep such a servant for?" as if he could have brought himself to send Will away from him, or persuaded Will to go.

When he had eaten a little he felt more kindly toward everyone.

"While I read he has nothing to do," he argued, on Will's behalf, "and so runs into mischief."

June 8

This day Christabel Cowper's younger brother was married for the second time, and she was at the wedding. She wore, as she ought not to have worn, a girdle woven with silver, and a silk purse hanging from it. Her veil, as it ought not to have been, was of silk, and the pins in it were of silver; she considered that this show was for the credit of the house. Besides, she was not as others, who wore such things in cloister, thus causing temptation to assail the younger ladies. When she was at Marrick these adornments lay in a chest, so now she could wear them heartily.

And over dinner, where the wine was good, she struck a most advantageous bargain with Master John Cocks, the tanner. To herself she said, "He'll be sorry for this tomorrow," but to him:

"It's good cheap for you, and a loss for us. But we poor nuns must take what we can get for our ox hides."

July 2

Lord Darcy did not take the King's order to the keeper of the Great Wardrobe till this day. He had been too much occupied with business to do it before. This business was disagreeable, and sent him to the law courts in Westminster Hall to answer feigned bills of that villain Banks, accusing him and Lord Hussey of wasting the goods of poor Monteagle. It cost my lord well over a hundred pounds before all was finished, what with the presents at court, and to certain of the King's council, the hire of the house at Stepney, and all the letters, messages, writings, and rewards to the men of law. But at the end of it he and Hussey, Banks and young Lord Monteagle signed an accord in the house of Master Cromwell, a servant of the cardinal's, and very deep in his confidence; Hussey had always said that there was no hope of coming lightly out of the business when he had heard that Banks had managed, by book or crook, to get this man for his friend. "Half lawyer, half moneylender," Hussey said, who knew more about him than Darcy.

"Then whole damned," Darcy muttered, who had suffered from both.

And this day, as he passed through one of the chambers in the Great Wardrobe beside Blackfriars, there was Master Cromwell, crouching over some rolls of silk and cloth of gold that lay on the floor. Gibson, porter and yeoman tailor of the wardrobe, was just slitting open the canvas cover of the last roll, and all about the two lay folds of the rich lustrous stuffs.

"Italian," Cromwell told Darcy, getting up from the floor. "There's none in Christendom can weave better such things." He was inclined to be friendly with Darcy, had Darcy allowed it. He was certainly very friendly with Gibson, calling him "Dick," and "gossip."

"And," said he aloud at the door, when he had taken his leave, "forget not, my good Dick, the clavichord wire." He smiled at Darcy, and said, "I confess I aim at defrauding the King's Grace to the tune of some yards of clavichord wire."

Then he was gone, a fat, cheerful, small man, with a ready laugh and a pleasant voice. His eyes were twinkling too, and merry, but Darcy had noticed, that day they had had to do with him and Banks, that every now and then he shot out of them a sharp, pricking look. And Darcy was nearly sure, that whether Master Cromwell was to have some of the King's clavichord wire or no, the roll of gray damask cloth of silver, which lay rather apart from the other silks, would go to Master Cromwell's house at the Austin Friars, and that it would never appear on the accounts of the King's Great Wardrobe.

When Cromwell had gone away, and the clerk of the wardrobe had been found, my lord showed him the King's order. He took Darcy to a closet where the spare chapel stuff was kept, and my lord chose a vestment, of black silk powdered with roses and columbines, for the chapel of his hospital.

September 26

Robert Aske was sitting on the step of the horse-block beside the hall door at Aughton, with a book on his lap, his elbows on his knees, and his head between his fists. The women were clearing out the rushes from the floors today, so as to straw new for the winter, and there was no peace for any man indoors. A dog or two lay in the sun near his feet; for the most part of the time they dozed, waking up suddenly to snap at flies or to scratch. From the farther yard beyond the old dairy there came the sound of someone chopping wood; a servant was drawing water from the well in the corner by the door into the kitchens; the rope creaked with a note higher than the whine of the winch, and now and again water slopped over the swinging bucket, and fell back into the well with a splash. From beyond the court came the tinkle of goat bells.

Aske took one hand from his head to scratch his thigh. Then he let out with his foot at a spaniel that had come too close.

"Keep your fleas on your own hide," says he, and the spaniel wagged, yawned, and lay down again a little farther away; Aske went back to his book.

When a shadow fell across the page he did not look up, but seeing Nan's gown he groaned, and, as if in anger, cried out on "You women who will never leave a man in quiet, but bound him out of doors with your brooms, and then come and deafen him with your clacking tongues."

Nan giggled. If Kit had said that she would not have known whether to laugh or go quietly away; but though she had found Robin rather alarming when he came home a month ago, she did not so now.

"Well?" he asked.

"Will you come and help to gather blackberries?"

"Nay, I will not."

"Then will you hold your godson for me?"

"I'll do so much. He'll mark my place as well as a straw."

He took the stiffly swaddled child from her and laid it down upon the book. "Perdy!" cried he, "he's wet!"

"They always are," she told him; and when he cried fie on her she laughed at him. "Keep him the right way up," she said, and went away.

He shifted the baby to the crook of his arm, and looked down into its unblinking eyes for a moment before he went on with his reading. Nan had been married to Will Monkton, eldest son of a man halfway between yeoman and gentleman. Will was a fat young fellow, slow-speaking and grave. Robert Aske was pleased to have him for a brother-in-law, though he guessed from something Jack had said that Kit did not approve of the marriage. "But if Nan likes him—" he thought. Nan was little, pale, and plain, and would always be, but Robert thought that her eyes looked happy.

"Sir," said he to the baby, "you stare too long for courtesy; and why you should bubble from your mouth when you are already so wet at t'other end—!"

October 1

Lord Darcy was returning out of London to the house at Stepney, when the Duke of Norfolk caught him up, going to try a new hawk in the fields beyond the village. The duke sent his gentlemen on, and rode softly beside Darcy's horse-litter, talking of the North Country, and of the young Duke of Richmond, the King's son, who had been sent there with a council and a great household to learn the trade of a ruler, though he was barely ten years old. "But," said Norfolk, "a singular gracious and wise child as all agree," and he waited a minute for Darcy to answer, and, when he did not, added that it was a pity his mother had not been the King's lawful wife.

Darcy said rather he thought it was a pity that the boy was not Queen Katherine's child.

"That is what I would say," Norfolk assured him, but Darcy had an idea that he had put it the other way to try what answer he would get. He wondered what the duke would be at, and wondered still more when they came to the end of the lane along which Darcy must turn. For the duke pulled up there, and began to ask about the house. Was it big enough, in good repair, were there stables and grazing in plenty? And every now and then as he talked he would nod and tip his head toward the roof and chimneys that showed above the orchard trees, and he frowned, and then winked one eye, so that Darcy knew that he wanted to be asked to turn in for a while, and see the house, though he could not think why the duke should want it, nor why he should make such a secret of it. But he said, "If you will turn in, my lord, to drink a cup of wine?" and he told his footboy to go on and fetch Norfolk's gentlemen back.

The duke would gladly turn in, he said, adding that it was as warm as summer, which was true, for, after a wet and windy September, October had come in with a light mist and still blue skies. So, at the duke's own suggestion, they drank their wine in the garden that smelt pleasantly of box, and apples, and sweet-briar warmed in the sun.

After they had finished their wine the duke brushed the crumbs of wafer from his knee and got up, but he waved his hand to his gentlemen, and taking Darcy's arm shoved him gently in the direction of the orchard. "Now," thought Darcy, "we're coming at it," and he was right. After a turn taken together, in which Norfolk spoke loudly of his own new grafted apple trees at Framlingham, he dropped his voice and asked Darcy did he know that the Cardinal's Grace had returned.

"Yea, I heard."

Norfolk looked down at the hooded hawk, restless, on his hand. "Everywhere in France he was shown great honor."

As he seemed to wait for a reply Darcy said that he supposed that was but natural, seeing he was the servant of so great a master.

"And so great a servant," Norfolk suggested, to which Darcy said nothing.

"Yet I have heard say, *'Non est Propheta inhonoratus nisi in patria sua,'*" and the duke looked sharply up at Darcy.

"How can that fit here, my lord, unless the cardinal thinks his honors—which, God knows, are many and great—are not enough for his services?"

"He did not think himself honored when he came to the King at Richmond," said Norfolk softly.

"Ah!" said Darcy. "This I have not heard."

Norfolk chuckled. "I shall tell you. He came there in the evening, having landed from Calais that morning, straight to give account to his master, as a dutiful servant should, and supposing that he should be joyfully received at his homecoming, as one who has made this new treaty with France. And coming to the palace he sent one of his people to the King announcing his return, and asking where and at what hour he should visit His Grace. I was with the cardinal, and I saw his gentleman go to the King, and I saw him return."

He chuckled again, and Darcy, not seeing why, said, "Well?"

"The cardinal's gentleman, when he came back, was as red as those apples on the tree. Yet he only said to the cardinal that the King would see him at once. 'Where?' says he. 'I will bring you to the King,' says the gentleman, and they went out, and I saw the cardinal turn to him, in going, and ask again, 'Where is His Grace?' but I did not hear the answer—not then. I waited, and I saw the cardinal come out of the palace and ride away. I asked one of his gentlemen how the King had received his master, 'Right thankfully, I'll wager,' says I. And he looked at me as awkwardly as if he'd stolen a purse, and said—'Right thankfully; very honorably,' and got himself away from me as quick as he could."

Darcy stopped walking, and they stood together under one of the trees, feeling the sun's warmth spatter through the leaves upon their heads.

"It's a long tale, but I come near to the end," the duke assured him. "It was from my niece—" "Mistress Anne?" put in Darcy; and, "Mistress Anne," Norfolk repeated. "From her that I heard the rest. For she came to me after supper in the gallery, and showed me a new jewel she was wearing, a table emerald with three hanging pearls, very pretty, very costly. She'd had it, she said, of the King's Grace that evening, and many gracious words with it. 'And kisses not a few,' says I, whereat she laughed, and did not deny it.

"'And then,' says she, 'one came in from my lord cardinal and asked where and when he might wait on His Grace.'" I told her I knew what he had asked; but what had the King answered?

"'It was not the King that answered,' says she. 'It was I. I said to the cardinal's gentleman, "Where else but here should the cardinal come? Tell him he may come here, where the King is."'

"'Mass!' quod I, 'was not the King angry?' She laughed at that and told me, no, not angry at all, but very merry, asking her if she would be one of his Privy Council."

"She is a very bold lady," Darcy said, not too cordially; but then, remembering how she had discomfited the cardinal, he laughed. "No other would have dared."

"Bold she is," Norfolk said, "and of a marvelous ready wit, and that the King loves her for. And," he turned to Darcy, "as I told you before, she loves not the cardinal." He held out his hand then, to say farewell. "You and I think alike over one matter; we should be friends," he said, and added, "though not too openly."

Darcy gave an angry laugh. "Thomas Wolsey knows that I love him little, and with great reason."

"Secret is best," said Norfolk, and went on to his hawking.

November 18

Master Cheyne had gone away into Kent to the deathbed of an uncle. He wanted to be sure that the executors did not cheat him of any inheritance that might be due to him. So Julian went up into the parlor after supper, and at bedtime with Meg into her chamber. Meg was in a kind mood, and let her sister take from an iron-bound box the precious and pretty things she kept there. Julian knelt before the big chest at the foot of the bed, and laid them out, one by one, on the lid, while Meg sat in her shift on the edge of the bed, combing her hair and humming a song. The shadow of her hand, and the comb, and her hair, went up and down the painted wall.

Julian bent over the trinkets, touching those she liked best with her finger, very gently. There was a girdle enameled white, red, and black in the Spanish fashion; she had taken it half out of the soft leather that wrapped it. Besides that there were gold buttons, each set with a tiny ruby, and beyond the buttons two rings, one with a hand gripping a cat's-eye stone, and the other plain gold with a rocky pearl.

Meg laid down her comb and began braiding her hair. July knew that she had not much longer till she would be sent away to bed. She fumbled down at the bottom of the box for a thing that she knew was there, and found it—half a gold rose noble, with a hole near the broken edge, and a thin gold chain through the hole. She knew that it was the token the Duke of Buckingham had given to the girl he had met on the shore at Southampton, before Meg was born—the girl that had become their mother.

She laid the coin in her palm and let the chain hang over her hand. For a minute it was cold on her skin, then grew warm with the warmth of her flesh.

"Meg," she said, not looking up from the thing in her hand, "what was our mother like?"

Meg's quick fingers moved among her hair so that the three tails leapt and shook as she braided it.

"She was only a simple creature, of no gentle blood."

"But—" Julian began.

"But she was very beautiful." Meg tied her hair with a rose-colored ribbon and looped the heavy rope so that it framed her face; she leaned forward and picked up the mirror, and smiled into it. She thought that she was more beautiful than ever her mother had been.

"Was—was she—good?" Julian asked.

Meg turned and stared at her, then laughed.

"Good? She bore us two bastards."

"Then," July persisted, "was she bad?"

"Oh!" said Meg lightly, and let the shift slip from her shoulders and stood up naked beside the bed, "I'd not say she was bad. But does it matter?"

July could not answer that. She began to put the things back in the box even before Meg told her to.

1528

January 1

This morning Will Wall came into the room at Gray's Inn that his master shared with two others. He had Aske's red velvet coat over his arm, for the Christmas Feast was not half over, and today was a high day. Hal Hatfield was not awake yet, and Ned Bangham lay with his hands clasped behind his head, but Aske was half dressed, and was just fastening the points that tied his gray hosen to his doublet; Will put down the coat on the bench near the dead fire, and began to tie the points at his master's back.

Hal wakened, yawned, stretched, and turned over.

"Well, Robin," he asked, "how did you get on with the young gentlewoman?"

Aske laughed. He sat down on the edge of his own bed, and stuck out his feet so that Will could lace the gussets of the hosen inside each ankle. "Not on—off," said he. "Last night was wine and candle to my wooing."

"Jesu Mary!" Hal rolled over the better to see him. "The end of it? My poor Robin! Is the heart broken?"

"To pieces!" Aske told him cheerfully; yet Hal thought he looked a little crestfallen.

"I never supposed," put in Ned Bangham from the other bed, "that wenches had so much sense."

"Now, master!" Will protested, "it's not sense to refuse a likely bachelor."

Aske winked at Hal over Will Wall's head.

"I'm best out of it," he told Hal. "Mating with such a merry gentlewoman would be too much for a quiet man like me. She told me roundly she did not care how many men loved her, and wooed, and went empty away, but she had no thought of marrying for another two years." He pulled a face, and spread out his hands, making a jest of it, but his pride was sore and Will knew it. He muttered to Aske's boots, which he was pulling on, that if he'd had a daughter spoke so, he'd think that she had not been enough beaten in her upbringing.

"At least," said Aske, "she sent me packing before New Year's Day, so I've saved the gift I bought her. See here, Will—you go out and buy wine for us to the cost of it, and then you'll have no quarrel with Mistress Clare."

"Ho!" cried Hal. "Me too, Robin," and he heaved himself out of bed. "How much have we to turn on? I've a costly thirst."

"He spent 12s. 8d. on a comb for her," Will answered disapprovingly.

Ned Bangham sat up and began to pull on his shirt.

"May you never prosper in love, Robin," said he, "if your friends can drink what your ladies refuse."

March 3

The nuns were in the choir, and Mass was almost at an end, while the wind whistled and moaned in the tower, and drafts tugged at the candle flames. Dame Christabel knelt with her eyelids lowered and her hands folded seemly under her chin. Yet she was aware that Dame Margaret Lovechild was occupied in quieting the little dog she had brought in on his yellow ribbon leash; that the prioress was frankly asleep; and that Bet and Grace, the two little novices, were whispering together though hardly moving their lips; it was an accomplishment they had learned since they came to Marrick.

The old priest stopped for quite a long time in order to cough; and then to hiccup because his digestion was now very bad. Christabel opened her eyes and looked at him as if she would goad him on by looking. She shut her eyes again and went back to her thoughts. She was wondering whether indeed

she had done well to choose to be a nun. If she had married—
She thought of a house—perhaps even of a manor house—with
new fine glass windows, comfortable, with jolly comings and
goings; there would have been many servants to rule, her own
children, a husband. Perhaps she could not have ruled him, but
at the worst most men could be managed. She sighed, sharply
and impatiently, and then with relief took up her part in the
singing. They were almost at an end now.

April 10

After dinner Lord Darcy had Lord Hussey's messenger into his
chamber for half an hour or so, and when the man had gone
down again to the hall, sent for his eldest son, Sir George. But
Sir George was out, and did not return till after dark when his
father was getting ready for bed and Lady Elizabeth already
lay within the drawn curtains asleep. My lord's gentleman had
spread the footsheet beside the fire, because the night was cold
and windy. He had taken off my lord's coat and doublet, his
shoes and black hosen, his shirt with the black Spanish work
about the neck, and his breeches. For a moment Darcy stood
naked, lean and bony, with the curled, grizzled hair pricking on
his breast at the cold; then the gentleman slipped over his head
the fine nightshirt and put on him a long nightgown of green
velvet, furred with red fox. He was just going away with my
lord's clothes thrown over his shoulder when Sir George came
in and sat down on a stool by the hearth.

While the waiting gentleman combed my lord's hair nothing
was spoken of except a horse which Sir George had just bought,

and of that they spoke quietly because of my lady, asleep in bed. "Luttrell has broken and half trained him already," said Sir George. "A right good stallion." My lord agreed that Luttrell had a way with horses.

"And in a week's time I shall sell him for twice that I gave. Luttrell's a fool at a bargain."

Darcy frowned at his son and tipped his head toward the gentleman, now beginning to slide the curtains softly apart along the cords of the bed.

"Let the curtains be, James," said Darcy, while George tossed up his chin and shrugged his shoulders at the rebuke. But he was silent till the fat yellow Paris candle had been lit and set at the bedhead for the night, and the dogs and an old tomcat that was a favorite of my lord's turned out. The gentleman paused at the door, bowed to my lord and his son and went out. Darcy bade, "Good night to you, James," and George nodded. Then there was silence in the room.

"You sent for me, sir," says George at last.

His father stretched out the iron-shod staff he walked with and struck roughly at a log that was out of reach of the flames.

"Will you not learn," he said, "if you must cheat one of our own people, not to brag of it? James and all my other gentlemen hold together as they hold with me, and Luttrell is one of them. Moreover I think it a wretched thing that any man should be glad to trick one of his own folk, that look to him rather for help than for such ill-natured doings."

George "pished" impatiently and muttered something about fools and their money, as if he did not care. Yet it was only a pretense; he took no account at all of his stepmother, disliked his half sister, was jealous of his younger brother Arthur, because my lord loved him; but my lord he greatly admired, and almost as much hated.

"Well," said Darcy, after another silence, "I sent for you. Here's news of how the King's matter speeds in Rome, and it speeds not at all. The cardinal has sent out Master Stephen Gardiner, and he hath threatened His Holiness with most unseemly freedom. But threaten he never so, he'll get no good, for the pope fears the Emperor too nearly to sing but as he calls the tune," and my lord chuckled and slapped his hand down on his thigh.

George did not so much as smile. He said, with his eyes on the fire, that he thought no loyal subject should rejoice that his Prince was thwarted in a matter so near his heart as the breaking of this ill-made marriage of his.

Darcy seized on one word, "Loyal? You say, or you think, I'm not loyal?"

"And you chide me because I profit by a fool's folly—"

"Now by God's Death, George," Darcy interrupted him, "I wonder sometimes that you are son of mine. My father taught me as I have taught you, that a man that is a lord stands by his friends and his men through flood and through fire."

"And not by his Prince?"

Darcy turned and looked at him, and answered after a while in a different voice, thoughtfully.

"You and some others have a new idea of a Prince. You think he must have his way, whatsoever it be, with the law or maugre the law. That was not the way of it in England when I was a lad."

"And a right merry England you made of it with wars and bickerings, and making and unmaking of kings." George got up and went over to the door and wrenched it open.

"Give you good night, sir," said he, and went out.

"Is that you, Tom?" my lady called sleepily from the bed, and Darcy said it was, and got slowly to his feet and to bed. But it was a long time before he slept, thinking as he did of old days when there was war between two Kings in England, and of his son, and of matters at court and in Rome.

May 3

"It's ten o'clock, and my lord cardinal in bed this half hour." The cardinal's gentleman fingered his chin doubtfully, looking Mr. Foxe up and down, and seeing, in the dust on the boots and shoulders of the King's almoner, evidence of his travels, and of his haste—and haste means always tidings of weight.

Mr. Foxe had sat stiffly down on a bench. He had come from Sandwich this morning. For more than a fortnight, since he had left the papal court at Orvieto, he had not slept twice in the same bed. He yawned, and said behind his hand—

"His Grace will be glad to see me."

The gentleman looked hard at him for another second, said, "I'll tell him," and went away with the servant bearing a candle before him. Master Foxe dozed with his head back against the arras, and thought that he had fallen off his horse upon a stony road, and that the horse looked round at him with the pope's face instead of the face of a horse. When the cardinal's gentleman tapped him on the shoulder he sprang up all amazed.

Two servants were lighting the candles in the cardinal's bedchamber, and as each new-lit flame spired up the light caught here a glow of color from the arras, and there a gleam of gold from the damask cloth of gold of the bed curtains. Master Foxe blinked in the swimming, trembling light, then he looked into the shadow between the half-drawn curtains of the bed, and went down on one knee. He could see the cardinal's head in its lawn nightcap, embroidered with black silk and gold thread; the cardinal's face was turned toward the room, one heavy cheek with the pouch under the eye socket plumped up by the soft down of the pillow upon which it pressed; the cardinal's eyes were open and gleamed in the candlelight. Master Foxe kissed the warm, soft hand, which came from between the sheets and was held out to him. Then His Grace wallowed up from the bedclothes like a whale out of the sea, and sat up against the pillows. "Bring me a nightgown," he said, and they brought him one of crimson damask and white fur.

When the gentleman and the servants had gone and Master Foxe sat on a stool by the bed, the cardinal said, "Well?"

Master Foxe had drawn out, and now laid on the bed, divers sealed letters. The cardinal flicked them over. "And letters to the King's Grace?" he asked.

"I have delivered them to His Highness." The cardinal's eyebrows went up. "I went at once to Greenwich," Master Foxe explained, "thinking to find Your Grace there, but you had been gone two hours."

"Ah! Well?" the cardinal asked sharply.

"The pope hath signed the dispensation without a word altered, and the commission; though *that* we strove for long, before they would consent. But at last, we, differing in two words only, demanded that *omnem* should be added to *potestatem*, and *nolente* to *impedito*, and so it was determined, Your Grace and Cardinal Campeggio being joined in the commission to try the cause of the King's marriage."

The cardinal stirred in bed and Master Foxe paused and then went on with his tale.

"But here began a new tragedy, for now the night being far past, and the pope sending to the cardinals' houses, they replied that they would look up their books tomorrow.

"Then after much spoken hotly on our side, Master Gardiner saith that when this dealing of theirs should be known, the favor of that Prince, our King, who is their only friend, should be taken away, and that the Apostolic See should fall to pieces with the consent and applause of every man. At these words the Pope's Holiness, casting his arms abroad so—" and Master Foxe threw his arms wide and clapped them on his thighs, "bade us put in the words we varied for, and therewith walked up and down the chamber, casting now and then his arms abroad, we standing in a great silence. After a while—"

He paused, stumbled, and lost the eloquence which was that of an overwearied man. The cardinal had moved again. He leaned forward in the bed.

"Master Foxe, tell me now this one thing. In this commission is it written that the pope shall confirm the sentence, and may, if he will, revoke the cause to Rome?"

Foxe said it was so written. "But except for those clauses we thought it as good as can be devised, though not in all so open as—"

"Then," said the cardinal, "it is nothing. Nothing."

"Sir, the King's Grace and Mistress Anne are right well pleased. His Highness sent for her that I should tell her the news, saying again and again, 'Here is that good news we have waited for.'"

The cardinal began to move his big head slowly from side to side, so that the heavy dewlap trembled a little.

Master Foxe grew more eager to reassure him of success. "I told His Highness how strongly Your Grace's letters had worked upon the Pope's Holiness, yea, and that without them we could have done nothing, at which His Highness and Mistress Anne were marvelous thankful, she saying—"

The cardinal raised a hand.

"Is the commission decretal or general?"

"It is general. The pope would in no wise—"

"Then I tell you that it is nothing."

"But—"

"Master Foxe," the cardinal leaned from the bed till his big face was close to Foxe's face; "it is nothing. If Queen Katherine appeal—and she will appeal—the cause will be revoked to Rome. Will the pope then break the marriage, if now he dare not sign a decretal commission giving full and final power to the commissioners to break it? No, by Christ's Passion."

He drew back, and for a long time said nothing, except that Foxe heard him mutter to himself, "It is useless. It is what I feared," and now he bit his fingers and now he fiddled with the gold buttons of the pillow-beres.

Foxe roused with a jerk to hear his own name, and realized that the cardinal was talking to him. "We must press His Holiness," he was saying, "with all possible persuasions to grant the commission decretal. For indeed, Master Foxe, it is for the very sake of His Holiness and the stability of the Holy See that I should be of such authority and estimation with the King that whatever I advise His Grace should assent to. His Holiness doth not know how matters stand here, in how perilous a state, and how tottering. For on the one hand the King, if he think the pope his enemy, may be wrought to some desperate course, and on the other the church is so eaten into and inwardly devoured of heretics—yea, like maggots in cheese, Mr. Foxe—that I fear—I fear—"

He bit his nails again, and began to devise arguments, one after another, to lay before the pope, and questions to lay before the jurisconsults of the papal court, so that Master Foxe, in a confused way, as his eyes blinked and burned for sleep, heard "confirmation of the sentence *per superiorem judicem* . . . the parties may *redire ad nova vota* . . ." and the like, as the cardinal out of his deep and subtle wit spun a new thread which might at last draw the pope to satisfy the King's demands.

May 16

When Sim, who was clerk to Master Cheyne, got drunk, he would sit in the kitchen singing and beating time to his own singing with a wooden spoon or a rolling pin or anything handy.

Mostly he sang merry songs, about young lovers or railing wives, but tonight he was in a melancholy mood—

> The life of this world
> Is ruled with wind,
> Weeping, darkness
> And hurting:
> With wind we bloomen,
> With wind we lassen,
> With weeping we comen,
> With weeping we passen,
> With hurting we beginnen,
> With hurting we enden,
> With dread we dwellen,
> With dread we wenden.

He was so affected by the words and by his own voice, which was a plaintive tenor, that he put his head down on the table and cried.

July was in the kitchen; she spent most of her time there those days; Master Cheyne thought it fittest for her, and she liked it better than those parts of the house to which he came more commonly.

She was pounding spices in a mortar but she stopped to listen to the song, with her hands lying slack in the lap of her shabby brown gown, which was now much too short for her, both in the skirt and sleeves. The words and the tune she had never heard before, but they met something that had been in her mind, she could not tell how long—it seemed to her for as long as she could remember. The song met that something that had been below the surface of her mind, as a leaf spinning down from the tree in autumn calls up in the water its own reflection; they rush together, faster and faster, touch, and are one. That was how it was with Julian.

Someone clapped Sim on the back, and they filled his cup. That cheered him and he soon was singing again; this time it was "The bailey beareth the bell away."

July pounded steadily away at the spices.

The lily, the lily, the rose I lay,

Sim sang, but she did not stop to listen to that song.

June 5

In the evening the rain took off, and after so many wet days the younger ladies at least were glad to be able to go out into the garden. Heavy purple clouds lay yet below the sun, but the air above was bright, and the blue of it lay in the pools which the rain had left. So they walked to and fro, lifting their gowns from the wet paths and the grass in the two little walled gardens, while the elders sat in the parlor with door and windows set wide.

Dame Christabel walked with Dame Bet Singleton, and behind came Dame Bess Dalton and Dame Margery Conyers. The garden was small, but they regulated their pace with a nice care, so that each couple walked separate until Dame Margery stooped to tighten the lacing of her shoe, and the other two nuns must either turn back or pause with her. They paused, and just then there came from within the parlor the sound of a door slammed, and a raised excited voice; Dame Anne Ladyman was crying out upon the serving woman, Cecily a' Wood, and now they caught the words, "A thief—a thief—a murrain on her! No, I will have justice. I'll see her in the stocks. They shall whip her at a cart's tail."

Someone answered. They could not hear the words, but the voice was Dame Margaret Lovechild's, and the tone was soothing.

It did not, however, soothe Dame Anne. "Why should I forbear?" she cried more shrilly. "They are mine. The gold hand holding the pearl my mother gave me, and the other—" She paused, and her voice dropped to a note they all knew well. "The other, the brooch with a heart and a ruby, it was a love gage given me—ah! me!—before I entered religion."

Dame Margaret spoke again. "But, madame, she has four or five children, little ones all—"

"And bastards all," cried Dame Anne.

"And who will tend them if the constables take her?"

"Let them fend. One of them's a big lass."

"Madame!"

But Dame Anne stamped her foot and cried, "I'll not forbear. A shameless hussy and a thief!" and came flouncing out into the garden and saw the four ladies standing there listening.

"Christ's Cross!" she said, still very shrill, "and will you also bid me let this baggage, this light-fingered trull, go free?" and she looked from one to another with her big black eyes snapping sparks.

Margery Conyers grew crimson and tears came up into her eyes; that was how it was with her always when she grew angry, and she was angry now because Cecily a' Wood was a Marske woman, and so it was the duty of any Conyers to defend her. For a few minutes she and Dame Anne raged at each other, then Dame Margery, whose position was weak seeing that she knew more of Cecily's misdemeanors than Dame Anne had ever heard, burst utterly into tears and went away, sobbing that here was a pretty way of keeping St. Benet's Rule, that talked always of holy poverty and nuns who owned nothing, no not so much as a shift nor shoes nor a pen to write with.

"St. Benet quotha!" Dame Anne cried, looking from one to other of those that remained, challenging them also to battle.

"Madame," said Christabel, "I hold you are right. A thief's a thief, whether it's a nun's goods she takes or another's."

They all looked at her, quite taken aback, for not one of them but had expected that if she spoke at all it would be to thwart Dame Anne, for the sake of the old quarrel between them.

"For," Christabel continued, too earnest even to be aware of their looks, "if she thieves here she'll thieve there and everywhere. And how can any order be if the poor may idle, not caring to earn their honest living, but getting their bread by thieving from them that have, by God's will or by the industry and providence of their own kin, goods, whether cattle or corn, gold, jewels, or whatsoever may be?"

"Mass!" cried Dame Bet and Dame Bess breathlessly, "How she speaks like a book! Like a book!" But it was not her eloquence that had taken away their breath.

"Mass!" cried Dame Anne too, "but it is sense she speaks, and the first I've heard. Then tell me, madame," she addressed herself to Christabel as amongst paynims one Christian to another, "tell me what you think I shall do."

Dame Bet and Dame Bess stood still; the two others drew together and moved off down the path toward the beehives.

"Holy Virgin!" said Dame Bet to Dame Bess, and turned and went into the parlor to tell anyone there, who did not know it, that Dame Christabel and Dame Anne Ladyman were walking together in the garden.

They walked there for some time. Dame Anne told Christabel all her suspicions, the traps she had laid, and at last the certainty of Cecily's guilt. She also told the whole story of the brooch with a heart and a ruby; this part of the discourse did not much interest Christabel. They did not go in till a drop of rain, heavy and chill, struck Christabel's face. More drops began to rattle on the leaves and as they reached the parlor door the shower broke full.

"After you, madame!"

"After you!" each told the other with great courtesy, and all the ladies within stopped talking to watch them enter.

August 18

Julian heard Master Cheyne ride out early, and some time later Meg went to Mass. Julian supposed that he would be out the whole day, and perhaps Meg too, but Meg came back quite soon with Sir John Bulmer and one or two other gentlemen, so Julian knew she must not go up to the parlor. As there was strife in the kitchen just now, on account of the cook's pursuit of one of the young serving women and the jealousy of his wife, she did not go to the kitchen. The hall was neutral ground, so she stayed in the window there till they came in to set up the boards on the trestles for dinner. Then she went out into the yard, and tried to make friends with one of the lank stable cats. It would not come near, so she threw a stone at it and it fled. She was sorry then, because she knew that it never would be friends now, whatever she did. Yet there had been satisfaction in the hollow rap that the stone had made on the creature's ribs.

It was afternoon when Sir John and the others went away and Margaret, a little flown with wine, called to them and mocked them from the parlor window. July saw that she had on her very best gown, of green damask with a lace of little pearls. One of the young gentlemen called her "Diana," and July wondered why the others let out such a shout of laughter, and why Meg pelted them fiercely with comfits, though she was laughing too.

November 10

Aske, Hatfield, and Bangham went up into their room, taking with them Wat Clifton, to mull some wine and to talk. It was a chill evening and Aske slammed the shutters to, and barred them, so they were in the dark, except for the glow of a charcoal brazier, until one of the servants came back with their livery of candles. But there was light enough for Aske to begin rummaging in the elm hutch at the foot of his bed for the three horn cups rimmed with silver, a silver spoon, and a little box clasped with silver in which were spices. Hal plumped down on a stool by the wall, the guest sat on Aske's bed, and Ned perched himself on the desk by the window and set his feet on the other stool. Presently in came Will Wall and Hatfield's servant with the candles, and Will stuck two prickets on the branch and lit them; but the gentlemen hardly knew that the room was light now, so deep were they already in one of their everlasting disputations.

"You're wrong, Robin," Hatfield said.

Aske, searching now in the hutch for the sugar, grunted, and then, because he would not let an argument go by default, sat back on his heels and gave Hatfield his whole attention.

"Find me then a case, Hal," said he. "As I told you before, find me a case."

"Ask one of the benchers," Clifton suggested. He always avoided unnecessary effort, though his fellows warned him that men of such a humor and of such a build as he, run early to fat.

Hatfield, who liked law less than music and verse, was aware that in knowledge he was no match for Aske, but he trusted in luck and said, "Well, and he would find a case," so he got up and went over to the shelf where Aske kept his books and took one down at random.

"No use looking there. I've searched."

"Oh! but you would!"

"There's a new one. A Year Book. Thirteen Richard II. I bought it yesterday. Where a plague is it?"

They discovered at last that Clifton was sitting on it. "I thought you slept on a mighty hard pallet," said he, giving it up without regret.

Hatfield took the manuscript in its white sheepskin boards, remarking that Aske spent some money on books. He opened it at random, looked at the morass of closely written, fantastically abbreviated pages, and drew back like a swimmer hesitating before a dive.

"Let's get it clear. You say disclaimer by parole should be enough. No need to disclaim feoffment in a court of record."

"Disclaimer by parole," Aske answered, "is enough."

"Ready to aver it," Clifton chanted, and they all laughed at the consecrated phrase of the courts.

"Ready to aver it," Aske declared, and clapped the sugar box down on the end of the bench.

"Oh! Mass!" Hal groaned. "Pray for me!" He bent over the book, complaining that it was a sin that the printers should never clearly print these wicked old manuscripts for us poor lawmen!

He might have searched for hours or for days, but he had been right to trust in his luck.

"I have it!" he shouted. "Robin's wrong."

"Am I?" Aske's surprise made them all laugh. "Read it," said he, but then he laid an arm across Hal's shoulders and leaned over the book to read it for himself as Hal read it aloud.

"'*Et nota*,'" Hatfield intoned triumphantly. "'*Et nota tenuz fuit par touz les justices*'—it was held by *all* the justices, mark you," and he dug Aske in the ribs, "*'que tel desagreer par parol saunz estre en court de record ne vaut riens.'* Couldn't be clearer. Disclaimer by parole is worthless."

Aske was bending closer over the book, and he laughed softly.

"Have you read the writing in the margin? Another good lawyer thought like me and wrote it down—*'Vide mirabile judicium.'* And 'Here's a marvelous judgment!' I say too."

The others looked at each other; Hal shrugged, Ned raised his eyebrows, and Clifton groaned aloud.

"Not against *all* the justices!" cried Hal.

"Against as many justices as you like."

Hal shut the book with a clap and spoke with solemnity, as if he were giving sentence.

"Never, Robert Aske, did I know a man so set as you be in your own opinion. If you hold a thing, you sink your teeth in it and grip like a boar-hound."

"So do all men."

"Not all. But you do. It will get you into trouble one day."

December 28

It had been a green Christmas, and on this morning Dame Margaret Lovechild gathered two small pink roses from the big bush in the northeast corner of the cloister; she put them in an earthen pot and set it on the low wall of the cloister, where they should catch the sun. Someone even claimed to have seen a bee, but this was not generally believed, though the ladies inclined always toward faith rather than incredulity. Certainly after chapter the cloister was so nearly warm that most of them preferred it to the parlor.

Only the old prioress, Dame Christabel, and Dame Anne Ladyman sat within by the parlor fire. The two ladies who had so long been at enmity were now quite reconciled and often together in company. The prioress dozed and nodded, muttering now and then, and feeling for her staff; when her fingers found it she would set it now on this side of her chair, now on that, and at once forget on which side she had put it.

Christabel caught Dame Anne's eye, and in a glance they understood each other.

"Poor Lady," said Dame Anne with propriety, but their eyes had spoken the dread each had of the ruin time makes of defeated human nature, and the hatred each bore to the prioress as the trophy and exemplar of that defeat. They drew their stools closer together and began to talk in low voices so as not to wake her. They spoke, not as any other of the ladies would have spoken, of Marrick doings, or of their own families in the world, but of great matters at court, such as had filtered through to this quiet place, and chiefly of the King's divorce. Each of them found the subject interesting in her own way. "They say," Dame Anne whispered, "that this Mistress Anne is a marvelous fair lady, but also marvelous free. They say that Sir Thomas Wyatt . . . they say that Mr. Norris . . . And of her sister too . . . They say that the King . . ." So, she went on, throwing up her hands in horror and greatly enjoying herself. Dame Christabel spoke of the cardinal's part in it all; she doubted he was no true man; she wished the King might have honest, faithful servants to send to the pope so that his case might be truly known. Neither listened with any attention to what the other said, but as they took turn and turn about, fairly enough, the conversation contented each.

Once Christabel got up to toss another log onto the fire, and before she sat down she peeped through the little window that opened on the cloister.

"The ladies are all sitting with their hands tucked into their sleeves, and I swear that they are rubbing their fingers to warm them."

"And each telling other," said Dame Anne, "how warm and pleasant the day."

"I heard two of them tell the rest that today is the Fourth Day of Christmas. 'Jesu!' said they, 'just think of it, the Fourth Day of Christmas, and here we sit out in the sun!'"

"They are very simple," said Dame Anne.

In the afternoon the sun went in behind what had been light flecks of cloud, fine and white as lambs' wool, but now had thickened and darkened into a muddy brown curtain hung across all the western half of the sky. It was time for the ladies to leave the cloister and come into the frater, which was warmed by braziers and decked with holly and bay, box and ivy, like any lord's hall. And they danced there to the rebec and flute of the minstrels who had been hired from Richmond. When they had danced enough they sang songs and carols of God, of Adam, of our Lady, and the little Christ.

❖

That same afternoon Julian was shaking out and brushing Meg's clothes that lay in the great chest in her sister's bedchamber. There were sleeves lined with fur or embroidered all over with little flowers, bees, butterflies, and running stags; there were coats of velvet, there were petticoats of damask and tinsel satin. July laid all out on the bed, lingering over them, touching them with her fingers, loving and wishing for them.

She had one hand on a white damask gown when she heard Master Cheyne's voice in the room beyond; at that she snatched her hand back and skipped away from the bed, and stood listening.

Master Cheyne was not shouting at her but at Meg and at Sir John Bulmer. He must, July supposed, at last have caught them kissing.

That did not make it much better, so great a terror to her was Master Cheyne. If it was Meg and Sir John now, it would be July after, and his temper would be sharpened because they had angered him. "O! O! O!" she whispered under her breath.

Now Sir John was shouting as well as Master Cheyne. There was a crash as if someone had overturned the big carved chair by the hearth. Then feet pounded heavily, and a door slammed.

After a long minute the door of the bedchamber opened. Meg came in, shut the door, leaned against it and began to laugh.

"Jesu Mercy!" she cried, "I shall die of laughing. He has thrown him clean downstairs. I doubt not he has broken a leg at least. They are picking him up now."

"Downstairs!" July gaped. It did not seem strange, though it was terrible, that the terrifying Master Cheyne had thrown

Sir John Bulmer down the stairs. It did seem strange, however, that Margaret should laugh.

"Aye. And then out of the house and away, before any of our knaves could be after him. I knew not Jack Bulmer could be so quick. Oh! I love him for it."

July understood then, yet she could not laugh. "But, Meg," she whispered, "what will he do to us—after." The thought of Cheyne's hoarded malice made her shrink.

Meg tossed her head and laughed again, so that July saw her white teeth in her red, open mouth. She was laughing like a fishwife, yet whatever she did she was beautiful.

"He may do what he will," she cried. "This has paid for all."

1529

January 4

Robert Aske came out of the monks' church at Westminster. Mass was just over, and he was bidden to dinner with them by Dom Richard Pickering who was a Yorkshireman and a friend of his father's. Dom Richard had told him to wait outside the church, for he himself must today give the great dole to the poor, which was given every day during the Christmas Feast.

So Aske stood in the rare winter sunshine in the empty court, feeling clean within, and happy and rich, since those things which he had heard at Mass he believed, and was possessed of. Yet, for all that, he did not know exactly what it was that he possessed, but prized it as a man who keeps a treasure in a locked box that he has never opened, because he has never needed to open it.

Dom Richard came out from the cellarer's door, and servants with him, bearing the dole; he was eating an orange and he rolled in his walk, an immensely fat man, whose bulk the abbey's moderate fasts could not at all reduce.

Just then the porter opened the gate, and in came the crowd of poor folk who had waited outside. In a minute the court was full. Dom Richard and the servants were surrounded, and even Aske was pushed this way and that by the poor wretches—cripples and blind, hungry, dirty and foul-smelling—they were all about him.

When the crowd was in he found himself shoulder to shoulder with a tall thin man in a shabby scholar's or priest's gown; marvelous thin he was, unshaved, with deep harsh lines running down on either side of his huge mouth and bony nose.

Aske's hand had been in his purse already, and now something in the man's look moved him to hold out a silver mark. "Take an alms, Master Scholar," he said.

The man turned, stared at him, shook his head fiercely, and rather struck than pushed Aske's hand away. Then he wrenched round and slunk away into the crowd.

Aske lost sight of him; but when Dom Richard came back, wiping his hands and then his brow with the edge of his sleeve, he asked, "D'you know the tall thin fellow that looks like a scholar, Father, thin as a maypole and hungry looking as a tinker's cur?"

Dom Richard remembered him well, since he came often to the dole, but knew nothing of him.

"And I remember him," said Aske, "or think I do, yet cannot think how."

"Well, to dinner, to dinner," the monk said, and as they went back into the cloister he cried, "Mass! where is my orange? I must have dropped it." But hearing the trumpets blow he forgot about the orange. "St. Joseph! there goes the boar's head and the brawn!"

�֍ *The Chronicle is broken to speak of Gilbert Dawe, priest.*

Gilbert Dawe, Priest

The name of the man whose face Aske half remembered was Gib Dawe, and he was the fifth son of Mat Dawe, the Marrick Manor carter. Of those five boys he was the only one that lived beyond eight years old, so Mat was very angry, and Gib got many a beating, when he began to steal away from the village and down to the priory to learn his letters from the nuns' old priest, who, in those days, was not so old, so deaf, nor so stupid as he grew to be later.

Before that time came the boy had learned all he could teach, and being of a sharp and impatient temper he began to grow discontented, and scornful of the old priest. His father had given up beating him; the lad was grown too big for that, and besides Mat could see that he would never shape for a carter. But neither would he, if he continued by turns so pert and so surly with his betters, get his clerkhood; and so he told Gib often, and as often got saucy replies.

It was a better chance than Gib deserved that he ever was priested. The archbishop of York came to Marrick Priory to make his visitation of the nuns. He had brought two clerks with him, but one slipped on a slimy stone and put his thumb out, and the other was busy with the archbishop's injunctions to the houses of religious which he had lately visited. So Gib was sent for to write letters for the archbishop. The work kept him at the full stretch both of his penmanship and latinity, and therefore happy, and because happy, well-mannered and serviceable. The archbishop took such a liking to the long lad with his bright, eager eyes, that when he left, to the wonder of all the village and of Gib's family in especial, he took Gib with him, to be a clerk in his household, and to get his priesthood.

Gib did not come home to Marrick till just after he had been made priest. By that time the archbishop thought less well of him. Able he was, but never at peace with his fellows, nor for long civil to his betters. Therefore instead of keeping Gib in his household he offered to set him to serve, with two other priests, St. Mary's Church at Richmond.

So Gib came home after great perturbation of soul, for the priesting had raised him to the height of heaven, and the archbishop's malice (so he thought it) had flung him down headlong. It was May when he came home, and he stayed till hay-time in a summer when the weather was the fairest that could be. Gib helped with the mowing, but always a little apart from the other young people, for they, both men and maids, sheered off from him, excepting one only maid, the miller's third girl, Joan. She, at first for kindness, and after for the stir and unquietness of her heart which drew her to him, would pause in her raking to speak, or sit near him in the noonday rest under the trees, or linger with him in the evening when everyone went slowly home from the hay fields. One evening they lingered longer than ever before—so long that the late twilight came down on them, and the dark with bright stars but no moon.

Gib, when he woke next morning to the gray light before dawn, and felt his arm stiff under the weight of her head, knew that the pillars of heaven had failed, and that he lay broken in the ruins. That very day, before noon, he had fled from Marrick, as a man flees from a pestilence which he is aware of bearing within him.

Late in the next January, Joan the miller's girl knocked at the door of the priest's house at Richmond. It was not that her father would have refused to keep her, though with hard words in plenty, but that she had loved Gib so well, and was (so he came to feel it) of a blind and mulish constancy. So again Gib fled, taking with him the unhappy partner in his sin, and, in her body, its fruit.

They went South; no one at home in the dale knew where, and few would have cared to know.

1529

Further of January 4

Gib Dawe passed out under the gate of the Abbey of Westminster with a cheat loaf, two herrings, a lump of cheese, and the remains of Dom Richard's orange, which he had picked up from the ground. He would not go empty today, nor cold, so mild was the air, but he was thankful for neither of these mercies. As he and the rest of the poor trailed away, some already munching their bread and cheese, rich and succulent smells tormented their empty bellies, as the monks' dinner was carried, to the sound of trumpets, from the kitchen to the great frater. Gib thought of the vast bulk of the monk who had brought out the dole; he hated him for his round paunch and for the fine rolls of fat that lapped his jowl like that of a well-fed porker. He hated Master Robin Aske too for his careless, indifferent good humor; he would not for the world that Aske should have known him for Dawe the carter's son of Marrick; and yet, since he well remembered the boy that he had used to see fishing in the Swale, or riding the manor horses back from watering, he rated Aske's forgetfulness as a kind of contempt.

So he called up contempt to answer it. He despised Aske for being a friend of the monks; for being a gentleman; for having but one eye. Having thus written him off, he felt better, and seeing that he had got as far as Ludgate he went on a bit and then turned down Creed Lane to find a quiet place in which to eat his dole, for he had not the heart to go back to his lodging, where, even before he had set out, the other men were already sodden with drink.

He found a good place at Puddle Wharf and sat down on the edge of the wooden staithes, with his feet dangling over the first widely lapping tongues of the incoming tide. The sun was warm, the river bright, and what wherries passed him were full of holiday makers; but there were few people about since most were keeping their Christmas indoors. Just opposite him, a little way out, a barge was moored; a sailor in a red hood sat eating bread and onions in the stern; as he ate he hummed, monotonously and out of tune.

Gib for a few minutes took comfort from the sun's warmth, from the gaiety of the shining river, from the thought of the bread and cheese he would presently eat, and even from the feeling of companionship which the presence of the sailor—apart, yet not so far away—gave to him. But before long the man's humming began to annoy him. Once or twice, when the fellow was forced to be silent because his mouth was full, Gib whistled the tune correctly, but the sailor could not or would not learn it.

At last Gib lost patience.

"Sing in tune, fellow," he cried, "or sing not at all."

The sailor stopped humming and seemed to consider. "I sing for mine own pleasure," said he, and turned his back, taking up his tune again, but singing a little louder.

Gib, under his breath, wished a murrain on the fellow, who, as so many now, had no godly humility, no reverence, even for the priesthood. That rankled, though Gib knew quite well that few would recognize the priest in him under his ragged, greasy gown. "But," he thought, "so is the world these days—naughty men in honorable places, and righteousness a mock and a scorn." Whose the blame was he knew very well, and in his mind he ran over the sins of the rich—prelates, nobles, monks. "No wonder," said he to himself, "that heretics abound," and he groaned in spirit, both over the heretics, whom he hated, and over the rulers of the church, whom he hated more.

And all the time the sailor went on singing, so that Gib at last could not endure it. He snatched up the bread and cheese to eat it hastily, and to be gone from here.

He broke the bread and found that it was green with mold within. He threw it as far as he could into the river, and then was sorry, because the crust had been good enough to eat, but now only the cheese was left, since he could not eat the herrings raw.

He looked down at the water, where the two halves of the loaf were wallowing. If he waded in he might reach it, but again, if he did he would be wet, and the loaf was by now sodden and salt.

Watching it blackly, and eating his cheese to the very rind, his mind tumbled back into its discontents. And now that moldy loaf seemed to sum up and set a seal on all.

"To this," thought he, "is Christian charity come; to this the hospitality of monks; and to that fat paunch of the Westminster almoner the simplicity and austerity of St. Benedict." He was empty as ever, though all the cheese was gone, and he saw the whole world, and more especially Christ's Holy Church in these latter days, in desperate case. Hunger and the distress of his mind pricked him like a goad, so that he sprang up and made his way toward Ludgate, going fast yet aimlessly, his thoughts distracted between his own need of begging or earning a meal, and the world's need of repentance and return to the virtue of the older times. "*Deus misereatur nobis*," he kept muttering, and the few he met in the streets glanced at him, and stepped aside, so wild and fierce was his look.

He came to the wall of the Black Friars' House, and passed a little group at the gate, but then he swung about and went back. There were two comfortable, broad-shouldered, soberly clad men there, just getting down from horseback; they looked like yeomen or merchants in a small way, in from the country.

"Sirs," said Gib, pulling off his cap, and trying to look serviceable, "I will hold and walk your horses for a penny."

They gazed at him with the slow suspicion of the country-bred, and he thought they would refuse; but just then a friar came out of the gate and they referred the matter to him. He was a quick restless man with glancing eyes that seemed to take in more than lay on the surface of things. He said surely they must leave the horses in charge of this—worthy man—he summed up Gib with a searching glance and hardly a pause, and then he was gone inside with his two guests, and Gib paced up and down the street beside the heavy beasts or stood and leaned against their barrel-like girth.

At the end of a weary hour out came the two, and Gib got his penny and no more. Still, it would buy a dish of eggs at an ordinary if he made haste, for dinnertime was almost over. He was turning away when the same friar who had welcomed in the two countrymen put a hand on his arm.

"Have you dined, Master . . . Scholar? Or is it 'Sir Priest'?"

Gib answered only the first question: No, but he was about to dine even now.

"Upon a penny," said the other, and before Gib could be angry—"If you come within you shall dine, and yet save your penny. Come, come in!"

He left Gib to follow or no, and Gib followed, wondering what the friar did it for. He could not know that Brother Laurence was one of those who like to interfere, kindly sometimes, and sometimes of malice, in the affairs of others.

To Gib he seemed incredibly, even, for a time, suspiciously, kind. But when a hunk of brawn, and a big piece of mutton pie, and close on a quart of ale had gone down Gib's throat he ceased to suspect, and to resent, and even to notice the sharp glances that Brother Laurence gave him, when, every now and then, the friar would raise his eyes from his lap where his fingers were fretting his beads up and down upon the string. Feeling himself at ease Gib flung one leg along the bench and leaning an elbow on the table began to talk, with the help of an occasional question from the friar, as he had not talked since he left Oxford behind.

He was, he told the friar, a man of Swaledale in the north parts, of Marrick on Swale, and son of a carter. A priest he was right enough, and scholar too, for after he was priested—he stumbled there, grew vague, and passed on to the time when he served in the Queen's College at Oxford, earning his keep and getting his learning as best he could. "And then," said Gib, taking another stride to cover another awkward part of his story, "I came here to London, since when I have none well sped."

"So you have studied at Oxford?"

"Seven years. To no end." Gib brooded, and the feeling of well-being waned within him. "To no good end, for how could learning serve in these days, but if I were willing to creep into favor of some rich priest as other men do? For in these decaying times—"

He jumped at the force and suddenness with which the friar banged his fist on the table.

"Master Priest, you have spoken the fit word. Decaying the times are, yea, decayed, corrupt, rotten."

At an opinion so congruous with his own Gib's eyes began to burn with their somber fire. For a little while he and the friar told each other what was amiss with the church, and the churchmen—bishops, priests, monks, and nuns. Then Gib held forth alone and the other listened.

"And who shall reform the whole of the spiritual estate?" he concluded at last, and brooded over his own question, adding after a little, "No wonder heretics are many among us."

He was startled out of his thoughts by the friar asking, and asking him again, what were these heretics. It seemed to him a foolish question. Everyone knew what heretics were—Lollards, those who would have no priesthood, no sacrament, no church; those who read books that were forbidden. So he answered stiffly, not understanding the reason of the question.

The friar sat silent a moment. It was quiet in the big, high, vaulted frater. The sunshine had waned now, and the light came dully through colored windows, five great traceried windows down each side. There was a smell of clean rushes, underfoot, and of wood smoke, of tallow candles, and of many meals.

"Friend," said the friar at last, looking very hard and piercing at Gib, "wot you what those two good men, whose horses you held, came to me for?" Gib shook his head. "They came to buy from me books of the Scriptures, Englished, and other books such as are forbidden to be read." Then he said, "Come up to my chamber. It seems to me you do not yet know rightly what are heretics."

The room to which he led Gib was small, but pleasant and warm, for it had a glass window, and a little charcoal brazier was burning there. There was a bed with a red say coverlet, a big chest at the foot of the bed, a stool, a bench, and a shelf with books; Gib went to the books, like a fish to a mayfly. There was a Mass book, the whole of Chrysostom and Gregory, a *Summa Angelica*, Gregory's *Moralia*, and a breviary. He sighed as he paused before turning back to the friar, as much with pleasure as with envy, and let his hand slip lovingly over the bindings.

The friar was smiling. "Those are not the books I would show you, and talk with you of." He took a key from his neck and unlocked the great chest, letting the lid fall back on the bed.

Gib knelt, and began to look at the books that lay within, together with an old sparver cloth, and some sheets, two or three linen shirts, and a lute. *The Burying of the Mass*, *The Psalter in English*, *An A.B.C. against the Clergy*, *The Practice of Prelates*, he read.

"All proclaimed against, whether to sell, buy, or read," said the friar.

Gib sat back on his heels. Yesterday he would have been horrified, but today it was different. As though his mind had been full of gunpowder, which it needed but a trifle to touch off, the tuneless singing of a sailorman and a moldy loaf had caused an explosion which had unbolted doors and window shutters. And now he would listen without fear to this friar who had fed him, and who spoke his own thoughts of the corruption of the church, and of the greed of rich men.

So, while the friar talked, he listened. At first it made his skin creep to hear the holy mystery of the Bread called "Round Robin," or "Jack in the Box." When the friar blamed much of the ills in the church upon the pope's court of Rome and said, "Yea, and the Hollow Father himself must shoulder it too," Gib crossed himself and blinked. But he grew used to such outrageous words, and was able to smile when the friar read aloud to him from *A dialogue betwixt the Gentleman and the Plowman.*

"So," the friar came to his conclusion, "these are your heresies, and I, no doubt, one of your heretics, but what do I hold but you hold it too, though maybe you know it not? And what is it that I would do to cleanse and reform the church, but you would do the very same?"

They were sitting now on either side of the brazier, Gib on the bench and the friar on the stool. Gib drew a deep breath. "By God's Soul!" he cried. "It is the truth," and he brought his fist down on the seat beside him.

"Let us," said the friar, "root out from the church all these proud prelates with their jeweled rings, and their tippets of satin, and their scarlet hats from Rome. And with them let us root out also all these fat, lascivious abbots that keep paramours, two or three, in their lodgings, and these ignorant and beastly priests that haunt brothels. . . ."

He ran on quite a time, but Gib lost him, because those words of the friar had thrown him back into his own past, and into the darkness of the old sore shame. So he sat, hearing nothing, but going hot and cold, and feeling the sweat start on his back, knowing he would speak, and telling himself there was no need to speak. Then, as if someone had jolted it out of him without his will, he cried, not in his own voice, which was strong and harsh, but in a wavering voice that sounded strange in his ears, though he had heard the like of it from the lips of others in the confessional, "Listen to me. Stop! I am one of them. I am a fornicator; I committed fornication with a woman, not once but often and for years, so that she bore me four children."

When he had said that he turned away upon the bench and let his head hang down so that the friar could not see his face.

Brother Laurence had pulled up short. The thread of his discourse, which had been at that moment of the feigned miracles of St. Thomas of Canterbury, was broken off, and he needed a moment to collect himself. During the silence Gib seemed to himself to live again through all those years with Joan, the miller of Marrick's girl, from the evening they first met under the hawthorn, with all the air heavy-sweet with the scent of the blossom and the milky scent of the cows that were swinging slowly by them—from that evening to the moonless night among the haycocks, and the winter day she came to him at Richmond, and their journey to the South.

All that was eight years ago, yet the same pang of shame went through him now, fresh as the memory of that time was fresh. What came after was more dim, more dully aching. The years of servitorship at Oxford were confused in his mind: he could remember the birth of his first son, and of the daughter that died; but when the second boy had been born he could not be sure. Joan was a servant at the Blue Anchor Inn in Ship Lane, and there the children were born, and there they had died, of the sweating sickness, just as Joan was brought to bed of a fourth child, a puny boy.

And suddenly he found himself telling all this to the friar, who, though a good talker, knew also how to listen, and let Gib stumble on halting, returning, now mumbling indistinctly, now shamelessly candid.

"And three years ago, when the three elder brats were dead, and the other weaned, she went away. I think it was with one of those gentlemen scholars; perhaps the children also were his, or another's. Nay. Nay. They were mine. But," he cried sharply, coming back to the heart of the matter, "never for one instant, no, not when I first sinned, never did I take joy in it, but always shame. Shame," he repeated, as if he savored the word and the thing once more.

"Tell me!" said the friar at his side, "Did you keep yourself wholly to this woman, or did you have commerce with others?"

"With her only."

"Then I count you as it were married unto her."

"I, a priest, married!" Gib gave a sharp bray of laughter, but the friar was grave.

"Let the bishop be the husband of one wife," he said. "And if the bishop, then why not the priest, or senior?"

Gib stared so that a smile went over the friar's quickly changing face. "Friend," said he, "read you in the Scriptures, and you shall know shame no longer."

"But—priests—to marry!"

The friar laughed outright at that.

"You shall read the Scriptures new Englished." He got up and went to the great chest that still stood open.

"I cannot buy," Gib muttered hastily.

"No; but I can lend."

Gib passed out of the Black Friar's gate in the early twilight with the New Testament in English clutched close to his side. As he went through the empty and darkening streets he was like a man newly come out of prison. Now he need not think of all the years when he had lived, the friar said, as a married priest. For it was not wrong to be a married priest, still less, he thought to himself, when he had never taken joy in it. Joan had not had much more joy than he, so greatly had she suffered from his bitter, tormented temper; but that, though he knew it well enough, did not seem to be a thing which he needed to consider.

May 1

A number of the gentlemen of Gray's Inn got up before dawn and rode out to the fields toward Islington to bring in Summer. They found and picked little tufts of budding may, for not much was in flower yet, and decked their horses' head stalls with them, and their own caps. Then they came on some young maidens sitting in a ring under a beech tree that was here and there splashed pale shining green with the young leaves, as if it had been with sea spray. The girls were making garlands of primroses, and purple orchis, and a few early cowslips. Four of the young gentlemen who were still together in company bought garlands, paying for each garland a groat and a kiss.

After that they would not let the maids remain under the beech tree, but had them away, not unwilling, to Islington village to eat cakes, and cream, and brawn, mutton pie and watercresses. By the time that they had drunk their ale each young gentleman had his lass on his knee, and there was a great deal of laughter and not a little kissing.

But May morning passes, and at last Robert Aske gave his tankard into his maid's hands, bidding her sup the rest for he must be going. The others cried fie upon him, for the day was early yet. But said he, no, look at the church clock, and that he must be at Westminster Hall before the courts closed.

"Oh," Hal groaned, "why did we bring this spoilsport in our company?" But he did not mean what he said, because Aske was always a merry companion.

They took their horses again, and the young maids went down the road with them a little way and then parted. They were all very good friends, and the men promised to come again soon, though but half meaning it, for May morning was one morning different from all others of the year, when gentle and simple, learned and unlearned, met in pleasant comradeship.

The other three young gentlemen, being not so willing as Robert Aske to return to the collar, said they would come with him as far as Westminster, and then lead his horse back with them; so they went merrily, lengthening out the holiday with teasing and talking. At Charing Cross they had to stop, because a great number of horsemen and footmen were going by; there were gentlemen and serving men all in scarlet, and after them a number of priests, and crosses that flickered and blazed when they passed the southward-leading streets where the sun touched them. After these went the two cardinals, the English on a white mule and the Italian Campeggio on a black.

When the gentlemen from Gray's Inn could move on again Robert Aske was silent, so that Hal asked, "What's amiss?"

Aske turned his head. "Do you like this business of the King's divorce?" He gave Hal no time for answer but said, "I tell you I do not."

"Well," said Ned Bangham, "it's the King's matter, and the cardinal's, the two of them, but certainly not ours." And Wat Clifton, who was a cautious man, asked whether it were not better for a wise man to keep his mouth shut.

"Ah!" cried Aske. "Wise!" in an angry voice, but all the same he did shut his mouth, and kept it shut, till they came to Westminster and parted.

May 12

Gib Dawe lived now in Thames Street at the house of a pastry cook, who had for his sign King David with his harp. Brother Laurence had brought him here from the very wretched hovel outside Ludgate where he had used to lodge, saying it was not fitting he should be there, but among friends, and honest, good folk.

Gib's new landlord was one of those called among themselves "known men" or "brothers in Christ." He longed as greatly as Gib to change things in the church, and indeed some he wanted to change which Gib would have retained, so they had great arguments in the evening when work was done and they sat on the doorstep in the twilight. They grew very hot in their disputes sometimes, for though Gib could have borne that people should go to church on any day of the week but Sunday (which alteration the pastry cook believed would bring with it a notable minishing of superstitions); and though he now thought it well that all holy water, and candles, and crosses should be done away, yet he could not agree that every man was priest as truly as those who had been anointed as he had been.

So they were arguing it this evening, about and about, looking down the street to the apple blossom in the orchards of the great merchants on the other side of Thames Street, and growing hotter and hotter. Then the cook, a lean man and irascible, drew his knife, but Gib caught his wrist and prayed over him so eloquently that the cook wept, and fell on Gib's neck. Gib was satisfied that he had demonstrated the potency of priesthood, but he did not say so to the cook. Brother Laurence, when he came to bring Gib more copying of forbidden books to do, was pleased to see the two men so friendly. From each of them he had heard complaints, and feared that Gib and his host would soon part. But this evening, a fair and mild one, dying gently in a clear sky, they talked amicably of the great iniquities of the rich, about which they all agreed, till you could hardly see the color of the apple blossom in the Thames Street gardens, and till the cook's wife called them in to supper.

July 1

When William Cheyne came out of his chamber this morning he locked the door behind him, and dropped the key of it into his pouch. Then he called down the stairs to the servants who were setting the tables for breakfast in the hall below that they should bring his meals upstairs that day. They came up with plates and cups and food for two, but he sent down all but what he needed for himself.

The servants, of course, talked. One of them had heard the mistress calling out, very angry, from the bedchamber, and beating on the door. But the master had only laughed, and cried out to her that if she fasted today, fasting would make continence more easy. "And as for me, sweet," he said, "it comes of you that I am a lame man now, and only able to have an eye on you if I keep you under lock and key."

But if he was cheerful in the morning by the time it was dusk he had sunk into a sour, self-pitying mood. Julian had been able to keep out of his way all day, but at suppertime the maids told her that since it was her sister's carryings on that were the cause of them having to bring up the master's food, wine, and candles, she should bear her share. So they pushed the candles into her hands, and sent her before them into the upper room.

Master Cheyne sat with his chin sunk on his chest, and the staff, on which he leaned ever since his fall downstairs, between his knees.

He looked up at July, and his lips moved so that she saw his teeth, as if a dog were snarling.

She came near and put down the candles where he pointed, but before she could get away he caught one of her wrists and held her, so she stood still, with her heart beating right up into her throat, because she was so frightened of him.

"You're her sister," he said, and then let her go, and spoke as if July were not there. "God forgive me," he cried, "and have mercy on me that ever I married a whore."

When July found herself free she got away from him to the wall beside the door, and stood there clutching the painted hangings with both her hands behind her back. When the maids had set down the dishes she scuttled away after them.

August 25

There had been no train of mourners at the burial, no file of poor folk bearing candles, no singing men and boys to bring music to the very threshold of silence. The body had not lain last night under a hearse stuck over with many lighted candles, and today, now it was laid by, there would be no great dinner, no great dole for the crowds that should have come to such a burial. All had been done quietly, quickly, almost in a secret huddled way, because, in a time of pestilence, Lady Elizabeth Nevill, second wife of Thomas, Lord Darcy of Templehurst, had died, suddenly and with the marks of the sickness upon her.

So now only my lord himself and Lord Sandys of the Vine, Lady Elizabeth's brother, stood together in the friars' church at Greenwich looking down at the green and silver pall that covered the hole in the paving into which the coffin had been lowered. One or two of the friars moved and stood farther off, and, unostentatiously beside a pillar, a couple of masons waited with their bags of tools, for the grave would be closed at once. At the door of the church my lord's gentlemen and servants hung about; they stood sadly, for Lady Elizabeth had been a good mistress and a great lady, and besides they were conscious of a lurking fear that dogged any household where one had died of the pestilence; yet there was upon them a sense of relief; it was grievous that a life was finished; it was well that the empty shell which had held the life was put away. When they saw my lord move and come slowly down the church toward them, they turned their faces, almost with eagerness, to the open air, the gray light and whirling dust of a dry but blustering and threatening day.

Back in the house at Stepney the two lords sat together in my Lord Darcy's privy chamber, and heard the twigs of a wind-thrashed tree outside tap and whine upon the glass. For a long time they sat almost in silence. Then Darcy said, "I always thought to be buried with my father and his father at Templehurst. But now I shall choose to be laid beside her."

And after a while, in which he had looked about the room as if he were learning it, like a strange room, he said, "I see now why the dead are commonly buried with such state. It is to make the living think that death is—something." He met Sandys's eyes, and then again looked about the room from which she had gone, and from which the careful servants had removed all traces of her—the bits of embroidery, a book she had read, her lute—so that her husband's heart should not be wrung. "Whereas," said Darcy, "it is far worse than anything. It is . . . it is the nothing of it that . . ."

He did not try further to put into words the plain desolation of that one absolute negative, but Sandys understood, and nodded, and they sat again in silence, letting the knowledge of loss flow over all that was in their memory and find its way down every passage of their thought.

At last Lord Darcy stood up.

"I shall walk in the garden," he said, and they went out together into the restless tumult of the wind, on which now and again came a spitting rain. There in the orchard they walked up and down, clutching their hats to them, and with the wind flapping and tugging the skirts of their coats and beating back the breath into their mouths. But each felt better, nearer to life, and nearer too, in a strange way, to the dead, so that they began to talk about her, and even laughed, gently and lovingly, over things which Sandys now remembered of his sister when she was a little girl.

Yet, in the end, it was the knowledge of loss that must triumph. Darcy stopped and faced his brother-in-law, and let him see the tears on his cheeks.

"As long as I live I shall mourn her. She was—" He paused to choose his words. "She was my truest friend, and has left me now alone."

"You have two sons, and Bess."

"And Bess is her mother's lass, every inch. But she's a Constable now, since she's wife to Robert Constable's son."

"George," said Sandys, in a voice that did not ring true, "George is a dutiful son."

Darcy looked up into the tossing branches. Some of the leaves, torn away by the wind, went spinning by as though it were already autumn.

"George? If there were a time when George could compass his own profit by my loss, he'd do me a shrewd turn, and rejoice in it, and call it by a fine name."

Sandys spoke no more of George, since he thought that saying only too true. Nor could he bring himself to mention Arthur Darcy, so lightly did he regard my lord's younger son. But Darcy himself went on: "And Arthur—he means no harm nor would do none so long as to be true to his friends and his kin is as easy as playing on his virginals and his clavichords and his regals. But if it were to be a matter of strife, and blood, and danger—"

He broke off and moved away, and Sandys heard him mutter that God should forgive him for speaking so of his own sons. "But it's the truth," he said, and after that there was nothing more spoken between them till the horns sounded for dinner inside the house.

October 24

It was a day of drizzling rain and a gray murk from dawn to dusk, so that no one remarked the small closely curtained barge that brought two gentlemen and two ladies, all muffled up in fustian cloaks, to the steps of York Place, the new great house built by the cardinal, beautified and furnished by him, and now left empty, but for a few of the King's officers and servants.

The four who had come by water from Greenwich climbed the riverstairs, crossed the privy garden and went into the palace by the small door that side. By this very door not a week ago the cardinal had come out, and stood, hesitating, dazed yet by the fall from the height of his precarious greatness. "Which way? Which way?" he had murmured, like a man lost, and it had needed a servant's touch on his arm to direct him to the barge that lay waiting. Then he had gone toward it, carrying, himself, a small trussing coffer, since only few of his household came with him to carry other of his stuff. He had not once looked back at the great palace with its gables and many gilded weather vanes catching the light, but had gone away and down to the barge walking with the cautious unsteady flat-footed pace of a very old man.

Today, once inside the palace, the King and the others cast down their cloaks.

"Now, sweet," said the King to Mistress Anne, "we shall see what goods this false servant of mine hath laid by."

"There is an inventory written?" she asked sharply.

"He was bidden write it with his own hand, that nothing should be forgot."

They came on the inventory in a little closet of my lord cardinal's own, very richly furnished, but desolate now, with the ashes of a dead fire on the hearth, and dust of the last days on the black velvet close chairs, and the cushions of velvet figury still crumpled in disorder in the window.

The King and Mistress Anne bent over the many pages of the book; he had his arm about her and his hand over hers at her waist. With his other hand he turned the pages so that their eyes caught out, from here or there, the record of something rich and lovely.

New hangings . . . 6 pieces of triumphs, counterfeit arras . . .
   the arms of England and Spain, roses and daisies.
Three blue velvet figury hangings . . .
Beds, one of rich tissue.
Quilts sarcenet, paned, with my lord's arms and a crown of
   thorn in the midst.
Pillow-beres of black silk with fleur-de-lys of gold; of white
   silk with red fleur-de-lys.

Mrs. Anne seemed to purr like a cat.

Cloth of silver and green satin sometime the lining of two
   gowns . . .
Blue and crimson velvet and it with green scallop shells of
   silver embossed with needlework and S S of gold on each
   of them . . .

But the King grew impatient and let the pages go with a run.
   "Where is the plate of gold and silver?"
   He found the page.

A gold cup of assay . . . a crystal glass garnished with gold . . .
   a gold salt garnished with pearls and stones and a white
   daisy on the knop.

He shut the book, and, turning, shouted for one of the royal
officers who had charge of the stuff. The man's voice answered
him hollowly in the great empty house.

"The keys! The keys!" the King cried, and when the keys were brought they went away with them to the chamber where all this most precious stuff had been stored.

There it was, set upon benches and cupboards, and overflowing to the floor, the dim light gleaming on the bellies of gold cups, gold salts, silver cups, silver salts, and catching the facets of jewels.

"Jesu!" cried Mrs. Anne, and the King said, "Passion of Christ!" at the sight of that sumptuous spectacle. Then they moved about, touching and lifting, here a gilt charger, there a gold cup with a cover and the top-castle of a ship on the knop.

"Ah! the pretty thing," cried Mrs. Anne, and pointed her finger at a bowl of gold with a cover, garnished with rubies, diamonds, pearls, and a sapphire set in a collet upon it.

The King stooped to look at it. Just near, upon the bench end, stood a tall gold salt with twined green branches enameled upon the gold, and scrolled letters enlaced together; the letters were K. and H. He gave the salt a shove with the back of his hand and it fell from the bench and clattered to the ground.

Mrs. Anne tittered, because she knew that K. stood for Katherine, but the King's face had reddened with anger. He caught her by the wrist and kissed her roughly and went on kissing. As his mouth lifted from her throat or from her lips he was muttering—

"Laugh? You may laugh. And she. And the pope. But none will laugh when it is seen what I shall do."

October 27

On this day the mermaid, (if she really was a mermaid), came to St. Andrew's, Marrick, just as the ladies were sitting down to their mixtum, which today was of fried eggs, and salt herrings soused, because it was a Friday. There was a strong wind blowing from the west, so the sound of the pack mules' bells did not reach even those messes whose chamber windows looked down the dale, until the mules were quite close. But as soon as any of the ladies heard the bells they knew them for those on the harness of the two priory mules, Black Thomas and the Bishop, and they knew therefore that Dame Margery Conyers the chambress, and Dame Bess Dalton and the three servants were returning from York, where the chambress had been to buy cloth for the ladies' gowns.

Knowing this, more than one of the ladies clapped a fried egg or a piece of herring between tranches of bread, and bearing these in one hand and a cup of ale in the other, made for the great court, to greet the arrival of the returning ladies; those who had been to York had been, they considered, into the world, and brought back news of miracles, of fashions of gowns and coifs, of the sweating sickness, of the Scots, of the prices of cloth; and besides news on these important subjects, other news which might be called little better than tittle-tattle, but the ladies loved it not less than any of the rest.

Dame Christabel was eating her mixtum with the prioress, and the prioress's chamber faced up the dale, toward Calva, humped and spined like a great beast under its brown heather and red-brown bracken. For this reason, and because of the great wind that was blowing, Christabel did not hear the mule bells; the prioress did not hear them either; but that was because she was growing very deaf.

The first thing which Christabel heard above the noises of the wind, which rattled the casement, and made strange whistlings among the rushes on the floor, was the clack of the latch. Then the door burst open, dry bits of rush rose and flew about, the fire swirled out from the chimney, and Christabel had to catch the edge of the board-cloth to prevent it flapping back across the dishes on the table. Dame Elizabeth Close came in, like a great ship before the wind, wind in her skirts, wind in her veil. For a moment she looked far too big. Then she caught the door and forced it shut behind her, and in the restored quiet of the room became her normal size again; which was big enough, Dame Christabel thought, for Dame Elizabeth was a very large woman.

"Our Lady!" cried she, casting up her hands. "Our Lady! A marvel! Here's a marvel. Jesu! it is a marvel indeed!"

She went across to the old prioress who was tremblingly trying to get up from her chair, for if she had not heard she had seen Dame Elizabeth's gesture.

"What is it?" she cried in her shaking old voice. "Is it the Scots?"

"No, no. Not the Scots. Lord! no. It's a mermaid!"

"Where?" The prioress looked vaguely round as if there might be one under the table.

"Here, in Marrick."

The prioress sank down again. She was not able to deal with such a situation. It was Christabel who asked, "How did she come?"

"Dame Margery hath brought her from York."

"She would!" Christabel murmured, but under her breath; and to herself she thought, "At least if any of them would, she would." But she had not expected that any of the ladies should have had the opportunity of committing such a rare foolishness.

She said to the prioress, "Shall I go down and see?" And the prioress nodded more vehemently than her ordinary ceaseless nodding, so Dame Christabel went.

The great court, as she went down the outer staircase from the prioress's room, looked as if today were the great spring washing day, so full was it of the flapping white of the ladies' veils. But besides the ladies there were a great many of the serving women, and even some of the farm men, and of course Jankin the porter in his green hood. And from the center of the crowd came now and then the chime of the mule bells, or the ring of a hoof on stone as the beasts fidgeted.

None of them, not even the youngest girl that tended the hens, took notice of anything but what was in the center of the mob, so, though Dame Christabel came to the outskirts of the crowd, she could see nothing, nor make any way in. "Perdy!" and, "Marry!" cried the wenches, and, "By cock!" the men. But beyond them Dame Christabel could hear Dame Margery's taut, excited voice declaring that, "Yea, truly she is a very mermaid and the skinner's wife of York would never have sold her to us but because of the great reverence her husband and she have for St. Andrew. Two pounds I paid, and we are to pray for them both every St. Andrew's Day."

"Two pounds," thought the treasuress, "for a mermaid!" She did not think that Dame Margery was one to have obtained at such a price a very mermaid. That would have cost far more, so the two pounds were sheer loss.

"Where," cried Dame Anne Ladyman, "shall we put her?"

"In the big fish pond," someone suggested.

"But she'll eat all the fish," young Grace Rutherford piped up, forgetting in her excitement that it was no novice's place to speak aloud among the ladies, still less so when there were men about.

"Little fool!" Dame Margery chid her, but not for the fault of speaking. "It's pike, not mermaids, that eat fish."

"Mass!" cried Dame Joan Barningham, with triumph in her voice. "What will the Ladies of St. Bernard say when they know that we have a mermaid in our house?"

Dame Christabel was now, by dint of shoving and some determined elbowing, in the thick of the group, though she still could not see what the ladies in the midst were staring at, for their great veils flapped and flew up in the wind, and thrashed like washing on a line.

That remark of Dame Joan's came to her just as she had her hands on the shoulders of two of the hinds, meaning to thrust them part. It made her pause.

Could this thing be true? Could this be the very mermaid that Dame Margery claimed? Then what a triumph for the chambress, though doubtless also a triumph for the whole house, as regards the ladies of St. Bernard.

Christabel's mind—usually so prompt at a decision—for an instant wavered. Suppose the chambress had somehow transported in a tub of water, balanced against the nuns' bales of cloth across Black Thomas's packsaddle, a mermaid, even now lazily combing her hair over naked shoulders with a golden comb, while in the depths of the tub her tail moved with the easy grace of a fish keeping itself head-on to the quietly running waters of Swale. If so, the triumph of the chambress was complete. If, on the other hand, it were some creature, human in shape, which the chambress's enthusiastic imagination had taken for a mermaid, would it be possible to rig it up somehow to impress the ladies of St. Bernard, and yet within the house of St. Andrew make it clear that the chambress had been soundly taken in. Certainly a fair young girl dimly seen in a tub in the warming house, and reputed a mermaid, would cause the ladies of St. Bernard to grow green with jealousy.

Dame Christabel pushed the hinds asunder with a tart, "Make way, fellows!" and, "Where's your plow today?" The ladies saw her then, and made way too, and at last she came to the space in the midst of the group.

She stood there a moment, looking down at the creature sitting on the grass. Then she laughed.

"A mermaid!" she said, "And why should you think that is a mermaid?" The creature, a woman with a broad flat face, pale blue eyes and a mouth half open, raised her head, and shrank away.

"Because—the skinner's wife was assured of it. She had her of a shipmaster of Bridlington, who took her at sea, swimming in a storm."

Dame Christabel had, however, infected with doubt some of the ladies. Dame Joan, leaning forward over the creature, adjured her to say whether she was truly a mermaid and lived in the sea.

She got no answer, except that the mermaid shrank still more into herself.

"There," said Dame Margery, as if the proof lay before them. "She can no English."

"Ask," someone suggested, "if she cometh from the middle of the sea or from near the edge of England, for then she might understand something like English—perhaps French or Low German."

No one knew any Low German, but old Dame Euphemia Tempest remembered that she knew the motto of the King's Lady Mother, and that it was in French. She did not know what it meant, but perhaps the mermaid would.

"*Souvent me souvient*," Dame Euphemia repeated several times, but without any response.

They tried Latin next, reciting the Paternoster to her, several of them at once, which cannot have made it easier to understand. At all events she gave no sign that she had ever heard it before.

"There!" said Dame Margery again, "you see."

"And what," Christabel challenged her, "do we see, but that the creature's a heathen? There are many such in Muscovy, or the parts that lie beyond the Emperor's lands."

"Fie!" cried some, and, "That's true," said others; but there was no time for them to debate it at length, because the bell in the tower just behind them began to ring, and it was time to go in to Lady Mass. Afterward there would be chapter, and there they would fight it out.

By Compline that night the blustering wind of the morning had dropped, and the evening was very still, though gloomy and overcast. The storm which had raged among the ladies had also spent itself: Dame Margery had been defeated; Dame Christabel had won; and most of the ladies were ready to laugh, though rather regretfully, over the absurd idea of calling the creature from York a mermaid.

Yet their incredulity had not spread beyond the walls of the house, and all that day little knots of people kept coming to the gate, some with fowls to sell, some with nuts, some with gifts of warden apples, or a piece of homespun—anything that would get them past the gatehouse, and give them the chance of seeing the marvel.

At Vespers the old parish priest came hobbling down from the parsonage. It was not often now that he troubled the parish church with his mumbled and garbled Latin. But tonight he went right through the service, as loud as he could, so that the Ladies, singing their own Vespers beyond the great screen, should hear him. When both they and he had finished he went round to the gatehouse, and, after a word with Jankin, into the great court. Along the line of windows the lights were already pricking out, so heavy were the clouds. From the kitchen came the clatter of wooden bowls and plates; the servants were fetching away supper from the kitchen to the various messes. Then Jankin, who had gone up to the prioress's chamber, beckoned to him and he went up.

He was not glad to see that it was Dame Christabel Cowper who tonight supped with the prioress, because she always made him feel what he was indeed—an illiterate and doddering old man. As he blessed them both, hurriedly, and stumbling over the words, his eyes were on the prioress. He and she had known each other for many years; there had been disagreements between them, and disapproval on the prioress's side; but in the presence of Dame Christabel they felt that there was an alliance between them. Neither of them was very bold, but together they were just a little bolder against her than either would have been alone.

And then the door opened and the ladies' servants brought in bowls of pottage from which a scented steam wreathed up. The old man's nose told him, "Hare!" as he sat down, and for a little time he forgot what had brought him down to Vespers.

It was the prioress, who, with an apprehensive eye upon Dame Christabel, told him that, "Dame Margery today brought back a creature from York who, 'twas said there, was a mermaid. But now she hath legs."

"Christ's Cross!" said the old man. He had heard enough from Jankin as he passed to know that he must go warily. Yet he very greatly desired to see the creature. Even if she were no mermaid, even though, as the prioress seemed to imply, she had grown legs between York and Marrick, yet still there was something marvelous in one who had been thought to be a mermaid. But his slow wits could hit on no way of asking to see her that would not draw upon him the scorn and anger of Dame Christabel.

It was Christabel herself who gave him his excuse, for she spoke to him, though she looked at an apple that she was peeling.

"She's a heathen. She does not know the Paternoster."

"God's Bread!" The old man took a bite out of his apple.

"It's for you, since our priest is away at York," said Christabel, "to make her a Christian soul."

"God's Bread!" he mumbled again, and then hastily swallowing the mouthful, "Then I must see her. I must be sure she is not christened already."

"You shall." Dame Christabel's eyes glinted with a smile at his simplicity. "You shall see this marvel."

So the creature was sent for, and came. She stood with her back to the door, where the servant had pushed her, and hung her head. The priest's hopes dwindled and died, but he began, though unwillingly because of the presence of Dame Christabel, to question the woman. "Are you christened, daughter? Can you say your Credo?" and so on. To all of it she gave no answer, only watched him through her matted hair.

"She can no English," he said at last.

"Or is an idiot."

Even a worm will turn. The old man was afraid of Dame Christabel but her scorn of him was so manifest that it pricked him into a moment's courage.

"She's no idiot," he told her quite firmly. Indeed the poor thing's eyes, though vague, had not the untenanted look of the idiot's. "But if she's a Christian soul she'll know this," and he crossed himself, which none of them had thought to do.

The woman was watching him but she did not move. It was almost conclusive. But yet he tried one thing more. On the beam across the chimney breast a little ivory crucifix hung. There was a touch of gold on the head of the cross where the monogram had been written, and red paint showed on the hands and feet. It was the work of a craftsman of old time, harsh and terrible, no King reigning, but a tortured man hanging on the tree. The old priest and the ladies knew it too well to see it for what it was.

He came close to the woman and put it into her hand. She bent her head, peering at it, then suddenly she gave a cry, and threw it down among the rushes.

The two ladies sprang up, and the old priest stepped back a pace.

"Jesu Mercy!" the prioress cried, and began to cross herself.

"*Retro me Sathanas!*" said Dame Christabel. She had not much Latin, but if she ever used it, it was with effect.

"Oh! why did she come here?" the prioress mourned. "What shall we do with her?"

For once it was the old priest who took charge. "I'll christen her now," he said, "and so shall the devil be driven out of her."

They christened her there and then, with water in Christabel's great cup Edward, and with Christabel and Dame Margery, fetched in haste, as godmothers, and Jankin as her godfather. Dame Margery tried to have her christened Melusine, after the mermaid lady in the story, but her position was too weak; the creature had not only a devil, but legs. When therefore Christabel said that her name was Malle, so she was named. No one asked why she should be Malle, but Christabel was thinking of the sheep in Chaucer's story, which belonged to the widow whose cock was called Chauntecleer and his wife Pertelote.

When she was a Christian woman they turned Malle out. She had no idea what had been done to her.

1530

January 15

My lord of Norfolk's long nose was still blue after his ride to Esher on the drab, raw January morning, but now the horn had blown to dinner, and he and the cardinal went up together. All the way up the stairs and the length of the great chamber (which indeed was not so very great), the cardinal was thanking the duke for his good will, kind offices, and merciful mind, in that, like the lion in his coat armor, he spared those he had pulled down. "For," said the cardinal, "of all other noblemen, I have most cause to thank you for your noble and gentle heart, the which you have showed me behind my back, as my servant well hath reported unto me."

The duke heard it all in a courteous silence, and if he rejoiced at so great humility in a man lately of such haut and proud stomach, or if he found it tragic, he gave no sign either way.

Then Master Cavendish, one of the cardinal's gentlemen, came near with water warmed and perfumed for them to wash their hands. The duke drew away, and though the cardinal beckoned that he should come and dip his hands together with his, he would not, for, said he, it became him no more to presume to wash with my lord cardinal now than it did before.

"Yes," said the cardinal, "for my legateship is gone, wherein stood all my high honor."

"A straw for your legacy," cried my lord, "I never esteemed your honor the higher for that," and he looked about as if he wished all present to take note that he had said it, so that perhaps one might carry it to the King, saying that "my Lord of Norfolk lightly regards the pope and his legate in this realm." But certainly he would not wash with the cardinal, declaring that "as archbishop of York and cardinal your honor surmounteth any duke in this realm."

Nor would he sit beside Wolsey at dinner, but on the less honorable side of the table, and there not opposite to him but a little beneath. And while they dined, all his talk, as he warmed and flushed with the wine they drank, was of how highly thought of were those servants of the cardinal who were faithful to their master, and how those were blamed who had forsaken him.

Altogether, though the day was so dark that the candles were lit all along the board, and torches here and there down the chamber, the cardinal and the duke dined very cheerfully, for the cardinal, receiving such honor from the duke, repaid by an eager, humble courtesy, bidding the gentlemen bring the duke always the best, whether of fish or eggs, since it was Friday, or of the wine.

But that night, when Master Cavendish came to the cardinal to make him ready for bed, he found him very shaken and uncertain in spirits, now up, now down, now declaring that the King's mind toward him must be good, or never would such a true, plain-dealing nobleman as the duke have spoken so honorably, giving him courage—yea—and hope that he should come again to the King's good grace and be as well as ever he had been; and now silent, plucking at his underlip with hasty fingers, shaking his head and knotting his brows.

When Master Cavendish had put upon him his fine linen nightshirt, the cardinal sat down so that he could draw off his hosen, and then as Cavendish knelt before him, the cardinal gave a great sigh—

"George," said he, "you know not why I am so sad."

Cavendish did not know, but he could well guess that it was due to something which had passed between his master and Mr. Shelley, judge of the Common Pleas, who had come to Esher even before the duke had left, with yet another message from the King, who, when he asked the duke to tarry and assist him in his message, the duke denied, saying, "I have nothing to do with your message, in which I will not meddle."

And so it was, as he guessed, for now the cardinal, having broken silence, told him all; all that Mr. Shelley had said from the King, and all that he had himself replied. The King's message was not very long but had a sharp sting. He sent to say that it was his pleasure to have my lord cardinal's house, called York Place, or more commonly White Hall, near Westminster. And the judge said that all the judges and learned counsel of the realm had told the King that he had the right to it.

"Fie!" cried Cavendish roundly, "right he hath never to it."

"Ah, George," the cardinal looked down at his bare feet upon the footcloth, curling and uncurling his toes much as he had done when they were new and he a baby on his mother's lap, but now with no pleasure in his skill in making the ten little pigs move. "Ah, George, so said I too. Or rather I drew a distinction, for it may be law, yet it is not conscience, and so Mr. Shelley himself admitted, that I should give away that which is none of mine, from me and my successors."

He fell silent again and motioned Cavendish away with his hand, who went about the room, laying by my lord's clothing and preparing for the night. It seemed that the cardinal would say no more, but just as Cavendish slid the curtains back along the rail of the bed, his master spoke again.

"So I said at the last, 'Master Shelley, I charge your conscience to discharge mine. Shew His Highness from me that I most humbly desire His Majesty to call to his most gracious remembrance that there is both a heaven and a hell.'"

"Aye!" thought Cavendish, "and that there is!" and he ground his teeth together, thinking of his master's enemies.

When the curtains were drawn again, and all lights but the great Paris candle beside the bed put out, Master Cavendish laid off his clothes and went to his trussing bed in the corner of the room. He could hear the cardinal often stirring and turning in bed, and once he groaned and muttered, and once beat with his hand on the pillow.

Cavendish lay waking long too, watching the candle flame swing in the draft, for the wind had risen now and sang thinly round the chimneys of the house. He tried in his simple, faithful mind to resolve his master's perplexities, and know those friends on whom he could rely; but where so much was treachery how could an honest man tell who was true? He could see that the cardinal trusted now in the Duke of Norfolk. Sometimes Cavendish trusted in him too, and sometimes, as the wind grew more boisterous and began to move the hangings and the curtains of the cardinal's bed, he thought that there was no man in the world save himself that his master could trust.

February 2

Dame Christabel knelt in her stall. The old priest elevated the Host, and the ladies bowed their heads.

"And she," thought Dame Christabel, who had been reviewing in her mind the episode of Dame Margery Conyers and her mermaid of three months ago, "*she* would have liked to cut up the old green cope of St. James, because of the cockleshells on it, to make a gown for the creature." She turned her head, slowly and only slightly, so that none should notice, and looked through her fingers to where, among the servants, close to the lower door, Malle knelt. Malle was not decked out in the sea green satin but in an old brown homespun gown, a worn-out shift belonging to one of the ladies, and a length of patched linen for a head kerchief. They had found her an old pair of shoes too; there was a hole in each sole, but Perkin the carter had patched them.

The bell rang in the tower to tell the dale that God, the Omnipotent, was in this place, this very place.

Dame Christabel smiled to herself, remembering Dame Margery's discomfiture.

March 16

Gib had been paid to sing Mass that day in the Chantry of John Chamber in the Church of Holy Trinity, Knightrider Street.

The church was small, old and ruinous, sheared up with props of timber, and the tower covered with ivy and full of noisy jackdaws. Jackdaws built inside too, so that sticks rolled and snapped under his feet as he moved about, making ready for his Mass in the chantry, which, like all the rest of the church, was dusty and decayed, with the paint chipping off the carved angels and little figures of mourners about the tomb.

Gib had been glad to take the money for singing the Mass, but now the dirt and disrepair of the church affected him to a gloom more savage than melancholy. He stood and knelt, did reverence and raised the Host, all without thinking of what he did, having willfully, though blindly, barred God out. For that morning he had quarreled again with the cook, his landlord, and he hated him yet. He hated him, he hated all men, and himself he hated most.

June 10

July shut the door very softly, and tiptoed away and downstairs. She did not know if Sir John and Meg knew that she had seen them, but she had seen, and now she shrank away, sick and soiled, and frightened lest something that was horrible should reach out and touch her. All that morning she lurked in the shed where the empty wine casks were stored, so that she did not know when Sir John went away, nor when William Cheyne came back, nor that there was a guest to dinner. But when she slunk in, a little late but not enough to be noticeable, there, beside William Cheyne at the table, sat an abbess, whose plump face looked very pink against the white of the Cistercian habit.

"Jesu!" thought July, scared, yet with a feeling of relief, "*he* knows" ("he" always meant Cheyne for her) "and he has brought this abbess to chide Meg and persuade her to do no more of—those things—with Sir John—or other."

So she fastened her eyes on the lady, but soon came to the conclusion that such chiding and persuasion were not to be hoped for from her, since she was a very merry, free-tongued lady, and also a little drunk.

Upstairs, when July was sent for to find a piece of music that Meg wanted, Meg and the abbess were laughing together over a story which the abbess told of a lusty, gallant prior, "not twenty miles," cried the abbess with a giggle and a wink, "from a house of religious women that I know of," and then an account of his carryings on, at which Meg laughed till she cried. But William Cheyne sat apart, watching them with a sour, thin look on his face that July knew, and her attention was more on him, wondering always, "Does he know? What will he do?" than upon the abbess. She only wanted to find the music quickly and get away before he would come out from his silence and stillness.

But when she had found the music at the bottom of the small painted chest, Meg wanted her box regals, and when July had brought those, and pulled up a stool to set them on, Meg told her to lay hold of the bellows and blow. And then, worse still, for it made her conspicuous, Meg bade July sing the song with her. July had a voice as small as a wren's tiny pipe, but as true and clear; it was her one grace, and of no pleasure to her, because she dreaded to be noticed for any reason, seeing that to be ignored was so much safer.

She sang with her eyes lowered and did not therefore have time to draw back before she found herself drawn by the abbess into her arms, hugged to a warm, soft breast, and kissed with moist, lingering kisses that July detested. "Nay," cried the lady, "I must kiss that sweet little mouth. Marry! and by our Lady! But the voice is the voice of a bird."

She held July off, staring at her, while July looked only at a little chain of gold with enamel flowers of blue and white which the abbess wore; it heaved up and down with the lady's breathing in a way that disgusted July.

"And this is your little sister, madame? By the Mass, little gentlewoman, I would I had you among my ladies to sing. Such a high, sweet note! It puts me in mind . . . Ah! me!" She did not tell them of what it put her in mind, but still holding July firmly she shed a few tears, murmuring, "Alas. I was young. I was young."

July stood very still, knowing that it would be unmannerly to pull herself away, but as stiff as a poker. The abbess loosed her at last, in order to wipe her eyes, and July drew back a little and felt enormous relief, but not for long. For the next thing was that the abbess leaned over to Meg, and put one of her plump hands on Meg's fine small one, and said, sighingly, that there was nothing would make her gladder than to take the young gentlewoman back with her and receive her into religion. "For I doubt she's not portionless, seeing, as ye say, ye come of such high blood," and at that she turned from Meg to William Cheyne, as though he were the one to deal with that side of the matter. But he said nothing, nor gave any sign that he had heard her, though his eyes were on the three of them, cold and unwinking as a snake's eye.

Meg looked at the abbess, then at July, and laughed.

"There!" said she to July. "You hear that? There are you provided for," and she began to thank the abbess and praise July more than July had ever thought to be praised. But when the two of them were making all arrangements—of how and when the child's dower should be paid, and what stuff she should bring with her, and whether it would go on one of the abbess's pack beasts or need a hired mule to carry it—July suddenly broke in on them.

"No!" she cried. "No! I will not go." She stopped because they turned and stared at her. But she cried again with a shrill, breaking voice, "No, I will not. I will not. I will never go with her."

Meg was angry, but the abbess said, no, no, not to chide her, and put an arm once more about July, promising her that she'd find it no harsh life: "For you shall have a rabbit to keep or a little dog, and when you are grown perhaps a gay scholar of Oxford for your true love, for we must have our pleasures, we religious, being for all our vows but women, and therefore weak, as all the Fathers knew, God wot, nor would Our Savior, who . . . but what was I saying?" She laughed a little emptily, for the wine was mounting ever more potently to her head. And then she said, very solemnly, "Even though it comes to a babe, that is no matter. And it has so come, more than once among us. For we're women, we religious, women . . . God forgive us."

July wrenched herself away. "I will not go. I will not go," she cried again, and then ducked her head because Meg had sprung up, and her eyes were flaming with anger.

But before Meg could catch her William Cheyne spoke, and his man's voice, coming so suddenly and so sharply, startled them all to stillness.

"No," said he, "she shall not go. But for you, mistress," he spoke to the abbess as though she were a person of no importance, "you shall be gone from my house."

Then there was a great to-do. The abbess was dignified, then wept. Meg raged till her voice cracked. But it was the abbess who went, July who stayed. In the charged silence after the guest had gone William Cheyne told his wife why he had refused to let July go. "For it is not right," said he, "that nuns should be so lewd, nor that such a jig as yonder abbess should bear rule." Those were the reasons he gave, but they were not the true ones. He had refused to let July go chiefly to thwart Meg, but partly also to have the opportunity to use words of the abbess and her wantonness that he dared not these days use of his wife; yet they both knew at whom he cast the ugly words.

Meg answered him that she would have let the child go for a religious, "because," said she, "well I can see that her being here irks you, and for her sake I would set her beyond reach of your ill tongue and your unkindly handling." But neither was that the truth. She had jumped at the offer partly because she thought if July were not there a few of Cheyne's east-wind angers might be scaped, but mostly because that morning she had seen the girl's face at the open door, though she was sure Jack Bulmer had not. But the girl had peeped in, and drawn back with such a white, sick face that she might even do so mad a thing as to tell William Cheyne what she had seen. "But Jesu!" thought Meg, tossing up her chin, "let her tell him."

They neither of them asked why July had refused to go, and she went away quietly, having realized as soon as Cheyne had spoken for her that if she had escaped the abbess she had condemned herself to prison with him for her jailer.

Yet she would have done the same again. For while she stayed with Meg that thing which she had feared this morning would, at most, reach to her and touch, and leave a slimy trail on her mind, like that of a garden slug. But if she went with the pink-faced abbess the thing might wind round her, catch hold, and hug her close. Down in the yard she pumped water into a bowl and splashed and scrubbed her face from the touch of the abbess's lips. Then she went and played hopscotch with a neighbor's child, and forgot, or covered over, what had happened. But one thing remained. She would have nothing to do with that to which Meg and the abbess took so kindly.

July 28

In the evening the new prioress, elected, and now duly confirmed by the bishop's letter, set about moving her belongings from the chamber she had shared with Dame Bess Dalton and Dame Elizabeth Close to the prioress's chamber overlooking the great court. Jankin had been called from the gatehouse, and two of the men from the stable, and between them they carried down, and through the cloister, and up the outside stair to the prioress's chamber, all the stuff which Dame Christabel Cowper had brought with her from Richmond, or had since received as gifts from her family.

The meditations of the ladies who sat in the cloister were much disturbed by the tramping back and forth. First Jankin and the two men bore out the new prioress's bed, which had carved oak panels, and an oak tester above; after these came the new prioress and Dame Anne, one with a pair of tongs and a fire pan, and the other with a couple of candlesticks. And so it went on: there was the feather bed, the big silver coker-nut cup, red and blue curtains, the painted hangings that Andrew Cowper had left his daughter, and irons, a pewter basin, sheets and blankets, two stools, and three worked cushions. Of course everyone knew the things by heart but to see them moved created a stir of interest in the cloister.

At suppertime Dame Anne ate with the new prioress. They were tired, but Dame Christabel was, and with reason, elated. After supper they sat looking about the room. It was strange and interesting to see Dame Christabel's painted hangings in place of the old prioress's red and yellow say, and to see the carved cupboard set up beside the window which looked out toward Calva, instead of the old square coffer of ash, with its faded paintings of the life of St. George, which was now pushed to the foot of the bed. On the carved cupboard the pewter plates, a little salt of silver, and the great cup Edward made a worthy show. It was a pity that there had to be a gap in the painted hangings above the fireplace, but the old hanging for the chimney breast had been so worn it was not worth putting up again.

So the raw stone showed there, and upon it in large old letters of dark red paint the monogram—I.H.S.

Dame Anne nodded in that direction. "You'll be needing new hangings." She could not keep a spice of malice from her tone. These two were now friends, or allies, but the old unkindness still ran below like a spring underground.

Dame Christabel smiled. She had not missed the tone. "I think to wainscot the room one day," she said.

"Wainscot!"

"And above the hearth, work in plaster, painted, such as I hear is done by these foreign craftsmen of Italy."

"And when," Dame Anne scoffed openly, "will such a craftsman come to Marrick?"

"But till I may find my man," Christabel continued calmly, "I shall hang between the wainscot a piece of arras, very choice."

She knew that she had triumphed. Dame Anne could not better a flight of fancy so daring. The new prioress had pity on her.

"Let us drink a cup of wine together," she said; and when Dame Anne had poured it out, waiting upon her who was now Lady of Marrick Priory, they drank and were accorded, each reminding herself that the other must be very tired after the excitements of the day, and that weariness sharpened the temper.

August 29

The King had been shooting at the mark with the Duke of Suffolk, Sir George Boleyn, and Sir Henry Norris. Lord Darcy was one of those bidden to watch the match, and when it was over—the King and Norris had won it—the King fell into conversation with Darcy of horses, and in particular of a stallion he had bought. So with Norris and Boleyn carrying the bows and quivers, for the King had sent the gentlemen and pages away, they all went in by the little gate into the privy garden, and that way to the stables.

Some of the grooms were leading out horses ready saddled. A very lively gray came sliding out with two grooms skipping along beside him, and all the gold fringes and tassels on the black velvet harness dancing and swinging. It was a very rich harness; besides the fringes and tassels it was studded with gilt buttons, shaped like pears, and all the buckles and pendants were gilt.

The King had been speaking to one of the yeomen grooms, an old gray fellow in a leather coat, with the cold eye and slit mouth of a man brought up among horses. But when he saw the dapple gray go bucking by he turned and cried—

"Ho! Who bade you put that harness upon that brute?"

The grooms pulled up, with some difficulty. It was Madame Anne, they said, had commanded the gray to be harnessed with one of the new harnesses sent from the Great Wardrobe, or else they had not thought to use it without His Grace's own commandment.

The King swore by God's Wounds that it wasn't the harness he cared for. "But it's not fitting she should ride that beast. I'll not have her on him. He's killed two stable boys—God's Death! Would she drive me mad?" He seemed suddenly to realize how the attention of all was fastened upon him, the gentlemen watching covertly, the grooms with a gaping curiosity. "Take the gray back and saddle the little bay with the white blaze. I'll tell my lady why." He was halfway across the stable yard, and called back over his shoulder to the yeoman groom to show my lords the stallion. He waved his hand and was gone into the palace by the Ewery passage.

The lords looked at and discussed the stallion; they were shown, and admired, other sets of harness which had come from the Great Wardrobe for Mistress Anne, while Sir George, her brother, stood demurely by. Afterward the duke, Sir George, and Norris turned back into the palace, and Darcy and Sandys went out by the tiltyard, to take a boat at the next stairs, and so across the river to Lambeth, where Sandys went to see a couple of hounds, my Lord Darcy going with him for the pleasure of so fair an evening.

Not till they sat among the box bushes and hollyhocks of the yeoman's garden at Lambeth, waiting for the dogs to be brought out, did either speak of anything they had seen at the King's palace of Westminster. But then Sandys said, putting down his ale can, and squinting into it, "The Black Crow goes very fine these days," and they talked a little of Mistress Anne, speculating as to whether she still kept the King off. Darcy thought yes, and Sandys no. "For," said he, "she's been openly in the palace close on a year now, and with the King when he hunts, and how could she?"

Darcy shrugged, and said in a low voice, his eyes narrowed against the light from the golden west, that he did not like these

Boleyns. "Although," said he, "at least the Black Crow helped to bring down the cardinal."

Sandys was still frowning. "They talk, and openly, of spoiling the goods of the church. Look how they favor Lutherans and heretics. Sometimes—" he hesitated, and then said it with a half laugh to excuse the improbability of it—"Sometimes I think they mean to pull down the church with the cardinal."

He turned to Darcy for reassuring derision but Darcy was looking at the holes he was prodding in the mossed path with his iron-shod walking staff. He did not answer Sandys for a minute.

"And if they so intend," said he at last, "let them but try."

September 13

Gib was sitting at his copying, in shirt and breeches only, because the day was hot, and the upper room at the sign of King David was close under the rafters and above the big fires where the cooking was done. So he set the door open, and the window shutters as wide as they would. Downstairs he heard people coming in and out, for the roast ribs of beef and hot pies were ready, and if he had listened he could have heard what they asked for and how much they paid, but he did not, for he was busy writing.

Dinnertime was past when he laid by his pen and thought of going down to eat with the Master Cook and his wife. But as he heard the voices of two men below who had entered the shop, he waited till they should have got what they wanted and gone.

They were, he heard them say, church wardens of St. Botolph's, and come to ask for the cook's charity for the church, for, said they, money was needed for furnishing the rood lights.

"Ha!" Gib thought, hearing the cook clearing his throat unnecessarily, "now will he give alms to their superstitious uses, or will he openly refuse?" And he guessed that the Master Cook would, in fact, hedge.

Hedge he did, pleading poverty; a dishonest servant had of late run away with a bag of silver. "Therefore, look you," said he, "I have nothing to give today, but come within and drink." So they went into the inner room and Gib heard the cook go down the steps to the cellar and heard the cans clink in his hand.

But when he came back to the inner room and bade them drink Gib heard one of the visitors say, "Master, what book is this lies in your window? For I read in it strange things."

Gib could guess what book it must be, since the Master Cook had, before dinnertime, been disputing with him over one of Friar Laurence's books. So now he sat very still upstairs, and leaned forward listening, but he could not hear what words the Master Cook mumbled, and Gib was angry and scornful. He said to himself that he had always known that such a prating fellow as the cook would not hold his ground.

"There are strange things in this prologue," said one of the two visitors. "Tell us, Master, what think you of baptism?"

"Now," thought Gib, "he will be silent or speak humbly of the sacrament."

He heard the cook give a kind of scraping cough, and then, in a wavering voice, say that no water, though superstitiously called holy, could save a human soul.

"Jesu Mary!" and "God's Bread!" they cried, and began to ask him of Transubstantiation, which he denied, speaking louder and in a shrill tone, and after that they said they need ask him no further, and Gib heard them go away.

After a few minutes he went down. The Master Cook sat at table drumming with his fingers on the board. There were three cans of ale beside him, untouched. At the fireside his wife was beating eggs, and as she beat tears fell down her cheeks and into the bowl.

They ate dinner very silently. The cook drank the three cans of ale one after the other. His wife wept without any sound. Gib was ashamed because he could not be glad that the cook had done valiantly. He said to himself that the bishop would not care that such a poor, ignorant fellow should talk heresy.

September 16

Gib came back to the sign of King David in time for supper; but he found no supper, and the place in confusion. Two of the servants had run away, and the wife and a serving woman were trying to do the work of those that had fled, and of the Master Cook too.

"But where's he?" Gib asked.

The cook's wife did not lift her eyes from the pastry she was rolling.

"They've taken him away, the bishop's officers have."

"Why?" asked Gib stupidly, knowing well why.

"For heresy."

If the woman had wept Gib would have thought less heavily of the business, but her hard flat voice, and her hands that never stopped their hurried dealings with the pastry, affected him unpleasantly. He mumbled something about returning soon, hardly knowing if it were his or the cook's return he promised, and then went out, to roam round the streets in a sort of aimless haste, which never outran the blank fact that the cook had been taken for a heretic.

November 8

The new nuns' priest had hardly been in the priory for half an hour before he sent word to the prioress that he would be ready to sing Lady Mass, thereby showing, as he intended, a commendable zeal.

The ladies had heard no Mass since their old priest died a month ago, save what was mumbled through for them by the toothless, ancient parish priest, drunk too, most of the time. They were therefore very ready to come into church. Besides they all wanted to have a look at their new priest.

They saw a round, cheerful, fresh-faced man, with a small, pursed mouth, which let out a loud and tuneful voice. His demeanor was most proper, but more than one caught a glance of his eyes, full of bright, friendly curiosity. When the Mass was over and they back again in the cloister, the ladies were able to tell each other, with confidence, that they were pleased, and would be pleased, with their new priest. They stayed rather longer in the cloister than they would otherwise have stayed on such a raw, drenched day, feeling that the presence of a new priest in the house called for a stricter observance of the Rule; but the mist closing in drove them into the parlor where they continued, in greater comfort, to discuss the new arrival.

Meanwhile the priest was exploring his two small rooms, with something of a dog's eager, prying interest. He did not sniff in the corners, or at the bed hangings, but being short-sighted, he brought his nose very close to everything he looked at, so that he did indeed seem a little like a brisk, cheerful mongrel dog. When he had examined everything he sat down by the fire and took out from his baggage his recorder and a music book. He played to himself till it was dinnertime, and one of the ladies, hearing faintly the sweet, musing, warbling notes, reported his occupation to the others, importantly and as a discovery. Soon the sound of his recorder would be nothing to them, but today everything about him was news.

When it was time for dinner he went across the great court and to the prioress's chamber, and they two, Dame Joan Barningham, and Dame Eleanor Maxwell dined together. The prioress, though more critical than most of the ladies, was very well satisfied with her brother's choosing. The little fat priest was of Easby just beyond Richmond, brother of a good worthy yeoman; his manner was attentive; his disposition obviously cheerful. She felt she had done well for the house.

November 30

Norris said, "What if he gains the King's ear once more? God knows he has the craft of the very serpent."

The Duke of Norfolk cried out, "Blood of God!" and wagged his hand at Norris to bid him be silent. He did not wish to hear put into words the fear that had gnawed at his mind since the King had sent for the Earl of Northumberland to arrest Cardinal Wolsey and bring him again to London. He was not going to tell Norris of the scene in the Privy Council yesterday; it would be common knowledge soon enough, such running tongues as most men had. But now, as he remembered it, he felt his face grow cold again, and stiffen, as it had done when the King thumped the board with his fist, leapt up scattering the quills and sandbox and paper all over the place, and then had stormed away from the room, crying: "Not one of you is worth what the cardinal was worth to me. Not one of you! Not one of you!" He had slammed the door of the council chamber behind him so fiercely that it had bounced open again, and in the silence that followed they had heard the King's quick footsteps go down the four stairs beyond, then along the gallery passage where the windows looked out today on nothing but the blank, drab fog. On the side of the gallery passage, facing those windows, was the door leading to the apartments of Mistress Anne Boleyn. Norfolk had listened—had guessed too that every other man listened—for the sound of the King's hand rapping on the door, and for the click of the latch. But the footsteps had not paused. The sound of them died away, and after a moment more of silence and a few moments of murmured, wary talk, His Grace's honorable Privy Council had broken up. Once again, as yesterday, Norfolk thought, "If she lose her power over the King and the cardinal again wins his ear—!"

He got out of his chair and went round to the fire. He heard Norris murmur that they said that "My lady, your niece, swears she will leave the King. And shall all then be for naught, and the cardinal rule again?"

Norfolk muttered, "When last I saw him he was much changed—aged. He's not the man now to recover that place he had." But there was confidence neither in his mind nor in his tone, and he stood staring moodily into the fire for a long time before he said, "There is the Italian's information to be used against the cardinal. The King will not take it lightly that his own subject and servant begged the King of France to intercede for him. We can raise that nigh hand to treason itself." He let out an impatient kick at a log, which, falling inward, sent a scatter of sparks up the chimney, and tattered flames leaping after the sparks. "I shall try the Italian again," he said, and leaving Norris hunched on his cushion in the window, went off to his own apartments.

There they presently brought in the Italian, Master Agostino de Agostinis, who had been my lord cardinal's doctor. He was a small, fragile man, fair in coloring, with yellow hair, and a quiet benign face; his looks, and his long, patient discretion were now turning profitable, for the cardinal had trusted him as a man trusts his confessor, so that he had much secret knowledge to sell.

The duke received him coldly, merely waving him to a small table where there was everything necessary for writing, and a candle set and lit, because of the gloom of the day within doors.

"Sit there, Master Augustine," said he; and no more for several minutes. Then he asked, bluntly, for information which would set the King against the cardinal.

"Shall it be true?" The Italian's soft tone was demure, but Norfolk caught a hint of a smile on the man's face.

He stared it down. "True?" he repeated.

"You prefer it true?"

"I pay for the truth," said the duke with a look and tone that would have quelled most Englishmen of Master Augustine's station; but then he was an alien, and, more than that, an Italian, so that these lords, even the greatest of them, were to him more than half barbarian.

"I remember," said the Italian, after a silence in which the duke twirled a big ruby on his finger and Master Augustine sat at ease, in calm consideration, "I remember the cardinal's words to me when he first went on embassy to France."

"Write them."

The duke picked up a book, and Master Augustine bent over the small table, writing down in careful English, and his elegant Italian hand, what the cardinal had said to him. He remembered accurately, not only the words, but the cardinal's hand on his shoulder, even the warmth of the cardinal's breath on his ear as my lord leaned close to whisper so that no one else, less trusty, should hear. But those things it was unnecessary to put down, only the words.

They were interrupted by a knock at the door, and the entrance of a gentleman in haste who began, "My Lord Duke—" and checked dead when he saw Master Augustine with his pen poised and face turned to watch.

The duke said, "Take your paper and candle into the little closet," so Master Augustine gathered up all from the table, and went within to a cold little room where the hangings smelt of dust, and there were many dead flies on the windowsill. He was still arranging his papers and preparing to write when the duke threw open the door and stood looking in. Beyond him, in the brighter light of the outer room, was the gentleman, also looking that way. Both had an air as of men, who, without any warning of an approaching storm, had been startled by a sudden thunderclap.

"You can spare your writing," said the duke; and while Master Augustine still stared, he added, "He is dead."

"The cardinal of York!" The Italian said it, not to be sure, but to realize what the news meant.

The duke said, "The cardinal. At Leicester." He turned away from the other two and stood by the fire. They heard him let out a long breath. Then he bade the Italian to go, and the other to, "Send me Bowman to make me ready to go to the King."

"My lord!" The Italian paused at the door. The duke leaned and looked into the fire, with one hand laid against the wall above the hearth; the fingers of that hand tapped restlessly upon the hangings. "My lord!" Norfolk only answered by a jerk of the head that meant dismissal. Master Augustine's voice rose several tones. "My lord, I shall be paid—I shall be paid notwithstanding?"

"Yes. Yes," said the duke, but in a manner so absent that the Italian got no assurance from it.

When both he and the gentleman were gone, and the door shut, the duke turned and looked about the room, seeing not those four walls, hung with the tapestries of the Quest of the Fleece, but the world itself over which brooded no more the fear of the cardinal's return. In spite of the dark day his world seemed bright as spring.

1531

February 11

The Queen was embroidering a green cope with white lilies and butterflies. Her ladies sat about on cushions; most of them were sewing, but a lute was passed round, and now one, now another, would sing. When there was no singing they talked of gowns, of sweethearts or husbands, of the weather; or else someone would tell a story.

The Queen listened, talked, and smiled, cheerful and pleasant as she was always; the Princess sat at her feet, nursing a small brown dog with flop ears. The Queen bent now and again to speak to the girl, and teased her, much as she was teasing the dog. Yet some of the older women, who knew the Queen well, thought that she had not her mind on anything that was said, but was listening. When the Countess of Salisbury came in, her eyes and the Queen's met.

"Madame," the countess curtseyed, "have you that pattern for a cushion I asked of you—that with the beast, and a tree, and a huntsman blowing on his horn?"

"I will give it to you." The Queen got up. "No. No," she said to the Princess, "stay here, and read in this book to the ladies."

She picked up a book from the floor, and gave it to the girl, then she and the countess went into the inner room, and, shutting the door of it, away to the farther side; it was but a small room and hardly more than a closet.

"They will not hear," the Queen said. Only the low murmur of a voice sounded through the door. "Not that it matters. All will hear soon."

The countess faced the Queen. She said:

"They have consented."

"Merciful God! It cannot be true."

The countess laughed sharply. "It is true. The Convocation of Canterbury hath acknowledged His Grace to be 'Sole Protector and Supreme Head of the Church and Clergy of England.'"

Katherine raised her hands and laid them to her cheeks in a gesture of horror. "But it is not possible."

"'So far as the law of God allows,'" the countess added, and laughed again; but the Queen caught at the phrase.

"Then—then is all well and this means—nothing."

"It means—so far as the will of the King intends."

The Queen turned away and looked out of the window. The privy garden of the palace lay below, covered deep and soft with snow. Not a foot had trodden it since the last fall, except the little dainty feet of birds; just then the big flakes began to spin downward again, a few at first, then myriads. Away in the garden they blew with the wind, sailing by in the opposite direction, slow, giddy, and uncertain.

"Meg," said the Queen, "Meg, what does it all mean? What is coming to us? Is he—is His Grace mad?"

"I do not know." The countess let that answer all for a minute, then she said, "What anyone may know is that hard times are coming to us. You and I, madame, though we are women, we shall have to fight."

Katherine turned then, and they looked at each other—the countess too spare, too rare for beauty, but exquisite as carved ivory; the Queen plain, plump, and heavy. The countess was of the blood of Kings and of the Kingmaker; the Queen came of the royal and fighting house of Spain.

"So I will," said the Queen, "when the time comes."

February 24

Dame Christabel came to the gate of Marrick Manor; old Dame Eleanor Maxwell was with her, and behind them a servant carrying a basket of warden pears. The porter at the gate yelled to the dogs to stop barking, and to a lad to take the ladies to my lady in the winter parlor.

They crossed the court, and went into the hall where a few boys were idling and squabbling on one of the benches. At the far end there was a short dark passage, and then the servant opened the door of the winter parlor, which was warm and bright with a log fire, and with sunshine.

Several women were there, sewing or spinning, but Dame Nan was busy making a hawk's lure, and a book on falconry lay open on the rushes at her feet. Her hands were stained with the medicines and ointments which she made for the horses, dogs, or hawks, and her skirts with hawks' droppings; but she did not care. When she got up, however, and greeted the ladies, you could see that she was the daughter of a great house.

There was a cradle beyond the fireplace, and Dame Eleanor went to it at once; she bent over it making those sounds which are traditionally held to be agreeable to infants. Little Doll, however, began to cry. Dame Eleanor could not hear, but she saw the child's face crumple and redden, and she drew back. "It's my black gown," she explained as one of the women lifted the baby to comfort her, and from a more discreet distance she smiled and beckoned, twiddling her fingers and crying, "Ah! the poppet! The poppet!"

The prioress sat down beside Dame Nan, and came at once to the point of her business. Did Sir Rafe know of any priest for the parish? Such a search she had had but a few months ago for a priest for the priory, and now here's all to do again for the parish. Yes, it was early days, she admitted, seeing that the old priest had died only yesterday, but she did not want the archbishop—who had no right—to put his finger into the pie. "The benefice is ours," she declared. "I have searched all the writings and it is ours to bestow."

Just then Sir Rafe came in; he was very cold for he had been up on the brewhouse roof watching the men mending the chimney. So the prioress had to wait till mulled wine had been brought, and wafers, while Sir Rafe stamped about warming himself at the fire. Then he was ready to listen.

But he knew of no priest. He seemed to think that it would be well to leave it to the archbishop; when the prioress was insistent, he offered to write to his brother Sir John, who, if he was not now in London, on business of a lawsuit, as he had said he should be, knew many in London who would be able to find a man.

"London? That's a far cry," the prioress objected.

"Have it as you will then. The archbishop—"

The prioress thought that perhaps she had not done well to ask Sir Rafe's help. But she must choose between him and the archbishop. So she capitulated. "I pray you ask Sir John to find us a man."

"And you'll have whom he finds?" Sir Rafe could be a close man at a bargain, and he knew that with the prioress there was need to be close.

"We will."

Sir Rafe and his lady saw the two away from the gatehouse, and both returned to the brewhouse to see that the work there was well done. The two ladies from the priory went down the hill in the sunshine; all about were the pure lucent colors of February; there was still snow on the northern side of walls and banks, which the shadow painted with lavender.

March 2

"Woman," said Gib to the cook's wife, "what can I do? Will you have me persuade your husband to recant and deny the truth?"

"No. Yes," she mumbled, being by now almost dumb with weeping; and then she said other words disjointedly and so low that he could not hear them.

"God's Bread!" cried Gib, "Let me alone. I will do nothing."

Yet when she had gone, fumbling for the door latch, and he had heard her shut herself into the kitchen, he went quietly out of the house and to Newgate, where the cook lay, having been handed over by the bishop to the secular arm. Tomorrow he was to be burned.

It cost Gib an angel, which he could ill spare, to be taken down to the dungeon of the prison, and the parting with so great a sum, and the foul air, the fear of the prison, and his old dislike of the cook all made him very resentful.

They had gone down a good flight of steps; it was quite dark when the warder took out a key and, while Gib held the torch, set it in the lock. It was very quiet down here, damp, and horribly cold; as the key turned and Gib moved he saw a rat's eyes burn green in the light; it scuttered away as the door opened.

Gib went in, and the warder shut the door on him and locked it. Gib's spine grew cold at the sound. The cook was sitting with his back to one of the old squat pillars, and upon a bed of straw. He had a tallow candle in his hand and a book on his knee. He got up, looking doubtful and not altogether pleased, but Gib greeted him as "brother" and took his hand; so they sat down together on the straw. Gib could not think now, any more than he had been able to think on the way here, how he would begin; but the cook did not wait for him to speak and asked eagerly if his wife had sent him meat or drink or something warm for to put on his back.

Gib had to say, "No," that she had not known he was coming, and at that the cook grew angry, because it would have been so easy for Gib to tell her, "And then," said he, "I'll be bound she would have sent me something to comfort me."

Gib resented the criticism, both because he knew the cook's wife had been fretting to send her husband a pottle of old Malmsey and a sleeveless coat of rabbit skins, and also because he thought that a man who was to be burned tomorrow for the truth's sake should not have his mind on such things.

So when he opened his business it was not in the friendly tone he had intended, but harshly.

"Tell me," said he, "the articles for which you are condemned, for no man should consent to death unless he has just cause to die in, and it were better to submit to the ordinances of men than rashly to finish your life without good ground."

"The first article," replied the cook stiffly, "is that I hold Thomas à Becket a traitor, and damned if he repented not; for he was in arms against his Prince, and had provoked other princes to invade the realm."

"Where," cried Gib, furious at the man's wrong-headed foolishness, "where read you that?"

"In an old history," the cook told him with his usual stubborn, downward look.

"And it may be a lie. So it were madness for a man to jeopardize his life for such a doubtful matter."

"It's no lie." The cook breathed hard through his nose, and Gib cracked his finger joints as he did when he was angry; but in a minute he was able to command himself and asked, "What else?"

"I spoke," said the cook in no friendly tone, "against pur-
gatory—that it is a word the priests use to pick men's purses
withal; and against masses to make satisfaction for sin."

"Hm!" Gib muttered, and again, "Hm!" because these were
matters in which he also believed that a man might stay his
soul so that he would die rather than recant. "But," he warned
the cook, "beware of vainglory with which the devil will try to
infect you when you come into the multitude of people and see
the high stake set up in the midst, where you are to die, and all
watching you."

"God's Body!" cried the cook very loud, and he jumped up
from the straw and rushed to the door and began to beat upon
it. When the warder opened it he begged him to take this man
away and leave him in peace.

Gib was ashamed then and tried to find something to say.
"The good woman your wife—" he began, but the warder
pushed him toward the door.

Then it seemed that the cook was sorry too, for he tried to
catch Gib back.

"Tell her—" said he, but the warder cried that he had no
patience with either of them, and he showed Gib out into the
passage and shut the door. Before it was quite shut Gib had a
glimpse of the cook standing there, holding out his hands, the
candle in one of them, and the light of the candle glittering on
the tears that were running down his cheeks.

As fast as Gib could he went from Newgate to the House of
the Black Friars, and there found Friar Laurence reading over

his charcoal brazier, nibbling raisins of the sun and spitting the pips into the fire. Gib plumped down on the bed and told him all that he had said to the cook, and the cook to him, while Friar Laurence murmured from time to time, "Do not speak so wildly, man," or, "Do not weep so." But Gib could not control himself, and in the midst of all his talk he would stop to knock his breast, crying loudly, "Who will deliver me from the body of this death?" meaning not only his own body but his own self that sickened him.

In the end he quieted down, and saw that the friar was weary of him, for, though Brother Laurence had a long patience, Gib had tried him too much and too often.

"I will go," said Gib, getting up from the bed. Then it came to him that if he could go far away perhaps he might somehow leave his self behind. "Where can I go?" he cried sharply. "Is there any place I can go to?" and burst out of the friar's room to roam about the streets till nightfall.

When he went back to the cook's house he found that a letter from the friar was waiting him.

Here but now was Sir John Bulmer praying me, for his brother, to find a priest for that very parish called Marrick, that you come of. Therefore, friend, if you will, you shall have this benefice, and bring the true light of the gospel into those parts which all men say are very superstitious.

Gib said to himself, "He would be glad to have me gone where I can no longer trouble him." And he could well understand that the friar should feel so. He wrote a letter at once, saying he would willingly go back to Marrick as priest of the parish, and finding a neighbor's boy, playing with his top in the street, gave him a penny to take the letter to the Black Friars' House in the Strand.

March 20

It was Master Cheyne's birthday, so he had to supper other Master Vintners and their wives. After supper, while the older men sat longer to drink, the women went upstairs, and Master Cheyne could not prevent two of the younger husbands, whose wives were merry and fair, going up with them, although he would have preferred that his own wife should have no man's company.

Up in the solar the wives sat down to sew and to talk; one of the young men found Meg's lute in the corner by the hearth, and so, while he played, they sang songs. Julian, who acted now as her sister's waiting woman, since that saved Master Cheyne a woman's wage, was sitting on her heels in front of Meg holding a skein of dark red silk which Meg was winding.

In a pause between the songs one of the vintners' wives began talking about the Queen. She was a fair fat woman who was embroidering a fine width of white silk for a petticoat, with little flowers of every color, and snails stitched in gold thread sitting on the flowers. As she bent over the work to snap off a thread of green with her strong teeth, she said: "That black-eyed whore of the King's came by the other day, from the royal barge, going with as much state as if she were Queen. But I and my maids, and a neighbor or two who were standing in the street, cried out on her, 'Fie! Fie on you, mistress, for a brazen hussy!'"

The others exclaimed at such daring, and the young men thought it a foolish thing to do, and one that might get the women's husbands into trouble. But all the wives there were for the Queen; and some thought the King was tiring of Mistress Anne and would put her away; and some said that the Holy Father would never let the Queen's cause fail.

"And what do you say, mistress?" one of them asked Meg, just as the door opened and the elder men came in.

"Marry, I think here's a coil the Queen makes to be the King's wife still. There are some women would do as much to be unwed."

She spoke very high so that all heard, and then there was silence till she laughed and said, "Goodman husband, you'll not spend money to have a divorce of the Holy Father. But if some man will buy me, will you sell?" She laughed as if it were a jest, but they all knew that there was no jesting in it. Master Cheyne ground his teeth, and said, sell her? Yea, that he would, and in a great hurry another of the men began to talk about the repair of Galley's Key, where the Venice galleys unloaded their wine, and no one said any more about the King or Queen or divorce. But Meg caught July a sound box on the ear because the child's hands were shaking so that it was difficult for Meg to wind the silk. July knew that at night, when the guests had gone, Master Cheyne would take it out of Meg for her words, and out of July too for being Meg's sister.

March 30

In the Church of the Black Friars, where the lords sat in Parliament, it was so dark that they had lit the candles; but even now those on the one side could hardly see the faces of those on the other. Above the high, painted vaulting, blue as blue heaven and scattered with golden stars, rain drummed on the roof.

The chancellor stood up, and the lords became silent and kept their eyes on him, but as Sir Thomas More spoke he looked neither to right nor left but only at the high altar and the steady light that hung in the shadows above it.

He spoke, as the King's mouth, and as the King had commanded him, declaring there were some who had put it forth that the King pursued this divorce out of love for some lady, and not out of any scruple of conscience. "But these," said he in a grave, steady voice, "these are lies, for His Grace is moved thereto only in discharge of his conscience, which, by means of all that he has read and discovered from doctors and from the universities, is sorely pained by his living with the Queen. And this will appear by the seals of the universities which I shall show you, and of which ye shall understand the tenor and substance by what Sir Bryan Tuke shall presently read unto you."

When Sir Thomas sat down Sir Bryan stood up and read loudly, in English, that which doctors in the universities of France, and of some other nations, had written of the King's divorce, declaring that his first marriage was incestuous and void. As he read the rain took off, and the sky so lightened that a fleeting gleam of watery sunshine swept through the church, dulling the candle flames. By the greater light many looked more narrowly at Sir Thomas, but could read nothing in his face.

"Ah! watch now, Talbot!" my Lord Darcy murmured in the ear of the Earl of Shrewsbury, sitting in front of him. "Soon will come in chiming other hounds of the King's pack!" For the bishop of Lincoln had stood up and began to speak.

"And now London," Darcy muttered as Lincoln sat down.

Shrewsbury made no answer, and shifted his shoulders uncomfortably. He, no less than Darcy, disliked all these doings, but he wished to be discreet, for he was a man who loved peace. Therefore he took no more notice of the other lord's mutterings than if it had been a fly pestering him.

"Those two," Darcy chuckled, "those two trust that as Bishop Fisher is not here to answer, none else will dare." Darcy did not think much of bishops, regarding their part in this controversy rather as the play of children. It would not be the bishops, he thought, who would check the King. Yet, when first the bishop of St. Asaph, and then he of Bath, stood up and spoke against the other two, he grunted approval, especially as they spoke both manfully and with subtle reasoning.

Bath, however, was not allowed to finish, for the Duke of Norfolk got up, so hastily that he knocked down the walking staff of an old lord beside him, which fell clattering; the little sharp echoes ran into the aisles and chapels and died there. The duke said that it was not the King's purpose that they should debate the sentence of the learned doctors of Christendom. "But," said he, "you have heard the King's mind by the mouth of the lord chancellor."

It seemed then as though no other would speak; Sir Thomas stood up as though to conclude the business, when someone said:

"My Lord Chancellor, you have declared the King's mind. What is your mind in the matter?"

Sir Thomas More turned about.

"My lord, I have many times declared it to the King's Grace."

They waited, but they got no more of him, and then someone behind Norfolk asked what my Lord of Shrewsbury thought, because they all knew that he and the chancellor agreed together on this. But Talbot would say no more than that it was not for him to give an opinion in such a matter.

Then, after a little uneasy silence, the chancellor went away down the church to declare the King's words to the Commons. Norfolk, Suffolk, the bishops of Lincoln and London, Sir Bryan Tuke, and many others went with him.

The rest of the lords sat waiting, without much talking, and heard the rain begin again to mutter on the roof.

April 1

In the evening Gib Dawe came home to Marrick. It was one of those days when a cold and winterly spring is, at one stride, overtaken by the heat of summer. The new chestnut leaves hung limp and very green. Roads were deep in dust, and for the first time the sweet smell of grass breathed in the air.

It was nearly a month since Gib had left London, and today he had walked from Richmond. He came from the open fells to the first of the village fields where the oats were pricking up. The sun had just dropped below the opposite side of the dale but the sky that way was of a flushed gold, like an apricot. All the way across the fells the air had been full of the crystal singing of the larks; now that he came near the big chestnut trees behind the manor he could hear a blackbird lazily spilling notes that were rich as honey.

He passed two little girls, naked, with water pots hugged to them, on their way to the well; they shied off the road at the sight of a stranger, and one of them threw a stone after him. He came to the green opposite the ale shop; the ale shop bench was full; he recognized more than one sitting there, but he hurried by, so that they should not know him, or should not greet him. The road now ran between cottages on one side and a stone-walled orchard on the other. At the town end, the very last cottage before the way went steeply down to the priory was the one in which he had been born. There were a couple of lambs under the tree, and a sow rooted by the wall. In the garden beyond the cottage he could see rows of onions, kale, and cabbages. He came abreast of the door and looked in. Smoke from the fire swam out, hot and blue in the bright warm air. His mother, small and very bent, stood over the fire. She stirred something with one hand, and with the other held up a lappet of her kerchief to shield her eyes from the heat of the flames. He went inside and greeted her.

They ate their supper sitting on the door step; there was pottage in wooden bowls, and black bread and cheese. Hankin, the old dog, sat opposite them, moving his eyes from one to another as Gib or his mother lifted hand to mouth. The brown and speckled hens picked at crumbs in the dust at their feet, moving with jerky nods that shook the fringes of their feathered hoods about their shoulders.

After supper the old woman brought out her spindle. Gib bent and pulled off his shoes. His leather hosen were of the kind that has no foot; he waggled his toes, and began to shift his feet softly to and fro in the warm dust, pleased to think that tomorrow he would not have to take his staff and wallet and trudge off again.

"That wench that you went off with—" said his mother behind him, and tittered. Gib jumped as though a flea had bitten him.

"How did you know?"

"She told me when she came back. But you needn't fear. She's told no one else."

"She has come back?"

"She came. Then she died. Last Martinmas."

Gib knew that he was very glad of that. Though now he believed that it was well for a priest to be married, he did not wish ever to see the miller's Joan again.

"And," his mother went on, "the little knave won't tell neither, for he's dumb, and a fool too. And moreover the miller sells him, if he hath not yet sold him, to the lead miners up beyond Owlands."

"The little knave—" Gib repeated as though the words were news to him. But indeed he had only forgotten. Then he asked, "How old is he?"

She cackled at that. "You should know." But Gib could not remember. "A four or five years child, by his looks," his mother told him.

A little while after she left him to milk the cow, and he sat there, his body at ease, but not his mind.

May 31

The ladies who were to undress the Queen had taken off the billement of pearls and sapphires that surrounded her neck and was tucked into the bosom of her gown, and it lay beside the rings from her fingers, and the collar of gold with the great table sapphire and three hanging pearls, upon the velvet cushion which another held, kneeling. Then someone knocked, and when the door was opened word came that, late as it was, a great company of lords were asking audience of the Queen.

"What lords?" she asked. They had taken off her velvet headdress and her hair, pale silver-gold now, was bare; she looked older so, and less stately.

They told her—"My Lords of Norfolk, Suffolk, Shrewsbury, Northumberland, Wiltshire—"

"That is enough. Friends, a few—and unfriends," she said, and broke off, to sit frowning for a minute. Then she motioned to them to put on again her headgear, but when they would have added the pearls she said, "No. Not those," and so went out to the lords, who, thirty or more of them, waited in her chamber of presence. She would have none of her own people to follow her, except two or three of her elder ladies.

The lords had come, as she knew well, from the King, and, as she might guess, with reproaches against her, for being the occasion of His Grace being cited to appear before the pope at Rome. They delivered their message, and she answered the reproaches patiently, having learned patience in a hard school.

But at last Doctor Lee, the archbishop-elect of York, spoke, saying that since her first husband, Prince Arthur, the King's brother, had had carnal knowledge of her, therefore the marriage between her and the King was very detestable and abominable before God and the world, as learned doctors and the universities had declared. At that the Queen flushed crimson, and then went white. Her hands closed on the carved arms of the chair she sat on, until her knuckles too showed white. Yet she let him finish.

Then she told him, in a voice not one of them all had heard before, so hard and sharp it was, that he could talk to others so, but not to her. "Nor are you my counselor, nor are you my judge," said she, "that I should believe you. Prince Arthur knew me not." She stopped there because her breath was short. "This," she cried, though her voice shook, "this is not the place to set forth such things. Go you to Rome, Doctor, if you will, and there you will find other than women to answer you; aye, men be there who will show you, Master Doctor, that you know not, nor have not read, everything."

After that they spoke more bitterly, and bitterly she answered them; telling them one by one to go to Rome, to go to Rome, and at last when all that wished had spoken, she reproached them all, so many and so great, for taking her by surprise, at night, and unfurnished of counsel.

Norfolk spoke up then, saying *that* she could not complain of, seeing she had the most complete counsel in England—as

Archbishop Warham of Canterbury, the bishop of Durham, Fisher, bishop of Rochester, and others.

"Jesu!" cried the Queen, "fine counselors! for when I asked counsel of the archbishop he answered that he would not meddle in such affairs, saying often, '*Ira principis mors est.*' The bishop of Durham said that meddle he dared not, being the King's subject. The bishop of Rochester bade me keep up my courage, and *that*," the Queen concluded, "was all the counsel I had from them."

After this, and some argument about her appeal, they asked leave to withdraw, which she gave them curtly. When they had gone, for a long while she sat in the chamber of presence, where the candles had been lighted. It was dark now outside, and from the garden moths swung in and whisked about, blundering into the flames and making them dip, sizzle, and flare.

At last the Queen got up, and went back into her privy chamber. Her head was up and her countenance serene, for all that anyone could see, but she moved slowly because of the heavy knocking of her heart, and as her heart knocked, so it seemed to her to ache.

July 25

The Duke of Norfolk, coming into the gallery that led to the King's privy chamber, recognized the voice of his niece, Mistress Anne Boleyn. It was raised and shrill, but he was certain it was hers, though he did not catch the words. And then, from a doorway at the far end of the great room she bounced out, cried, "I will not! I will not! I will not!" on a rising note that ended as high as a peacock's scream, and slammed the door behind her.

The duke made as if there were nothing strange in all this. As she swept by him with a whistling of silk, he saluted her gravely, though unnoticed; and rebuked, by a long hard look, the stares of the gentlemen and pages who had got to their feet from games of dice or cards.

He went the long length of the room slowly and with dignity, but in his mind he was wishing that the elderly and rheumatic gentleman who followed him had not arrived in time to see that bit of business, since he came as a messenger from Queen Katherine. As for his niece, the duke thought, "Mass! The girl's out of her wits. She'll lose all by this manner."

"Wait here, sir," he said to the elderly gentleman, and knocking gently on the door, went into the privy chamber.

The King stood looking out of the window. He did not turn, and the sunshine, streaming past him, threw his broad shadow across the strewn rushes on the floor.

"Your Grace," said Norfolk, down on one knee, "here is a gentleman come with greetings and a letter from the Queen, who—"

Then he saw that the King had his dagger out in his hand, and was stabbing with it at the wooden sill of the open window. The silent violence of that repeated gesture was like a blow across Norfolk's mouth. He gasped and was silent.

"By God's Death!" The King plunged in the dagger and wrenched it out again. "She will not. Will she not?" He swung round suddenly on Norfolk. "This girl's your niece. Yours! Did you teach her this manner duty? The Queen never spoke to me so. I've made—I can unmake her."

Norfolk's eyes flinched from the King's face. He muttered something about "love" and "loyalty" and held out the Queen's letter. When the King whipped it out of his hand and flung back to the window Norfolk told himself that soldiers, aye, brave men, men that feared nothing, were afraid of their Prince, so great is the majesty of kings. Yet he felt the flush on his cheekbones, and was glad that none had been there to see and to hear.

The King said "Tchah!" and crumpled the letter into a ball. "A very dutiful letter. She asks how I do, laments that I left her at Windsor without the consolation of bidding farewell. Very dutiful!" He dropped the crumpled paper on the floor and set his foot on it. "And it's she that will have me cited to Rome, and thinks I'll forgive. God's Blood! I'll not see her face again."

He sent Norfolk away and remained alone in the small sunny room where still lay a scatter of bright silks and a piece of embroidery that Mistress Anne had thrown down when their quarrel had begun. The King tramped to and fro, rolling a little in his walk, concocting in his mind the cruelest answer to the Queen's letter that he could devise. There were two women who crossed him, and he would make one pay for both. For already an uneasiness was growing in his mind and a restless craving. Supposing that other should—mad wench—leave him after all? He could not endure the thought.

October 30

Julian had been sent out to buy lemons and therefore was not present when Master Cheyne sold Meg to Sir John Bulmer. Nor was Meg herself in the room when the business was transacted, but only Master Cheyne, Sir John, and Gregory Cheyne. Gregory, who drew up the deed, was a notary and second cousin to Master Cheyne, and therefore, he considered, privileged to titter as he wrote out so strange a document, and to mutter pleasantries which he took care Sir John should not quite hear.

William Cheyne, who felt the cold sadly since his leg was broken, sat hunched in his chair beside the fire. His head was sunk deep into the warm fur of his collar, and fur lined the wide sleeves of his dark red cloth coat. Sir John was dressed no more richly than he, for Master Cheyne, whose ships went to and fro between London and Bordeaux, could have put down gold for gold against the knight. But Sir John was far gayer; in green, with a yellow hood and scarlet hosen.

Gregory giggled to see how neither of those two faced the other, nor seemed to be concerned in the business afoot; for Master Cheyne sat with his back to the room and his hands held out to the fire, and Sir John was astride the bench by the window, with his long thick legs stretched out; he looked, and meant to look, insolent and disdainful as he turned his big heavy head this way and that, staring about the room, and then through the window again. The room was on an upper floor and you could see, over the scanty yellowing leaves of an orchard opposite, a glimpse of the river. There were ships lying there, swung one way by the tide, and now and again a wherry went by.

Gregory Cheyne finished the writing, and paused, his pen still poised over it as he looked aslant along the lines. The tip of his tongue had been showing between his teeth as he wrote, but now he drew it in and pursed his lips, and opened his eyes very wide, as if he were astonished or shocked at what he had written. Then he giggled.

Sir John turned on him, but he was serious again, and intent on sanding the ink. He had sprinkled sand over the page, and now he tilted it neatly back into the pounce box, and snapped the lid shut. Next he began to root in his pouch, and brought out, and laid on the table, a medley of those things which notaries carry always with them—a twist of plaited threads and some ribbon for scales to hang on; a tinder box; two or three lumps of wax, scarlet, green, and yellowish white. But he wanted none of those just now—only a pair of scissors. He found them and then began to snip the parchment across the middle in pointed jags, exactly where he had written in large, fanciful, flourished letters, the word "Chirographia," so that fragments of the letters remained on one half and fragments also on the other.

There was no sound in the room except the snip of the scissors and the soft fluttering of flames on the hearth, till Master Gregory said, "There!" and, "God's Bread! Never till today have I drawn up such a deed."

He got up and handed them each a half of the paper. Sir John seemed for a moment to intend to cram it into his pouch unread, but he thought better of that and spread it out on the table. Gregory bent over his cousin's shoulder, his pen pointing along the lines till William Cheyne struck his hand away, and then he went back to his stool.

Sir John nodded. "That is good enough."

"Now pay for the trull you're buying," William Cheyne said.

Sir John took a bag from the bench between his knees, and opening the throat of it let the gold pieces, marks and rose nobles with occasionally an old angel of the last King's time, slide out on to the table.

"Count it, Greg," Master Cheyne bade, turning in his chair.

Gregory had put a foot down on one gold piece that had rolled over the table edge and fallen into the rushes; but Sir John, who was neither so slow nor so careless as he looked, said unpleasantly, "Under your foot. A rose noble." William Cheyne smiled for the first time.

The money was counted and stood in piles on the table. "Now," said Sir John, and stood up, "send for her, and I'll take her away."

"Fetch her, Greg. She'll be listening at the door," and he pointed to the door of the inner room. As Gregory went to do as he was told, William Cheyne said, "And you'll take her away in her shift."

Sir John was very angry at that, and so was Meg, who had been busy decking herself in the rose-colored velvet with a cloth of silver petticoat, which was her best gown, and with jewels about her neck and hidden in her bosom. She was so angry when she knew that it must be so, and that William Cheyne would not yield, that she began to tear at her clothes, as if to strip herself before the three men.

"God's Teeth!" she cried shrilly, "then I'll go out naked and shame you."

That drove Sir John wild, what with Gregory's chirrups of delight and Cheyne's cold smile. He pushed her back into the bedchamber, throwing his own cloak after her and bidding her roughly, "Take off your clothes and wrap you in that."

"You see betimes," said William Cheyne, "what you have bought. God give you grace to be glad of your bargain."

Julian did not know till suppertime that Meg had gone, for she had dallied over the buying of the lemons till it was nearly dusk. But when she came in the kitchen was humming with the news, and supper not near ready. She listened, at first struck into a sort of blind and dark helplessness by the news. Meg was gone, and here she was, alone. It was long, black minutes before she thought, "I'll go after her. I'll find her." But that only brought her heart into her throat for haste and fear. She came to the group of men and maids who were all talking it over, and clawed at this girl's elbow, and the skirts of that man's coat, crying, "Where does he live? Where does he live?"

Only after a time one turned and thrust her off, but told her, "In Yorkshire."

"Where is that?"

"In the North Country."

"But when he is in London?" They did not know or would not tell, and so Julian left them, and went into the empty hall where the trestles were set up, but nothing on them. Master Cheyne was limping down the stairs; Gregory Cheyne came after him. In an ordinary way Julian would have bolted back into the kitchen at the sight of him, but today she went straight forward and dropped a curtsey.

"Sir," she said, "where is he in London? Sir John Bulmer?"

She got less help from William Cheyne than from the servants, since the sound of Sir John's name drove him into a fury. After he had managed to lay his stick across her shoulders once or twice he shouted at her to go, to go to the devil with her sister.

When she saw the way clear to the street door, beyond the screens, Julian ran for it; she got the door open somehow and shut it behind her with a slam. Then she ran on till she could run no more, thinking that Master Cheyne was after her.

So there she was, out in the streets in the owl-light, knowing only that Meg was with Sir John Bulmer, but not where to find him.

She began by asking here and there, where he lived, but no one could tell her, and some were angry, shoving her out of the way, and some did not seem to hear her, and others frightened her more by trying to catch hold of her. A fat, wheezy fellow did that, and so she ran again, and apprentices shouted after her and threw dirt picked up from the kennel. Then she met a monk and asked him to tell her, catching at his sleeve, but he pushed her away and shook his head and told her she was a bad wench—so young and all. He was deaf, but July did not know that.

Once she knocked at a door because the candles were lit inside and the shutters not yet barred, and she could see a pleasant painted room with a couple of apprentices and journeymen, and maids, two or three, and the mistress of the house sitting by the hearth, while the master, a jolly merchant with a curly beard, drank his wine standing astraddle, with his back to the fire.

When she knocked, the boy who answered the door said he'd ask, and went in, and after a minute out came the merchant, and seemed surprised, and as though he had expected to see someone else. But she told him whom she was looking for, and why, at which he laughed and said, "Yes, yes," he'd take her to Sir John, but just now—he turned his head over his shoulder and seemed to listen, and then whispered, "Slip in, and through that door, and up the stairs and stay still as a mouse. I'll come as soon as I can."

But just then out came the mistress, and the merchant gave July a push in the chest, and shut the door on her. So when she had picked herself up she knocked at no more doors, and inquired of no more folk, but went on, because she must go on till she could go no farther.

After a long time, seeing the steps and the dark shape of the great cross in Cheap, all its niches and images hidden by the dusk, but the gilded cross at the top just showing a shadowy pale gleam against the deepening blue of the night sky, she sat down on the top step and made herself as small as she could, and thought that perhaps in her gray gown she might not be noticed there.

But she had forgotten her white head kerchief, and how it would show up, and hardly had she sat down when one of two men going by glanced aside, and he told the other, and they both stood, looking at her. All July could do was to turn her face toward the stone of the Cross, and then hide it in her hands. But she knew that one of them was coming toward her, and now stood over her, and she knew somehow that his hand was stretched out to touch her.

He did not touch her though, because he saw how she shrank. He only said, "Little maid, where's your home? What do you here alone at this hour of the night?"

She took her hands softly from her face and peered up at him, catching her breath when she saw he had only one eye. But she did not care for that; his voice was what mattered, which she thought was the most beautiful she had ever heard. Even though he spoke so gently it had a ringing note in it like a well-tuned bell.

"Oh! Sir!" she clutched his fingers, and then, with her other hand, his arm. "Tell me where is Sir John Bulmer?"

"Mass!" said he, "and you have asked one that can tell, being myself a man of the North Country. And in a manner, though distant, a kinsman, for my name's Aske, and my grandfather married Elizabeth Bigod, who was Sir John's wife's aunt," and he went on a little about the Bigods, Askes, and Bulmers, not because he conceived that the child would be interested in such an excursion into genealogy, but having himself young sisters he guessed that it would be well to give the little thing time to stop shaking so.

"There now," he said after a minute, "now let us go softly over to Sir John's lodging, and as we go you shall tell, if you will, how you come to be seeking him."

She told him, all in a rush, and he gave a soundless whistle in the dark. He could not now, being kinsman to Sir John's wife, like the business, nor feel quite so sorry as he had felt for the little girl; but when Will muttered that they might well leave

Sir John's drab's sister to find her own way, Aske told him to hold his tongue, and spoke gently to July, telling her that the place was not far off.

So they went out through Newgate, and along Holborne. Here there were fields, and houses with gardens, and here gentlemen would take lodgings who preferred to be out of the noise of the city, and free from the bustle of taverns, or who for some reason wished to be private.

It was nearly dark when they stopped at one of these houses, and Will knocked on the door.

July caught Aske's wrist. She had just remembered again to be frightened.

"Suppose they will not let me stay."

Aske said, "I'll come in and see they do."

He had not intended to come in, saying to himself, "Let the fellow keep his whore, but for my kinswoman's sake I'll have nothing to do with him or her." All the same, since he must go in out of pity for the child, he was not a little curious to see this wench that Sir John had bought. He was ashamed of the curiosity, but it was there.

An hour or so later he got up from the bench beside the fire in the room upstairs, and said he must be going. Sir John at once set Margaret down from his knee; he did not seem to be very sorry to part with Aske, but Margaret said he must come again, and soon.

At the door Aske paused. "Where's little Mistress Julian?"

Meg laughed. "To bed this hour ago. She was all eyes for you, and you never looked her way."

Aske grew a little red, because he knew where he had been looking; but he sent his duty to July, and kissed Meg on the cheek with Sir John standing close at her shoulder, and then went away.

As he and Will walked back through a night as black as the inside of a bag, he did not exactly reckon up whether by mortgaging his manor at Empshott in Hampshire, and selling the farms his father had given him at home, he could have raised the price which Sir John had paid for Meg, and which Meg had told him, laughing. But he did feel suddenly sorry for himself, a younger son of no great house, and not yet even a barrister. Also he felt considerable dislike for Sir John Bulmer, yet intended to cultivate his acquaintance.

November 3

Gib came back with the flour from the nuns' mill. He drove the donkey on very fiercely, and reached home breathless and red though it was a chill evening with a raw wind from the east. Yet when he had dumped the sack into the big flour bin, and turned the donkey out to graze, there seemed to have been no need for hurry at all, for he sat down on a stool by the fire, with his fingers idle and no book on his knee.

When his mother came in and asked had he got the flour, and good weight, and no mixing of rye flour like that naughty fellow the miller was like to make, Gib only grunted. But when she was just going off with the pail to milk he said, "Miller said he's sold the brat to the miners."

"Did you ask?"

"No. I heard him say."

She went away then, nodding her head, and muttering, but to herself, that it was good hearing, for now there'll be no talking. Gib sat still by the fire, scraping out the dirt from under his nails with a thorn, and with thorns pricking into his mind so that he shrugged his shoulders and wagged his head to be rid of them and could not.

At last he gave a sort of groan, pulled on his shoes again, and picked up his staff from the corner of the room. Just then his mother came back with the full pails, and "Where are you going?" she asked him.

"To fetch the brat," he told her.

She slopped the milk over, she was so surprised, and that angered her as well as the anger she might well feel at such foolishness. So she railed at him: Would he have all the village and the ladies know that he had taken that trull from Marrick, and got children on her? And see how he had made her spill the good milk. And if the miners had taken the child, what then? Would he to Jingle Pot mine this night, with the dark coming on, and the miners naughty men that cared for none, neither priest nor layman.

Gib, as answer to all that, told her that it was right for a priest to have a wife, and she laughed at him, and asked whether the miller's wench had been his wife. He said no, and let her talk on. But at last he shouted at her, "I'm going. And I shall bring him back," and went away, as angry as she was, and more unhappy. He did not want the little knave. He did not want it to be known that he had taken the miller's girl with him when he went. But he knew that this thing was laid upon him, and he must do it.

He came back by starlight, dragging after him a boy of five who whimpered and moaned, but who could speak no word, and whose voice was not like a human voice. Gib had paid a price for him, and all the way from Jingle Pot the child had struggled and cried. Gib's patience was out long before they got to the cottage, where all was dark and the fire dead. He shut the boy into the lean-to beside the house with the donkey and the sow; there was no window and he barred the door so that he could not break out and run away.

December 26

Sir John's men, and the maids he had hired to serve Meg in the hired house, had been busy in every corner and on every stairway making garlands and swags of holly, bays, ivy, box, and yew. Now these hung from the row of wooden pegs at the top of the walls on which the painted cloths and the tapestries were stretched, so that the gods and goddesses, the virtues and vices, the huntsmen, woodcutters, falconers, and hunting dogs looked out from under real instead of pictured branches.

The kitchen had been furnace hot for a week past, and there was still, every day, a great business of baking. July, slinking about the house in the quiet way she had learned, came there, and stood beside one of the maids who was beating batter for a cake, full of raisins of the sun and spices. Her plump fingers showed pink through the batter, which was richly yellow, sticky with honey, and spotted with plump raisins and the black eyes of currants. About the wooden bowl lay the broken shells of a score or so of eggs. The woman bade July hold out her palm, and slapped into it a lump of sweet dough. July drifted off again, licking it with her tongue.

In the hall they were laying places for dinner, so she did not stay there. In the solar, she could tell by the noise that came from it, there was a merry company. She meant to slip by the door, but it opened just too soon, and Meg burst out, laughing and running. After her Master Aske came, his hands stretched out, his face muffled in a hood, for he was Hoodman Blind. After him the other guests crowded the narrow passage, laughing and calling on him to catch Meg, or on Meg to give him the slip.

Aske caught Meg just beside July and threw his arms about her. For a second Meg tried to drag away, but could not; then she turned and drove her fist at his covered face.

He let her go, stepped back against the wall of the passage and stood there so long that July thought, "Oh! She has hurt him!" and for a minute she thought to strike Meg. But just then he pulled off the hood, and he was laughing.

Meg and he went back into the solar, and the door was shut, but July knew that he was angry (though he laughed); very angry, as if he had wanted to hurt Meg. July was not surprised at that, because Meg had hit out hard, yet somehow she was frightened. And as for Meg, her sister knew very well that warm shining look she gave to a man, and the way she leaned toward Aske as they went back into the solar together.

1532

January 1

The clerks of the Great Wardrobe were busy already setting down in fair copy the gifts which had been sent that day to the King, by nobles, gentlemen, and commoners. They had their rough lists, made out when the servants brought the gifts from their masters, but now they must go through all again, weighing, counting, and carefully describing the stuff before it was carted away to the Great Wardrobe. Some of the gifts were not in the gallery at all: "A pair of geldings, gray and a black bay," had been led off to the stables; "a beast called a civet" and a leopard were jolting away in their cages to the menagerie at the Tower.

But in the gallery, all over the floor, on the windowsills, upon chests and benches lay the King's New Year gifts, and amongst them moved certain of the clerks, while others sat with their lists and their pens ready; these last would call out the name of a giver, and the other clerks would answer with the gift. The names were first those of royal persons, for the lists went strictly in order of precedence.

"By the Queen," the list began, but there they must leave a blank, and a blank also for the Princess's gift, for the King would accept nothing from either of them. After that there were the bishops' gifts.

"Carlisle?" "Two rings with a ruby and a diamond."
"Winchester?" "A gold candlestick," and so on.

Next came the dukes and earls, and first among these, though he was neither, Sir Thomas More. "The lord chancellor?" said one old clerk, and another answered, "A walking staff wrought with gold." These, the noblemen's gifts, were mostly of gold—gold tables and chessmen, a gold flagon for rose water— "The weight?" asked the old clerk who was writing the list—and they weighed it and told him.

"Ten sovereigns in a glove." "Have you counted?" The old clerk checked his pen till the sovereigns were tipped out and counted.

Then there came the gifts of lords.

"The lord chamberlain?" "A pair of silver-gilt candlesticks."

"Lord Darcy?" "Gold in a crimson satin purse."

"How much?" "Six pounds, thirteen shillings, and four pence."

"Lord Lisle?"

Again there was a pause, a long pause, for the clerk counted twice.

"Twenty pounds lacking six pence," he said, "in a blue satin purse."

"Lord Audley?" "A very pretty gift. A goodly sword, the hilt and pommel gilt and garnished."

"Tchk!" says the old clerk, "I have writ as you said, 'A goodly sword.' But no matter." He peered at the sword in the other's hands. "It is, as you say, a goodly sword."

After the lords came the duchesses and the countesses.

"The old Duchess of Norfolk?"

The clerk had opened a little gilt and enameled box, very curious work.

"'The birth of our Lord in a box' is what I have writ here," the old clerk prompted him, and they left it at that.

And so they went on, through the ladies, the chaplains, the gentlewomen, knights, and gentlemen, down to "A dumb man that brought the jowl of a sturgeon."

Master Aske came in with another gentleman from Gray's Inn. Those two and Meg, and one of Sir John's boys who had a sweet voice, sat by the fire singing while Meg played on the box regals Sir John had bought for her. Sir John sat by her, toying with her neck, or arm, or the gilt ball of her girdle. Now and again the servants brought wine, and spiced ale, which they drank till they were pretty merry, and very well pleased with the world.

Just before the candles were lighted July came in and sat down beside Meg's woman, away from the fire, but below a branch candlestick so that they could see to sew.

Meg saw her, and called out to her that here was kind Master Aske who had brought her a New Year's gift. Master Aske was singing just then; he smiled at Meg, and with his hand that was beating time he made a little gesture toward July.

At the end of that song they began another, and after that talked, and then asked riddles. When it was quite dark outside Master Aske and the other gentleman got up and said good-bye. Master Aske stood looking down at Meg, one hand on his hip; he was telling Meg about a masking there was that night at Gray's Inn; July bent her head and kept her eyes on the shift she was sewing, because she knew that he had forgotten the New

Year's gift, and she would not remind him, not by so much as a look. As he went out she sat as still as a stone and a stone seemed to her to be sticking in her throat.

January 6

As Sir John and his household sat down to dine on Twelfth Night Master Aske came in. He had been invited, and now made his excuses for being late. "And it's not," said he, "that I stayed to see whether I could have a better dinner at Gray's, but my man did, and drank himself to sleep, so that I had to dress myself." He was dressed in crimson cloth, and crimson satin, under a black coat—all pretty well worn and carelessly put on, but his shirt was very fresh and fine with black Spanish work round the collar.

All that July saw, and then kept her eyes on her platter, because Master Aske's eye was looking about the room as though he sought someone.

"Sit down then. Sit down," Sir John Bulmer cried.

"A moment, pardon me. Ah—there she is."

July knew that he was coming toward her. He stretched out his hand over her shoulder, and there were a dozen gilded sugar plums in it.

"See, mistress, a New Year's gift that a careless fellow brought, and then forgot."

July raised her head. He had been looking down at her with a smile, but now he was looking away, and July knew that his eye was upon Meg.

"I do not like sugar plums," she said, in a voice that was not her own.

"What! you do not like—"

He stood behind her still, and his hand was still stretched out with the sugar plums in it. He began to toss them up and down on his palm as if he were wondering what to do. "My niece Julian would give her soul for sugar plums," he said; and then, "See, I'll set them here, and you shall do as you will with them."

He tipped them out on the table and they rolled between a dish of stewed eels and a big mutton pasty.

Then he went away, and sat down where Meg made room for him beside her.

When dinner was over July found a place where she could be alone. There she laid the sugar plums in her lap and wept over them silently and steadily, till a good deal of the gilding was washed off them. Now and again she ate one, but that only made her more miserable, because they tasted of tears, made her throat ache, and gave her hiccups as well. Altogether her misery was extreme. Either she had hurt Master Aske or made him angry; probably the latter. She imagined him telling Meg, or his friends at the inn, of the girl who behaved herself so unmannerly. Next time he came he would look at her with cold disapproval, or else speak a hard word. Yet the worst he could say was better than that she should have hurt him. The catastrophe of her wickedness loomed over her, darkness without a star, unbearable and irremediable.

January 8

There was snow on the wind, but sunshine in between the squalls, and the prioress chose a sunny interval to go across the

orchard to the workhouse to look over the new flails which the
carpenter had been making. One of them hung ready on the
wall, and the willow hand-staves for two more, peeled, and
dried in the oven, lay beside the holly swingles on the bench.
They waited only for the cap and thong of ox hide which would
join swingle and stave. The prioress, who liked to oversee these
things herself, picked up each stave and swingle, one after the
other, and turning toward the doorway looked along it to see
that it was duly straight.

It was so that she saw Gib Dawe, who was passing the door.
He had come to ask the nuns' bailiff for some of the priory
dung for his garden, and he was not pleased to see the prioress, because he knew that she did not like those who asked for
priory stuff, even for dung. "And of that same grudging humor,"
thought Gib, "are all the rich of the earth."

He had almost got by, but heard her call his name, so he
came back and stood in the doorway, peering into the brown,
dusty twilight of the shed where the sunshine struck in, smoke
blue, and where there hung always a pleasant mingled smell of
sawdust, oil, and leather.

"Sir Gilbert," said the prioress, "what is this I hear of you?"

Gib wondered what it was; she might have heard more than
one thing that would not please her.

"How can I tell, madame?"

"For a priest to stumble into fornication," the prioress told
him, with her cold gray eyes narrowed against the sun, "is one
thing. And it is long ago and all but forgotten. Yet it's another
matter that he should make an open scandal of it."

Gib knew now that she had heard the talk about him taking into his house the dumb child. He had his answer ready.

"Madame," said he, "I count it no scandalous thing, but meetly right for priests to marry and beget, even as other men. For if you read in the Scriptures—"

"And what," cried the prioress, "have the Scriptures to do with it? Priests do not marry."

"That is in these latter times. But in the first, most holiest ages of the church, as we may read in the Scriptures—"

The prioress took fire at his schoolmastering tone, and tossed the hand-stave clattering down on the bench.

"What is your Scriptures against the fathers and doctors of the church? Yea, and if that were not enough, popes of old time and every time, that are successors of our lord St. Peter."

"Ha!" Gib was triumphant. "Peter Bar-Jona was himself a married man."

He thought that would end it, but the prioress was stouter of heart and quicker witted than he knew. It took her a second to realize of whom he spoke so lightly, as if he spoke of Jankin the porter. But then she answered like a flash: "Was he then pope of Rome when he had a wife? Was he priest at all?"

A man might have given him time to find a retort, but not a woman—certainly not the prioress. She laughed in his face, and waved her hand as if to brush him and his argument away. Her sleeve was lined with fur, and as she moved a smell of musk came to him.

"The Scriptures—" he began, in a voice that should have frightened her, but she laughed again.

"Lord! You and your Scriptures! You've but the one word, like my brother's talking popinjay bird. And will you tell me that your Scriptures say the blessed St. Peter was a fornicator like you?" She looked up into his face quite unperturbed by his glance of smoldering fury, and now she spoke in a tone casual, reasonable, almost friendly, that galled him more than any other could have done.

"Go your ways, Master Priest, and hold your tongue about your sin, and the fruit of your sin. If the miller put force on you to take the brat (though what they say is that you sought him out willfully), then keep the lad, but keep your mouth shut as to who begot him. Say that you needed a boy in the house to help the old wife, your mother. Say what you will that's not the truth. But how will you curse me the young maids and men when they fall into incontinence, when you declare yourself, unashamed, a fornicator?"

She stepped forward then, and Gib must move aside to get out of her way. He stood awhile after she had left him, biting at his nails, and then went home, still raging. "It's easy," he thought, "for a woman's tongue to outrun a man's." But that comforted him little. "She would not let me speak the truth, being a woman benighted in the old ways," he told himself, but that only spread salt on his raw self-respect. And truly the grudge he had against her was deeper. He told himself, "It is for mine honest dealing in taking charge of the lad, and for avowing the true pure knowledge of the New Learning that I am rebuked."

He should have rejoiced so to suffer for righteousness. He had brought the lad home, laying on himself that penance for the old sin, that he might be at peace with himself. A little also he had taken pleasure in braving, as one having the New Learning and new light, the censure of the ignorant. But the presence of the dumb brat in the house nagged at him like a toothache, and for a toothache few men would endure to be chidden.

January 30

Meg had gone out with Sir John to buy stuff for yet another gown. She had already, hanging from the perches in her chamber, gowns of green velvet and carnation satin, of white silk and blue silk, of black cut velvet with cloth of silver, and now she must have a gown of cloth of gold of Lucca. Sir John had pledged a gilt cup and a collar of enamel, and they had gone off to buy the stuff for it.

Master Aske, when he heard they were from home, said, "No matter, no matter, he would sit and wait awhile," and went into the hall. July was there in the sunshine of one of the windows, with a piece of sewing, and old Mother Judde sat spinning by the hearth; she had a tuneless sort of song which she sang to the buzz and rattle of the wheel, and her attention was divided between the thread and a twelve-months infant belonging to one of the women, which was crawling about by the hearth.

Master Aske went over to the fire. Mother Judde looked up at him, but her head went on nodding to the working of her treadle, and she did not interrupt her crooning. He stood for a few minutes, warming his hands, and looking about the room, before he saw July. He took off his cap to her, hesitated, and then came across the room toward the window. July, her face burning with embarrassment and distress, scrambled off the seat and curtseyed to him. It seemed to her that there was nothing she could, and nothing he would, say to heal the unforgivable slight she had put upon him.

He said, "Good morning to you, Mistress July," and pushed aside July's thread and scissors from one of the cushions in the window seat. When he had sat down she still stood in front of him, looking only at his shoes, her sewing hanging from her clasped hands. He took up the hem of it.

"Do you like sewing?" he asked.

July shook her head, but could not speak, so he asked her again, did she like sewing, and then, glancing up, saw her with her cheeks burning and tears in her eyes, and thought that she was a strange child, and was sorry for her because she was such a skinny little thing and her eyes so big.

"My niece July," he said, "loves to sew."

"I know."

"How do you know?"

"You said so."

He laughed. He remembered now that he had said so, talking to Meg, quietly, by the fire, a few nights ago.

"Then," he said, "you are a good girl to sit sewing, and with such neat small stitches that a man with one eye can hardly see them." He did not know what pains July had taken since she had heard of his July, to shorten and straighten the great staggering stitches she generally made. But as if he knew he put his arm about her and drew her to his knee and spread out the shift, smoothing it over his leg.

To July it was as if a miracle had been performed. In a breath, and without a word said, all was forgiven. She began to grow bold.

"Sir—" she whispered, staring at the thick springy hair that fell across his cheek as he stooped over the piece of linen.

"Anon?" He glanced up at her, half smiling.

"Why have you only one eye?"

"Because someone came for me with a fishing rod and struck out the other."

"Who?"

"One of my brothers. Kit. The second one."

"Oh!" July twisted her hands together. "Did it hurt?"

Master Aske, glancing up, saw her face, and his arm tightened about her for a second. "Oh yes," he told her lightly. "But never mind. It was a long time ago."

"Was he sorry?"

"Kit? He was. And the more when my father beat him."

"Is that—" July asked, having no sorrow to spare for Kit. "Is that why you are not a knight?" To her mind he was like that Sir Lancelot whose preeminence among all knights she had learned by listening to a book from which Meg sometimes read aloud.

"No," Master Aske explained. "But I am the third son, and that is why."

July gave up the mythical Sir Lancelot without a pang. "What are you?"

He told her, "A barrister—utter barrister, and I hope one day inner barrister." And then, without knowing why, he said what lurked in his thoughts these days, pricking him with uneasy shame. "Once I thought to have been a monk." He had not long intended that, and only years ago, but he could not rid it from his mind just now, seeing that now his desire was for a thing so different. And after he had spoken he sat silent, frowning.

It took July a little while to make up her mind that his frown did not mean that he was angry with her. Then she wriggled in his arm, and put a finger on the haft of the small knife that hung at his belt, so as to recall him from his thoughts.

"That's what I sharpen my pens with," he told her, but it was not the knife she was interested in.

"How many brothers have you?" she asked, "and sisters?"

"D'you want to know?"

She nodded fiercely, so he stuck out one hand with all the fingers spread, and bent a finger for each one he told her.

"There's Jack—he's the eldest, and my little July's father. Then my big sisters, Bet and July, who are dead." He paused to cross himself, and bowed his head, saying something in Latin. July crossed herself too.

"Then there's Kit, then me, then—"

"What is your name?"

"Mine?" He seemed surprised that she did not know it, as if it were written all over him. "Why! Robert. And then—"

"Do they call you Robert?"

"Sundays and saints' days," he told her, "but working days it's Robin."

"Silly!" she cried delightedly, loving him very much, and having quite forgotten her awe of him. She began to laugh and dabbed her nose against his, and put her arms round his neck meaning to kiss him.

She did not, because just then Sir John came in, and Meg. Meg made very merry over July's lover, and said that they'd have a wedding before Lent began. It was not July she was teasing, for the three of them went on together to the solar, leaving July alone. Aske, who was hardly ever at a loss, was now a little put out, but he answered Meg's sallies as best he could, as they went up.

February 12

The lords whom the Duke of Norfolk had bidden to his house stood about the fireplace in the gallery, waiting for him to come to them. Their waiting should not have been tedious because there were many rarities to look at in the gallery: enameled clocks, carved gems, some books most exquisitely printed by a press in Venice, and the arras hangings themselves, which showed the story of Ulysses, with gods and goddesses, ships, and many strange sea beasts. Though it was a dark day the room was bright with candle flame and firelight and the duke's gentlemen served his guests with cakes and plenty of very good wine.

But the lords, who knew pretty well for what kind of business they had been summoned, talked only in low voices, and not at all when the duke's gentlemen were near, unless they spoke of trivial things.

At the end of about half an hour the duke came in. He looked smaller than ever, with his face peering out of deep furs that faced and lined his long coat of purple and crimson velvet.

He greeted them all with a sort of plain, blunt courtesy that made those who did not know him well think him to be the simple, honest soldier. Those that knew him better were aware that there were in his head too many schemes, and too great, for a man of that humor. Yet, whether they knew him or no, his manner always worked on others. The lords disposed themselves to listen patiently to business which, they could well guess, would be unpleasing to them.

And unpleasing it was, for the duke, standing in the midst and stretching out his fine, small hands to the fire, set before them how ill the pope had treated the King in not remitting to judgment in England this cause of the King's divorce, since here at home it should be judged according to the privileges of the kingdom. "And," said he, turning a ring with a great sapphire round and round on his finger, "even without those same privileges the cause should be judged here, for there are doctors, learned and many, that say matrimonial causes belong to the temporal jurisdiction, so that the King, as Emperor in his kingdom, hath the judgment of them, and not the pope. But come," said he, looking round at them again with the same candid air, "give me your advice, for well I believe there is no man here but would spend life and goods maintaining the King's rights."

After that there was a silence, so complete that they could hear the ticktock of the German clock measuring time away. Someone coughed; someone shifted his feet in the rushes and stirred a sweet scent of rosemary, strawed along with other sweet herbs. When Lord Darcy spoke they all turned quickly toward him, and each man was glad that another had spoken before himself.

And what Darcy said pleased them too, for he promised the duke that for his part life and goods were at the King's service. "But on the other part," he said, and met the duke's eyes, "I have heard tell, and in divers books read, that matrimonial causes are spiritual and under the church's jurisdiction. And, my lord," said he and now the duke turned his glance away—"surely the King and his honorable Privy Council know what is right in this matter without coming to us to—" Darcy paused and laughed, "to pull the chestnuts out of the fire for them."

Many of those there murmured that yea, that was their counsel also, and none spoke against it, for the cunning old lord had shifted back the burden which the duke had hoped might be shogged off onto the shoulders of the noblemen. The duke was put out and showed it. He had thought by this device to threaten the pope with the word that the lords of England were in agreement with the King's Grace in this matter. It would have set him high in the King's favor had he succeeded where all others had failed; besides, if he had succeeded, his niece would have been Queen.

February 13

Meg lay late in bed, so Sir John sent up July and one of the women to bring her the bread and fish and ale that other people were breakfasting on this first morning of Lent. When the woman had gone down July stayed, laying Meg's cloth of gold petticoat in the big hutch at the foot of the bed, and hanging up her carnation satin gown, all of which had been cast down anyhow when Meg and Sir John came back, late last night, from the masking at Gray's Inn.

While July was busy Meg began again to tease her about Master Aske. July, as usual, took it in silence, because she knew well enough that if she answered, Meg would strike harder and probe deeper with words. But she heard how Master Aske, "your lover," was dressed last night, all in tags and tails and skins. "Cyclops he was. I asked him what Cyclops were, but he would only laugh at me. He said that was his part since he had one eye."

Meg stopped talking to drink some of the ale and July took the opportunity to curtsey and get to the door. "May I go now, madame?"

"No—no—stay a little. Come here, sister."

When July came to the bed Meg surprised her very much by taking her in her arms. July stood very still while Meg held her cheek to cheek.

"Nay, sister," Meg whispered, "listen and I'll tell you a secret. It's your lover that I love much more than I love that great ox downstairs. Oh, he's a witty man, not a block of wood. And though he's but a third son, yet by the Mass I think he will be greater than Sir John one day, for there's—there's a power in him." Meg sat with her proud, lovely face lifted as though she looked into the future and saw fame there and heard horns blowing.

July tried to draw away and Meg let her, except that she still held her by the wrist.

"I think," said Meg, with one of her bright wild smiles, "I think—nay, by Cupid! I know he loves me. Shall I tell you what he said? 'You're too bright, Mistress Meg,' he said, 'for a man with but one eye. You'll make me blind.' 'Then, sir,' I answered him, 'you'll have to go tapping along the roads with a stick; 'tis pity, but the maids will be the safer.' 'It's not the maids I'm after,' says he, and then he laughed and said right under Sir John's nose, 'A word in your ear. When *he's* out of the way one fine night, send me a token, and I'll come.' 'Holy Virgin! I will,' I told him; and when he asked, 'What will you send?' 'A whetstone,' I said, and because we laughed, and because I said 'A whetstone,' that fat ox thought I was promising Robin the prize for a lie."

And she began to sing, sawing July's hand up and down in time with the tune—

> I saw a dog seething a souse,
> And an ape thatching a house,
> And a pudding eating a mouse.
> I saw an egg eating a pie,
> Give me a drink, my mouth is dry.
> It is not long since I told a lie.
> And I will have the whetstone if I may.

"But," she said, and suddenly flung July's hand away to cross her arms over her own breast and hug herself tight, "But he—Robin—when there was dancing caught my fingers hard—aye, cruel hard—and whispered to me that he meant it all." She laughed softly. "The dear fool! His voice was angry and his face as red as fire. 'I mean it, you bawd!' he said, as though he hated to mean it. But I'll make him love to mean it. He shall love me better than he loves our Lady and all the saints. Aye, even the prettiest little she-saint in the calendar."

July was at the door. "You're jealous, sister," Meg cried. She did not mean what she said, because July was a child, but July had a scowling way with her, and Meg loved to tease. As the girl went out Meg began to sing, very softly, to herself

A! Robin, gentle Robin—

March 8

Will Wall came bustling into the room at Gray's Inn, waving a letter and crying that here was the York carrier in, "and news for us, master, from home."

Robert Aske took it; "Less noise, fellow," he bade Will, and slipped the letter under his thigh on the bench, and, though Will hung about, would not read it, but went on with his law book. Hatfield and Wat Clifton, who had looked up, returned to their occupations. Will, giving it up at last, crept away, shaking his head and pursing his lips. Master Hatfield and Master Clifton might guess what ailed his master that he was so surly these days, but Will knew.

After a time Aske took up the letter and broke the seal. He read it through twice, and then laid it on his knee, and opened the book again. But now he did not follow the learned arguments of justice and counsel long dead and gone, but instead he saw the house at Aughton and the fields about, and his father, on a hundred chance and trivial occasions: cracking nuts in his teeth by the fire; kneeling in church; drinking with the reapers at the harvest home. He could hear his voice too.

Presently he got up and went out. Will was in the little closet halfway down the stairs, where he slept; he was polishing the silver studs on his master's best belt. Aske went in, shut the door, and laid his hand on Will's shoulder from behind.

"The news is—my father's dead."

"Master Robin!" said Will turning to him, and then away. So they stood in silence, neither looking at the other, but Aske's hand hard on Will's shoulder.

"My mother," Aske said, in a stifled voice, "will be glad of his coming there where she is." And that made Will weep too, and they sat down together, as if they had been boys again, on Will's pallet, and spoke of Sir Robert, and of Aughton, with the long silences of old friendship.

But after a time Will began to fidget and grow uneasy, and at last said, "Master, may I speak?"

Aske turned to him, stared, frowned, and said, "No." But Will did speak.

"Master Robin," said he, "what the master leaves is all good— good name, good memory, good sons to carry on the name."

"Hush!" Aske told him but he would not.

"It's for you to leave sons as good," Will said, and then Aske sprang up, and went away from him to walk about the streets till dusk. Will was an unaccountable fellow, a sloven, a drunkard, and quarrelsome too sometimes, but he had spoken the truth. Marriage and sons—that was the right, sound, clean way for a man. But for Aske there was Margaret Cheyne, Sir John Bulmer's minion, and there was nothing else but her. He was in as great shame as he was in pain that it was so.

March 25

It was the last Sunday in Lent, but the fast had not enabled
Robert Aske to call back his thoughts and desires from rushing,
like flames on a wind, always toward Meg Cheyne. And in the
evening, as he and another man had come back in the twilight
to the gate of Gray's Inn, a boy was waiting for him, in a patched
green coat, with cheeks as red as a strawberry and eyes as bright
as a bird's.

"Who sent you?" said Aske, who had never seen the lad
before.

"She told me not to say."

That set the other man laughing and he went away mocking
and railing at Aske over his shoulder.

Then the boy took out of his pouch a thing wrapped in a
scrap of carnation satin. It was heavy in Aske's hand, and he
knew without opening it that it was the whetstone which is
the prize for the greatest liar, and the token which Meg had
promised.

"She bade me say 'tonight,' and she said you'd give me a
groat, or more maybe."

Aske gave him two groats, and went up to his room; he was
glad that neither of his fellows was there, and that he could
cast the whetstone unseen into the coffer, still wrapped in the
bright satin. He was glad also that they should not see him
begin to dress himself hastily, without calling Will Wall, in his
best clothes.

It was while he searched in the bigger coffer for his silver-
studded belt that he came on the old sword which had belonged

to his great grandfather, Sir Richard Aske, and which his father had given him when he was between boy and man. His fingers met the hilt, and he drew them away quickly, and sat back on his heels. He had not till this moment contemplated anything but to go to Meg. Now he remembered that he had sent no word at all by the boy. He need not go. He thought, "I'll not go," and then, "O! God forgive me!" He reached out his hand again and searched for the silver-studded belt till he found it.

March 26

Before it was light old Mother Judde came into the dark chamber, shielding with her hand the flame of the wax taper she carried. She lit with it all the candles in the room, and then pulled back the curtains of the bed, but softly so that the rings did not knock together.

"Come now," she said, and tittered as she looked down at the tumbled bed. "Come, my turtledoves, you must part."

Aske started up. He neither felt nor looked like a turtledove, but like a young man who has a bad taste in his mouth from drinking too much wine last night, and a worse taste in his mind.

He did not glance at Meg, but flung out of bed and began to drag on his clothes. The room was at once cold and stuffy, and as the candles began to gutter and smoke the air grew worse.

"Dear heart," said Meg from the bed, "let me be your servant to tie your points," and she held out her arms.

"No," Aske told her. He managed to knot one pair of points, then, in tugging at it, broke it.

"I'll call Mother Judde," Meg said.

"No." Aske hated Mother Judde as much as anyone in the whole business. He finished dressing somehow, and then stood hesitating.

Meg held out her arms again, and he looked at her once and turned his head away, yet he went unwillingly to the bed, and let her take his hand.

"Kiss good-bye," she murmured, trying to draw him toward her. "No, nor it's not good-bye, for do not fear but I'll send again when I may, Robin. But not a whetstone this time. What shall it be?"

She was playing with his fingers, and now lifted his hand toward her lips. He snatched it away.

"Nothing. You shall not send, for I will not come."

When Mother Judde came back from letting him out by way of the brewhouse door she found Meg in tears.

"Nay, nay," she tried to pat Meg's shoulder. "What a pair of true lovers. Here's one crying her eyes out, and the other gone off like a man to his hanging, as glum as a death's head. But heart up! There'll be other times."

Meg lifted her face. "No. He says no. And I love him. He doesn't know how I love him."

"Tchk! Tchk!" Mother Judde sat down on the bed and began to expound the ways of men, about which she knew a great deal. She promised Meg that the sweet gentleman should come again. She herself would be sorry if he did not, for Meg had paid her well, and Aske had crammed a gold piece into her hand as he went off.

March 29

In the afternoon, which was the afternoon of Good Friday,
many of the Marrick people came, by custom, into the nuns'
church. On that day the door in the screen between it and the
parish church was set open, so that all who chose should come
in with their baskets and bunches of wild violets and primroses,
to straw on the Easter sepulchre. So there was quite a crowd
there to watch the nuns' little brisk, round priest, as he washed
the rood from the rood screen in wine and water, wrapped it in
a pall of green silk, and laid it, together with the Host in its gilt
pyx, in the Easter sepulchre. The nuns' priest moved about nimbly, bowing and prostrating himself very properly, but, every
now and then, as he came near to the place where the prioress
sat, he spoke to her, though in a low voice, for he was a very
cheerful and garrulous man.

Gib came to the door in the screen and watched for a while;
the Marrick smith was with him who, like Gib, was one who
called himself one of the "known men."

"Ha! See!" said the smith, speaking behind his hand, when
the nuns' priest laid the pyx beside the hidden crucifix, "there
goes little Jack into the box."

Gib smiled at the joke, but sternly. Here in the dale, where
folk were so ignorant and superstitious, he was fortunate, and
knew it, to find even one who had seen the light of the New
Learning. Yet the smith's bludgeoning wit did not please him,
nor did it please him that the fellow, because he could slowly
spell out the English Scriptures—at least if they were fairly

printed—thought himself sufficient to debate points of doctrine with Gib.

The women and children were now about the sepulchre, casting on their flowers. Among them was the priory servant Malle. She had a round basket full of violets, white and blue, and now she was throwing great handfuls among the rest, jumping up and down on her feet and laughing, with squawks like a hen.

"Tchah!" said Gib, and turned back into the parish church; but the smith stayed, and began to call out to one or other of the crowd in the nuns' church, jesting with them, since the prioress had gone away now, and the priest was never one to spoil other folks' enjoyment.

April 12

Dame Anne Ladyman came back from a visit to her brother's house, where his youngest girl had been married. Her brother lived beyond York, so she had spent some hours in the city, and came back therefore not only with news, but laden with stuff from the York shops. This she produced first in the parlor for all to see: a little frail of figs, some spices, a jar of green ginger, three bobbins of silver thread to work the new black satin cover for the Gospel book, half a pound of pins, and a fine large new book of paper for the cellaress's accounts.

The news she kept back, at least most and the best of it, till she and the prioress sat down to supper together with the priest. Then Dame Anne had much to say of the wedding, of this one's surly husband who beat her, or that one's unfaithful husband who kept his whore in the house, or that other's undutiful son who wasted his money on harlots. She had, in a short time, acquired an amazing knowledge of such happenings. The little priest crowed with laughter, or clucked with the correct amount of horror, at her tales. The prioress listened with half an ear. Nowadays, since this kind of thing had ceased in any way to interest her, it had ceased also to shock her. She let Dame Anne have her head; they two understood each other now.

By the time they sat round the fire, eating walnuts kept fresh all winter in salt under damp hay, Dame Anne had disposed of scandals among her acquaintances, and was touching on the King's affairs. For at her brother's house had been a man of the bishop of Durham, a very courteous gentleman but of a free tongue. "Oh! Jesu Mercy!" Dame Anne threw up her hands, "I would I could tell you some of the words he said. But I could not for shame. I promise you I chid him more than once. 'For remember I'm a religious,' I told him, and he said—" She whispered what he had said, which did not amount, the prioress thought, to very much, unless it had a meaning which she could not be bothered to seek out.

"But I would tell you," Dame Anne ran on, "how he spoke against this lady of the King's, calling her no better than a common stewed whore. 'Fie, sir,' says I, 'not in my hearing!' But he would have it she was a common stewed whore that ruled the King, and made all the spiritualty to be beggared, and the temporalty too. 'But,' says he, 'when the great wind shall rise in the West we shall have news afterward.'"

"What news?" the priest asked, but Dame Anne did not know, and now clapped her hands together and said: "And should I

forget to tell you what that same servant of the bishop told me?"
The prioress yawned discreetly behind her hand. Dame Anne,
she thought, was sometimes hardly to be borne. She began to
wonder why she did indeed bear with her so frequently.

Then she found herself listening. For among all his gallant-
ries the bishop of Durham's gentleman had spoken at least one
piece of sense. He had told Dame Anne that if any in England
be converted from any erroneous faith and misbelief to the
Christian and Catholic faith, then will the King pay yearly, for
and toward his or her relief and finding, during her life natural,
three halfpence every day. So Dame Anne reported the bishop's
gentleman, and the prioress had no doubt but that those were
the very words he had used, for she knew Dame Anne to be possessed of a most remarkably accurate memory.

"Malle!" said the prioress, and Dame Anne nodded, "Malle!"

The prioress stood up, shaking the walnut shells from her lap
into the fire where they crackled sharply.

"Let us write now to the King's Grace," she said.

The priest sighed and drank up his wine hastily. He knew
that he would have to write the letter, for the prioress's penmanship was crabbed. So the servants were sent for to clear the table,
and Malle was sent for to tell what her name was before she was
christened, since the bishop's gentleman had instructed Dame
Anne that it would be necessary to write this in the letter.

Yet when they had questioned Malle, bidding her repeat her
old name over and over, and had at last sent her away, the priest
hesitated with the pen in his hand.

"It is no name at all," he objected. "I cannot write it."

"Do as well as you may," the prioress urged.

He wrote, scored it out, wrote, altered it, and shoved the paper over.

"I cannot say it," the prioress confessed, after she had tried once or twice. "It is, as you say, no name at all, yet it has a most heathenish look," and she passed the paper back to the priest.

"I never thought," she said softly to Dame Anne as he bent over his writing, "that the priory should be the better for the creature Malle."

May 20

M. de Montfalconnet, the Emperor's messenger, was brought through the base-court, where some hens were picking, to a little inner court, and so into the house, which was small and dark, having been built in the old days when windows were few because all houses must be defensible.

The Queen got up from among a few of her ladies, and came toward him. She had been at prayer half the night, and her eyes were red; never careful about dress, she now looked no finer than any citizen's wife, and not so neat. Indeed she made a jest of her disarray at the sight of the Emperor's messenger and said that he found them like busy housewives at their sewing and spinning. But when she had laughed her lips shook because it was so seldom now that she saw a friend. M. de Montfalconnet, angry and sorry (and he did not know whether one more than the other), went down on both knees and kissed her hand.

When she had sent the ladies away she asked him many questions about the Emperor, her nephew, for monsieur was the master of the imperial household. And then she sat smiling, her eyes distant, her hands idle in her lap and her mind far away in the past. Only after some time did either of them mention that which lay at the core of the unhappy present—namely, the business of the King's divorce. Then monsieur listened while the Queen urged on him arguments, appeals, and encouragements. If the pope would only give sentence, she said, twisting her hands together, the matter would be settled, "and I do assure you that the sentence, whatever it is, will increase and reestablish the friendship between—my—between the King's Grace and the Emperor."

Montfalconnet was silent. He could not think it, but he inclined his head, torn once more between anger and pity, and answered only that he would surely do all he could to explain her advice to the Emperor.

But the Queen seemed hardly to hear him, so eagerly did she continue to pour out her arguments. "You see," she interrupted herself with a half apology, "I have so long time to think of all these matters. My nephew—the Emperor—has many other cares, but I have none but this. So I think I see clearest."

Yet with very little of all that she told him could Montfalconnet agree. She would have it that if once the sentence were given the King would obey. ("Not now. Not now, whatever might have been once," he thought.)

"The pope," she said, lifting her chin, and showing him for an instant the face of an indomitable woman, "the pope does very wrong so long to delay. And if the decision goes against me I'll bear it for the honor of God, for monsieur, I have not deserved it."

After she had sat brooding for a while she began to say: "If I could but speak once to the King, if—" but on that she had to get up from her chair and go to the window so that he could not see her face. "If I could speak to him," she said, with her back to Montfalconnet, "all that has happened would be as naught—because he is so—good." Montfalconnet turned away at the sound of her voice. She said, with difficulty, "He would be kinder to me than ever. But they will not let me see him."

Montfalconnet would have been glad to get himself out of the room at once, and in silence, but ceremony forbade it. He could only go down on his knee and keep his eyes strictly upon the cap in his hand till she came back to her chair and he could take his leave.

June 20

Gib found the door of the Marrick church standing open.

"God's Body!" he muttered, thinking that as likely as not he would find the sheep in the sanctuary, dropping their dung everywhere. But when he went in there was no scurry and stampede of small hoofs; only a sudden quiet, after the living air outside, and a twilight that kept him standing for a moment till his eyes were used to it.

The parish church at Marrick had been painted round about the walls at the same time as the nuns' church, that is to say nearly two hundred years ago. But whereas the pictures in the nuns' church were all of the life of St. Benedict on the one side, and on the other the prophets, here, for the instruction of the people, were shown the precursors of Christ, two on the north and two on the south wall, on either side of the iron grille which divided the two parts of the church, and from these, coming east toward the chancel, were pictures of the birth, life, and death of Christ, and of his rising from the dead. Of the precursors, Isaac unfortunately was almost swallowed up now with creeping stains of damp; only his father's curved, menacing knife showed above the fringes of the mold, and in the corner a very large ram in a very small thornbush. David too had suffered, though not so much as his neighbor, but his fine kingly blue mantle had deadened to pale gray, because the damp of the wall had caught the lime with which the paint had been laid on.

The two precursors on the south wall were however both of them in good fettle. There was Joseph, as master of the household to the King of Egypt, neat as a grasshopper in a green surcoat of the old fashion, with a heavy jeweled belt round his hips, and his yellow hair rolled up in a curl on each side of his face. And next to him stood Solomon, with the temple on a hill behind him, but it was very like the friar's church at Richmond. Solomon was bearded and handsome in a purple robe sewn with golden bees.

At the feet of Solomon knelt Malle, the serving woman. She crossed herself many times, and then held out her clasped hands, and bent her head before the picture.

Gib went down the aisle toward her. She did not notice him till he was quite near and then she jumped up and backed away a little, because she could see that he was angry.

"What," he said, "is this idolatry?"

She shook her head.

"What are you doing?"

"I pray to this saint," she told him.

That made him angrier, but now he was not angry with her but with the prioress, the ladies, and their priest—with all those who wore warm, fine clothing, and lived delicately, who were proud, who despised the poor, who worshipped the painted images of saints, who left this christened soul so deep in ignorance that she worshipped King Solomon.

"Did they not teach you the faith?" he asked her.

"Oh! yes," she said, "they did indeed. The priest, the old man, brought me in here and told me. He told me of those—" and she pointed up the church to the rood screen. The screen and the paintings on it were much newer than the pictures on the walls, having been set there not much more than thirty years ago by old Sir Roger Aske. The colors were much fresher, and, as they were painted with oil and resin in the paints, more deep and glorious than the frescoes, and besides that picked out with much gold leaf, so that the burnished haloes of the apostles, who stood in rank along the screen, shone darkly, even in the dim light of the church; and their robes were scarlet, green, azure, purple, and rose color.

Gib looked at them and snorted. "You shall not make to you gods of silver, neither shall you make to you gods of gold," he said, but Malle had left him, and was moving toward the screen. She stopped before the picture of St. Philip who stood against a background of scarlet patterned with gold. His prettily tousled hair showed up in curls against his halo; his cloak was green as new beech leaves, and under it was a sumptuous gown of brocade, the color of ripe corn, with the pattern of a huge vine growing all over it, curved and notched stock, leaves, tendrils, heavy grape bunches and all.

"These," said Malle, as Gib came up behind her, "are the holy apostles, that sit on thrones in heaven." And she began to recite their names, but when she had pointed at St. James she faltered. "The priest was called to dinner and could not stay," she said, "so I do not know them all."

Gib looked at her. Her face was dirty, her kerchief torn, and her toes were coming through one of her shoes. He looked at the row of splendid and pompous figures that stretched across the church, glowing with color and gold. Then he raised his arm, and pointed to where the tortured Christ hung, half naked between the blue, starred mantle of the Virgin, and St. John's crimson cloak.

"*He* said, 'How hard it is for a rich man to enter into the kingdom of heaven.' And *he* said, 'Woe be to you that are rich.' And again *he* said, 'The rich man also died and was buried in hell.'" Gib was thinking of the prioress and the nuns' priest, the bishops and great abbots, and his voice grated. "For these," he told Malle, sweeping his hand along the length of the screen, "were fishermen, he, and he, and those two. And the Lord" (he pointed again at the great rood), "He was a carpenter's son, and a carpenter."

She looked at him with her mouth open, foolish, but most intent.

"God." He jabbed his finger toward the Christ. "A poor man, a carpenter!" And warmed by his triumphant indignation against all the great and the rich, he seized her by the wrist and dragged her toward the font, where, painted on the wall, the angels told the news to the poor shepherds, first of all men.

So he began to instruct her, going from picture to picture, and she listened with strained attention, for the sake of which he bore with her foolishness, though now and again he must chide her. For when he was telling her of the child in the manger she laid a finger on the brown dog, which sat, upright and very respectful behind the youngest shepherd's feet, calling him "Trusty," which was the name of one of the convent's sheep-dogs. "Listen to what I tell you," he bade her sharply. Again, when they stood before the picture through which Christ rode, in the midst of a crowd of folk in mushroom-colored hoods, upon a donkey not much bigger than a dog, she wanted to know whether that was the miller's donkey. This time he was less patient, and struck her with the flat of his hand between the shoulder blades, and bade her hold her tongue.

In the end they came again to the rood screen, and stood below the rood. Gib had had enough, and was for leaving her, but she caught at his gown and he waited.

"Who is—that one—and that one?" she asked and nodded her head to the picture of the baby in the hay, and then lifted her wide, vague eyes toward the rood.

He cried "Mass!" angrily, and told her, "God," but when she murmured after him "God?" he was not so much angry as amazed at the vacancy of her simplicity. It was not even, he thought, like pouring knowledge into the little cup of a child's understanding, but into a pail that had holes in it. How could such a one learn to know the incomprehensible? What in her twilight mind was God?

"The living God," he said, and he spoke aloud, but more to himself than to her, the words that came into his mind. "'I am the first and the last, and am alive and was dead, and behold I am alive forevermore.'"

She stared at him, with something of light in her look that was usually as vague and dim as the colorless, half-transparent jellyfishes that bob about in the clear fringes of the tide as it slides in over a sandy shore.

"Sir," she mumbled, "what for did he this thing? What for?"

Of course she could not understand, and he pushed past her as he said, "To shew us the face of God. To brast the chain of sin. To be the glory of his people Israel."

But at the door she was beside him.

"Where is he—now?"

He lifted his arm and pointed up to the sky beyond the steep woods, and beyond the edge of the fells where a huge white cloud stood in the blue, leaning its head toward the dale.

She did not follow him any farther, but when he looked back from the gate of the churchyard she was staring up under her hand toward Gawnless Wood where a woodcutter was working. The ringing of the axe on the tree came faint but clear in the summer silence.

July 15

Master William Cowper had come to Marrick Priory to buy wool. Last night he had supped with the prioress and been pleasant with her and those nuns that were her guests; but today was for business; he must weigh the priory wool-clip and be off to the next seller up the dale.

He had begun the day by a brief, and, he had reason to believe, a private interview, with the priory bailiff. At nine, just as the bell began to ring for chapter Mass, he came into the wool barn where the scale beam hung from the roof and the wool fells lay in piles ready for weighing. His man came after him with the two seven-pound weights slung over his shoulder by a leathern strap, and the other odd weights in a bag. The inevitable knot of little boys closed in from the wide open doors; a gray goose approached, stared about with haughty disapproval and went away into the sunshine.

"Now," said Will Cowper, speaking very short and brisk, "to work, Master Bailiff. Where's your stone for the weighing?"

But the bailiff had forgotten to bring his book in which to write the tally of the convent's wool, so his man had to be sent to fetch it, and consequently only Will and the bailiff were at the weighing of the big fourteen-pound block of stone against Will Cowper's two weights; the stone was that same which had been used in wool weighing for longer than any could remember. It was but a form to weigh it, so they two did it while the two priory servants went to fetch the fleeces to the scales.

When the bailiff's man came back Will and the bailiff stood opposite each other, watching the scales swing under the first tod. The wool scale dipped, so Will put into the weight pan a two-pound weight from those in the bag, and—

"Two to the wool," said he as the scales steadied; the bailiff nodded, and they went on with the next lot of fleeces.

The bell in the church tower rang faster, so they knew it was nearly time for Mass, and that all the ladies would soon be piously occupied in church. The bell rang on. Will sang out, "Five pounds less three due to the wool leaves two pounds to the weights."

Just then the prioress came into the barn. She had on a riding hat above her hood, and gloves on her hands.

Will and the bailiff turned. They stood so still that the two men loading fleeces on the scales turned too, and stood, and stared. There was a short but pregnant silence, during which they heard the after-song of the last stroke of the bell hum through the sunny air and die away.

Will Cowper stammered, "Not—not at Mass, sister?"

The prioress looked from one to the other of them; she smiled.

"I thought this morning when I saw your heads so close laid together that it were well I came to the weighing."

"You saw—" Will looked at his sister in dismay and dislike; but there was respect in his glance too.

"Well, no—I should not say I saw you. But I saw your shadows on the stable wall, and your chins wagging. So I said to myself— 'It is time my father's wool weights were brought to the sheriff for assay, seeing that they are old.'"

No one said anything, until the prioress asked Will would he not go with her. Then he began to bluster, asking her did she think the weights were loaded?

"Why," said she, "whether loaded to my loss, or overlight to yours, brother, neither thou nor I would be willing to defraud other."

"No!" cried Will, "No!" and swore it by Cock's Bones.

"Well then—"

"Well then," Will wiped his brow, "A God's Name, if you have other weights—"

"There's weights in the kitchen."

"Then we'll use those for this time. It's true that these are old, and may be not—not—" He picked up the seven-pound weights by their strap, and slung them away into a dark place beside the wall. When weights had been fetched from the kitchen they settled again to the weighing. The prioress sat at one end of the bench by the door, Will at the other; each had a book to enter in the number of fleeces weighed. Will's man stood by the scale calling the weights; the bailiff sweated carrying the fleeces from the pile to the scale, and away again. No one had said that he should do his man's job, but he did it. No one spoke all through the weighing except the necessary words, as when Will's man would call, perhaps, "Two to the wool," if the fleeces weighed heavier than the 28 pounds of a tod, or "Three to the weights," if the three-pound weight was needed to bring the fleeces down to the level. When they had weighed this year's wool-clip the bailiff began to bring out last year's, and, when that was weighed, yellowed fleeces from the year before. Will fidgeted with his feet and scowled over his book, but he said nothing. When the prioress said, "All at one price," he said, "Aye."

Will and his man went away, after they had all, the bailiff as well, drunk a cup of ale together. The prioress turned
back from the gate. The bailiff's man and the two servants, still
goggle-eyed from the events of the morning, took themselves
off; the prioress nodded her head cheerfully to the bailiff.

"All the old wool sold, and at the price of this year's clip.
That was good."

The bailiff, crimson from heat already, managed to color
deeper.

"Madame—I—I—"

The prioress went on as if he had not spoken.

"Since we have sold so well I look to do a thing I have some
while intended. Know you of a good craftsman who could wainscot my chamber fairly?"

The bailiff, though unable at once to credit and understand so strange an oblivion, could tell the prioress of a good
Richmond craftsman, a right worthy man.

"An honest workman?"

The bailiff choked, and said, "Yea, honest," and would have
said more but that he realized in time that the prioress was that
rare woman, one who will let facts work in silence. She did not
even tell him what he knew very well, that she would watch him
like a hawk, and the next trick he tried to play her, if ever he should
try, would be the last. She only bade him look to the scythes in
good time for the harvesting, and then went up to her chamber
with the wool book, which he had used to keep, under her arm.

The story of the bailiff's excursion into double dealing leaked
out, but not through the prioress. It spread like damp on a wall,

upward, from the bailiff's man. So it was the ladies who last heard it, and more than a week after Will Cowper had gone. Among them, when the topic had been privately but exhaustively discussed, there were two schools of thought. The more timorous were shaken to their very souls by the knowledge that such wolves as Master Cowper and their own bailiff wore doublet and hosen and walked the earth on two legs, but ravening. One or two even said, but erroneously, that they would not sleep easy in their beds, knowing that wickedness prowled so near. The others, more adventurous, triumphed in the triumph of their prioress. "Mass! If we could but have seen the bailiff's face!" they cried, "down on his knees clutching at the Lady's habit, praying for mercy!" "And Master Cowper, he wept they say."

So they relished the affair, each after her own manner. But there was about it something not one of them could understand. Neither soon nor late did their prioress speak a word of blame, either of her brother or of the bailiff. Indeed, to deepen their incomprehension, it was whispered, on the authority of Dame Anne Ladyman, that Dame Christabel had said, Perdy! she loved Will for it, the rascal! That was beyond them.

August 3

Robert Aske had just parted from a client after walking and talking with him a while in Paul's, when he came up against Sir John Bulmer, whom he had not seen since April, and who was the last man on earth he wanted to see. He regretted now that he had stayed for the summer vacation lectures at Gray's; Hal had gone off weeks ago; Clifton last Thursday. However, he neither would nor could run away from Sir John, so they turned and walked together out of the cathedral into the sunshine of a day of heavy, thundery heat.

"One told me that I should find you here," Sir John began. "Often I have meant to seek you out, but never—"

Aske interrupted him by standing still.

"Well, you've found me. What would you have of me?"

Sir John, facing him but not looking at him at all, pulled off his cap and began to fidget with the brooch in it, a pretty thing of Europa riding on a golden bull. He began to talk in starts, jerks, and half sentences. "None of the servants will tell, but maybe—not even Mother Judde, not a word, and she, if any of them—by God's Death, I don't trust her. Only the boy spoke clear enough, yet he's only a child." He put up a hand to tug at his hair, and then cried, "Did you come to the house and lie with her that night I rid to Dorking the first time?" and he looked Aske in the face at last.

Aske did not pretend he did not know who "she" was, but he was by no means so simple as to answer such a question either with yea or nay.

"And what night was that?"

"Lady Day night."

"And other times you rid to Dorking, you say. What of them?"

"The lad—he says you ever said nay but that first time he was sent. Besides, I had set watch."

"And what," Aske fenced, playing for time as he wondered whether, if put to it, he could speak a flat lie, "And what did I say to the lad that one time?"

"He says you gave him a groat."

"I see," said Aske, "that I must beware how I give groats to boys," and he began to walk again; for a moment he thought he had shaken off Sir John, but he came up behind and caught him by the elbow.

"Wait a minute, for I need counsel. I must go home northward soon. I have thought much of how my wife will bear the matter of a bawd. So I consider whether to take her with me or fairly turn her off here in London."

Aske could have laughed aloud at such a simple cunning, though indeed laughter, in this nasty business, was a dismal thing.

He said: "I'm a bachelor. I've neither wife nor bawd. Go you to others for counsel."

"Well," Sir John watched him narrowly, "I think I shall turn her off."

"Since," said Aske steadily, "I am kinsman to your wife, though distantly, I think you would do well."

It was a comfort to be able to speak the exact truth, and he could see that whatever answer he had expected, Sir John had not expected that, and was now at a loss, for he put up his hand again to tug at his hair, dropped his cap, stooped for it, and came up very red.

"No, by God's Blood," he cried, "I'll not believe it of you," and he caught Aske's hand and wrung it, crying, "Forgive me, but I think I'm crazed with loving her. You do not understand, she—" and he ran on, doing his best to make Aske understand.

When he could escape from those undesired confidences Aske set off alone, and at a great pace, for the river, though not with any other purpose than to keep moving. It was noon, and the dogs lay panting in the shade; Aske felt the sweat run down his back and his shoulders prick at the touch of the hair shirt he had worn since Lady Day.

October 14

Sir John and his household started for the North early in the morning in a cold downpour of rain. They came along Holborne toward Newgate because they must strike the road for Highgate and the North, and so they passed the end of Gray's Inn Lane.

July, riding behind one of the servants, peered through the driving shower; she could see the tops of the trees tossing in the garden of the inn; she could see the smoke of the kitchen chimneys driven aside by the rain. Master Aske was there, asleep yet perhaps; or drinking his ale and eating his breakfast before going off to the courts at Westminster. But she was being taken away to the North Country, and she supposed she should never see him again. He had not been to the house for months now; no one had told her why, but July knew: it was because Master Aske had at last found out the things that Meg did. She thought, as they rode out from the gate into the slanting cold rain and the drowned countryside, that she could not endure to be so unhappy. All the same she had to endure it.

October 18

Sir John Bulmer held the manor of Pinchinthorpe, eight miles or so from his house at Wilton. There was a little house at Pinchinthorpe, but old and in disrepair, for it had not been

used for some time. However it was a convenient distance
from Wilton; neither too far for Sir John to ride easily between
one and the other, nor yet scandalously close. Meg mocked at
him, but angrily, when he told her why he would leave her at
Pinchinthorpe. She could not move him though in this; he said
that it should be so. "My son is at Wilton," he told her.

"Lord! and what of that?"

"I will not put him to shame," he said, and scowled at her.

They came to Pinchinthorpe at dusk and rode into the little
grassy courtyard where brambles sprawled in the corners. The
hall itself was opposite them; they could see winking lights in all
the windows, for the servants whom Sir John had sent forward
had got the fire lit there.

Yet when they went in the hall was very cold. There was no
furniture but trestle tables and a few benches, and in a corner a
heap of teasels and some sickles and a little painted cupboard, in
which they found two cracked earthen pots.

Sir John was surly, because now that he was so nearly home
he could not but be thinking what he would say to his wife,
Dame Anne, when he saw her; whether to tell of Meg or leave
her to find out he could not decide. Meg was angry because
she was tired, and because Pinchinthorpe was such a poor and
rustic place. "Goodman John," she called Sir John, as if he were
a farmer, jeering at him. "Shall I brew and bake and milk the
kine?" she asked him. "Jesu! had I known before I came with
you I'd have gone—"

He struck her then and she snatched at his dagger and tried
to draw it against him. July left them, creeping out quietly into

the chill and now dark night. She was hungry, but it was better to be quiet than to eat. She felt her way up the outside stair to the room where they would sleep, and found that the servants had set up the beds, though not the sparvers and curtains to them. She crept into one in the farther small chamber where she supposed she would lie with Meg's woman. She was too tired and too cold to sleep at once, and the strange nakedness of sleeping without curtains kept her waking long, watching the slant of moonlight that edged across the floor. To all her old and usual fears of Meg, of Sir John, of the devil, had been added a new one—the fear of Sir John's wife. Meg laughed at Sir John's discomfort, but July could not laugh, being herself in the grip of a shame more disabling than Sir John's own. As she lay cowering in bed she said over and over, "Oh! we should not be here. We should not be here." For Dame Anne was kinswoman to Master Aske; he had told her so on that evening when he had found her at the cross in Cheap; and if Dame Anne was angry and all her kinsfolk angry, July was undone. She could not distinguish in blame, and did not expect any other to distinguish, between herself and Meg.

1533

February 24

Lord Darcy sat in the house at Stepney reading a book of devotion by the light of the branch of wax candles which stood behind his chair. He kept his eyes on the page faithfully enough, but his mind wandered. Thoughts about Templehurst mingled with his meditations on mortality: the roof of the great chamber that needed mending, the young fawns that should be fed in the lower close; or there would come clear and near before the eye of his mind a glance of the chequer chamber window, of the steps going down to the chapel, of the trees beyond the distant river, sleeping on a summer evening with the light dying behind them.

At last he dropped the book beside the chair and went over to the window. Outside the rain fell, steady and dark; it leaked through the casements, running in heavy drops along the iron bars of the windows and splashing down on the sill. In places it bubbled and spat upward from the corner of the window frames. The gentlemen who were with him in the room watched him, then turned back to their occupations.

"By the rood!" said Darcy, half aloud, "I would I were at home in the North Country."

He did not turn when someone knocked at the door, supposing it to be the servants with more lights; but as well as the lights they brought in his brother-in-law, Lord Sandys of the Vine, who slung off his heavy red felt coat which was dark across the shoulders where the rain had soaked in, and below that all silvery with the standing drops. He shook it before he tossed it to one of the gentlemen, and the wet flew off it and spattered the dogs that had run forward to greet him, so that they backed away.

He kissed Darcy, and said, holding him hard by the shoulder and looking him in the eye, "I'm soaked to the bone. Will you lend me a dry gown to put on?"

"That I will. Come within." Darcy led him toward the door of his bedchamber, then, over his shoulder, bade one of the gentlemen, "Bring light, James."

In the bedchamber, when James had lit the fire, and set candles, Darcy took Sandys by the arm and brought him to the high-backed bench in front of the hearth where two green cushions were set, worked with the buck's head in silver.

"Now, tell me your news," said he.

Sandys leaned toward him so that their shoulders touched, and said in a low voice, "She is with child."

"You mean the King's—"

"Sh!" Sandys looked over his shoulder at the gentleman, leaning against the door, and paring his nails with a little knife.

"Keep me the door, James," said Darcy, and when the young gentleman had gone out—"Well then, the Marchioness of Pembroke."

Sandys nodded, and spat in the fire. "Nan Boleyn," he said.

"Who told you it?"

"She did."

"She? Told *you*?"

"She told us all—all that were waiting outside the King's chamber."

"Who?"

"God's Body! a dozen or so—Exeter, Huntingdon, Norfolk, Wyatt too."

"Who was her lover once."

"They say so."

"Well I can believe it. And it's not *credo quia impossibile est*."

Sandys shrugged and went on.

"I was talking with Wyatt as we warmed our hands at a brazier, when the door of the King's chamber opens, and out prances my Lady Marchioness, the Queen's jewels all over her, aye, even some I can remember to have seen Her Grace wear when first she came from Spain. And this one had more too; they say the King gives her jewels every day. She'd as many as the Virgin of Conques.

"So out she comes, twisting her hands together like this," and he wrung his hands daintily together.

"She looks round at us all, and then cries out to Wyatt, naming him by name—'Sir Thomas! Sir Thomas! By the Holy Virgin you'll not guess what the King says.' Wyatt began to stroke his beard like he does when he's thinking out one of his pretty sayings, but she didn't give him time.

"'You know what I told you yesterday, how sharply I long for apples? I told His Grace, and he says it means I am with child,' and back she skipped into the privy chamber, cackling like a hen."

"God's Soul!" said Darcy, "and did she clap her hands to her belly like that?"

"She did, Tom."

They sat together in silence for quite a long time before Sandys murmured, "Will he marry her?" and then answered his own question. "But he cannot, unless the pope at last should give sentence against the Queen."

Darcy leaned his head near and spoke with his lips close to Sandys' ear. "I was told—but did not then believe it—"

"Tell me first who told you."

"No, never mind. I was told that about a month ago now this new archbishop, Cranmer, married them. It was very secret, but folks will talk."

"But," persisted Sandys, "no archbishop can, while the appeal lies at Rome."

Darcy looked at him with his head tipped back and angry dancing lights in his eyes.

"You may say he cannot, but this Cranmer will do it. And will declare the King's first marriage void, if he is set up to judge in the cause."

"I know," said Sandys, "that he was Nan Boleyn's father's chaplain. But he cannot. It is not possible."

Darcy laughed at him, but grimly.

"You shall see what he can do, and what the King can do now that this child is begotten."

May 17

Thomas Cranmer, archbishop of Canterbury, walked in the fields, for it was evening, and Saturday, and all day he had sat in the court at Dunstable, trying the matter of the King's first marriage. Now he took the air with one of his gentlemen. They walked at the foot of a gentle slope that ran up to a small oak wood. The little hill was a hill of gold, so thick the buttercups grew, and the oak trees themselves were greenish gold. A black puppy went with them, flopping and galloping, making parade of having to attend to affairs of great weight, with mischief shining in its eyes; when it came back to them, blundering against their legs, its muzzle was golden green from the gold pollen of the buttercups. On the fringe of the wood the milkmaids were busy among the kine; their voices and laughter came pleasantly, and one of them began to sing. All the birds were singing too, so many and so merry that there was never an instant's silence; single amongst all their flutings cuckoo called, and called again from the distance.

"Would," said the archbishop, pinching his lower lip between his fingers, as he did when he was troubled, "would that I could have pronounced the King's first marriage incestuous this day, before the court closed."

"But, my lord, you have brought it to a final sentence which—"

"Which I cannot give till Friday next, seeing all the days between are ferial; so that the court cannot sit."

"But," the gentleman objected again, "on Friday—" and again the archbishop interrupted him irritably.

"Supposing *she* hears the bruit of it—Queen Katherine. She hath not appeared to answer her summons—but if she should—"

He brooded over that, teasing his lip.

"I have written to the King," he said. "I must write to Master Cromwell. But I shall pray either of them to make no relation of the matter lest she should be stirred to appear afore me in the time, or afore the time, of sentence. For if she came I should be greatly stayed and let in the process, and you know time runs on, and this marriage must be broken before our gracious Queen Anne is crowned."

He started forward, going toward the house.

"I shall write now. See to a messenger for me," he cried over his shoulder, and went in to write to Master Cromwell of how nearly the process of the King's divorce was accomplished, and how fearful he was lest Katherine of Spain should appear in the court to answer in her own cause, in place of that docile and complaisant counsel whom the King had appointed to answer for her.

May 29

As well as the house at Mortlake, which Lord Darcy now rented instead of the one at Stepney, he had hired a small house at Westminster to use when Parliament was sitting. The house was old and crushed in between one of the tall kitchen offices of the new Palace of Whitehall, and a house that belonged to the abbot of Westminster. It had no garden at all, which was strange for Westminster, a countrified place where the palace sat among greenery, like Richard Crookback's crown on a thornbush, but the cardinal had bought and built upon the little garden which it had possessed, thus almost choking the house on one side of light and air. Because Lord Darcy did not care to be without a garden he hired one that lay at the end of the lane, and nearer the river; it was called the Vine Garden, because there was a very old vine in it, fantastically and harshly knotted, but still fertile, and now breaking out with exquisitely innocent and gay young leaves.

On this day, which was the Friday before Whitsuntide, my lord came in from Mortlake in his litter. The servants had been sent on hours earlier, so as to have the house ready, but when my lord came it was all hugger-mugger; in the room beyond the hall, where the ancient windows had pointed arches, and stone seats under them in the thickness of the wall, the hearth had not yet been cleared of the pale ash of the last fire, nor filled with green boughs for summer. When my lord sat down on a cushion on the seat below the window, he could hear feet scurrying overhead, and heavy bumps now and again, as the servants set up the beds in haste.

Presently Lord Hussey came in, so the two lords and several of their gentlemen chose to repair out of the confusion of the house to the little Vine Garden at the end of the lane.

The Vine Garden, though small, was a pleasant place. As well as the old vine on the wall there were trim hedges of thorn and box, and a trellis where the first monthly roses were pink and white like raspberries drenched in cream. Close to the gate by which they entered there was a cherry tree, whose fruit, plump, polished, and yellow, was already flushing with scarlet; a blackbird scrambled noisily from among the leaves, and flew away, shouting with fright and proprietary anger as they came in. At the other end of the walk a honeysuckle hedge and arbor were backed by a low wall, and as Darcy and Hussey sat together in the arbor they could hear the slap of the Thames' tide upon the stones behind them. A salt smell mingled with the scent of the honeysuckle, and seagulls drifted by, golden white against the blue, turning their heads from side to side as they spied about for garbage.

While the gentlemen sat, or strolled about the garden, the two lords talked, securely private in the honeysuckle arbor. Hussey could tell Darcy all the news there was of Princess Mary, for he was chamberlain of her household; he could also tell much of the Queen, for letters had been passing between Katherine and her daughter, even though they were forbidden.

"The Princess"—Hussey said, and checked himself, not for the first time; that title was forbidden. "The Lady Mary," he began again, and then struck one palm with the other fist. "Blood of God," he cried, but keeping his voice low, "if you knew how I live now between my wife, whose sweetest name for me is 'coward,' and these lords who come from the court to bid me call the—call my lady—this or that or t'other! She," he explained, and Darcy knew that he meant Lady Hussey, "she is passionate for the Queen. Oh God! the Princess Dowager I mean, and for—her daughter. But what can a man do other than obey his Prince?"

Darcy prodded the ground at their feet with his walking staff. He murmured, "Women are like that," remembering how his dead Elizabeth had, from the beginning, taken this same business of the King's new marriage. How many years ago was that beginning? Why, the thing had hung over them for close on six years. And now it was come to an end, but to a different end, and by very different paths than any which he or others had dreamed of then.

For a breath Darcy could have believed that his wife had been right, and all was as simple as women saw it. "Here's a man married. What if he be a king? Here's his wife and his true-born child. What if she be a lass instead of a lad? There's a whore. What if she be crowned queen and wear a collar of pearls about her neck as big as chickpeas?"

He sighed, and Hussey beside him swore softly again and went on complaining of how his wife goaded and reproached him. Darcy only half listened. He was thinking that this "great matter" of the King's, so long ago begun, was perhaps not yet ended. It had spread so far as a flood spreads, that none could say now where it would cease to undermine, to bring down, to efface. No. Certainly the women's simple way was not for a man to take when all known paths were hidden, and he must feel about for foothold. "But," he comforted himself, "all will return into place one day," and when he thought—"If it does not—?" he answered the doubt promptly. "Aye—but it must."

In the evening he was promised to supper with the Marquess of Exeter at that same Manor of the Rose which had once been Buckingham's. Just past Temple Bar the preparations for shows began. The streets too were graveled, and along one side a railing had been set up, so that the Londoners would not be hurt by scared horses trampling in on them. The conduit in Fleet Street was freshly colored, as bright as a Book of Hours; the shields of arms were sticky with paint—scarlet, blue, green—and the angels all new gilded. A sort of gallery had been built out above, like a little walled town with a turret at each corner, and the sound of instruments of music and the voices of singing boys came from it and mingled with the noises of the street. A few men of the city stood below, listening and looking up, with the script of the music in their hands, for it was their pageant.

A dray unloading hogsheads at the conduit held up Darcy's litter for a while, so he leaned out to watch while he waited. The instruments and voices sounded pleasantly here, and the setting sun made the conduit and its fanciful adornments like a picture of the New Jerusalem. But now something had gone wrong; the music faltered, the viols and recorders played a phrase alone, then played it again, but raggedly. Someone from below cried out in anger, and, when a boy put his head over the rail above, complained, "You there, Justice! We don't want you. That's Temperance his part."

The boy glanced back over his shoulder: "Well, Sir, Temperance is—Temperance—Marry! Sir, one of the casks of the conduit to run wine tomorrow was stove in, and Temperance—he's very sick, sir."

Darcy let out a laugh, and someone else beside him laughed too. When Darcy looked round to see who it was, he found a gentleman on horseback close beside the litter, with many in livery following him; and then he saw that it was not a gentleman at all, but Master Cromwell, keeper of the King's jewels.

"Temperance," said Cromwell, "will have not only a sore head tomorrow, but a sore backside," and he nodded at the enraged citizen, already climbing the narrow ladder, with such a pleasant puckering of the eyes in his laughter that Darcy could not, for the moment, dislike him.

So they rode up the Strand together, talking pleasantly, and indeed Master Cromwell was a good talker, ranging easily from praise of the great arch the Venetians were busy setting up, to the whole city of Venice itself, thence to speak of the more ancient Italy, with talk of the Cave of Scylla, "which," said he, "I have with mine own eyes seen, but no monster therein, only a row of sea birds sitting and looking out, very solemn and wise, like justices on the bench." By the time the keeper of the King's jewels pulled up his horse in Candlewick Street and said that here must he take his leave, Darcy had decided that this was a much pleasanter rogue than he had thought.

And Master Cromwell lingered after dismounting, as if unwilling to part with my lord. He stood talking, shading his eyes with one hand against the great flood of swimming dusty gold that the sun poured down the street, leaning an elbow on the side of Darcy's litter, and idly flicking to and fro a pair of new and costly Louvain gloves, dove gray, like his dove gray satin coat, and stitched with silver.

The streets were still very full, though it was past suppertime for merchants and working folk; everyone was about, staring at the decorations, though not, Darcy noticed, with that free hilarity that such shows usually brought. People moved slowly, and spoke low to each other. But the shows were plentiful, and every house along the way had hung out lengths of colored stuffs, or painted cloths or devices. Below the windows of the house opposite, almost hiding the twined roses and pomegranates carved along the timbers, hung damask velvet of crimson red. And even now some wenches and an apprentice or two were leaning out from the windows, to better it with painted shields, white and green, each with two letters interlaced—an H. and an A.

Master Cromwell twinkled at Darcy, said farewell, and moved away. Darcy told the boy on the leading horse to "Get on!" and he looped up the reins in his hand ready to obey. Just then among the crowd there came three young gentlemen, arm in arm, going toward Westminster, with the sun on their faces.

They were opposite the litter when the midmost of the three suddenly stopped and pulled the others up.

"Look you!" he cried, and freed one arm to point at the lettered shields that hung a little drunkenly. "Look you there!" He had a notable voice, deep, but with a clear note in it that rang above the noises of the street, so that people looked round at him. "Why! That's what we all say of this coronation, and now they write it for us to read—H and A. That spells Ha!" and he let out a great, derisive "Ha! Ha!" Someone in the street laughed, and then more than one, and a shrill boy's voice echoed the "Ha! Ha!" and there were catcalls and more laughter.

The litter stopped and Darcy found that Master Cromwell was beside him again. "Wait!" said he to Darcy, "Who said that? Which way did he go? What manner of man?"

Darcy leaned out and peered eastward toward the Tower, and then westward toward St. Paul's. In that direction he could see the red cap of the young gentleman who had said, "Ha! Ha!" Then it was hidden by the stiff white coifs of a couple of citizens' wives who had gone by with an apprentice boy following them. "By the rood!" he answered slowly, "I could not say who. Nor I could not say which way. Nor what manner of man."

"Ah!" said Cromwell, after a silence. "I see. And it matters—but little."

His eyes, sharp and small and full of consideration, seemed to be looking through Darcy's head, as if he were adding up a sum that was written on the green and tawny curtains of the litter behind it. He said farewell again with no less courtesy and sweetness than before, though without a smile.

Darcy went on to the Rose, and chuckled more than once as he went. The trumpet was blowing for supper when he got there, and he had time only to wash his hands and join them at the board. But after supper, when the candles were lit, he and the marquess stood together in a window, in a shadow that lay between the cold turquoise of the sky and the warm light of the fluttering candle flames. The marquess asked for news, but when Darcy began to tell him what Hussey had said he knew it already.

Then Darcy told him of the young man in the street, and of Master Cromwell's concern. The marquess laughed, but at once his face fell again into its expression of tired and fastidious melancholy. He had royal blood in him, and he looked royal, but as if an exiled and weary king.

"Who was he—this young man? Did you see him?" he asked with so little interest that it was enough for Darcy merely to shake his head.

"I fear that Master Cromwell has notched a tally against me in that working brain of his," said he, and at that the marquess exclaimed with disgust upon Cromwell. "A petty usurer," he called him in such a tone as one would speak of a louse. "Never fear for him."

"Fear?" Darcy had not thought of fear, and something made him turn his eyes from the marquess for kindness' sake, as from the face of one who has betrayed himself without knowing it. And, because that other, the saucy young man, was so different, he remembered again his face, which indeed he had seen well, and not forgotten. For if a man has but one eye it is easy to remember him; and easier yet if the eye is sharp with scorn, and bright with laughter. Darcy had caught its glance for an instant, and his lips twitched now as he remembered the liveliness and mockery of that single eye. "By the rood!" he thought to himself, hearing again in recollection the northern broadness of speech, "By the rood! he's a Yorkshireman I'll swear, and that's a bold, true man." And he thought with warm love of the North Country, and the men that were bred there.

June 8

This Sunday, the next after the Queen's coronation, almost everybody went to court, and Lord Darcy one of them. As he paused on the landing of a stairway, Master Cromwell came out from a door which he locked carefully behind him. He seemed greatly pleased to see Darcy, and urged him to "Come up, my lord, come up," as though he spoke for the King. They went on up the stairs together, and Darcy saw that Cromwell had a little crimson velvet casket in his hand, a pretty thing with gilt hinges and a tiny gilt key.

"A jewel for Her Grace," said Cromwell. "The King sent for it, and it came but yesterday." He stopped at the next window, and opened the box in the sunshine. Darcy bent his head and saw a great emerald flash back the light and hold it in depths of undersea green that glowed as if with fire. There were three pearls hanging from it, large and elongated, the shape of plovers' eggs.

"Hm!" he said, though not much interested, "pretty."

"And of great price." Cromwell prodded it with a forefinger. He had fat hands, with dimples at the knuckle joints, yet they looked strong too. "It was the Princess Dowager's. She brought it from Spain. It was a jewel, perhaps, of those Kings of the Indies. Now His Grace will give it to Queen Anne."

He shut the box, and they went on together. Darcy guessed that Cromwell expected him to say something, either to approve or deplore, or discreetly to turn the conversation. He did none of these, being too honest to approve, too wary to deplore, and at once too practiced and too bold to fear a silence.

He had thought that when they reached the presence chamber Cromwell would leave him, but instead the master of the jewels laid a hand lightly on his arm, and twinkling at him with the smile that Darcy could not dislike, said that he would he were of the number of my lord's friends, few men of these days being so stout and honest. "And," said he, "as I would earn your love I will essay a small thing thereto. I will bring you, without pain of waiting, at once to His Grace." And he began to push his way, not roughly yet with determination, between the wide puffed shoulders of the men, and the spreading stiff gowns of the women, crowded into the long room and all looking toward the far end, where hung the cloth of estate above the King's chair. Darcy followed him, but not now liking either him or the times in which such an upstart could lead a nobleman to his Prince's presence.

When they reached it the chair of estate was empty, and Cromwell, catching the eye of a gentleman in silver and green who stood on guard at a closed door, led Darcy there, knocked, and went in.

The room was small, hot with sunshine, and fragrant with strewn flowers and perfumes of musk, ambergris, and orris.

There were two small chairs, covered with purple velvet and fringed with silver, set below one of the windows, and the King's Grace and the Queen sat on them. The King's hand with its rings was laid on hers or touching or toying with her all the time, whether he greeted Darcy or spoke to the French ambassador or argued with her father about the voice of one of the singing boys of the Children of the King's Chapel.

Cromwell knelt, and presented the jewel to the Queen. "It is," said he, "a gift from His Grace."

"For me," she cried, and turning her head tipped up her face to the King who hung over her. Darcy thought, "She knows what will prick a man to desire."

The King lifted the jewel out of the box. He leaned closer and set the chain about her neck. Then he must settle the jewel so that the midmost pearl hung plump above the cleft between her breasts, which showed where the jeweled edge of her gown ended. His fingers lingered on her flesh; she let herself droop toward him.

"A born harlot!" Darcy thought, and guessed that Cromwell thought no other, though the master of the jewels kissed her hand and took leave with due humility.

But he had to acknowledge that she had wit, for she began to talk about her coronation in the abbey of Westminster, and had them all laughing because she so pricked through the splendors and solemnities that she pierced to the folk behind them, and as she talked these were no more reverend than a rout of villagers at a May game.

When she finished, ". . . And so we came away to dinner," the King wiped his eyes, though his bulk still shook with diminishing gusts of laughter. He flung his arm across her shoulders and bade her tell them more. "What of the dinner?" he pressed her.

She let herself be pulled toward him, then put both hands on his breast and pushed him away.

"No, but I'll tell you what I saw at the abbey. But you'll be angry."

"Not with you, sweetheart."

"Faith! but you will. You'll say, 'To the Tower with her.'"

"Madcap!" The King looked about at them all, and then again at the Queen's father, a mass of slashed green velvet and cloth of gold, set upon a pair of thin legs.

"This daughter of yours!" he cried dotingly, and then to her, "Well, you little rebel? I shall not be angry. Or you shall have a pardon."

"Shall I? But you will be angry. See. I will wager you a prince to a collar of rubies that you are angry."

"A prince? How will you pay with a prince?"

"The prince I bear in my belly."

"Ho!" the King laughed. "You'll pay with him at your time, will you, nill you?"

"And isn't he enough to wager against a collar of rubies?"

The King swore by St. Edward that he would be enough, and then asked again, "Sweet, what did you see? Tell us now."

"I saw jewels."

"God's body! so you should. Here have I been writing orders to Master Cromwell for this, that, and t'other for you. And now today I have given you the emerald. My lord," said the King to Darcy, in high good humor, "should these not be enough?"

"Sir," Darcy answered, "if women be as insatiate as the sea, it is that they know our weakness, and their own worth," and on the last he bowed to the Queen. She inclined her head but he had seen her eye snap at his guarded courtliness.

The King however was growing impatient.

"Jewels?" he urged. "Are there not some few on the crown and the scepter?"

She pouted her lips, and blew all those away with scorn.

"Jewels! Not those. But the jewels on the shrine. Jewels in the lord abbot's mitre. Jewels in his staff. And there was a great ruby in the cross on the altar. I saw none in the crown nor in scepter like to these."

The King had withdrawn his arm from her neck.

"I think, madame," he said, "that you forget."

She flashed a look at Darcy that said, "You would be glad to hear me rebuked," and then turned her eyes, sparkling and reckless, upon the King.

"You owe me a ruby collar, for indeed you are angry."

"The devil I do!" The King got up quickly, but she did not move. He turned back. "One day, madame, you'll go too far."

"And then," she smiled at him, "you will send to Ampthill and bring Dame Katherine back."

The King had been angry, but now it was as if he had been hit with a stone between the eyes. He looked at her, but if he hoped to beat down her glance he failed. Darcy thought, "She can stare like any cat." And it was with the same bland sweetness of malice.

The King went back to his chair.

"I believe you would not fear the devil."

"Not if he wore a beard. And shall I have my rubies?"

"Ask the keeper of the jewels."

"Not the abbot of Westminster?"

The Queen's father cried, in an agony, "Peace, girl! Madame, I pray you, peace!" but the Queen did not so much as look at him.

"You'll get none of my lord abbot." The King's tone was gruff.

"These monks," the Queen murmured softly, "have all, and give naught. And the King can't take. Yet the cardinal took."

"Body of God!" the King turned on her. "The cardinal took only a few little priories, some of an ill name. But to speak of Westminster! By the Blood of Hales!" he cried, "I won't have this talk." He got up and went out of the room with his arrogant walk, swinging his wide, white satin shoulders.

When Darcy stood waiting for his litter and looking at all the coming and going in the great courtyard between the palace and Master Holbein's new gallery and gate, he found Cromwell at his elbow, and thought as he greeted him, "How the man sticks!"

"How sweet is the sunshine," Cromwell said, as though in idlest talk. "Truly I think this fair summer shows that God's favor is upon this marriage. That, and already so blessed a hope of issue."

"Already," Darcy repeated drily.

"Ah! my lord, how I love the bluntness of you men of the North Country. But at least," he murmured, "at least, even you, my lord, will confess we have a Queen now, young, witty, beautiful, and, let us hope, fruitful."

"And bold," said Darcy. "She wants the King to do with the Abbey of Westminster what the cardinal did with the priories."

"She said that, did she?" Cromwell remarked, in a tone almost innocent of meaning, and yet something in Darcy's brain pricked an ear, and he thought, "It's not the first time that same has been said, nor was she the first to say it." He was just thinking that this man was perhaps more dangerous, though not greater, than the cardinal, when Cromwell spoke again.

"But, my lord, there's a thing I'd ask of you. That young gentleman in Candlewick Street the other day, did you see his face?"

When Darcy did not answer he went on, "I thought I had heard his voice before. I'm sure I have heard it." He rapped with his knuckles on his forehead, and then bit at them angrily. "It was a voice that one should remember, and I cannot."

He waited, and then ran on again, begging pardon for keeping my lord when his litter waited, "But it would be well I should know of any young gentleman so quick, bold, forward, as that one seemed to be. It was a young gentleman, you said?"

"*You* said," Darcy corrected him; and then with a sharp smile, "Master Cromwell, if I tell you, shall I have the reward they proclaimed for those who informed against any that speak evil of this marriage?" He looked at Cromwell, and laughed; the keeper of the jewels was not often out of countenance, but now he was quite taken aback. He began to justify himself; it was necessary, he said, that quiet should be kept.

"Therefore I keep watch. People murmur at this marriage. Her Grace was displeased that so few caps came off, and there was so little shouting when she passed through the city. And there's a nun in Kent sees visions—foretells the King's death—" He paused and seemed to recollect himself, and laughed. "So perhaps I make too much of the idle jest of a saucy young man."

Darcy said, "Perhaps," in a tone that made Cromwell glance at him sharply, and then they parted. As Darcy looked back from below the new gateway arch, he stood there, still sunning himself on the steps, a sober, quiet figure, in his gray silk and black fur. Darcy thought he was like one of those floating spots which trouble a distempered vision, and which the eye can neither quite catch, nor yet be rid of.

June 30

The nuns' shepherd had come down from Owlands for goose grease, or butter, or swine's grease to mix with pitch and tar for sores upon his beasts, but before he went back to the lonely hut on the fells he turned into the kitchen where the cook and his man and the maids all greeted him well. The cook sent off at once to draw ale for him, and he sat down on the bench with a great heap of lettuces on the floor between his feet, and his dog at his heels.

Beside him on the bench were two strangers; one gray-haired, with a weather-beaten pleasant face; the other younger and clearly of less importance. The elder of the two was stirring a white treacly mess in a pail beside him; at intervals he tipped down his throat deep drafts of priory ale.

For a long time Shepherd said nothing, for his way of life had made him more ready to listen than to talk. But at last, in a pause in the talk, he nudged the strange man, and pointed at the stuff in the pail. "What's yon, goodman?"

The stranger turned his broad, red face.

"Yon's lime, and a heel of old, poor cheese."

Shepherd looked at the stuff in the pail, and from one to another in the kitchen. "What beasts," he asked in his slow way, "will you feed or physic with such?"

They all laughed at that, but the stranger answered seriously.

"It's for no beast, seeing I'm a master carpenter; but 'tis to glue wainscoting. For there's no glue like lime and cheese and spring water to hold wood together. It'll last you from now till doomsday morrow."

"Lord!" said Shepherd, and stared at it long before he asked, "And is it in frater or cloister, or maybe in church, that y're setting up wainscoting?"

The cook answered that, telling him that it was for the Lady's own chamber. "Painted hangings nor yet arras aren't good enough for *her*." He stood up and scratched himself inside his doublet. "Time to get dinner," said he, and sweeping the flies from a piece of meat on the table began to pare off a long dark red sliver, that flopped back over the fingers of his left hand as the knife moved. A boy came into the kitchen and squatted down on the floor in the corner with a basket of peas between his heels; he shelled them into a wooden bowl; pop went the pods and the peas rattled against the sides of the bowl.

"And it's time you and I got back to work," the master carpenter said to his mate, "or the Lady will be wroth to find us idling." So they went away, back to the prioress's chamber, and not too soon, for she came in and found them there five minutes after.

The furniture in the room had been moved into the middle of the floor and shrouded in sacking. Everywhere sawdust lay, soft to touch, and fresh smelling. But already except for one corner the wainscoting was in place upon the walls, clean pale golden wood, cunningly carved in the panels with softly flowing, scroll-like curves. Nor was that the whole of its beauty. All over the carved undulations of the pattern as well as over the firm uprights and horizontals of the paneling, the wood was alive with the living pattern of its own grain. Here swam, it seemed, a shoal of little fishes; there shining blotches floated like tiny clouds in the sunset; there you could trace wavering tongues like flames, or like the soft sleek trails of water weeds, swayed by a slow river; and there the wood was dappled as if it were shallow running water. It was beautiful wood and beautiful work.

That was what the prioress thought of it when she came in, and having shut the door stood looking about at the strange and fine new clothing of the familiar walls.

The carpenter, when he saw her, stopped whistling between his teeth, and laid down his T square and charcoal. He came forward with a sort of rough and breezy gallantry, not disrespectful, yet with a spice in it of laughter. He had had many dealings with women religious, being known for an honest fellow and not given to too much drinking. He was wont to declare that there were but two kinds of such women; the fools he overawed by a frowning look, and talk that none but a carpenter could understand; the masterful women he courted in the same manner in which he now set himself to court the prioress.

Certainly it went well here, but then the two already had a respect for each other. He did good work, and she knew and acknowledged good work when she saw it. So now he moved confidently beside her, as she let her hand slide over the smooth, sleek curves, and cast a penetrating eye on the joints to see that all were close.

As they went he talked, giving her news of folk in Richmond and the dale; she heard him, raising her brows or faintly smiling, but never letting herself be distracted by his talking from her examination of the work.

"And have you heard," said he, "of mighty great doings down at Easby?"

"That peg stands too high. I can feel its head."

He moved his fingers over the surface. "You'll not feel him when we've taken the oil and sand over all. . . . I hear there's them that say Master Oldbarrow won't last the summer out."

"That joint," the prioress said, "could be tighter," and then though they were alone in the room she brought her mouth close to the master carpenter's ear. "Show me the hidden place you have made."

He showed her the panel low down in the darkest corner of the chamber, where there was a lock cunningly concealed by a fold of the carving. When you knew where to look for the lock you could see that there were also hinges, and a little door. He opened the door, and showed the small secret cupboard.

"That is good," said the prioress.

July 11

Lord Mountjoy, Queen Katherine's chamberlain, her almoner, and others of the household, paused with one consent at the door of her chamber. None looked at another, but each knew that his neighbor squared his shoulders, or took a deeper breath than usual, or clenched his teeth, before Lord Mountjoy lifted his hand and knocked, and they must go in to do a business that they hated.

She lay on a bed in the vaulted room which was a somber place in the dull light of an overcast and stormy morning. A few days ago she had pricked her foot with a pin as she had got out of bed, and gone barefoot, in the middle of the night, to pray before the crucifix in her chamber; now the foot was inflamed so that she could not put on a shoe. When the gentlemen came in she cast the hem of her heavy skirts over it, and tried to pull herself up on the bed. Yet it did not need those small attempts at dignity to make them go down on their knees, as much in reverence of her sorrows, as of her birth and station. But for all the propriety of their behavior, her ladies, drawn away together to the empty hearth, some of them clutching embroidery, book, or instrument with which they had been employed, gave angry and grudging looks to the gentlemen; in this pass to which their Queen was come, they, as women, stood by her, a woman wronged by men. So a fundamental and eternal cleavage split in two that unhappy household.

Mountjoy spoke. They had, he said, come to her as she had yesterday commanded them, to read to her their report of that interview, before they sent it to His Grace's honorable Privy Council, to give account of the performance of the commission enjoined on them by the same honorable council.

"Shameful commission!" cried one of the younger ladies, then flushed crimson, and nearly burst into tears when the Queen rebuked her with a frown.

Yet the faces of the gentlemen seemed to give color to her words; yesterday they had felt shame in declaring to their mistress that her marriage with the King, in which she had lived blameless, honorable, and honored, was a thing "detestable, abominable, execrable, and directly against the laws of God and nature." And today they looked as hangdog as any collection of respectable and well-intentioned persons might look.

"To whom," asked Queen Katherine of Mountjoy, "do you say in your report that you have discharged your commission?"

He told her, looking on the ground, "To the Princess Dowager."

Queen Katherine drew herself up on the bed till she sat upright.

"Bring me the report!" she said to the gentlemen, and to the ladies, "Bring me pen and paper."

She was obeyed by both, though all in that room knew what she would do. When one of the ladies knelt by her, holding the ink, she set the report on her knee and scribbled out the words, "Princess Dowager," wherever they came. As she did it the sharp complaint of the driven quill and the Queen's harsh coughing were the only sounds in the room.

The gentlemen received again the report and asked leave to depart. But before they went the Queen spoke, while they stood twisting their caps and looking more like schoolboys in disgrace than any of them had looked for many years.

As she spoke she was shaken more and more by her cough, and inwardly by the thought of all the injustice she suffered, so that in the end she was crying out almost incoherently, that if she agreed to their persuasions to call herself anything but Queen she would be a slanderer of herself, she would thereby confess to have been the King's harlot for twenty-four years. She stopped a moment because she must, and when she could speak again it was in a whisper. The King had said that her case should be heard in some place indifferent, "but now it is determined by a man of the King's own making, the archbishop of Canterbury. And how much impartial he be," she cried, "God he knows. Nor is the place impartial, since the King has taken upon himself to be *supremum caput ecclesiae*, with greater authority than our lord the pope himself."

They waited for a while when she was silent, but she waved her hand to them to be gone, only to beckon them again to stay.

"I am," she said, in a voice whose bitterness pierced them, "I am, you know, no Englishwoman but a Spaniard, and having no counsel may err in my words. But you shall say that if anything else there is in the report prejudicial to my cause I protest against it."

They went away then, and the Queen bade that one of her ladies who had been reading aloud find her place again and read on.

So it would have seemed that nothing had happened in the dull room, except the failing and increase of light, as the wind outside gathered or drove away the clouds. But none of the ladies heard much of what was being read, and none of them could look at the Queen, though they knew that her face was composed, and that her needle moved steadily.

August 31

In the last of the twilight a man came and knocked at the door of the parsonage at Marrick. Gib was in, sitting at his supper of bread and cheese, beans, and a salad of cresses and radishes.

The stranger said, "Friend, are you the parson of Marrick?"

Gib stowed half a radish in his cheek, and said that he was.

"Sir Gilbert Dawe?" the stranger persisted, and again Gib said "Aye—that's me."

The other man came in then. He was very dusty and hot, and brown as a nut; so brown that his hair and sandy beard were paler than his face. He shut the door, in spite of the warmth of the evening, and said, "Ned Tanner of York told me of you. He said you were of us, a 'known man.'"

Gib kissed him and sat him down to supper. When it was dark, and the old mother had gone to bed, they barred the door and the shutters, and lit a rushlight, and so together read a chapter from the Apocalypse in an English translation of the Scriptures that the stranger brought out from a pocket very cunningly hidden in the back of his pouch. It was a different translation from the one that Gib kept under the floor. The stranger made a twit of that one, saying that it was old and rude, and the one he had, much better. So they read in his.

> And the sun was as black as sackcloth made of hair, and the moon waxed red as blood, and the stars of heaven fell into the earth, even as a fig tree casteth her figs when she is shaken of a mighty wind. And all mountains and isles moved out of their places. And the Kings of the earth, and the great men, and the rich men, and the chief captains, and every bondman and every free man hid themselves in dens and rocks of the little hills.

The stranger stopped here to explain that King Henry was not such a King, for he was a noble Prince, and executor of the wrath of the Lamb upon wicked men and fools, such as those who believed that the bishop of Rome had any primacy among other bishops.

September 1

Next morning Gib saw him take the track across the fells toward Washfold while it was still barely light. Then he went back to the bed where they had slept together, but his thoughts followed Master Trudgeover; that was what the stranger had called himself, and though Gib did not believe that it was his real name, one name was as good as another. Gib thought with envy of him tramping through England empty almost as an animal of the care of worldly things, and full of the marvelous riches of the spirit; less a man than a trumpet to sound to judgment and to destruction of God's enemies. Here lay he, Gib Dawe, as eloquent, as fervent, as truly grounded in the truth, but shut up in the narrow dale to preach to clods, who thought small beer of him because he was a Marrick man born, and no stranger like Trudgeover. And besides being shut up in the narrow dale, he was shut up too in the parsonage, with an old woman and a dumb brat.

September 4

The Princess Mary sat at dinner in the royal house of Beaulieu in Essex. Only the Countess of Salisbury dined at the same table as the Princess; the other ladies, and those gentlemen who were not on duty carving or waiting, sat at a table nearer the door. They were cheerful enough, though subduing their voices out of respect for their betters, but the Princess sat silent, and the countess did not try to rally her. She herself knew what lay like a shadow across the girl's mind, for it darkened her own too as they waited for the news that might come any day now. But besides that, Master Hugh Pennington was serving at table, "and although he's a good youth," thought the countess, "and of gentle conditions, yet he has the most careless and chancy hand at waiting of them all." She fixed her eyes upon the plate he was setting down before the Princess: he had carved the pork well, cutting it finely without disturbing the almonds that were stuck all over the crackling. But the gravy, rich and full of raisins and spices, all but swam over the roped edge of the silver plate as he set it down. The countess breathed deeply in relief, and then because she saw the Princess's hands suddenly clutch upon the table, she looked up and forgot Hugh Pennington.

Mary was staring down the room to the door which was just closing. Now she turned to the countess.

"Madame, I saw Charles. I know I did. Send for him to come in. No. I'll not wait. At once."

The countess frowned, though not because it was unnatural in a girl of seventeen to be impatient for her mother's message. It was natural, and it would have been right, if things had not been so wholly and shamefully wrong. But as they were so wrong this royal child would have need of a fortitude greater than natural, and it had been the countess's aim, in the last unhappy years, to train her charge to such a self-command that nothing should shake her. The countess, herself of the old blood-royal, and of a masculine courage, had wished, during wakeful nights, that she could somehow give to the girl of her own strength; that could not be done, and now she doubted if there would be time for the Princess to acquire it from practice or precept, for she believed that the hour drew near.

She raised her hand, and told one of the servants to bring in the man Charles.

He came in, and knelt before the table opposite the Princess. When she asked him how the Queen did, he said, "Well," and no more. When she asked him, "had he a letter," he said, "No. No letter."

"Then," said the Princess, "what message?"

He glanced over his shoulder, and the countess too looked down the room. At her glance the ladies and gentlemen at the lower table turned quickly to their food again; David Lloyd, making music with two others, had just shaken out his recorder and now held it to his mouth again, his lips pursed to blow, but instead of blowing he only stared and listened. When he caught her eye he put the instrument so hastily to his mouth that it let out a faint, involuntary toot.

"The Queen's Grace," said Charles, in a voice too low for any but the Princess and the countess to hear, now that the music was playing again—"The Queen's Grace sent me to tell Your Grace that the Marchioness of Pembroke hath been brought to bed of a child."

"Man or woman?" It was the countess who asked the question.

"A girl."

"Ah!" Mary sighed, and they guessed how much she had dreaded to hear the other. But Charles said, "The heralds proclaimed the bastard 'Princess of Wales' at the cross in Cheap."

There was a silence in which only the gay warbling of the recorder and flutes made a fountain of bubbling sound. Then the Princess said, neither to the countess nor to her mother's servant, but to the food on her plate, "It may die." And then, "I have heard, and am persuaded, that it is not my father's child at all."

The countess said, "Hush!" though Charles was discreet as death, and no one else but herself could hear.

Mary looked at her with a little elderly, poisoned smile, which even the countess, good hater as she was, found shocking on so young a face.

September 6

Queen Anne lay propped up with pillows in the carved, painted, and gilded bed that had been brought from the King's Great Wardrobe for the occasion of the birth of the heir. The rings of the curtains, drawn wide apart now, were of silver gilt and ran along silver gilt rods. The hangings of the bed were of white and green brocaded velvet, and the counterpane which they had thrown over the bed for the King's visit was of cloth of gold. It lay very heavy upon the Queen, making her think of the leaden shrouds in which the dead are wound—the great dead, who lie in proud tombs—but as cold as any beggar. Her cheeks and eyes were still bright with fever, and fancies such as these, each of them tainted with horror, filled her mind with moving shadows. Beside her, upon a cushion of cloth of gold, lay the small tight shape of the one-day-old child, swaddled to the neck, and wearing a little tight cap exquisitely worked in silk. Between the swaddling bands and the cap, the puckered, querulous, aged face was of a dusky red.

There was a stir at the door, and one of her gentlemen announced the King. He came down the length of the chamber, tall and immensely broad in his puffed and slashed doublet of sanguine velvet, which to her fancy suddenly took on the likeness of raw, bloodied flesh, while the white satin that showed at the slashes was white bone. He came alone, having, by a motion of his hand, stayed those that were following him. The Queen's people, seeing this, also drew away. They stood in two groups, not mingling, hers by the hearth, his just inside the door.

But she was looking only at the King. He came on, his head a little bent, his shoulders swinging, till he stood beside the bed. He asked, courteously and formally, after her health. She said she did well. He said that he rejoiced therefor. She thanked him for his gracious visit. He said that she should command him in anything she wished. She replied that there was nothing she desired but only his gracious favor. That, he told her, she had, and promised that not only in the royal chapel, but in all churches and chantries, her welfare should be petitioned for. Then he went away.

Her ladies came back. They removed the heavy coverlet and laid over her instead one of velvet brocaded in a pattern of true lovers' knots and roses. One of them asked her, "Shall we leave with you this noble lady?" rocking in her arms the child who had wakened with a shrill, piping cry.

"No," said the Queen, "I shall sleep."

She shut her eyes so that they should think she slept. He had not touched, he had not once looked at the miserable little creature that had caused her all that wasted pain. She could, for the present at least, feel nothing but loathing for the girl who should have been a boy.

September 11

Dame Anne Ladyman had been to Grinton. As she climbed the stair to the prioress's chamber she wiped her hot face with a lappet of her veil, for the weather was like high summer, and anticipated with pleasure the long, cool drink of ale which, she confided, would soon be slipping down her throat as they two sat together, she resting her tired feet and retailing all her news—and today one piece of such laughable news.

But when she opened the door she knew that all her anticipation had been vain. Opposite Dame Christabel sat the prioress of St. Bernard's Ladies from down the river, as erect and as iron as the firedogs on the hearth.

The dale grudgingly credited Dame Euphemia with a kind of sanctity; for how could any woman so completely ignore every comfort of life unless she had at least some tincture of holiness? But if she were holy, she was not beloved. Those who might kept clear; those who must be about her endured with what philosophy they could muster. She marched through life, rigid, cheerless, dispensing gloom, and not even taking pleasure in that. The whole world lay under her condemnation; her nuns were soft indulgent creatures, yearning for worldly delights; laymen were close-fisted wretches, careless of the hardships of St. Bernard's poor ladies; her own house she grudged at for its poverty, Marrick Priory for its plumper endowments; her kin she condemned for proud men who believed that ancient and noble blood would save a man at the last tremendous day (which day was perhaps the one occasion to which she looked forward with any enthusiasm); those of lower degree than herself and her family she despised. She was of the few people who could, by means of sheer blind, bludgeoning, remorseless pride, set down Christabel Cowper, prioress of Marrick.

So now, when Dame Anne Ladyman came in, she found St. Bernard's Lady with her usual look of one who has tasted

verjuice; the prioress of Marrick was flushed, but maintained an
expression of smooth, controlled politeness.

Dame Anne found herself affected, as everyone else, by the visitor's temper. Some were struck silent by it; but she took refuge in
loud and rapid garrulity. So, while Dame Euphemia's deep and
burning eyes looked down her important nose, Dame Anne rattled through the heads of the less startling items of news which
she had gathered when in Grinton: how that the harvest was the
greatest that any could remember; that the wheelwright's wife
had twins; that one of the hinds who had sliced his leg reaping
was now doing well; that parson's rheumatism was better. Then,
breaking off, she tittered, and struck her hands together.

"And now, I'll tell you greater news than all these. I wager
you knew not, madame, that we have a holy woman among
us—one that sees visions of heavenly things."

When St. Bernard's Lady had arrived Dame Christabel had
been reading "The Death of the Duchess" in an old, beautifully
written copy of Geoffrey Chaucer's poems that had belonged to
her mother. She had seen how Dame Euphemia's eyes fastened
on it, yearning to know by the title what book it was that occupied the Marrick prioress's leisure, but unable to read it upside
down. Now, because she guessed what satisfaction Dame Anne's
loudness gave the other woman, she determined to flaunt her
own frivolity, ramming down the visitor's throat, as it were, the
worldliness of St. Benedict's nuns. So she laid the book on the
rushes at her feet, carefully disposed so that the title was easy

to read, and even, with a provocative smile, pushed it nearer to Dame Euphemia with her foot.

"No," she answered Dame Anne, "I know none such. A woman who sees visions?"

"And what will you say when I tell you that this same is our serving woman Malle?"

"By St. Eustace!" the prioress began, but then Dame Anne burst out laughing, her high trilling laugh which the prioress so hated. Nor would she stop, except to interrupt herself with such exclamations as, "The holy Malle. . . . Her feast will be All Fools' Day. . . . If she have a halo it will smoke like the kitchen fire. . . ."

"And what," asked Dame Euphemia, so suddenly and harshly that Dame Anne fairly jumped about to face her, "what hath this wench of yours seen—or says she hath seen?"

It was those last words, spoken in a tone which stripped the ladies of St. Benedict of any right to hope for heavenly favors, which gave the prioress of Marrick her cue. When Dame Anne's eyes came back to her she nodded. "Tell us," she said.

Dame Anne took a moment to recover, and then began, stumbling a little.

"I'd been to the mill, to ask if the young goslings we're to have are ready. They are ready and I told her—but that was after. Well, I'd come nigh to the bridge and there I saw Malle, among a crowd of idlers and children, staring into the Blackburnes' yard.

"There's a wedding there this day," she added, with a side-long smile.

The prioress knew that smile well. "So I heard." She was curt.

But it took more than a tone of voice to shoulder Dame Anne off from the subject of a wedding.

"A bonny, bouncing lass, that one of Chris Blackburne's, but I'll warrant that when she goes to bed with a man this eve it won't be for the first time."

The prioress did no more than raise her eyebrows at that, and Dame Anne went on, with story and supposition, things seen by this or that one of the servants on summer nights or at winter ales. The prioress of St. Bernard sat with her eyes cast down in a dangerous stillness, which Dame Anne missed but the prioress did not.

"Well, there was that fool peeking and peering in." Dame Anne stood half crouching, her hands on her bent knees, and swung her head from side to side with goggling eyes and mouth open. "Like that," said she, and laughed.

"So I called to her, to have her away—wasting her time, the idle slut! She came to me, but then she caught my sleeve in her dirty hands, crying out, 'He's there within.' 'And who?' says I, very short with her, and, 'Get you back to Marrick at once,' says I.

"But she had me by the arm dragging me toward the gate and I could not but go. 'Look,' quod she, 'here they come again to the well to draw water for the wine.' 'Fie,' quod I, 'Goodman Blackburne won't have wine at the wedding, even with water in it. Wine's for gentles.'

"But she says, not listening to me but staring in at the window, and speaking very quiet, 'I can't hear his voice for all that din they make. They are so merry to have among them the King of Heaven. But when he comes out we shall see him.'

"'The King of Heaven,' quod I, and I boxed her ears soundly and bade her not be a fool, and she cried and whimpered a deal, but I said, 'Off with you to the mill, and bring those goslings back to the priory' (for the miller's wife had told me they were ready for the fetching). 'And if you linger,' says I, 'you'll be beaten.'"

"Madame," said Dame Euphemia to the prioress of Marrick, ignoring Dame Anne as completely as she ignored a bluebottle which swung about the room, "Madame, will you suffer such idle talk? It were strange that such a one as a serving woman—" she paused, and added, "of your house" (meaning clearly "of any house but mine") "should see such holy things."

The prioress of Marrick did not even look in her direction.

"Tell me," she said to Dame Anne, "did she see a light, hear heavenly music, fall into a trance?"

Dame Anne stared. "Lord," she cried, "it cannot be that you believe—? Why, she's mad as a goose. I asked her why she should think to see our blessed Lord at Grinton, and in Chris Blackburne's house. Quod she, 'He went to a wedding. And I saw the light shine.'"

The prioress bent her head, crossed herself, and said, "*Benedicite.*"

That brought Dame Euphemia to her feet.

"What! Should our Savior come to the house of a plain yeoman, nor no good sober man neither, but a lousy, upstart, swilling fellow—"

"We read that he went about," said the prioress with smooth satisfaction, "among common folk."

Dame Euphemia gulped. It was true. Yet she was sure that if those had been common folk they had been so in a different way from the people of the dale. That impropriety, however, was not the worst of it. She could have borne that a vision should have been seen in the Blackburnes' house if only it had not been a Marrick serving wench that had seen it. For a moment the outrage held her dumb, and into the silence Dame Anne let forth another of her high trilling laughs.

"'Light?' quod I. 'What light? Why,' quod I, 'what you saw was the sun dazzle on a pewter plate on a shelf within.'"

The prioress of Marrick rose.

"It may be so," she said, very stately and judicial. "I shall look into this. I shall question this woman. If God in his grace hath favored our poor house with a very holy thing, the world shall know that it is no feigned vision, no trumped-up relic that we claim to have received."

Dame Euphemia stood up; her white cheeks were patched with red. That matter of the horse harness, or the belt of St. Maura, whichever it might have been, lay years behind; it should have been by this time forgotten. Now she knew it would never be forgotten.

She moved to the door. The prioress opened it for her. The two religious ladies kissed, cheek laid not very near to cheek, and lips sucked in to make a noise like young chickens cheeping.

"God," said Dame Euphemia over her shoulder, "God grant this holy vision may be for your comfort. Yet remember, if you mell in such matters, that the nun of Kent is sent for to be questioned of treason."

St. Bernard's Lady went out; she was defeated, but a scorpion's sting is in its tail. The prioress of Marrick might give no sign. She might not even know that she had been touched. But soon she would know.

For a while after the visitor and Dame Anne had left her, Dame Christabel leaned at the window, her hands on the warmed stone of the sill, and looked out, not up the drowsy, blue-misted dale, but at things closer at hand. That patch of new slate in the stable roof; it had cost what she could ill spare. A man led in two horses from the field and brought them to the trough in the court below; he leaned against the rough quarter of one of them as they drank with long breathings and gurgling noises. She herself had bought that near horse at a great price; he was from Jervaulx where the monks breed the best horses of the North; but good beasts are costly.

If only the house might become a place where men came to pay honor to God, for the sake of its particular holiness, then, she thought—but her thought was no more than the clear sight, in her mind, of the last page in the priory accounts.

Her eye was caught by someone moving slowly through the fields from the direction of Grinton. It was Malle, driving the young geese before her with a long lissom willow switch.

"Now," said Christabel Cowper to herself, "I must have her in, and question her."

But even as she thought that, she shut the window and turned away, knowing that she would not question the woman, for least said about this matter of visions, soonest mended. She sat in her chair by the hearth, and bit her fingers. It seemed to her most unjust that when this hope of prosperity and honor was offered to the house, for caution's sake it must be allowed to go by. Better safe than sorry, but the necessity galled her soul; the more so because she felt, though illogically, that it was Dame Euphemia who stood between Marrick and the pleasant prospect of gainful holiness.

October 10

At breakfast Sir John Bulmer swore at the mutton pie for being mutton pie again, and then sat eating it savagely, leaning his head on his hand so that he should not see his wife's face, because her mouth, with the black moustache along the upper lip, was shaking, and now and again jerked down at the corners before she could steady it. That Dame Anne looked ridiculous in her grief, as fifteen stone and forty-five years old must look ridiculous, made Sir John yet more angry.

He had a right to be angry, he thought, stabbing a bit of the pie with his knife so fiercely that the point grated on the pewter plate. For while the eldest son had been at home Sir John had not ridden to Pinchinthorpe for more than a couple of nights at a time—or only when the boy was away at Settrington, hunting with his mother's nephews, the Bigods. But now that the lad had gone to London to keep his first term at Gray's Inn, why should not his father stay a while at his own Manor of Pinchinthorpe? Must not a man see to his lands and farms? And what right had a man's wife to suppose that he was tiring of his bawd, just because he was too nicely considerate of his eldest son to linger with her when the lad was at home? And again what right had she, when after so long he went once more to his bawd, to snivel over her buttered eggs at breakfast time?

To show that he was at ease in his conscience he told young Rafe Bigod, his wife's younger nephew, who was staying with them, a very merry story that had been going round the taverns of London last spring. He himself laughed at it loudly, and Rafe laughed feebly, crimson to his ears, and never raising his eyes from his plate. "Tchah!" thought Sir John. "Mincing young fool!" and included Rafe in his anger. "If he dared," he thought, "he'd chide me for his aunt's sake, but he daren't, and so he chafes and frets."

He finished his ale and a dish of fried eggs, and then stood up in the midst of a company grown suddenly silent.

"Tell them to bring the horses. I'll ride the Blackbird today," he said to the servants.

He made himself look at his wife. She had both hands laid flat on the table, and bent forward with her head lowered like someone who is preparing to speak. But she was silent.

"I'm riding to Whitby," he said, more loudly than he meant. "D'you want aught?"

She jerked up her head. "No. Yes. Oh, sir! the herrings," and began to cry openly.

"God rot the herrings!" He stamped out.

Young Rafe Bigod leaned at the door of the hall when Sir John had ridden away, and the household was busy about its ordinary tasks. The autumn sunshine fell pleasantly on his face, but Rafe's look was black. He wriggled his shoulders in his over-fine green hunting coat, and knew that he was a gawky lad, with a fair skin that flushed as easily as a girl's. He knew too that he did not dare rebuke Sir John for his own aunt's sake, and that he had not dared even rebuke him for a bawdy story, by silence, and a stern, unsmiling face.

He turned to find Dame Anne beside him. She did not look at him as she spoke, but her voice and her lips were quite steady.

"Rafe," said she, "I go to Pinchinthorpe. Will you go with me?"

He gaped at her. "Pinchinthorpe? For why?"

"I must," she said, "look on her." She added quickly, before he could speak, "And I need a—a kinsman with me."

That made him feel a man. "I'll come," he said grandly; and awkwardly, but with honest feeling, he caught and kissed her hand.

Pinchinthorpe was a very different place from the empty and deserted house to which Sir John had brought Margaret in the autumn. The little green court was shorn and neat; the brambles had been grubbed up, and by the hall door Meg's hawk sat on a perch in the sun. Inside there was change too. There were painted hangings all round the wall, and in the parlor two new chairs with cushions. The little elm cupboard now held a salt of silver, two silver cups, a couple of bowls, and three silver spoons. On top of it sat Meg's regals, and under-neath it her lute.

It was all very trim, and on a morning like this with the sun shining in, a pleasant place, but the house in which Margaret

Cheyne lived was like a house without doors and windows, through which a high wind blew. The wind could be warm, or shrewdly biting, but it was never still.

This morning the wind blew fair. Meg had ridden out before breakfast, and come back glowing; after breakfast she played in the yard with a litter of pups, was in and out of the kitchens and dairy pretending to be a good housewife, pulled out all her gowns from the presses saying she would make ready against the time when Sir John would take her to York and she would want to go gay. She had soon tired of that, and now July, in the old orchard, could hear her singing about the house.

The old orchard was still waiting to be tidied up, and remained a pleasant wilderness, and a refuge for July, who withdrew here when she wanted to be quiet and to feel safe. It lay tucked under the wall of the house, so close that she could hear if she was called and hurry in, but so well screened by trailing clumps of bramble and the crowded old apple trees, that she was out of sight, and, with luck, might thus be out of mind.

Today the late apples, high up and already warmed in the sun, smelt sweet, and the brambles were coloring, scarlet, yellow, and purple red; they and the grass alike were soaked in a foggy dew, for the sun had not yet reached them, so that the grass looked as gray as if hoar frost had touched it.

July picked up a windfall apple and went down the little twisting path that led to the gate; there had been a moat all round the house at one time, but this side was dry, and planks had been laid across so that people coming from Pinchinthorpe village might take this shortcut instead of going round by the road.

July stood on the second bar of the gate, clutched the top with her elbows, and began to eat her apple. From here she could see one of the big fields of the village, pale where the stubble yet stood, but with brown ridges of plowed land spreading over it. Four of the eight ox teams were working there now; one was so near that she could hear the creak of the yokes as the oxen plodded by. Gulls, swinging in the sunshine and dropping lower, settled on the new furrows, followed by crowds of smaller birds; above, the blue sky was stately with white clouds sailing.

Then from beyond the sandy bank below the pines, round which the road ran, two riders came—a man and a woman. That was all that July could tell at first, but as they drew nearer she could see that the woman was huge; a vast bulk in a flowing plum-colored cloak; the man was not so much a man as a boy, thin and angular, with straight fair hair and a cheek of as pretty a color almost as Meg's own. July stared, wondering who they were, and where were their servants, for they were not the kind of people who should have been riding unattended.

She was so lost in the security of her solitude, that she was still hanging over the gate when they drew abreast. Only, for shyness, she dropped her eyes, and bit deep into the apple. Then she looked up because they had halted.

"That's no Pinchinthorpe lass," said the lady.

"But she's no more than a child," said the boy.

The lady pushed her big brown horse close to the gate. July, looking up at her, thought that she had never seen anyone so bulky; she wished she had run away before they had come near.

"Are you," the lady asked, in a voice astonishingly high and harsh for one of her comfortable looks—"Are you Sir John's strumpet?"

July felt her face grow cold. She knew now who the lady was. "No," she mumbled.

"Then who are you?"

It had come to pass, that which July had dreaded. Here was Dame Anne Bulmer, who had for distant kinsman Robert Aske. And here, at Pinchinthorpe, were Meg, Sir John's strumpet, and July, Meg's sister.

She said, "I am her sister," and felt the blood flow up into her cold cheeks until she burned visibly with her shame.

There was a long silence which seemed to her worse than anything, and then Dame Anne said, "Poor child, you should not be in such a house. You—I have a mind to carry you—" She stopped. July was staring at her. She hesitated and then said again, but as if she had intended other words, "No, indeed you should not be here." And then hastily to the young man, "Come, Rafe."

She rode on, but he lingered.

"Is—she—within?" he asked July, in a low voice, and July believed that he would have been glad to hear that Meg was not.

It came to her suddenly that they must not go in to Meg.

"No," she cried. "No. She rode out. Do not go in."

The young man shook his head; clearly he wanted to believe her but could not. "We'll do her no harm," he said loftily, and went on after the lady.

July clung to the gate watching them out of sight. "Harm?" Those two gentle, good people—she knew that they were gentle and good, it was written all over them—those two, so kind and so defenseless, were going to see Meg. And Meg, impossible to bind as a fish or a flame, cold as the one and cruel as the other, Meg, who could stab with words, would be as cruel to them as she knew how.

The nearest of the plow teams passed and repassed twice before July moved from the gate. Something new had come into her mind, so new that time was needed to consider and accept it. Meg and she were separable. All her life till now July had counted them inseparable, but Dame Anne had separated them easily, with a few words. It was a great thought that made July feel free, as though she had passed over a threshold, and come out from a close room into open day.

She went back at last up the little slope of the orchard, into the old postern, and along the passage that led to the yard. But she stopped before she came out into the sunshine. The young man and Dame Anne had not yet gone. He was just now heaving up the great bulk of the lady into the saddle. At the wellhead some of the Pinchinthorpe servants stood and tittered, and July heard Meg's laughter, musical and wild; she must be watching from the door of the hall.

For the first time in her life July was aware that she hated Meg.

November 3

Most of the ladies of Princess Mary's household were gathered about the big fire when she came in; they drew back, leaving place for her, but she only bowed her head in her shy, awkward way, and hurried through the room. But Mistress Mary Brown, who had followed her, told them that, "My Lady's Grace has a letter from the Queen," which silenced their talking and laughing for a few minutes, and made more than one of them stare at the door which the Princess had shut behind her.

It was dusk when the Countess of Salisbury came into the Princess's chamber, for she had been out riding. She saw Mary stand, a dark shape at the narrow, deep-set window, for this was not the pleasant house at Beaulieu, but the Castle of Hertford; the King had given Beaulieu to Queen Anne's brother, and had sent his daughter here.

Mary turned, saw the countess with a candle in her hand, and turned back to the window. But she spoke, jerking the words out as though she could manage only a few at a time.

"A letter—from my mother—and a message for you. Read it." She stuck out a hand behind her, and the countess took the letter from it and read.

> Daughter,
>
> I hear such tidings today that I do perceive, if it be true, the time is come that almighty God will prove you, and I am very glad of it.

She read on, the delicate proud stillness of her face untroubled, though many would have wept at the courage and nobility and tenderness of the letter. She came near to the end before she found any message for herself.

And now you shall begin, and by likelihood I shall follow. I set not a rush by it; for when they have done the uttermost they can, then I am sure of amendment. I pray you recommend me unto my good Lady of Salisbury, and pray her have a good heart, for we never come to the kingdom of heaven but by trouble. Daughter, wheresoever you be come, take no pains to send to me, for if I may I will send to you. By your loving mother, Katherine the Queen.

"What," asked the countess, "does it mean?" She guessed that some message must have come with the letter.

"That my father will send me to the household of the bastard."

The countess was silent.

"I am," said Mary, "to be one of her waiting women." Her voice was steady, but, as she spoke out of the shadows, it had no more body than if a shadow had been speaking.

"His Grace," she went on, "is persuaded that you—that my people—encourage me to resist his will, calling myself Princess of Wales."

"By God's Death! so we do, and so we shall."

Mary went on to the end of what she must say. "Therefore I am to go alone."

This time the countess did not use any oath. She stood silent, and without movement, except that she turned the letter over and over in her fingers. She was a woman very strong in silence; therefore till she had resolved what to say she would not speak. The thing might not be true; but she could not say that, lest it should be true. She could not say, "Poor child," because this child had been born too high for pity. She decided upon something that must be said, and, taking the Princess hard by the wrist, she spoke at last.

"You must fear nothing, and you must yield nothing."

Now that she touched Mary she knew that the girl was shaking, but she only tightened her hold.

"In Her Grace's letter one thing is most true and most grave—"

"That I should obey my father?"

"That, of course." But it was not of that the countess wished to speak, nor of those little tender trifles of advice, such as that the girl should keep her own keys if there were need, or recreate herself on her lute and virginals, if they allowed her to have any. "No," said the countess, "but it is 'that you should keep your heart with a chaste mind, not thinking or desiring any husband.'"

"Yes," said Mary, "yes," but the countess knew that she turned her head away.

"What?" she thought. "Not yet! She cannot favor any yet!"

She ran over in her mind all the men, young or not so young, here or at Beaulieu. Of preference toward any of them the girl had given no sign, and yet the countess guessed rather than knew that she was one who would need greatly to love.

She said, because she must somehow find out what the averted face meant, "It is of course fitting that Your Grace should be married before long. But you cannot regret any of those betrothed to you by this treaty or that. The Emperor— you only saw him once, the Dauphin—never."

"No."

"Then," said the countess, and let the girl's wrist drop. Mary turned away and leaned her hands on the stone sill, staring out into the garden which she could not now see.

"It is not any man. But I have thought of children—of a child—a little boy best," she said in a whisper.

The countess went away across the room till she stood beside the bed. She laid her hand on one of the curtains, and stared at it as though she learnt the pattern by heart.

"Your Grace," she said at last, "Your Grace must put away such thoughts."

When Mary was silent she added, "For the love that you do owe to God."

"To God—" said Mary.

"And to your mother, the Queen."

"To my . . ." the girl began, and then hurriedly—"Go. Leave me. Yes. I will be alone."

1534

January 1

Dame Anne Bulmer sat for a long time in front of her mirror, though not because she took thought for what she saw in it. She sat there because she needed time to be quiet, and once the mistress of the house launches herself upon the day she has little hope of quiet, especially during the Twelve Days of Christmas, when the house is full of company, and every meal is a feast. So when her woman had pinned in place the red velvet, looped-up hood, with its gable-shaped frame of gold wire and little pearls to lift it from the face; and had put round Dame Anne's neck a chain with a ruby hanging from it, and a shorter chain that carried a little gold case in which was a hair of St. John of Beverley; and had clasped the gilt and enamel girdle with its swinging pomander ball, Dame Anne told her to go, and sat still in the cold room. The bed, in which she had slept alone, was disordered; a thin mist crept through the window shutters, so that the candles burnt in a haze. The huge, heavy woman, with her square, swarthy face, sat still, leaning her elbows on the arms of the chair and staring straight in front of her; you would have said that she thought of the bread, beef, or beer needed in the kitchen, or of subtleties for the master's table; but it was not so. She had put all thoughts of these out of her mind and now she meditated upon Calvary.

When her nephew Rafe knocked and came in she turned her face slowly toward him, and smiled. Rafe being, as she was, a Bigod, neither missed nor misunderstood the beauty of the smile, but it made him angrier, and more determined to say all that he had come to say.

She let him go through with it, listening patiently, not look-ing at him, but now and again moving the powder box on the hutch in front of her, or the comb or the nightcap, in her slow heavy way. And when he had finished she took her time before she answered him.

"I bear it because it is that which our Savior has laid upon me to bear, and—"

"But it dishonors us—it dishonors you and Frank and me—that he should have brought his bawd into this house."

She shook her head, rebuking him for the interruption, and finished, "and so I follow him, though a long way off, and halting."

"God's Death!" cried Rafe, in a hot rage, but when she hushed him he was ashamed, for he understood her, since he shared with her, and with his elder brother, that same quality which made some call them the mad Bigods—as if a lute string had been tuned to a note too high for ordinary ears.

Dame Anne lumbered up, like a cow rising in the meadow; she laid her hand for an instant along his cheek, meaning that the touch should speak for her, and it did. Rafe caught her hand to kiss it, and muttered, "Then we can suffer it too," while the blood ran up, bright as a girl's, to his hair.

"And now, nephew," Dame Anne said, going away from him to a chest at the foot of the bed, "you shall do an errand for me, if you will."

He said he would, and willingly, but when she told him what it was he was astonished and reluctant.

"Yea, yea," he cried impatiently, "I can see that it is not the child's fault that her sister is a bawd, but that you should send her a New Year's gift—it seems—it seems—"

Dame Anne came back and laid on his knee a little gay bunch of ribbon points.

"Give them to her and bid her Merry Christmas. I chose them of bright colors such as children love." She went away from him, her heavy crimson gown hissing over the rushes. "Rafe," she said, not turning to him, but fingering the dribbled wax that had run down the side of a candle, "Rafe, she is not like a child, that poor little maid. I have watched her since—they came. None of the servants will speak with her, not one. And the lads tease her. One of them threw a dead cat at her. She didn't cry out, or run, like a child. But she went past me, white as a ghost, and her eyes cast back like a hare's when the dogs are close. A child should not look so."

"Oh!" said Rafe. "Well, I'll give it to her," and he went out.

July was hovering at the kitchen door, looking and smelling. Inside the cooks ran about very hurried and hot, yet today never out of temper, and always with time enough to change jokes with any of the guests' servants who sat along a bench, each man dandling a cup of ale. On the long spits at the fire there were rows of small birds, as well as capons and partridges, which whirled slowly this way, then that way as the scullion boy turned the wheel. Below them on a bigger spit were rounds of beef, and a young pig, cut off at its middle and joined to the body of a fat goose. All these things hissed and spat, and smelt most toothsome. There were piles of mince pies on the table, and veal collops waiting for their sauce, and eggs, saffron, raisins of the sun, half a sugar loaf, and a lot of little bottles of spices waiting to flavor the sauces: from the pastry came the sweet scent of pies and tarts baking. July's mouth watered, and then someone came up behind her and touched her arm, and she jumped round and away in the same movement.

"Mistress," said Rafe, "I am to bid you Merry Christmas and to pray you have this gift from my Lady Anne."

July looked at the little bunch of bright ribbons, and Rafe looked at her and saw what Dame Anne had seen, a child too young to have the right to that look of fear with which she had sprung from him. He was not only a Bigod, but also very young, and his mood changed in less than a breath from condemnation and disgust, to pity and rage for her sake. In the perturbation and enthusiasm of his feelings he cast the distance of the five years that were between them, and spoke like a boy of her own age.

"Mistress July," he said, "have you seen that room where they found the bones of the man long dead, with gold pieces between his fingers?"

"Oh!" she whispered. "No!"

"Shall I show it to you?"

"Oh!—Yes!"

The little room he led her to was in the oldest part of the house, and Rafe pointed out the arched doorway which had been walled up and forgotten for many years. The room beyond was small, and even by day almost dark, because there was nothing to light it but a slot window, set high up in one wall. Rafe had to make a light and set it to a candle that stood on the heavy table. Besides the table there was only a trussing bed, a small iron-bound coffer, a few old swords in one corner, and a mousetrap in another.

But here, at the table, Rafe said, they had once found a dead man, or at least his bones. The bones had been dressed in a gown of red silk such as came from Cathay, with patterns on it like feathers; a heavy belt had hung sagging about the thigh bones, made of square gilt bosses of goldsmith's work and a precious stone in each square. On the table the dry white finger-bones had clutched gold pieces of more than a hundred years ago.

July shuddered with a not unpleasant horror. She was indeed so warm with happiness that even the terror of a dead man could not chill her. Dame Anne had forgiven her for being Meg's sister.

She sat down beside Master Rafe Bigod upon the bed. She was shy of him now, and would look nowhere but at the pretty ribbons as she turned them about her fingers. He, though she could not have supposed it of one so old and important, was shy too; his long sensitive face was bright with embarrassed color. There were, he was discovering, so few things that he could say to her, seeing that she was Meg Cheyne's sister. He wished, with passion, that he had not brought her here, then remembered his motive, and thereby found a topic which was not forbidden.

"Mistress July," he broke out abruptly on the silence, "you should thank God that has given you license to live in this time, for the Gospel of Christ was never so truly preached as it is now."

She looked up at him, startled and quite uncomprehending, and in the blankness of her surprise he read her need of instruction. He lost his shyness, and began to talk eagerly, looking at her, or beyond her, but always with a strange lit look, as though the things he spoke of were bright as a colored sunset. July did not miss that look, but could not guess what caused it; he was telling her that the Mass was nothing, priest nothing, the pope nothing, our Lady nothing. Such a sweeping elimination left her disturbed and a little shocked, but not otherwise moved, for these matters were not such as she was used to give much thought to.

Yet when he told her to come to the little room again tomorrow she promised him that she would.

"I'll read to you in a book I have. It is a godly book called *The Prick of Conscience*."

July did not find the title promising, but Rafe was Dame Anne's nephew, and he and his aunt were the only people in the world—that she could remember—who treated her as herself, and not as Meg's sister.

January 5

July came back to Meg's room in the dusk. There was a little table near the fire set for two—that meant Sir John Bulmer would be coming to sup with Meg. Two boys with viols, and a flute player, whom Sir John had sent up, were tuning and trying their instruments, and even now the little fat lad, whom Sir John had given Meg for a page, was on his knee before her with a bowl of water, and the towel for her hands laid ready over his shoulder.

July had hoped to slip in unnoticed, but Meg saw her directly, and called, "Sister! Sister!"

July went near, till she stood behind the kneeling page, who turned his round apple-blossom face and blue eyes to stare at her; the women stared too, and July's heart sank as she curtseyed.

"And where," asked Meg, with her wild laughing glance that took in all the room, "where have you come from, creeping in so quiet as a nun?"

July looked at her with her dark, unchildish look, but was silent.

"Marry!" Meg lifted her fingertips from the water, and, laughing, splashed a few drops in July's face. "Marry! Mistress Sly, but I know, and I'll tell you—where, and who, and what. And when too—and when is today and every day of this New Year."

She told them also, truly enough, where and who, but when she began to tell what, July, whose face had changed from burning to white, stopped her.

"We did not—he did not—I sat beside him on the bed, but—"

The women so screeched with laughter that she stopped. Meg laughed too. "What then did he—and thou—and the pair of you if you did not that?"

"He talked to me—of—of—he said the Mass was but a May game."

They cried "Fie! Fie!" but they laughed again, perhaps believing her, for all knew the two young Bigods for the maddest heretics, yet teasing her. At last, hearing Sir John on the stairs, Meg hushed them. "Not a word more. But," she whispered before the door opened, "next time perhaps there'll be a different tale to tell, for even godly young men may wax wanton at Christmastime."

That night July lay long awake. Meg's two women lay in the same room; one snored steadily; the other muttered now and again in her sleep. Outside the wind had risen; it moved like a great beast in the valley; sometimes by the sound it seemed to turn over and over and thrash about with its tail; sometimes it passed roaring by.

July, cold and very unhappy, listened, trying to resolve what she must do. If she went not to the little room tomorrow Master Rafe would think her ungrateful. If she went—Meg had so soiled her with the words she used that July believed he would see it in her face. Besides, it seemed that Meg had soiled him too.

The wind flung drumming showers against the window; after that there was a steady hush of rain as the wind ebbed; at last came the empty silence which wind and rain had left behind them, and in which snow began to fall. July slept. She had made up her mind that she could not bear to go.

January 6

It was nearly suppertime and already dark. July had sat all afternoon and evening industriously sewing, or obligingly singing, according as Meg desired silence or music. Now she began to believe that the day would pass safely, and perhaps tomorrow would take Master Rafe hunting, and the day after that—but she would go no further than today.

Then the hue and cry began after Pourquoi, Meg's little dog, who had a French name because he had been brought from Calais, and who was very dear to his mistress. They sought everywhere, under beds, on beds, in the attics, and at last Meg said that July and the women should go round and about the castle and even through the yards and outbuildings, carrying lights and whistling and calling for Pourquoi.

So July went, but would in no wise part from the elder of the two women, though Gill had bidded her several times, "Go seek you in that direction and I'll go in this." "No! No!" July would say. "Let us go together."

They were crossing a little yard between the old spicery and the carpenter's shop, when two gentlemen with a lantern came out of one of the buildings. At the sight of July and Gill standing in the midst calling, "Pourquoi! Pourquoi!" the shorter and stouter of these raised a laugh and a shout.

"Mass!" he cried, coming swaggering over to them. "What's here? Bring the light, Rafe." Gill, giggling delightedly, would have boxed his ears; he caught her by the wrists, laughing, then swearing, then silent, because she was a strong wench and bold. They struggled together, in a violent, unseemly fashion that grew more and more ugly, until his foot slipped in the trodden snow of the yard, and then he stumbled and loosed her. She fled, but when he had recovered he was after her. The other two heard her scream, heard him laugh, and then there was silence, and they stood alone in the little yard, Rafe Bulmer still stupidly holding aloft the lantern that the other had bidden him bring near.

By its light July could see that he was dressed very fine in brocade the color of ripening corn; she saw too that his face was flushed and loosened with wine.

He looked down at her. After what they had just seen her shrinking was a provocation. He remembered also that her sister was John Bulmer's bawd.

"I—I seek my sister's little dog," she said breathlessly, hoping to fend off with words that which Meg loved to angle for.

"Why did you not come to the little chamber this forenoon?" he asked. When she only shook her head, "Nay. You shall tell me," he persisted.

Her eyes, avoiding his, were caught by the gleam of the jewels in his cap. She tried, faintly and clumsily, to fence with him.

"What is that pretty thing?"

"What thing?"

"In your cap."

He pulled off his cap and looked at the little gold and jeweled brooch.

"Leda and her swan," he told her, and met her eyes and saw them flinch. "No, by the Mass," he thought, "she's no innocent."

He was sure of it when she persisted, with a smile he took for brazen, "Who—who was she?"

"I'll tell you the story. Come up with me to the little room."

She went, dumb and helpless. She was helpless because he was Dame Anne's nephew—one of the good people, quite different from Meg. She knew that he was so, therefore if she said she would not go, she could not tell him why. Indeed there was no reason, for surely there could be nothing to fear. Yet she shook with fear.

There was a little stair leading up from the old spicery into the ancient part of the castle. They climbed up it, by the light of Rafe's lantern, July going first, he coming after with his hand on her all the time.

❖

Dame Anne had gone down to speak to the clerk of the kitchen because when Sir John had called for figs to eat at the fireside in the great chamber, where he and his guests sat together talking and telling stories, and singing now and again, the clerk of the kitchen had sent back word that there were no figs.

So Dame Anne went down, found the clerk and took him with her to look; she moved about in the dark corners of the storeroom, while he carried a torch after her.

"I know there was a coppet of figs," she muttered. "I know it was not opened. What is that?"

"A coppet of great raisins, madame."

"I know," she repeated, dogged and distressed, "that there is a coppet of figs." Then she turned, to tell him to bring the torch nearer, and saw that he had backed a little away, and was staring out along the little passage, staring and smiling. She did not like the smile.

"What is it?" she demanded.

"Madame, nothing." He was grave at once, and came near again with the torch.

She went to the door and looked out.

"There is no one there." Her mind returned to the figs. Sir John was displeased that they were lacking, displeased too that she had come to look for them. He would be more displeased still if she were away long. She turned again into the stillroom, and as she turned remembered the little dim room along the passage. She guessed what sort of thing it was that the clerk had seen, and was angry.

"Did you," she asked him, "see someone go into the chamber there?"

He hesitated, and she stamped her foot.

"You did? Who? Who?"

He mumbled something about Christmas.

"And you think the men and wenches have license to be wanton because it is a holy feast. But I'll not have it. Not in my—" she stopped short because it came back into her mind with a new shame and desolation that her own husband thought he had license to be wanton, in her house. But though she flushed a hot, ugly red before the man's face she did not turn away.

"Go and knock on the door," she told him. "Bid them come out."

"Madame," he said, hastily and confusedly, "let alone. It is nothing. They have come here each day," he added, as if that made it better.

She went out of the stillroom, and he came behind her, half sorry, half relishing the humor of it. When she had thumped on the door and flung it open he was at her shoulder, peering in.

But Dame Anne did not let him stay, and when she had driven him off she sent Rafe also away. He, who had never before seen his aunt angry, was frightened by her. He tried to hold his ground, tried to assure her lightly that a few kisses were all; all he intended, all he'd got, and that they were nothing. "There was no more." He turned to July for her to confirm that, but she had her hands still over her face, and they could see her whole body shake.

He shouted at her, suddenly angry.

"As if you knew naught of such things. As if you had never seen, nor heard—you with a sister who—"

He went then because Dame Anne said, "Go," and he dared not linger. She shut the door behind him, and then she turned and spoke to July. She had suffered her husband to bring his bawd to the house where she lived. She would not suffer that another of that corrupt blood should befoul Rafe—Rafe who was almost more her own than her own boys, being Bigod as she herself was Bigod. She proceeded, slowly and implacably, to maul July with words. If she could have killed with words, she would have killed.

January 8

Lord Darcy had with him his steward, Thomas Strangways, who had just reached London. They had turned their backs on the table, littered with papers, pens and ink, rolls of accounts, and the sheepskin pouches that held wax, seals, laces, scissors, and all the things needed for letters or chirographs. Now they sat side by side on the settle before the fire, with a dish of winter apples between them, exchanging news of the North for news of London where doings were greater and graver.

Strangways listened while Darcy talked, rasping his forefinger down the bristles of his hard weather-beaten cheek. He was a man of a few years younger than Darcy, with a look open, choleric, and bold. They had been good friends ever since the days when Darcy had been captain of Berwick Castle and Strangways gentleman porter of the city.

"And so," said my lord, "this Parliament is set to do fine things, at the King's bidding. For the King will make bishops now, and is head of the church, and not the pope."

"That," said Strangways, "he cannot be. How can a secular man be head of the church? Will he be head of all Christendom?" His face was flushed up to his hair by the heat of the fire or by indignation.

"Not of all Christendom, but of the church in England only."

"But there's no more than one Church Catholic." When Darcy let that go in silence Strangways muttered, "Will this thing be suffered?" and a little later, "If man will not, then shall we surely see God himself take a hand."

"There was—" Darcy spoke at last, "this nun in Kent with her visions that the King should not live, but he has lived, and she and those that trusted her are like to die instead. Soon there will be a bill brought in to attaint them."

He looked sideways at Strangways as if uncertain whether to say more or hold his tongue. Then he said:

"I did myself, with many others, think that God might speak by that poor soul. If it had been so—" He broke off. "When I was a younger man than I am now, I took upon me a Crusade." Again he glanced at Strangways, sharply, as if with suspicion. "But in this matter I know not—I know not—" he muttered.

Strangways shook his head heavily. He said that there was a woman that they talked of in Swaledale at a priory there, that had seen a vision of late. Or so it was said in those parts.

Darcy swung round at him. Who was she, this woman? Nun or no? Who had told Strangways of her? Was she known for a person of holy life? Last of all he asked, "What was it then that she saw?"

Strangways said that it was a showing of shepherds and angels on Christmas Eve.

"How? Tell me as you heard it."

Strangways crossed his legs, and picking up an apple from the dish dandled it in his palm as he talked. The woman had seen—no, had heard, and partly by starlight seen—said she had heard and seen the blessed shepherds go by as she looked out at a little low window; they were going to find the Holy Child. And she said also that she had heard the angels sing that same night, though the words they sang she could not rehearse, "being a simple creature, as I was told."

"Go on," said my lord.

"The fellow told me that the woman said, 'It was deep, deep dark, smelling of frost, with stars by the thousand. I heard them laugh and shout, and their dogs bark.' And she says, 'The shepherds sang "Ut hoy," and "Tirly Tirlow."'"

"And the singing of the angels?"

"That was after."

"She saw them?"

"They say, no. She said, 'I saw them not, for I suppose they had put out all the lights of heaven and set open the windows that they might see him in the stable low down in the dale.' She spoke much of peace also, so they say." Strangways pulled down the corners of his mouth and shook his head, but sadly.

"It will serve," said Lord Darcy, and he laughed softly.

Strangways turned and stared. The old lord had his chin on his fist, gazing into the fire. As he sat there with his fine features, proud head, and hair warmed again to gold by the light of the fire, he looked almost a young man.

"You cannot," said Strangways, "give the tale credit! Why! Shall she not have heard some fellows go singing by to the ale-house. And as to the angels, what of the ladies at their Matins and Lauds?"

"Many will credit it," said Darcy. "Shall I tell you for why? Listen then. This nun of Kent saw, or said she saw, devils whispering Queen Anne Boleyn in the ear; and when the cardinal died, a disputation of devils. Such things move discontents. Such things may be feigned of men, using a fool, in order to move discontents.

"But this talk of angels and of shepherds—it is so simple it smells all of truth indeed."

Strangways fidgeted on the bench. "Yet," he said, "there is in it nothing to our purpose."

"She can be taught to utter some words of solemnity, and so we can use her and her visions." Strangways scowled and muttered something about, ". . . like this poor fool of Kent." Darcy looked at him quickly.

"You would not have me use her?"

"They spoke of her as a very simple poor creature."

"Ah! Tom," said Darcy, "none would think, to look at that leathern face of yours, that it hid so pitiful a mind. You'd not have me bring another poor fool into peril of her life?"

"If the North rise for a right cause," Strangways grumbled, "what need to use her?"

Lord Darcy did not answer. A strange doubt had touched him. For if these things were indeed of God, "It is my own soul I bring in peril," he thought.

After a moment he laid his arm across Strangways's shoulders, and said, "God forgive us worldly men, and bless the poor humble folk, for Christ was born in a manger."

January 9

Meg stopped July at the door of the winter parlor. She caught July's shoulder and pressed it so hard that her rings bit on July's bone.

"Now mark and remember!" she whispered. "Whether or no there was more than kisses I shall say there was, for so shall I wring out advantage for you. And do you say the same."

July wriggled in silence; Meg loosed her shoulder, opened the door, and marched in, braving them all with her heavy body, great with a seven-months' child, and her face quick as bright flame.

Sir John stood with one foot on the hearth; Dame Anne sat opposite him, her fingers straining at her beads; Rafe straddled a bench under the window, and glowered down a little toy of a dagger he wore. His brother, Sir Francis Bigod, older, thinner, and with a kind of noble ferocity of look, sat on a settle, and kept his eyes, blue and hard, upon his brother. Beside Sir Francis on the settle was Sir John Bulmer's brother, Sir Rafe Bulmer of Marrick, and beyond him Sir Rafe's wife Nan followed with her finger down to the page of a book on her knee, reading how best to shoe jennets.

There was no place for Meg, except Sir John's own great chair, and Dame Anne, sitting broad as a crouching frog, dared

Meg with her eyes to take it. But then Sir Francis sprang up, and
Meg, going by him with a very sweet, kind look, sat down in his
seat. He met that look with one of such disgust that even Meg's
cheeks tingled at it, and on the settle Sir Rafe slid himself away
from her, crowding up on his wife. No one marked July, stiff as
wood by the door.

Meg looked round at them all and laughed her high wild
laugh, and plunged at once into battle.

The clamor of tongues died after a while. Meg sat panting,
her hand to her side, biting her lip at Sir John who had just bid
her be silent for a fool; she was mad to think that Rafe should
marry the little bastard—no matter whether the lad had—

Dame Anne broke in there in her harsh deep voice, speaking
only to her husband.

"And no matter whether, either she or I shall go from Wilton."

"Fie!" cried Meg, "turn from the door a gentlewoman so
wronged!"

"A wanton and a bastard."

"God's Death! Peace!" cried Sir John, for this was to begin
all over again, and then he repeated for the third or fourth time
that there'd be no harm done, and no blame if they married the
little wench to a good, sober yeoman.

"Disparagement!" Meg cried once more, and shot a flaming
proud glance at them all. "Bastard she may be, but of a house
that overmatches any blood here."

Sir Rafe Bulmer of Marrick had said nothing all the time,
but now he broke in with a laugh, liking Meg for her beauty
and her spirit.

"Make the lass a nun," said he.

"No!" said Sir Francis Bigod.

They all turned to look at him. He came and stood in the midst, and again said, "No." There was on his face that shining look July had seen in Rafe.

"Will you," he asked, "so choose them that are to serve God? If my brother have deflowered the maid he shall marry her."

"Frank!" cried Dame Anne, "I'll not endure it."

"Aunt," he rebuked her, "you and I and he alike must endure it. It is the punishment of his sin."

"But," Nan Bulmer's cool light voice came gently upon a shocked silence, "if the little wench should choose to be a nun?"

"She? She will not!" Dame Anne looked at July and the look said, plain as words, "A whore, and a whore's sister."

"But ask her."

"Do you then," Rafe Bulmer told his wife.

"Would you," said Nan, "be married, mistress, or be a nun?"

July, seeing all their faces turned on her, grew white and choked. She had not followed all that was said, but now this was clear.

She cried suddenly, shrill as a whistle—

"I will not be married to him. I will be a nun."

When all the rest had gone out, July the last of them and least noticed, Rafe Bulmer drew his wife to the window.

"How will this fadge?" said he. "Bastards should not be nuns."

"Dame Christabel will not care for that, so as the wench brings her dower."

He whistled. "Dame Christabel! You mean—fetch her to Marrick? 'A God's name, why?"

"I do not like her sister," Nan told him; and when he laughed at her and said that was because Meg was so fair and beautiful a creature, she said no, it was not for that reason. "You know I like well that women should be fair. But I like not her."

He pondered over that a moment and then came back to the matter in hand.

"The other ladies may not be willing to have the girl."

She smiled. "Dame Christabel will not care for that neither." After a moment she gave a small laugh. "Those mad Bigods! There goes Frank braying out that young Rafe must suffer for wronging the wench, and the wench was never wronged."

"How dost thou know?"

Nan looked at him with her faint grave smile.

"I asked her, since none else thought to. She said, 'No.'"

"Then why—? But she may have lied."

Nan said no, she was sure July had not lied, "And she is virtuous."

"What! With that sister? Though she's but little more than a child."

"Child or woman, so she is," Nan told him positively. "And that is why she hates her sister."

January 20

Those two of Queen Katherine's ladies whose duty it was today to fetch food for the Queen's breakfast met again near the door of the pastry. Both had pink noses and blue fingers, for the air was sharp, and the perpetual winter chill of the waterlogged country all round made it colder still in the late dawn. One of the two had been waiting for the milking; watching from the door of the dark shippen, where the lanterns cast huge shadows, and caught here the crossbeams of the roof, there the wide shining eye of a cow, and there the thin steam of its breath, puffing, spreading, and fainting from sight. Now she brought again the pitchers full of the warm, frothed milk, and found the other waiting, stamping her feet, with a white loaf and some eggs in a basket, and on top of the eggs a fish.

Neither of these ladies was young, and therefore there was nothing amusing, either in having to fetch the food, or in having to cook it over the fire in the Queen's chamber. They did what they had to do in silence for the most part, and with set lips; they beat the eggs for the posset with anger and impatience, and having set the fish to broil, fastidiously wiped their fingers. From the farther side of the room a yet older lady came and looked down at the fish, already hissing and steaming in the heat.

"Is that—safe?"

The lady who had brought it nodded. "Quite safe. I took it from among those for the chamberlain's own table. I tumbled off all that were on top. No one could have known that this was the one I would take. And I did the same with the loaves."

"Well," said the elder lady doubtfully, "I suppose there can be nothing unhonest therein." Not for worlds would any of them have used the word "poison."

"Jesu! You'd have Her Grace live wholly upon eggs, I think," the other replied sharply, having been a little proud of her foraging. But then they were silent, because the door opened and Queen Katherine came in from Mass. She smiled at them all, a smile which was sweet as it had always been, but which left her face dead when it faded. She sat down at the table and leaned her head upon her hand; even when they served her she still seemed to need that help to bear it up, and so toyed with the food listlessly, with one hand.

While she was eating there came to the door the new servants appointed by the King to her household, with dishes for her breakfast. They were told that my Lady's Grace was already served, and went away without surprise or demur; it was well known to them by now that the Princess Dowager would now eat nothing but what was fetched and cooked by her own people.

February 1

The setting sun was flooding the top of the fells with gold as Sir Rafe Bulmer and his people came back toward Marrick. Near Langshaw Cross they caught up with the shepherd bringing back the manor sheep. The servant behind whom July rode stopped to talk to Shepherd; the sheep stayed about him; when you looked at them against the golden light they seemed all to be steeped in violent purple.

By the time the servant had finished his talk with Shepherd, and gone on after the others to the manor, and was ready to bring July down to the priory, the sun had set, though the sky was still bright and warm over toward the west. But as they dropped down the hill twilight met them; soon all the air was washed through with a kind of clear darkness. The earth was turning back from day toward its nightly privacy, and man, who had during the light been master, now moved as a stranger, ignored rather than unwelcome, upon whom, departing, doors were softly closed. July, riding pillion behind the silent servant, lifted her eyes and saw the first star prick out among the bare sharp branches of an ash tree, in a sky as green as it was blue. Another light, nearer and warmer, caught her eye, and when she turned she could see the lit windows of the priory. Candles burned in the upper rooms with a clear, twinkling flame, but the painted windows of the church were lit with a colored steady glow.

She looked back down the dale, and would have been glad to stay hidden there, unnoticed in the deep tranquility, and covered by the rising dark. But the servant rode on to the gatehouse.

He sat awhile with Jankin the nuns' porter, while July went in to wait on the prioress in the parlor. He told Jankin a great deal about July's sister; Jankin would not believe that she was so beautiful as he said, but did not doubt that she was as bad. As to July, the Bulmers' man admitted that one said this and another that; but Jankin was always happy to believe the worst.

February 18

Robert Aske shifted some crumbs on the table one way and another with the curve of his hand; he made them into a neat pile, and scattered them again with his finger. The Hall of Gray's Inn was full of barristers and benchers at table, of the good smell from their supper, of the sound of their talking, and of the trembling flames of many candles.

For once Aske himself was not talking but listening, his heavy brows drawn together, his big mouth pouted forward and very tight at the corners. His neighbors were disputing as to how that clause had come into Magna Charta by which *Ecclesia Anglicana libera sit*, and what was meant by it. Those round about him spoke of the words as words written in ink upon parchment, which, like pieces in a game of chess, would be set against other words; to move words thus against each other made a very good game. It was a game too that Aske liked well to play, but not tonight, not with these words, because these meant something too real to play with. If Parliament should give, as Parliament was busy giving, all power over the church in England into the hands of the King, how should the church in England be free?

Aske covered the crumbled bread with his hand, and stared unseeing at the thin gray beard on a bencher's chin that wagged between him and a candle flame as the old man talked. These new laws that were being made overshadowed his mind with something of the unease and oppression that goes before a thunderstorm. And away down below that and almost out of hearing there was a voice that asked a question—"If these things were done, what should a man do?" But that meant, "What shall *I* do?"

When supper was over and all stood up he shook his shoulders as if he shrugged off a cloak, and went away to his own chamber. Will Wall was there, turning some clothes out of a chest. He had in his hands an old velvet coat of his master's, and as he looked up, his long, dark, melancholy face was so full of trouble that Aske cried out to know what was wrong.

"Perdy!" said Will, "the pile of this velvet is so rubbed as a rye field beat down with rain. I don't like to see you go so poorly, Master Robin, as to wear such a thing."

Aske laughed, and, on his way to the bench by the fire, flicked Will's shoulder lightly with his hand, feeling a sudden warmth of relief and assurance in the old and close tie that bound the two of them. Parliament nor the King could not change Will, nor change all the settled faithfulness between man and man— so settled that you forgot about it till you found yourself stand in the midst of change.

He said, as he got down his book from the shelf, "Then take it for yourself, Will. It'll trim your gray camlet gown."

Will's face lit, but he hesitated. "It'd trim that red doublet of yours, master."

"Lord!" Aske said, "I'm beautiful enough without any such adorning," and grinned at him, and began to read. Will went away with the velvet coat over his arm, to get his supper.

After a while Aske laid the book on his knee and reached for a bundle of parchments, the evidences of the Kentish squire who had briefed him lately—charters and chirographs all tied together by a hawk's creance, and kept in a soiled bag of white leather. He had forgotten the troubles of the times and now was whistling through his teeth, for he saw the way he could plead, to establish his own case and undermine the other; argument and counterargument came so trippingly to his mind that suddenly he drove his fist down upon the end of the bench, swearing, "By God's Passion, I'll have them there!" and felt power, like a shiver, go right down his spine.

April 16

The benchers and barristers of the inns were called to Lambeth this day, to take the oath. There was a great crowd in the hall of the archbishop's palace, mostly of men of law, but also of other gentlemen; those of them who stood near the fire steamed like a wet washing day, for the rain had beat on them as they crossed the river, and now it rattled upon the windows of the hall, and hissed in the swirling flames of the fire.

At the upper end of the room the archbishop, the chancellor, and the Dukes of Norfolk and Suffolk sat behind the table. They took no part in what was going on, except that at times one or another of them would lift his hand to his cap in answer to a greeting from some bencher or sergeant-at-law among the crowd. For the most part the lords talked softly together; the archbishop did not talk but seemed to watch each man's face as he came up to take the oath; there was a pewter pot in front of him with daffodils and sprigs of rosemary in it, and now and then his fingers fidgeted with the flowers. In front of the table two clerks stood; each had a book in one hand and a copy of the oath in the other; not that they needed any copy by now, so well they had the words by heart after having repeated them to so many.

Hal Hatfield and Wat Clifton found themselves at the head of the slowly moving line. The clerks bent their heads, listening, then made a motion with their hands, and the two barristers passed on toward the door. Aske had come in with them, but the three had got separated in the crowd. He had just now come to stand before one of the clerks; Hatfield and Clifton muttered,

"Stay a moment," each without hearing what the other said; their eyes were on Aske.

The clerk repeated the oath, phrase by phrase, as he had done for each man; Aske said it after him; they could hear his voice over the shuffling of feet and the subdued sound of talking. He joined them at the door and together they went out.

The shower was taking off as they came slowly from under the gatehouse. Hal drew in a great breath of rain-sweetened air.

"There are," he said, "many good reasons—many good reasons in law why no man should scruple to swear."

"Aye," said Clifton. "Many."

Hal ran through a few of them; they were at his tongue's end, for at Gray's Inn the matter had been fully debated ever since Parliament had, more than a fortnight ago, ordered that every man and woman in the kingdom should take the oath to uphold the King's second daughter for his lawful heir, born of a lawful marriage. That meant that his first marriage was no marriage at all, and that, again, the pope's dispensation for the marriage was nothing. Matters such as these, of great moment and of as great complexity, had provided ample material for argument.

"I," said Clifton, glancing at Aske who was silent, "I took the oath adding 'so far as the law of Christ allows.'"

"They did not stickle at it?" Clifton shook his head. Hal turned to Aske. "Did you the same, Robin?"

"No," said Aske, and they looked away from him.

But next moment he had put his arms so roughly about their necks that he bobbed their heads together.

"Come," he said loudly, "let's drink! This taking of oaths makes me thirsty."

They sat in front of their pint pots till it was past noon, with not another thing said of the business that had brought them to Lambeth. When they went down to the river to take a boat across they were arguing about fishing. Each was extolling that fly, which above all others, so he said, was beloved of trout and grayling. They came down to the Hard which, as the tide was low, stretched a long way out through the washed, smooth sands. The wind had dropped, the rain was over, and against the gray, quiet sky the gulls showed coldly white. Aske brought the dispute to a sudden and tame conclusion.

"Oh! well, maybe you will take them as well with one fly as with another. Though," he muttered, "in our fenny waters—" He broke off there, shrugged, and let it alone.

He was silent for a minute and then said, as if he were in a hurry to have it spoken before they stepped into the wherry, "Sir Thomas More and the Bishop of Rochester lie this day in the Tower. Yet is their conscience clean."

April 20

When chapter was over and everyone back in the cloister the two other novices, good little girls who had not received correction in chapter, drew themselves away from July. They had known that she told lies, and mimicked the ladies behind their backs, but now that everybody knew it and July had been birched before all the house they did not wish to be seen associating with her.

So July stood alone, smiling, because that was the way to hide anything that hurt. But it is difficult to maintain a smile for a long time, especially when it is only for the sake of defense; the smile became a grin, then a grimace. She was very glad when the bell rang for Terce and they must all go into church.

When they came out from chapter Mass lessons began again. July, crouching within herself, did not for some time observe that her companions seemed to have forgotten that she had on her something which she had supposed to be indelible as the mark of Cain. But when the novice mistress dropped her book, and almost overset her chair as she bent to recover it, the other two novices, confining their giggles by hands pressed over their mouths, turned their eyes, shining with laughter, upon her, to share the fun. And a little later the novice mistress, who had laid on the birch, commended July's reading.

At first July was incredulous. Yet it was true. These people here were as kind as happy. And that evening old Dame Eleanor Maxwell, deaf as a post, slow as a cow, and sweet as new-made bread, gave July a little carved box. Dame Eleanor had been one of those whom July had mimicked, and when the old lady put the box into her hands she almost dropped it, and blushed up to her veil for shame. But Dame Eleanor, muttering, "To keep your bobbins in. To keep your bobbins tidy," patted July's hand and closed her fingers round the box. July went away, still with a very hot face, glad that Dame Eleanor had missed that part of the accusations in chapter, and dreading lest someone should now tell her.

She went away to the room where she slept and took out from the trussing coffer her bobbins and her thimble and laid them in Dame Eleanor's box. The twilight was coming in very quietly, and here and there in the woods birds were singing which had felt the first motion of the spring this sweet still day. July lingered. There was a doubt in her mind; it was vaguer than a question, but yet it was there. Was there any need to tell lies and to mock in this quiet place? The doubt, even though she did not try to resolve it, brought a kind of ease like that which the quiet evening had brought to the dale; outside the windows, as dusk gathered, fields and trees turned to sleep too softly even for the release of a sigh.

May 14

The ostler of the White Horse at Cambridge tossed up the saddle of the bay mare onto the peg and looped the irons over it. Then he came back to take off the bridle, but his mind was not on that but on the argument that had risen between him and Mr. Patchett's servant, who now leaned against the door prodding at the cobbles with a faggot stick he had picked up in the yard, and declaring that the pope should put all right, and make King Harry take his own wife again.

"There is no pope," cried the ostler, and jagged at a buckle so sharply that the bay threw up her head and laid back her ears. He left her and went to the doorway. "There is no pope," he repeated, "but only a bishop of Rome." A few loiterers outside, hearing the note of controversy, came nearer to listen.

Mr. Patchett's servant ground the end of the faggot stick into the crack between two cobbles. "There is a pope," said he, "and they that hold the contrary are strong heretics."

"Hah!" cried the ostler. "If I am a heretic yet I have the King's Grace who holds of my part."

"Then are both you a heretic and the King another. And this business never would have been if the King had not married that strumpet Nan Boleyn."

"Fie!" cried the ostler, who was a little man but stringy and tough, whereas Mr. Patchett's servant was a large, soft man.

The loiterers outside closed in; a dog came and skulked about round the outside of the group. In the midst the two were arguing ever more hotly. "Knave!" the ostler called his opponent and then Mr. Patchett's servant raised the faggot stick and broke the ostler's head.

At that moment a company of grave gentlemen were coming out of the door of the White Horse; most of them were doctors of the university, but among them was the mayor. He stopped, and then crossed the yard.

"What's this?"

The ostler with his hands to his head clamored, "Master Mayor! Master Mayor!" When the mayor had heard his story he looked very grim. "For it smelleth to me of treason what you, fellow, have said," and he frowned on Mr. Patchett's servant.

"Mass!" said he, being a man of temper and courage for all his fat look. "Mass! then is half the realm in treason with me; for as I say, they think."

June 2

"Now," said the novice mistress, "we shall read again in *The Revelation of Divine Love* of Dame Julian of Norwich. The first

revelation—the fourth chapter. Take you the book." She gave
the book to the eldest novice, who began to read:

> And in this, suddenly I saw the red blood running down from
> under the garland, hot and freshly, plenteously and lively, right
> as it was in the time that the garland of thorns was pressed on
> his blessed head, right so both God and man the same that
> suffered for me.

July leaned her elbows on her knees and slid her hands up
inside her veil so that she could press her fingers into her ears
to keep out the words. She succeeded so well that she nearly
got herself into trouble, because when it came to her turn to
read, Bridget had to jog her arm, and, even when she took the
book, she had no idea of the place, for instead of following over
Bridget's shoulder she had shut her eyes tight too.

"Where?" she whispered urgently, and Bridget's finger came
down on the page—

> Notwithstanding, the bleeding continued till many things
> were seen and understood,

she began breathlessly, but Bridget jogged her again, and
pointed.

> The plenteousness is like to the drops of water that fall off the
> eavesing of an house after a great shower of rain, that fall so
> thick that no man may number them with any bodily wit.

And for the roundness, they were like to the scale of herring
in the spreading of the forehead.

These three things came to my mind in the time: pellets,
for the roundness in the coming out of the blood; the scale of
herring, for the roundness in the spreading; the drops of the
eavesing of an house, for the plenteousness unnumerable.

This showing was quick and lively, and hideous and dreadful, and sweet and lovely.

July gabbed on as fast as she could, trying not to understand
what she read. To her the showing was hideous and dreadful
indeed, but it was nothing else.

When the novice mistress said, "Enough," July shut the book
with alacrity. "Now it is time," said the novice mistress, "that ye
should turn to your broidering. But in your minds ponder that
ye have read."

They sat thereafter in a demure silence. The cloister was empty
of the ladies, who, this fine warm day, were gone out to the daleside to sit among the young bracken and in the shade of the thorn
bushes, spinning and sewing. Only the sacrist's big striped cat lay
at ease in the sunshine on the paving of the north cloister walk.
From the great court came voices of servants, men and women,
and sometimes the soft gabbling of ducks. There was also a steady
hum of bees in the flowers of the cloister garth.

July, glancing up sharply from her work, tried to read the
novice mistress's face. It was absorbed and serene as she stooped
over a little purse of scarlet silk. July did not understand how
it could be serene after the horror of pain that the book had

laid bare. She grew angry with the novice mistress—did she not understand what she was doing, to make them read such things? The little priory between the daleside and the quick running Swale had become for Julian a lodge of leafy branches built on a summer day, so pleasant, so flimsy as that. She did not want the woven branches torn open to let in the sight of God suffering. She wanted not to know—or rather to unknow—that there was suffering everywhere.

July 12

Early in the morning the haymakers set out from the priory to carry in from the last and farthest of the priory closes. The cellaress went a little later, and with her the three novices, and the mother of the youngest of them. It was only because she had asked it of the prioress that the three were allowed the treat of spending the day in the hay field. Jane's mother knew what little girls liked; she was young herself and pretty, and plump; not heavily plump, but with something of the soft, airy roundness of a dandelion clock.

So with bread and meat, cheese and beer, and a pannier of cherries, they set off from the priory gate across the open field to the gate at the foot of Marrick Steps. Here and there in the grass at their feet there shone a soft blink of wet gold, where the sun caught a dewy cobweb. But in the woods the shade was thick, and the air damp and green. Jane, who lived in her own private world of marvels, heroisms, and holinesses, walked behind the others with her finger on her lips and treading softly because someone, she was sure, had said "Hush!" to the trees, and there was somewhere under a great stone a monstrous fairy toad, with a gold crown on his head. If the trees kept quiet long enough he might look out from under the stone. Her mother and the cellaress talked pleasantly of grown-up matters. July and the eldest novice forged ahead to reach the hay making quickly.

After a long morning in the open, burning field, and dinner eaten in the shade of an ash tree with all the haymakers, the girls were content for a while to lie idle, watching the women move along the swathes with their rakes, the men gathering the small pikes into kyles, then tossing up the kyles onto the wains. Their voices came pleasantly in the heat, and pleasantly too the thin hiss of the hone on a scythe blade from a nearby close, where one of the Marrick yeomen was cutting his hay.

The two elder novices dozed, slept, wakened, and dozed again. Jane had curled herself up against her mother's thigh; whenever the other two wakened they heard her talking.

She said, "Madame, there were many knights that had their pavilions set at the ford below the priory . . . where the stepping-stones are . . . I saw a dipper there yesterday; he told me he had three eggs in his nest . . . He said he would show them to me one day when he had leisure . . . . There was a red pavilion, a gold pavilion, and one all stripes of blue and green. Every day the knights ride into the dale to find Paynim knights to joust with, and damsels to deliver." She paused to stretch and yawn like a puppy, then laid her cheek down on her mother's knee. After a while, "Madame," said she in a drowsy voice, "wot you that there is a mermaid at the priory?"

Her mother, never surprised, never incredulous, remarked placidly, "Nay. In truth?"

Jane sat up to explain that "she was a mermaid but the Lady said she could not be so she was not." She hesitated, then said, "Some say she is a fool, and some that she is a holy creature though foolish. But we must not speak abroad of what she has seen, because the Lady will be angry."

She wriggled herself nearer. "I asked her, madame, how it was to live beneath the sea, and of the caves and palaces there. She would not tell. But she told me what she saw last Twelfth Night. Can I tell you?"

Her mother snipped off a length of green silk, puckering up her eyes against the light. "Tell me, but not others," she said.

"Malle," said Jane, "—her name is Malle—Malle went up to the manor that night to fetch a feather bed; there were so many guests at the priory that there were not beds enough, and then Dame Anne Ladyman's sister came." She giggled. "July and I had to sleep in the same bed, and we talked till the ladies woke for Matins." She turned to smile at July, but July's eyes were shut.

"It was the time of the great snow, and the moon shone, Malle said. And as she came back by the wood side there ran two boys after her down the hill, and about the snowy field, the one chasing the other. He who was chased was laughing full sweetly, Malle said. She said that when she heard him laugh she knew it was God's little Son. She said none other but he could laugh so happily as that, since none but only he knew joy so nigh. And, madame, Malle said—"

"Did Malle say that?" Jane's mother asked.

Jane stopped, considering. "I think she did."

The eldest novice, who had wakened, interrupted here, with brutal frankness.

"Jane is making it up. Malle doesn't talk like that. She is only a fool, and stutters when she talks. She would not say such things."

Jane flushed. She shrugged the eldest novice off with her shoulder, and spoke only to her mother.

"That is what she meant to tell me. That is what she saw."

"And," said the eldest novice, "you know, Jane, that we are forbidden to tell her foolish sayings."

Jane's mother turned the conversation easily and pleasantly by reaching out a dangling handful of cherries from the little pannier, and bobbing them against Jane's lips. The others sat up too, and all ate cherries, and soon after tied on their straw hats, and went out again to help with the hay.

As the two elder girls went raking one after the other along a swathe, the eldest novice spoke gravely of Jane's disobedience in talking of Malle's crazy sayings.

"Humph!" said July, and would not, though the other tried to persuade her, say any more for a time, only, "Let her alone. There's no harm in that."

"Dost thou then," the eldest novice asked, "believe in this foolishness?"

July thought, "If it is true! If God knows joy! If we coming toward him come nearer to joy, and that without fear!"

To the other novice she said, "Nay."

"For," said that young lady, who had reached her priggish age, "if any were to see such a vision it would not be a wench like Malle, but the prioress, or one of the ladies, or even . . ." She stopped there, without mentioning novices.

July thought, "Jesu! Mary! St. Andrew! Let it be true!" Then she thought, "I shall find Malle and make her tell me that it is true." But very soon she knew that she would not dare do that, for fear she should find out that it was a lie.

August 20

The King came in to sup with the Queen in her apartments. In the antechamber one of her ladies was playing on the virginals, others were reading, or whispering together; two of the youngest were playing with a kitten. Everything seemed as usual, but when the King had looked sharply round, not one of them, as they rose to curtsey, would meet his eye. He indicated with a wave of his hand that no one should follow him into the privy chamber beyond, and went by quickly.

The Queen sat there, alone, between the yellow candles and a lowering red sunset. She got up from her chair and curtseyed very low; her eyes were on the ground but at the look of her the King knew that he had guessed right, and that though in the antechamber all seemed pleasant pastime and cheerfulness, a storm had raged here lately. Besides, it had by no means escaped his notice that one of the Queen's maids who should have been in attendance was not.

"Madame," he said, lowering his head, and going straight at the point, "where is—"

The Queen did not even give him time to speak the girl's name.

"She is not here. She is not here," she burst out; and now she raised her eyes and braved him. "I will not have her here. Oh! I know. Jesu! But I can see. And I'll have no rutting here among my maids. She shall go home." She gave a sudden sharp cackle of laughter. "Christ! Now you will say that it means nothing that you must sit by her, and lean over her and paw her—Ah!"

She stopped because he had moved so abruptly.

"No, madame," he said, not speaking loudly at all, but— she could not help herself. She started back as if he had raised his fist to her, and could only hope he did not see how fast her breath went.

"No, madame, I shall not say that. But I shall remind you of what I have done in raising you, and what you were before I raised you. And I shall counsel you to be content with what I have done, the more because if it were to do again, I would not do it."

He smiled at her unpleasantly, and she covered her face with her hands, and sank into the chair again. She looked beaten, but as she sobbed, partly from the trembling of her nerves, and partly for design, she had indeed snatched her courage to her again.

"It is my great love—my great love for Your Grace," she murmured.

He began to fidget about the room, and she let her sobs cease, but she fetched a trembling sigh.

He said, "Well, well. Come to supper."

She caught his hand and kissed it, and then covered her mouth with her fingers, because he had pulled away from her so sharply that the claw setting of a great ruby on his finger had torn her lip.

August 28

Robert Aske was coming back from Aughton Landing. One of the barges which brought goods up into the country from Hull had arrived there after dinnertime, and Aske had hoped that among the stuff for Aughton would be a ream of paper that he had sent for. But the master of the barge knew naught of it, though he had set ashore barrels of fish, several casks of wine, the lock of the parlor door which had gone to be mended, and two sugar loaves. Aske left the servants to bring these up, and started for home alone.

The evening had fallen quiet after a windy day, and white clouds, plump and pillowy, wallowed lazily across the sky. In that huge open countryside it was like being below the water of the sea, and looking up at the hulls of a fleet of ships sailing by above. Beside him his shadow, stretched and lean, slid smoothly, or flickered over unevennesses in the grass of the ings. Just before he left the river bank he startled a swan which had been standing there; it tottered clumsily toward the water, leaning forward with its wings spread; in a second more it was in the air, beating with great slow wailing flaps down the course of the river; only when it had gone far along did it rise, and then for minutes he could see it still, sailing toward Bubwith, white against the white clouds that lay low on the horizon there.

As he came near to Aughton the church bell began to ring; it must mean that the harvest was over, and that the great open field from which the corn had been carried was now broken, so that the cattle could be driven in to pasture upon the stubbles. But as well as the clanging of the bell he could hear, as he came up beside the old grassy mound where the de la Hayes had had their castle, that there was an unusual stir in the house. Dogs were barking and men shouting; he walked more quickly; it would surely be Jack, come home after a fortnight's visit to Marrick—both to Marrick Manor and to the priory, since Dame Nan Bulmer at the one and old Dame Eleanor Maxwell at the other were both kinswomen, the one on the Aske side, the other on the Clifford.

Jack it was, and very pleased to be home. At supper all the talk was of what had happened at Aughton since he went away—to the children, the harvest, the beasts, the dogs. After supper he and Robert went out in a late clear afterglow, so that Jack might have a look round; he was not content to wait till morning, so eager was he to be truly Aske of Aughton again.

Yet as they leaned on the stack-yard gate looking out on the lane Jack did not talk at all, for a while at least, of Aughton, but of their people at Marrick. As Robert listened, hearing news of Dame Nan's hawks, and Dame Eleanor's rheumatism, he wondered if Jack knew that it was better not to talk before his wife of Aske kin; he wondered too how anyone could be so jealous, and with so little cause, as Nell.

But then—his mind wandered—Nell's tempers were small things, sharp and sudden, like flaws of wind on the water, but like those only shaking the surface of life, which, here in Aughton, was all unstirred below. Here, but for such shallow troubles, was a great familiar peace. He looked down the lane; the elms were gathering twilight in their dusky leaves; tags and streamers of the harvest hung from their lower branches to show where the wains had passed; now a herd of cows came lazing along, driven by a young fellow in a green hood, who gave out now and again hollow, owl-like cries, which in no wise hastened the slow beasts. With the boy was an old man, who carried aloft on his shoulder a dumpling-faced infant. Both young man and old must have sworn that oath that every grown person in England had sworn, except so very few. Jack too had taken it, and Robert dared not ask him what he made of it all. Yet here perhaps it might seem to Jack and the others that there was no force at all in the oath; what King Harry did in London came to Aughton as no more than hearsay, and would not change a thing. "At least," Robert Aske thought to himself, "nothing has changed here. At least here for a while I need not to think that it has changed. At least I can forget London where I know that all has changed."

The cows were passing. Jack, forgetting for the moment Marrick matters, told Robert the age, the parentage, the quality of each beast as they went by, swinging their heads, switching tails, and casting a wild look sidelong on the men at the gate. When they had gone the whole air was sweet with the smell of milk.

Jack turned so that he leaned his shoulders against the gate. "Tell me, Robin," he said in a doubtful, hesitating way, "what think you of visions?"

"Visions? What visions?"

Jack laughed, as it were apologetically. "You'll call me a fool for thinking on it. But there was that in the poor creature—though they say she's crazed—yet there was that made me—"

When Robert interrupted, demanding to know what in God's name he was talking of, he said, "Of that poor fool the nuns call Malle." He twisted his head to look down the lane, and added, "I'd not use the nuns' cows to lay a patch on ours."

"What visions?" Robert Aske rapped out, so sharply that Jack turned toward him. But he, lest Jack should see his face, had hitched himself up to sit on the top bar of the gate. "What visions?" he asked for the third time.

So Jack went on. "This Malle, who—well, I'll tell you it, Robin, as it happened. I was up at Marrick, coming back to the manor at dusk, in a great rain that drove so hard that I had my head down and saw nothing till the horse turned aside. *She* was in the way; she'd a great bundle of faggots on her shoulder, and she stood in the rain, as soaked as a washing-day clout, but she never moved, only stood staring.

"Staring at what?"

"Into the window—but it was shuttered—of the last toft of the village, for I had come just to the town end.

"She said, without looking at me, 'He is within. He blesses the children.'"

"Wait a moment," said Robert. "You said the last toft. That's where that wench Cis—"

Jack held up his hand. "I know what you'll say, Robin, but let me end. Quod she, 'I looked in. The shutters weren't close. Cis was stirring the pot for supper, and the pigs and hens were driven in for the night. I could see the sow lie in the corner, and the hens roosting.' Then she said—but, of course—however—she said—'I saw him, a young man by the fire, tired from way-faring. He had his boots off to ease his feet. One of the little wenches leaned against his thigh and the babe was on his knee, and two of the little knaves played in the ashes at his feet. I saw him,' quod she, 'lay his hand on the little wench's head.'"

When Robert said nothing at all Jack said:

"I know you'll tell me it were no strange thing to see a young man, or men not so young, in that toft at night. Her husband's dead now—not that it made much odds when she had a husband. The Bulmers say not more than half that string of brats were his begetting."

"Did you," said Robert, "see in? Was there—was there—one with her?"

"No. The shutters were close when I came." Jack turned now, and looked up at his brother. Robin sat humped on the top bar of the gate, watching, with his one eye puckered up, the bats that swung busily in the darkening air.

"I knew," said Jack, "that you would laugh. And indeed the common talk is that the woman is crazed."

"I? Laugh?"

"Robin! You believe that indeed she saw—"

Robert Aske had jumped down from the gate, and now moved away toward the house. As he went he said:

"I warrant that when he went about in Jewry he did not deny to bless bawds' children, being so merciful as he was."

"But," Jack persisted, "you believe it a true vision?"

"If ever," said Robert, marching on ahead and speaking in a voice that sounded angry, "if ever there were a day in which Christian men needed a sign to ensure them of God's forgiveness, and if ever there were a place, that day's today, and that place England. And if any man needs it in special—"

"But such a simple creature, so ignorant."

"I shall go to Marrick, and find out for myself."

"When will you go?"

"Sometime," Robert Aske answered, roughly, because as soon as he said he would go he knew that he would not go. He would not act the lawyer with God's word, to doubt it, to haggle, and probe. "No," said he to himself, "I'll take it, thanking God for his mercy."

September 30

M. Eustache Chapuys looked up from the letter he was writing, stared, with eyes that did not see, at a cupboard with a jug of wine and a silver pot on it, and stroked his lips with the end of the quill he was using. These long dispatches of the imperial ambassador to his master took up both time and thought. He bent again to his writing, and for a while the pen chirruped almost as steadily as a cricket by a warm hearth.

At last M. Chapuys cast down the pen, yawned, stretched elaborately, and picking up a glass of late carnations sniffed deeply at the spicy scent. Then he threw one leg over the arm of the chair and began to hum softly. Now and again he glanced over his shoulder at the letter; it was a good letter, he thought. He was of the opinion that the Emperor Charles was lucky to have such a man as himself in England in these difficult times. An ambassador here today, he thought, needs to be fearless, subtle, ingenious, perspicuous; he must be such an one as is able to keep on good terms with the King and Thomas Cromwell, now master secretary; for otherwise he could do nothing to help Queen Katherine and the Princess. All these qualities M. Chapuys conceived himself to have. And, being no fool, but a good judge of men even when it was himself he judged, he was right. Not exactly young, he had a young man's nicety in dress, as well as other qualities which a man usually leaves behind him before he reaches middle age. He was still sanguine, flippant, and eager; he was also wary, or he would not have served the Emperor Charles, but it was as though he played a game in which caution was necessary, and amused himself thereby.

After a little while he swung to his feet and went across to the window. It was a large window, of five casements in a row, with wooden mullions between. If he had opened one and looked out and up he would have seen, as well as a row of empty swallows' nests, a tangle of rich and various carvings—vine leaves, grape bunches, twists of ribbon, peacocks, unicorns, and wild men whose hair became vine tendrils and whose bodies tailed off into fishes. Opposite, on the far side of the Cheap, the houses were adorned with similar, though even more opulent, carving; for on that side as on this the goldsmiths lived, and their houses, not so very long builded, were the pride of Londoners and the admiration of strangers.

Below M. Chapuys's chambers were the workshops, as well as the kitchens, hall, and shop of his host. When his door was open he could hear the gasp and roar of the furnace as the bellows governed it; but the stammering tap of the goldsmiths' hammers came to him all day long, whether the door were shut or open. So now for the noise they made he did not hear the footsteps of one coming up the stairs outside. At a knock on the door he turned quickly.

"Ah!" he said to himself, and more loudly, "Enter!" and the man he was waiting for came into the room, and straight across to the table. Chapuys met him there.

"Did you see him?"

"Yes, M. l'Ambassadeur."

Chapuys said, "A moment," and opening the door shouted for Gilles. There was a muffled answer. Chapuys said in a low but clear voice, "Gilles, I wish to be private." When he came back into the room he was smiling.

"From the sound of Gilles's voice," he observed, "I judge that he had his face in a pint pot. Being a Fleming he takes kindly to this barbarity they call beer."

He sat down at the table, resting his elbows on the letter which lay there, and became at once serious and intent.

"You can speak freely now."

The man, who was tall, pale, and bald, shifted his feet among the rushes, and paused a moment before he said: "I saw him."

"Lord Darcy himself?"

"Yes, monsieur."

"Secretly?"

"Very secretly."

"Where?"

"In a privy chamber. His steward brought me there. Only my lord and he go in."

"Did he know you, this steward?"

"Yes, monsieur. But he is safe."

"And my lord? Is that true which Lord Hussey said of him? He'll do more than talk?"

"He said he would."

Chapuys said "Tchk!" under his breath. To get news out of this Burgundian was like pressing a cheese. Screw, a dribble. Screw. Another dribble. Screw. A little flow of whey. Yet if he had not been so discreet he would not have been so useful.

"Tell me all he said to you."

"First he made me swear to be secret, or it might be death to him. He said not even his sons must know."

"God forbid they should. One stands so well with Cromwell that he hath lately made him captain of one of those islands . . ."

"Jersey," said the Burgundian, who always had his facts clear.

Chapuys stretched out his hand suddenly, and jabbed the table under the other's nose with his finger.

"Tell me. Have you heard any say that it was my lord himself who asked this favor, the captaincy of this isle Jersey, from Cromwell?"

"I have. It is true."

"But—" cried Chapuys. "Then is Darcy then playing with us?"

The Burgundian shook his head.

"Monsieur," he said, "I was once at Etaples in France and there I heard the bishop of Meaux read in French from the Bible. It was not forbidden then."

Chapuys nodded. "I know."

"He read a story of how the people of Israel came out of Egypt. That day they left they took from the people of Egypt jewels—rings, brooches, collars."

Chapuys waited. After a while he said persuasively, "Yes?"

"My Lord Darcy wishes very much, monsieur, to go back to Yorkshire."

Chapuys chuckled. "Out of Egypt."

"And before he goes he would spoil the Egyptians." The Burgundian allowed himself a faint smile. He took his fingertips from the table, and spreading his hands under his eyes, seemed interested in the trimming of his nails. "I think—" he began.

Chapuys did not move.

"I think, monsieur, that my lord remembers the time of the wars, when there were two kings in England."

"He's past seventy. Yes, he must remember."

"I think he remembers it well."

"But what of that?" Chapuys asked.

"Kings were cheaper then. He thinks of kings not as men think now, but as a man of those past days."

"I see." Chapuys tapped with the tips of his fingers on his teeth.

"Yes. I see," he repeated.

"And there is yet another thing, monsieur. It may be the greatest thing."

Chapuys did not interrupt by a question. He only lifted his eyebrows.

"My lord said that in this quarrel he would raise the banner of the crucifix beside the Emperor's banner. He said those very words."

Chapuys's face lit with excitement and then became appropriately solemn.

"It's true. This King is nothing but a heretic." He added quickly, "Did he say what force he could raise?"

"Sixteen hundred Northern men. He said, monsieur, that I should tell you this—that he is more loyal to his Prince than most men, in matters that go not against his conscience and honor, but seeing that things are done here contrary to reason and hateful to God, he cannot be consenting thereto, neither as an honest man nor a good Christian."

Chapuys bowed his head. "I count it myself," he said, and crossed himself, "even as a Crusade." He struck the table with his fist and laughed. "And what a stroke at the throat of France if we could pull down this King and set up the Princess Mary."

When the Burgundian had gone Chapuys turned again to his letter, writing out first in rough and then fairly what the man had said. When it was done he sent Gilles for a taper, sealed the letter, and shoved it inside the breast of his doublet. The rough copy he held to the flame of the taper till it blazed, then threw it on the hearth, and watched while the paper writhed, and blackened, and lay still, making the tiniest sharp ticking sounds. When he had broken the frail thing down to finest black ash his caution was satisfied.

November 6

At chapter the prioress told the ladies that the King's commissioner would be at Marrick this morning to take the oath of each one of them to the Act of Succession.

"And of the servants too?" Dame Anne Ladyman asked.

"Of the servants too."

"Mass! How should their oaths matter?"

The prioress was shrugging her shoulders over that when Dame Margery Conyers stood up, and said that she for one would not take the oath.

They all stared at her and someone, in a loud whisper, mentioned the Tower.

But the prioress said, "Nonsense. Why should you not swear? All but a very few have sworn, throughout the whole realm. Will you be more careful of right than they?"

Dame Margery had grown very red, and shut her lips tight; she shook her head in silence, because, as usual when she was excited, tears were gathering in her eyes.

The prioress looked at her, and then at the faces of the others. Dame Elizabeth Close was leaning forward; her hands were gripped tight together; in a moment she would be on her feet. The prioress saw that Dame Margery's refusal might be an infection to spread.

She said, speaking calmly, but as in a matter of grave moment: "Yet before you refuse consider what will fall, not only upon you, but upon the house. For to refuse is treason, and if you and others should refuse, that will happen at Marrick which has happened to the Franciscan Observants. The priory will be suppressed."

In the dank chill of the November morning cold shivers ran up the backs of several of the nuns. In the minds of all what the prioress had said was a blast of bleak wind, not to be endured.

Dame Margery sat down, then stood up again.

"Madame," she said rather grandly, "then I discharge my conscience and I charge yours."

The prioress bowed her head. Her conscience was ready to bear the charge.

That afternoon in the old Frater, they took the oath tendered them by the Commissioner, a portly, cheerful man, who before the business began had talked over wine and wafers of his little girls at home, and the first boy, the heir, still in swaddling bands. Such humanity and kindliness had greatly eased the ladies' minds; they could not but feel that an oath proffered by such an individual must be innocuous.

When they had taken it the servants came in, and after them the men from the fields. Dinner was late, but when the ladies sat down to it, hungry but cheerful, they looked back at the day's work with equanimity.

1535

January 1

None but his own servants gave New Year gifts to the Emperor's ambassador on the first morning of the New Year, for his friends and his kin were not here, and the English lords knew better than to make presents to one whose master was so ill a friend of their master.

But soon after dark had fallen a little gray-haired priest came to the door below, asking for Gilles the Fleming. He spoke English like a stranger himself, being in fact a Hainaulter, so there was nothing out of the way in his coming. Gilles, however, when he had brought him in, led him upstairs and into the ambassador's room, where M. Chapuys sat throwing dice, one hand against the other. After that Gilles sat down on the stairs outside the door.

The priest from Hainault wished the Emperor's ambassador "A happy Christmas from my lord," and laid in his hands a long slim parcel lapped in leather. When Chapuys undid the wrappings he found a fine sword in a sheath of crimson leather.

"It's a choice gift," said Chapuys, "and I send many thanks for it to my lord." His eyes were on the priest's face, as though he waited for something more.

"What will be in this New Year—" the priest began, and then spread his hands and let them fall.

"No man can tell," Chapuys ended for him. "But I think my lord sends me this gift because he'd have me know that the time is near when we shall play with steel."

The Hainault priest shook his head heavily, and said that the times were very ill.

Chapuys slid the sword out of the scabbard, laid it to his cheek, and looked along the blade. As he lowered it the firelight shone red upon the clear steel.

"God help us to mend the times," said he, and the priest said, "Amen."

February 2

Lord Abergavenny murmured, "Bring me your ear closer," and the Earl of Huntingdon stooped over the brazier where they warmed their hands, so that their faces were near together.

"In my hearing," said Abergavenny, "my Lord of Northumberland called her 'the great whore.'"

Huntingdon raised his eyebrows and pulled down the corners of his mouth but made no answer.

"So many," Abergavenny went on softly, "hate her, and what she has brought on this realm. If the King tire of her—"

He stopped because Huntingdon had whispered "Sh!" at the King's name, and they both turned from the glowing red of the charcoal to look between the crowd to where, at the far end of the great gallery, the King and the French envoy, M. Palamédes Gontier, treasurer of Brittany, moved to and fro in front of the great hearth. A monkey with a jeweled collar slunk and gamboled inconsequently after the King at the end of a gilt chain; it chattered with rage when the chain pulled it up at every turn and it must follow whether it would or no.

The King was all in white satin, stitched with gold thread and sewn over with emeralds, in honor of the feast, and the envoy beside him in his black velvet and gray satin looked like a long thin evening shadow. It was pretty clear to anyone who knew the King that he was growing testy; now and again he leaned upon the Frenchman's furred shoulder, but for the most part his hands were behind his back—not clasped, but with the back of one laid flat on the other palm, and he kept clapping them together in a fidgety, impatient way.

"The business," Huntingdon murmured, "goeth not well."

Abergavenny took a discreet look over his shoulder at the King and the Frenchman, turning just now at the window.

Huntingdon went on, as though he spoke to the thin blue smoke of the charcoal. "I have heard that the French will have none of the Princess Elizabeth, but require the old treaty to be kept, and the Lady Mary to be given to the Dauphin. That will not please His Grace."

Abergavenny turned slowly back.

"His Grace seems to me," he whispered, "to go halt upon his left leg."

"Sh!" said Huntingdon sharply, but when Abergavenny muttered "An ulcer?" he nodded, and said, "The physician told one of my gentlemen so. There are two things I would know—" He broke off there, and said in a different tone—"Ah! my lord duke!" as the Duke of Norfolk, huddled to his long nose in fur, joined them beside the brazier.

"And what be those two, my lord?" said he, with the frank smile that he could use when he chose.

"One is—whence they have that fine gravel for the tiltyard," said Huntingdon promptly.

"That I can tell you," said the duke, and the three began chatting lightly of such matters, now warming their hands over the brazier, now tucking them under their arms, and most of the time stepping gently with their feet among the rushes to keep the blood coursing, for the day was very cold.

That same afternoon Mr. Thomas Cromwell brought the French envoy to Queen Anne. She was in one of the smaller rooms leading off the presence chamber, yet the room was large enough to have two fireplaces, one at each end, and for thirty or forty people to be able to divide themselves into two quite separate groups. The larger group by far was that about the King, who stood with his back to one of the fires, pulling tight his white satin trunks across his broad backside, and now and again bending slightly forward, the more exquisitely to toast his rear.

The Queen sat beside the fire at the farther end of the room with a lute on her knee, and some of her ladies and a few young gentlemen about her. The fire sent out puffs and gushes of sweetness for they had not long since scattered spices on the logs.

One of the young gentlemen near the Queen had the King's monkey by its chain, and he and a gentlewoman were feeding it with sweetmeats while most of the rest looked on and laughed. As M. Palamédes came near he noticed that the Queen was watching the monkey too, but with loathing; and so intently that she did not see the two gentlemen approach.

As they paused the strange creature sidled over to the Queen till it stood crouching before her. She shrank back. "Mother of God! I hate monkeys!" It laid one of its long, wrinkled, dark gray hands on the strings of the lute, and with the other grabbed at a sweetmeat in the Queen's fingers. Then it was away, with its paw at its mouth. The discordant twang of the strings under the tiny clutching fingers was echoed by a cry from the Queen, who brought her own hand up to her mouth in a gesture strangely like that of the animal.

"Oh! He scratches!" she said, just as M. Palamédes bowed and went down on one knee.

Neither he nor Cromwell missed the start that the Queen gave. Cromwell glanced round at those standing near; he did no more but it was enough. The group about the fire broke up and drew away, leaving the three of them alone.

As the Queen's hand lay upon Gontier's and he stooped to kiss it he knew it was trembling. He lifted his head, and his eyes, caught by the shifting sparkle of jewels, rested for a second on her bosom. Her blood-red velvet gown, brocaded with gold, had an edging of pearls and small sapphires along which the firelight ran with a broken flash, quickly gone, and then running again from point to point in time with the Queen's quick breathing. The woman, M. Palamédes realized, was panting—no less— yet when he looked in her face she smiled, and as she spoke in French of how she had loved France, and how ill she now used his lovely French tongue, she laughed, shrilly, a laugh with as little meaning as the strained smile, while her eyes darted past his head to watch what was going on at the farther end of the room.

Then, with desperate urgency, but always with that same smile on her face and with laughter that tinkled emptily, she began to press him "to use dispatch in this business of the mar- riage of my daughter the Princess Elizabeth's Grace." Dispatch! Dispatch! That was the word, over and over. "For if you do not

I shall be in worse danger than before I was married. Worse danger!" She laughed with fear looking through the mask of her face. Her head jerked and she craned her neck to see beyond him. Gontier felt his flesh creep, and yet he knew that nothing had happened of more moment than that the musicians in the room beyond were tuning their instruments and that the King had moved away from the other hearth.

The Queen held out her hand; the Frenchman bent and kissed it again and felt her nails nip into his flesh.

"I dare not speak longer," she said breathlessly. "I cannot tell you more. The King is watching us. Someone said I should not anger him. But if I did not he would think I am afraid." She seemed to choke, then said, "As (dear Mother of God!) I am afraid."

She did not seem to know that she was still clutching his hand, but he freed it gently and asked if he might wait on Her Grace another day.

"No. No. I can't see you again—or write—or stay longer. He has gone. They are dancing already."

She sprang up, laughing again. The room was nearly empty. Only a few of her ladies were there to follow her as she moved toward the door through which came the sound of fiddles and recorders.

February 12

When the physician had gone out Queen Katherine sat for a long time pricking with her needle at a leaf on the corporax case she was embroidering, but making no stitches. From time to time she sighed. It was hard enough to be separated from a daughter; it was worse if the child were ill; and she had been ill for months. The child—the Queen realized that the girl of fifteen whom she had last seen, would be nineteen in four days' time.

She thought, "If I could go to her! If only he would go!" meaning her physician. But he had seemed not eager to go. He had said he could not leave Her Grace, and indeed, thought the Queen, "I had done ill without him while I was so sick. But now—why will he not go?"

As an answer to that came into her mind she grew very still. For a minute she sat stiff in her chair, staring straight before her while her face whitened, and her mouth formed a silent "Oh!" which she did not utter. Then she snatched up the little bell on the table and rang it, and went on ringing it till the door opened and two or three ladies, with scared faces, looked into the room.

"Quick," said the Queen. "Bring me pen and ink. Quick. And one of you find Charles. He must ride to London at once."

They had thought her ill. Now they almost thought her mad.

"Go! Go!" she stormed at them. "Don't stand staring. Pen—ink—paper." She began to walk up and down the room and to bite her nails. But before any of them came back she had drawn out a crucifix from her breast, and sitting herself down at the table, bowed over it. When the eldest of her ladies came in, shutting the door softly, the Queen looked up at her with a gray face, but calmly.

"I think," she said, "that he does not dare to go to my daughter because he fears there is poison given her, and that if she—if she die, they will lay it at his door."

The elderly lady cried out at that, but the Queen hushed her with a word, and began to write to M. Chapuys, ambassador of the Emperor's Majesty.

For a while there was no sound in the room but the complaint of the driven pen. When that stopped for a minute the lady-in-waiting looked round, and caught a glimpse of the Queen's face. It was less like a living face than a carving in stone, chiseled to represent, changelessly and for years on years, the uttermost of woe. She did not look again.

So [wrote the Queen], because it appears to me that what I ask is just, and for the service of God, I beg you will speak to His Highness, and desire him on my behalf to do such charity as to send his daughter and mine where I am; because treating her with my own hands, and by the advice of other physicians and of my own, if God please to take her from this world my heart will rest satisfied; otherwise in great pain.

You shall also say to His Highness that there is no need of any other person but myself to nurse her; that I will put her in my own bed where I sleep, and will watch her when is needful.

I have recourse to you, knowing that there is no one in this kingdom who dare say to the King my lord that which I desire you to say; and I pray God reward you for the diligence that you will make.

She signed it then, "Katherine the Queen," and dated it, "Kimbolton, the first Friday in Lent."

May 4

The King sat in his study at York Place in Westminster with a small harp on his knee and music on a desk before him. His hands, white, fat, yet at once both nimble and powerful upon the strings, plucked out from the instrument its voices of trembling sweetness. He played first a love song, then a Nunc Dimittis—very gentle and slow; he swayed his head to the plaintive measure and his face was calm and purged.

Someone knocked at the door, and without pausing in his playing he bade, "Enter." But when he saw Mr. Norris come in he set down the harp so roughly that the strings tingled in one soft discord.

"It is done?"

Mr. Norris shut the door. "It is done," he said. Then he tittered. "There are four fewer Carthusian brethren in the realm to refuse Your Grace's Supremacy and hold by the pope. Four fewer alive, that is, but if every piece of every monk of these four were to count a whole monk then hath Your Grace increased the sum to—" he reckoned on his fingers, "four quarters each, and their arms torn off, and every man his bowels and his heart—" He began to laugh noisily.

The King pressed the lips of his small mouth close and his eyes roamed about with the lowering hot glance of a boar. He said, "And they lived yet when they were cut down?"

"One of them lived even till both arms were off. But all while they were opened and drawn."

The King bowed his head. He seemed to consider with attention a diamond on his finger.

"The executioner did his work with a will?" he asked.

"With a will. He rubbed their very hearts, hot and steaming, over their mouths."

"Ah!" said the King, and after a while stood up. "Shall we make a match at the butts?" He went to the window and opened it. The day was more like April than May, with a racing wind, blue sky, and light flying clouds. Just now one covered the sun, and it was as though he had shut an eye. The King said, "The wind's strong, but steady. I'll use that new great bow." Yet he stood still staring out of the window.

"Did they cry for mercy?" he asked suddenly.

Norris said that they did. It was a lie, but the King nodded as if pleased, and that was what Norris cared for.

This evening Robert Aske came late into the room where Clifton and Hatfield sat over a flagon of wine. When they asked him where had he been he said only, "Riding." He would not drink with them, but sat down on a bench and took a book on his knee, but after a little Hal nudged Wat and motioned with his head toward Aske, and Wat saw that the book lay upside down.

Presently Wat said:

"If you have ridden out into the country you may not know that the brothers of the Charterhouse were executed this morning."

Aske moved so sharply that the book fell between his knees.

"I do know," said he. And then with a jerk, "I was there."

"Mass! You were there!"

Aske's face twisted into a sort of grin. "I was not the only one. Many of the court were there to see the brave sight."

"Tell us the truth then," said Wat. "Were they hanged in monks' frocks—not degraded from their clergy?"

"They—" Aske began, but instead of answering the question he said, huddling the words together, "Let them tell you who were not there. I cannot say it."

He put down his hand to take up the book again and then stopped and they saw him stare down at his wrist where the sleeve had drawn back as he stretched his arm; there was a dark brown stain on it. He looked up at them with a sick face.

"I did not know I was spattered with it. But I stood so near as that." He got up hastily. "I must wash it off."

At the door he stopped and they saw him draw the fingers of one hand across his eye and shake them as if he would shake off something which clung like a cobweb. "I can wash it from my wrist," he muttered, and then went away.

May 7

Gib went up the stair from the houseplace to the chamber that was above. There he prized up a board in one corner and took out a book. This was his latest hiding place for his latest purchase—a small old manuscript of Wycliffe's Testament; it had painted initial letters of red and blue, but the back was shabby, and besides that scorched right through the leather to the board beneath in one place.

Gib did not intend to read indoors; both discretion and the fair morning urged him out. When he came downstairs again he laid the Testament in a basket, put a handful of hay over it, and called to his mother that he was away to Kexwith to fetch the sitting of eggs that the burleyman's wife up there had promised him.

It was a morning of brisk wind, warm sun, and bright sailing cloud that might darken and gather later. Just now the sun was pleasant, and more than one of the old women of Marrick stood at the doors, each with the distaff tucked under one arm, and the spindle swinging and whirling at the end of the lengthening thread. Gib gave them good-day sternly, and was glad to be through the village. These ignorant old souls were, he knew well, irrevocably sunken in superstition; he could do nothing with them.

Beyond the last fields he reached the crest of the rise and suddenly all the fells were open before him, blue and green like the sea, with grape-purple shadows of the clouds lying here and there; for miles on every side but one there was nothing but wave after wave, with Mozedel rising higher yet in the far distance; only nearby, ahead and to the left, the ground fell away to the trees and the profound sheltered peace of the dale.

The nuns' bailiff and his man came into sight near Langshaw Cross on the road from Owlands. Gib knew the bailiff even from this distance by his white horse and the big brown dog that ran alongside. He did not wish to meet him or anyone else, so he left the road for the turf, taking the green track that joined the way up from Grinton. When he was out of sight beyond the swell of the ground he sat down, and took his book from the basket, secure in the austere emptiness of the fells, and in a great quiet, for here the wind passed in silence and of all the birds only the larks had confidence to fly strongly and sing aloud; the rest made short flights close to the ground, and spoke with small stony twitterings and chinkings. Nor were there any flowers up here, other than the tiniest sort among the grasses, except where the golden wild pansies were spilt upon a sunny bank.

Gib opened the book and began to read.

He entered into a synagogue and a man was there and his right hand was dry. And the Pharisees espied him if he should heal him in the Sabbath, that they should find cause to accuse him. Soothly he wist the hearts of them.

"Black hearts," Gib thought, who saw the Pharisees as a row of abbots, sitting in their carved stalls, each man different in face, yet each with the same air of command and confidence.

He saith to the man that had a dry hand, Rise up into the middle and stand.

Gib smiled at the thought of the discomfiture of that rank of grave and scornful prelates; his imagination increased their number now by two or three bishops.

> Soothly Jesus saith to them, I ask of you if it is lawful for to do
> well in the Sabbath or to do evil, for to make a soul safe, or for
> to loose? And all men looked about—

At that Gib gave a small sharp laugh; he could see their proud
yet shifty eyes glancing from the rushes on the floor to the brass
eagle that carried the Gospel book on its wings, and then up to
the painted vault of the roof, not one of them daring to catch his
eyes, not one with a word to answer.

> He said to the man, Hold forth thy hand, and he held forth,
> and his hand is restored to health.

"Hah!" said Gib half aloud, and then jerked his head up because
a shadow slid across the grass beyond his feet. Malle, the priory
servant, had come near and now stood, red faced and puffing;
she had a very young calf in her arms; its ears flapped, and the
long, heavily jointed legs dangled helplessly.

"This one," said Malle, and dumped the creature on the
grass, "this one ran away. He came out of the ox house only
today, and the world frightened him. So when he found a hole
in the wattles he broke through, and ran, and never left running
till he had no breath left. But at last I caught him."

The calf, after trembling and quaking for a moment, flopped
down, its forelegs doubled under it; it looked softly at them with
its large, shining eyes, and swept a thick tongue over its nose; it
lowered its head and they heard the gentle sound of its breathing
as it nuzzled at the turf.

Gib frowned at the little beast, and frowned at Malle's bare feet; he had his hand over the page, yet knew it was not hidden, and was angry to know that he feared lest it should be seen; he looked up at her face, and saw that her eyes were on the book.

"Sir," she cried, and came close. "Is yon the book in which you find news of him?"

He shut it then, shuffling it between his knees before he remembered that Greek, Latin, Hebrew, or English, it was all one to her who could read no letters. He said, the more harshly because of his fear, and the shame it left behind, "The book is not for such as you to read in." He said that, and suffered at once from a sharper twinge. It was of the very breath of the New Learning that it should be open to all; yet, he told himself, not to this woman, who was utterly a fool.

She laid her hand across the two tight knobbed curls on the calf's brow which would be horns later, and he could not be sure if it were she who sighed or the creature who breathed a deeper breath in the turf. Then she smiled.

"Perhaps he will come again," she said, and then, "Up, little one!" and gathered up the calf into her arms, and lumbered on.

Gib opened the book again.

"And it is done afterward," he read, "that Jesus made journey by cities and castles—" but he could not keep his mind to the words. He looked after Malle, trudging along with her head kerchief flapping in the wind; he even drew his breath to shout after her and bid her come back, but then he saw beyond her, and quite a long way off, the Marrick flock of sheep and lambs, like the white edge of a wave lapping toward him over the green turf;

the shepherd walked before them; his dog, restless and quiet as the shadow of a moving leaf, slid beside them, now on this flank now on that. Gib picked up his basket, and huddled the book under the hay; when the shepherd came alongside, five minutes later, Gib was beating with a stone at a nail in his shoe. He waved his hand, put on the shoe again, and stood up. They walked along together then, the sheep following them, the dog circling on noiseless feet, but the whole air full of the plaintive bleating of the flock as that above sea cliffs is of the gulls' yelping.

Gib said he was going to Kexwith for a sitting of eggs. He said that a nail in the sole of his shoe had galled his toe. The shepherd, walking alongside, with his pipe to his mouth and fingers moving but playing only a soundless tune, bowed his head and made no answer. He was a very silent man and so used to thinking his own thoughts that often he forgot to listen to what others said; sometimes too, when he did speak, he seemed not to know if others listened.

"How many lambs this year?" Gib asked, and got no answer.

"'Most white. That's right,'" said Gib, "but black ones enough for black hosen too."

Shepherd nodded. Then he said:

"She said she saw him. Yet it's strange—here—in these days."

When Gib asked who "he" was, and who had seen "him," the shepherd did not answer, but stopped, and turned to look back the way he had come. Malle was by now out of sight, but as they looked the bailiff rode over the crest of the rise, and disappeared, going down into the village.

Then, leaning on his long hooked staff, with his wind-puckered eyes looking into the light of the sun which had even yet not risen very high, Shepherd said:

"I was over to Harkerside Moor t'other day, and coming back I saw yon wench hoving by the roadside. I thought 'twas far forth of her way, so I stopped and asked what she did there."

After that he let so long a space of silence pass that Gib felt himself forced to ask, "Well, what did she?"

Shepherd's eyes came to him, and then seemed to look through him.

"Quod she, '*He* hath gone by below,' and she pointed at the corpse road going toward Keld. 'A young man,' quod she, 'with twelve other young men, all talking merrily and walking fast this shining afternoon. But *he* went ahead of them all; I heard the iron shoe of his staff clack on the stones of the road. And the birds,' quod she, 'sang Osanna fit to brast their throat.'"

Gib said something, hardly a word indeed, but it brought back Shepherd's eyes to his face. "And then?" cried Gib.

"Naught else. Except she said: 'They know not yet with whom they walk, but only have great joy to be with him.' I thought," said Shepherd after a moment, "that a priest'd know if such a thing could be. But there—" He met Gib's stern look, and sighed.

Gib turned away. He would not let Shepherd see how mightily this thing had moved him. But surely here was a sign from God, spoken and shown to his very soul. Those young men, following that other young man up the dale, they were going forth into the world to preach. Well—and if he could not go after them, could he not write? And did not books, coming fast now from printing presses, speak to more—aye, and more surely—than the words of a preacher? His heart went up like thistledown floating in autumn, and he heard in his mind, as if someone had spoken—"There is much ripe corn, and few workmen; therefore pray ye the Lord of the ripe corn that he send workmen into his ripe corn."

He said, in his harshest voice, "I will call the woman, and inquire further of this matter. The truth shall be proven."

They walked on together a little way, but then Gib said he must make haste so as to be back at noon. So he left Shepherd moving slowly, his shadow and the shadows of the sheep slipping smoothly over the short turf in front of them. As all good shepherds do, he would lead the flock westward till the noon sun stood high; in the afternoon, when it had a little declined, he would turn and bring them home again, so that always the sun shone from behind them, never in their faces.

Gib swung on again at a great pace; he was a fast, impatient walker, and besides that, the way was far. Yet he walked faster even than usual, so buoyed up was he with that which Shepherd had told him.

Sweating, with his face harshly red, he came to Nungate Top, and began to go down toward Dales Beck. A couple of small children stumped along just ahead, carrying a bag of flour on a pole between them. They were not ill-looking children like Wat, but fair and sturdy; he noted himself taking pleasure in watching them, and that confirmed his confidence. "Jesu Mary!"

he thought to himself, "If I may be free to proclaim his word, I shall love all his creatures, every one." But something trembled in his mind when he thought—"Even Wat."

Yet he went to Kexwith and back in very good cheer, in a settled mood of confidence, too exalted for any grip of fear. Only in one matter did his mind change. When he came to think it over he decided he would speak no word of this vision to the woman Malle. What Shepherd had told him was enough. "If I speak with her," he thought, "it may puff her up to believe that this seeing comes to her by cause of holiness. Thus shall she lose her humble meekness which, manifestly, is that in her which is pleasing to God." So he told himself, but he knew that he could not endure to ask her of her seeing—as if she, the poor fool, stood closer to God than he who was priest, and God's chosen messenger.

May 10

Summer had not yet come to Yorkshire. Today was cold, with cloud, strong wind, and occasional flaws of sunshine. When the sun shone the river winked with light, and far up the dale you could see a bright white flicker come and go upon the water. Gib met the nuns' priest near the East Close. He was walking with his head bent against the wind, and pinching his hood tight under his chin with one hand to keep it on and to keep his ears warm; so he did not see Gib. But Gib, who was bringing his two cows back to the milking, held out his arms across the track, and the nuns' priest jerked up his head with a start when he felt someone in front of him, and came to a stand. The cows slewed to the right and left and maundered on toward home with their swinging, dilatory gait.

"Sir," Gib said, leaning on the hedge stake he carried, "Sir, last Sunday I heard you pray for the bishop of Rome."

"You heard me—?"

"I was in the parish church. I heard you well through the grille. You said quite clear, '*Oremus et pro beatissimo Papa nostro.*'"

The nuns' priest ruffled up and became very dignified.

"I shall so pray," said he, "till I have further command to the contrary."

Gib heard footsteps behind him above the tumult of the wind. He turned and saw that the smith was coming up and was indeed quite near. In a moment he ranged up alongside Gib and stood looking down at the nuns' priest.

"It is forbidden that any priest should pray for the bishop of Rome," Gib said in his grating voice, and hearing that the smith cried, "Ho! Marry! Say you so. Doth he pray yet for the bishop of Rome?"

The nuns' priest had grown red and a little flustered, but he held his ground, saying again that he would so pray till commanded to the contrary.

"Yea! Cock's Bones!" shouted the smith who had been drinking at Grinton. "Will you pray for Dr. Pupsie though it's forbidden?" and he began to slap his thighs and to laugh uproariously at his joke, repeating, "Dr. Pupsie! Dr. Pupsie!"

The little priest grew nearly purple and he spluttered.

"Mass!" he cried, "and if it be forbidden by these new laws! Yea, nowadays we have many new laws. And if we take no heed I trow we shall have a new God shortly," and he put his head down and moved forward with such decision that both Gib and the smith made way, and the nuns' priest went on toward the priory.

Gib and the smith continued along the road in the other direction. The smith was very noisy, laughing and hooting and shouting, "Dr. Pupsie." Gib stalked on in silence, angry almost as much with him as with the nuns' priest and all other idolaters.

May 15

"What does it mean?" said the old treasurer of Paul's who had kept one of the three keys of the cathedral treasure for the last thirty years. He turned over the letter of Master Cromwell, the King's chief secretary, and peered at it upside down.

"Surely," one of the canons told him, "it means that the King has been informed of this precious little crucifix of ours and hath taken a high affection and pleasure of the sight of the same, even as the letter saith."

"And," said another canon, a big, gaunt man, with a sour face, "it means that seeings will be keepings."

"Fie!" the first rebuked him, while the old treasurer looked from one to another. "It means that we shall tender the same to His Grace as a free gift, trusting in his charitable goodness toward our Church of St. Paul."

"And as little daring to refuse," said the tall canon, "as any wayfaring traveler dare refuse a robber his desire."

"Fie!" the first canon cried again, and others too. "To liken the King's Grace to a robber!"

The tall canon denied that he had done so. "It is the chief secretary that writ the letter," he argued.

But all of them felt that the less said the better, and that, whether they liked it or not, they had no choice but to make the gift. So the first canon was set to write a letter to Master Cromwell, and the old treasurer together with the dean and the sacrist went with their three keys to open the treasure house, where the precious little crucifix lay.

And when he had taken it out the old treasurer dandled it in his hands, trying, with his bleared old eyes, to see it by the light of the torch they had brought. It was very precious and beautiful, for it was of pure gold, with a rich ruby in the side, besides four great diamonds, four great emeralds, four large balases, and twelve great orient pearls. The old man began to cry over it, because indeed he could not think that it was right that the King should have it, seeing that it belonged to God and to St. Paul.

May 20

Of a sudden it was summer. The sun shone and cuckoo shouted day long. Among the thornbushes below Gawnless Wood the grass was clouded blue with bluebells. The nuns' priest climbing the stairs to the prioress's chamber felt the delicate stir of the gracious season, which was warmth and a vibration, and a note of singing just too high for human hearing; but he sighed as he raised his hand to knock.

The prioress was feeding the small brown bitch which had whelped lately, so she heard him first with only half her attention. But when his meaning became clear she put down the platter for the animal to feed or not as it would. He was asking her whether she would have him disobey the King's command, and continue to pray for the pope.

"Disobey?" she cried, at once seeing danger to the house. "No, you shall not."

"I have till now disobeyed," he said.

She had not noticed it, but then one did not attend to every word that was said in church.

She repeated, "You shall not disobey. It might imperil the house."

He fidgeted with his feet and ran the thong of his belt backward and forward through the buckle so that the leather made little sharp slaps as he drew it tight.

"I thought—" he began, "I fear—madame, I cannot think it well, that which is now done. There is the whole Church Catholic which prays for His Holiness; how can we alone forbear?"

The prioress sat down in her chair and looked him over with more attention than she had given him for many a long day. She could not have expected, she thought, to find such a strain of scrupulosity in a man so round, so pampered, so easy. His gown was of very fine cloth of a dark crimson, and the sleeves were lined with silk; his fair hair, thin now, was as carefully laid in waves as ever; but his little mouth was troubled. She was honestly sorry for him, but he must not be allowed to damage the house. She tried subtlety.

"Sir," said she, "I think you are in the right. But these things which are new—I do not look for them long to endure. Soon we shall see them laid by, and all return as it was."

"You think so?" he cried. He was ready to think so himself. He had said, miserably, what conscience had goaded him to say, but he had no lust for the martyr's part. He had been a sorely frightened man when he came in to the prioress, and here was balm.

She told him she did think so indeed, and truly!

"Then what shall I do?"

She was going to say "Conform!" but something obstinate about his look made her alter that into, "Go away from here for a little time. Let me say you are sick. Go and stay with the good yeoman your brother. There you can sing your Masses to the sheep and none wiser if you pray for the pope or no."

He demurred a little, but not much. Only, what would the ladies do for a priest? The prioress said, "Sir Gilbert can sing our Masses for us."

The priest frowned at that and muttered that he thought sometimes Sir Gilbert was half a heretic.

"Then," cried the prioress gaily, "when you return you shall convert and lead us back into Holy Church. And we'll all bear faggots on our necks and wear white shifts."

She would not take the matter seriously anymore, and soon the priest cheered up, and drank some wine before he left.

He stood for a moment outside the prioress's door and felt again the touch of the sweet day on his face. When he had paused here before the chill of fear had impaired the sweetness. Now, as well as a blessed relief, there was only a very slight twinge of dissatisfaction in his mind; but that, he was sure, would pass.

July 1

The flecks of blue and ruby and thin grass green which the sun cast on the pavement through the colored windows of Westminster Hall had slid only an imperceptible distance when the jury came back, so short a time had it taken them to decide on their verdict.

Sir Thomas More saw them file in and lifted his head to meet what was to come.

When they were silent Lord Chancellor Audley asked them, "Guilty, or not guilty?"

"Guilty," they said, and the chancellor stood up and pronounced the sentence of death.

More, who had sat so still, shifted now in his chair. He unclasped his hands from the little ivory crucifix on his knee, laid them instead upon the arms of the chair, and leaned forward. They all watched him and silence fell as the crowd in the hall hushed itself to listen.

"My lords," he said, "since I am condemned—and God knows how—I wish to speak freely of your statute, for the discharge of my conscience." Audley opened his mouth and shut it again. "For the seven years that I have studied the matter, I have not read in any approved doctor of the church that a temporal lord could or ought to be head of the spiritualty."

"What, More!" cried the chancellor now, and laughed derisively, "You wish to be considered wiser and of better conscience than all the bishops and nobles of the realm?" and he picked up the posy of sweet-smelling flowers and herbs before him, and smelt at it, and laughed again, glancing at the other lords for their approval. Sir Thomas waited till a few of them had laughed, and then began speaking again.

"My Lord Chancellor, for one bishop of your opinion I have a hundred saints of mine; and for one Parliament of yours, and God knows of what kind, I have all the General Councils for a thousand years. And for one kingdom, I have France and all the kingdoms of Christendom."

"Now," Norfolk broke in, and beat his fist on the table before him, "Now is your malice clear!"

"My lord," said More, "what I say is necessary for the discharge of my conscience and satisfaction of my soul, and to this I call God to witness, the sole Searcher of human hearts.

"I say further that your statute is ill made, because you have sworn never to do anything against the church, which through all Christendom is one and undivided, and you have no authority, without the common consent of all Christians, to make a law, or act of Parliament, or council, against the unity of Christendom."

He paused and seemed to have finished, but as Audley half stood up he raised his hand, and the lord chancellor sat down again, and then fidgeted upon his chair as though the seat were red hot; but much as he might have liked to interrupt, he did not.

"I know well," said Sir Thomas More, "that the reason why you have condemned me is because I have never been willing to consent to the King's second marriage."

He looked along the row of his judges, his eyes dwelling longest on Audley and Norfolk, and there came into his face the flicker of a smile only a little merry, but very gentle.

"I hope, my lords, in the divine goodness and mercy, that as St. Paul, and St. Stephen whom he persecuted, are now friends in paradise, so we, though differing in this world, shall be united in perfect charity in the other. And I pray God to protect the King, and give him good counsel."

They all knew that he had finished there, but you could have counted ten before the lord chancellor stood up.

"Take the prisoner away," he said.

July 3

Gib came back with the other men from the harvest; it was dusk now and they had been out since daybreak, yet still the fields were only half cut, and if this short spell of fine weather broke in thunder, as it was threatening, there was little hope of saving a quarter of the hay, after all the weeks of rain. It was of this that the men talked, looking up at the heavy sky, as they tramped homeward, weary as dogs that have hunted day long. One by one they turned off to their houses; by the time Gib came in sight of the smithy he was alone.

One of the smith's little girls stood inside the wide door; he could see in the dark the glimmer of her shift, which was all she wore. As he came nearer she skipped back into the shop, and when Gib came abreast of the doorway the smith was there. "Hi! Sir Gilbert," said he. "Come in."

"Not now," Gib was saying, but he saw the smith make a sign with his hand; it was a sign Gib understood, so he turned in at once. The little girl had been lurking in the shadows of the smithy, but she slipped away into the yard behind as Gib came in.

"When did he come?" asked Gib, as the smith laid his hand on the latch of the house door.

"Not half an hour ago."

He opened the door and Gib saw Master Trudgeover sitting by the hearth, with the smith's two youngest, one on each of his knees, his big rough bristly face bent over them while they looked up at him with eyes as round as birds' eyes, and chirped to him in their small voices which were almost the voices of birds.

The smith wanted Gib to sit down to supper with them all, but Gib would not, and would have Master Trudgeover come along at once to the parsonage, "for he'll be safest there," said he; but what he wanted more was to have Master Trudgeover's attention drawn from these piping youngsters and turned instead upon heavenly things. Gib wished to discourse with him upon the blessedness of the new knowledge of God, and with that upon the rewards prepared for those that accepted it, and the vengeance for those who refused.

So, though Trudgeover seemed a little unwilling, Gib insisted. "Bring the others with you when it grows dark," said he to the smith. "If they came here there's no knowing who might not chance in." That was true enough, while on the other hand few knocked at the door of the parsonage, except the smith and these same known men, who would come there to read together in their books.

Trudgeover put down the two children and laid his large hands on their heads; Gib heard him bless them. They went out into the twilight. Once Trudgeover stopped and looked back; the smith's children were strung out right across the road waving to him, but in silence, because even the smallest knew that he was a secret; he waved back, and kissed his hand.

A minute after Gib heard him sigh and say, "I've five childer at home in Norfolk."

Gib had never known that Trudgeover was a married man, and it meant little to him now. He thought of him only as the tramping preacher, whom sometimes he despised for his lack of learning and clumsy schoolboy jokes, and sometimes admired to the pitch of reverence for his way of kindling the simple, heavy countrymen till they glowed like the iron on the smith's anvil, and laughed or shed tears, as Trudgeover chose.

"I've heard no word of them for this four month," the preacher told him; but Gib said nothing to that, and in a few minutes asked what the news was where he had come from, and Trudgeover began to tell him how Master Cromwell, now the King's vicar general over the whole Church of England, was with the King in his hunting this summer, and, as the King hunted, Master Cromwell visited the monasteries, making record of their treasures, turning away those monks and nuns that had taken the vow too young, giving license to depart to any who chose, and threatening the rest with such an enforced strictness in keeping the Rule that none would be able to abide it. Trudgeover was very merry at the expense of the monks, and Gib endured it with a bitter smile, because it was good news to him, but nothing to the purpose for making jokes.

At the parsonage they found supper behindhand because Wat had gone off on some business of his own without drawing water. "And I," said Gib's mother, "must needs wait an hour or more till Goodman Tod came by and I could ask him to bring me a pailful." The old woman could not now do all that she had used to do, being often ailing, and sometimes in great pain.

Master Trudgeover said that for his part he was well content to wait for supper, but Gib was very angry. He went out into the garden, and they heard him calling for Wat, each time more fiercely. After a while he gave up calling, and soon came back with his hands full of salad stuff from the garden. "We'll begin with cheese and these," said he, "while the bacon's seething." He lingered at the door for a minute and said, "The rain won't be long." Then he barred the door.

The rain began while they were still eating bread and cheese and the cool, dripping salad stuff. It was very heavy. Soon after it began they all heard the latch rattle.

The old woman tittered. "There's my fine varlet." Trudgeover looked at Gib, but Gib helped himself to more cheese and said nothing. Trudgeover fidgeted, kept looking toward the door and losing the thread of his talk. At last he broke off.

"Brother, let the little lad in to his supper."

Gib crunched a radish between his teeth. "There's no supper for him." "Then let him in to bed." "He can bed with the pigs. He's an ill-conditioned knave."

Trudgeover laid down his knife.

"I shall let him in."

Gib stood up too. He met Trudgeover's eye, and then, to his extreme anger, found that he could not meet it. He unbarred the door, and Wat came slinking in; he had his cap in his hands, full of wild raspberries.

Gib caught him by the collar of his jacket, and, when he had driven the door to with his foot, shook him. The lad was so thin and ragged, and now so drenched, that he looked like an old clout hung on the line and shaken by the wind. Then Gib hauled him over to the little closet under the stairs and throwing him in shot the bolt on him.

They finished their supper in silence, and even when the smith and the other "known men" had come in Master Trudgeover seemed different—less eloquent than usual, speaking of mildness and mercy rather than of God's glory or God's judgments. And when the rest of the company had gone, in the last of the dwindling rain, he and Gib did not sit up together reading and talking by the rushlight. Trudgeover said he would to bed betimes against the morning, and certainly he was yawning, so that all his big yellow teeth showed. Gib said he was weary with the reaping, and they went up together in silence, and in silence undressed.

Trudgeover soon fell asleep, but Gib could not. At first he said to himself that it was the heat, or his bedfellow's snoring, which was indeed prodigious. But at last he admitted to himself that it was neither of these which kept him awake. How could any man suffer patiently a dumb fool like Wat, an ill-conditioned, idle, malicious imp? Lads must learn by beating. He himself had been beaten often enough. But for him Wat would have been a miners' lad, and what was that better than a slave? Yet always, as he disputed with his own thoughts, he knew clearly at last a thing he had long blindly known: in Wat he had brought the old sin to dog his steps close as his own shadow; he hated Wat, and that was a new sin. With horror the thought came to him that he had, as it were, begotten sin upon sin.

July 5

Gib heard the women from the priory pass by before it was light. First, even before they came near, he heard their voices, then the jangle of the chains by which the wooden pails swung from the yokes they carried, last of all their footsteps, for they all went barefoot, so that they made less noise upon the road than as many sheep. They were going up to the priory flock which the shepherd kept just now above Gawnless Wood, to milk the ewes for summer cheeses.

When they had gone by he got up, and lighting a candle sat down by the window to write. He had in his head many and piercing arguments against the usurped power of the bishop of Rome; when he woke they would begin to move in his head so that he could not sleep again. So it was better to leave his bed and write.

As he wrote the dawn came without his noticing it. Only when he heard the women coming back he raised his eyes from the page, and saw that the candle flame looked sickly in the daylight, while outside the window the shadows lay long and pointed across the fields, and the sky was delicately blue and full of brightness.

He thought—"I could do well with a draft of milk"—but to ask a gift of anyone grated on him, and it would be worse to ask from one of that cackling crowd. He heard them laugh and call to each other, and then shriek louder to the men out in the fields.

Gib got up and began to put on his coat, meaning to shake Wat from his bed and send him out to milk the cow. But he heard Wat stirring and opening the door below, so he sat down again.

"Ho! Priest's bastard!" cried one of the women, and, "Fie on the ugly brat!" another; then there was a squawk and a shout. "Drop that stone! Let me get at thee!" and Gib saw Wat go across the road, running doubled almost like an animal. He was behind the big elm tree; a second stone flew and there was another squawk.

Then the women began to go on again; he heard their angry voices; they spoke now not only of bastards but of heretics. He took up his pen but laid it down again when he saw that one of them was still below. She stood in the road, holding out a hand toward the tree, from which Wat danced out for long enough to fling another stone.

It caught the woman Malle on the arm, and she gave a little cry and began to rub the place, then she held out her hand again.

"Nay! Nay!" she said, and had to dodge a clod of earth. After that she gave it up. Gib saw her shake her head, and go trudging off after the other women with the milk lipping at the edge of the swinging pails, and now and again slopping out to make blue-water patches in the dusty road.

July 6

Just before dinnertime an elderly serving man in a greasy torn coat and leather hosen turned into the gate arch of the house at Mortlake which Lord Darcy had rented. He asked for my lord and was told "Within," but when he came into the house they said, "Without in the garden." So he went straight on, though more than one tried to detain to ask, "What news? Is it done?" But he would not stay to talk, being a discreet man, nor even to shift the old coat for Darcy's bright popinjay green livery with the Buck's Head badge; he knew that my lord waited for his news.

He found his master walking in the little walled rose garden where the fountain, forlorn and cheerless, wept softly under the gray sky into the gray water of the basin, or was flung spattering by a gusty wind that made the roses shiver and flutter. A couple of women knelt together, weeding; when they saw the servant come in under the arch they sat back on their heels to stare.

Darcy, looking the man hard in the face, raised his eyebrows. The fellow nodded with a very grim mouth.

"We'll go beyond." Darcy led the way down the yew alley to the riverbank. Yet when they had come there they stood in silence. Darcy's mind was searching back into the past, thinking of this King Harry, and of his father, and of the King whose naked hacked body had been brought into Market Bosworth tied on the back of a rough-coated farmer's pony. "But now," he thought, "is no man to set up his will against this King; no, not one."

The old serving man at his shoulder was seeing a crowd and a scaffold. His chest tightened again at the silence that had fallen when the headsman swung up the axe above the neck of Sir Thomas More; and again he heard the blade chop down with just that sound, only louder and greater, that housewives hear unmoved as they stand by the butchers' stalls talking of the weather and of the children's ailments; but this time there were few, men or women, whose breath did not catch at the sound. And then, with a bump and a rustle, the head, which had been one of the wisest and wittiest in Christendom, had tumbled forward into the straw.

"Did they suffer him to speak to the people?"

"Aye."

"What did he say?"

"Not much."

"God's Passion!" Darcy shouted at him, "What?"

The elderly serving man screwed up his face and braced his shoulders as if for a heavy bit of work.

"He says, leaning on the rail, and speaking slow, 'Good people pray for me, and I shall pray for you whither I go. And you shall also pray God send the King good counsel. As for me, I die a loyal servant of His Grace, but God's first.'"

Darcy pondered on that, recollected himself to make the sign of the cross and murmur a prayer, then pondered again.

"Well, it was enough. And yet—maybe they had commanded that he should use few words." He was, indeed, a little disappointed. This man who had died for conscience's sake might have left behind him words that could be passed from mouth to mouth to hearten other men, if the chance offered, for a different, armed resistance. Then he thought, "There's no chance—yet—or the chance is past," but if past he did not know when, nor how it could have been seized. He turned away along the riverbank, saying over his shoulder, "Go and get off those rags," and then halted to ask, "Did you know any that were there?"

The man named the lieutenant of the Tower, and the King's great chamberlain. Darcy interrupted.

"Not them. Any that were friend to Sir Thomas?"

"A serving man of my lord marquess, and of Lord Montague. And a man of the Emperor's ambassador."

"In their liveries?"

"Nay," said the fellow, and with a sour smile plucked at his own ragged doublet. "Only the ambassador's."

Darcy gave an angry laugh. "The rest of us don't dare show even our servants' noses." He struck his staff into the ground; the sodden earth clucked and hissed as he pulled it out again. He waved his hand, to dismiss the man, and then, as the horns blew in the house for dinner, turned and followed him in.

At table no one spoke of what had been done that morning on Tower Hill; no one spoke much at all. Darcy, observing the faces of his gentlemen, could see in them a look as of men unsure of their way; he knew how they felt. Under his own feet what had been the solid, known earth seemed now to crack and splinter like ice breaking. He could just remember times when there had been in England men marching or skulking in the lanes, charging across the quiet, familiar fields, dying on the banks of the brooks where as children they had used to fish for minnows. But this was a different thing, for there was peace, and in peace Cromwell—whose pale face, placid but for the quick eyes, was very present in Darcy's mind—Cromwell pulled down, one by one, those who resisted the King's will.

After dinner, in the privacy of his bedchamber my lord gave instructions to the Hainault priest for Masses to be sung, secretly, for the soul of Sir Thomas More, and John Fisher, bishop of Rochester.

"A very noble death—a martyr's death," said the priest, whose face showed that he had been crying. "God give us grace to follow such an example."

Darcy crossed himself. "God rest his soul. *Miserere Domine!*"

But he thought, although he did not say, "How would that serve? It is not martyrs that will bring down Cromwell. If every good man died a martyr, who would profit but heretics and harlots? How would God be served?"

When the priest had gone he sat long on the side of the bed, considering in his mind the power and the clogging burdens of the Emperor, the strength of French friendship for King Harry, the chance of an attack from Scotland. The longer he thought, the more sure he became that, without the Emperor would move, the only thing to do was to bide the time.

August 20

The nuns' church at Marrick was, of course, small, but since Dame Christabel had been prioress it was very neatly kept. There were hangings of green say with a trellis pattern of flowers all round the chancel now, and the big silver cross that had used quite often to be brown and discolored had always in these days a high polish.

Just now the nuns were not in church, as it was the time for parlement, that is, for good and religious conversation in the cloister for the ordinary nuns, and for the officers of the house the ordering of their particular charges. Both the doors from

the cloister into the church—the prioress's door at the east end
of the north cloister wall, and the nuns' door at the west end—
stood open, but so still was the day that no breath of wind came
into the church, only the sunshine, stained and enriched by the
painted glass where it fell upon the floor, but in the air nothing
more than ghostly slants of something paler than the general
brown dimness of the church.

Julian Savage knelt at the chancel steps, telling her beads.
She had already said twenty-nine of the fifty Paternosters which
were her penance for bringing Dame Margaret Lovechild's rabbit into the cloister, and she was keeping up a very good pace,
being anxious to be done, and then perhaps the novice mistress
would let her go out with the others into the field where the first
reaping was to begin today among the oats.

Then she heard the clack of the latch on the door of the parish church beyond the screen, and the unmistakable wheeze of
the door opening, and a man's voice said:

"Sir, take an offering and sing me a Mass for the soul of the
founder of this church and the house of the nuns. For I'm a man
of that same family, though of the younger branch."

After the first two words July knew the voice, and a shock
of delight and, somehow, of delightful dread, ran through her,
so that she heard the voice only and not the words, until Master
Aske said, in a different tone, "Why! I have seen you before."

"Since I was born in Marrick," Gib growled, "that's not
strange," and July, listening now with all her ears, heard the
priest go away to the vestry. As she could not hear any other
footsteps she did not know what Master Aske was doing, but

she guessed him to be down on his knees, as she was, and some-where quite near.

For a while that was enough, but then she thought, "I must see him."

She did not know how she could do it, but one thing was certain: she must be out of the church as quickly as she could. She got up and tiptoed down to the nuns' door. There was no one in the west walk of the cloister. She peeped along the north walk. Dame Bess and Dame Margaret sat with their heads close together presumably in good and religious conversation. Beyond them there was a knot of ladies near the prioress's door. They also were engaged in conversation but the tone of their voices was high and sharp.

July clutched her beads to her so that not a click should betray her, drew a long breath as though she were going to dive into deep water, and stole out into the cloister. She knew that she must not look round, but the skin of her back prickled as if she felt the ladies' eyes through her habit. Then she was in the little low passage between the cellaress's office and the church tower—almost safe—then out in the great court, and shutting the door of the passage behind her—for the moment quite safe. But what was she to do next? She had never thought of that, but must think of it now, and the shelter of the stable oppo-site seemed a better place for thinking than the open court; but while she still hesitated she heard a knocking, and his voice cried at the gate, "Ho! Porter!"

She forgot all about shelter then, and came out in the middle of the court. He stood in the shadow of the gate talking to

Jankin and leaning one hand on the wattled wall. She could hear the sound of his voice, though no words, and she could look at him. Instead of the crimson and black, watchet blue and murrey which she remembered in London, he was dressed today in an old patched coat of the dull colors that men wore for hawking, and a hawk sat on his left hand. July learned him all over again as she watched; yet really he was just the same, and in herself she was aware of no difference.

After a moment Jankin left him, lifting a finger to the edge of his hood, and went across the court to the cloister door. Master Aske came out into the sunshine and sat down on the horse-block in the sun. For a moment there was no one else in the great court—only the hens picking and scratching, and on the roof of the gatehouse a few pigeons which sidled, dipping their necks, or rooted with their bills under their wings, or lifted a coral-colored foot to scratch; on the horse-block there was Master Aske, and by the stable door July, all under the warm still blue sky.

She went quickly across the court till she stood in front of him.

"Master Aske!" she said, and then, "Oh! you've forgotten me."

"Mistress—" he began, puckering up his one eye against the brightness behind her head. Ought he to remember her? He did not. Then he did, and, so quick is thought, he remembered the last time he had seen her, holding a mirror for Meg, who laughed at him with her eyes over the mirror and over the girl's head; and he remembered the last time he had seen Meg, with her hair spread all over the pillow. That recollection made his mind sick.

July stood in front of him watching his face. If she could have gone away she would. If she could have cried she would

have wailed aloud. But she could do neither, and so she simply
stood and looked at him, dumb as a stone.

A more stupid man than Robert Aske would have seen that
he had hurt her, and a less kindly man would have been sorry. He
struck himself a sharp slap on the brow with his open palm.

"By the rood!" he cried, so loud that the hawk jerked and
flapped on his fist. "It's my other little July! I didn't know
you, grown so great a girl. But I did not know you were here
neither."

July came to life again. "I knew you were here. I heard you in
the church. I was doing penance for bringing Dame Margaret's
rabbit into the cloister. I live here. The ladies let me feed their
rabbits." She heard Jankin coming up behind her, and the prioress's door opening.

"Where have you come from?" she scrambled out quickly,
determined to know. "Do you stay here? When did you come?
For why are you here?"

He laughed at her with the bright teasing eye she
remembered.

"Mistress, one at a time and that the last. I'm come to see my
kinswoman, Dame Eleanor."

That struck July dumb. To think that she had never known.
To think that she had once made a laughing stock of his
kinswoman.

The prioress's voice called her by name and bade her begone
to the cloister. She went, not looking back, but she had the look
of him with her, laughing, browner than she had known him, in
his old stained, gray-green hood. She thought that if she had to

do more penance the look of him would last her through many Paternosters.

August 29

July walked to Grinton with Dame Eleanor and Dame Bess; two menservants came behind to carry for them. The day was very fair, after many days of rain, warm but with a pleasant breathing air to temper the sun's heat. The two ladies were pleased to have an errand to take them out on such a fair day, but July, who was in herself one of the motives for the expedition, found the sunshine as cheerless as black night, since she was going to Grinton to have a tooth pulled out.

To step into the cottage where the deed was to be done was like stepping into prison. The monk from Bridlington, who had the knack of drawing teeth, got up from beside the fire where the wife was busy with white puddings seething in the pot. He put his hand (he meant it kindly) on July's shoulder, and led her to a bench under the window. The two ladies abandoned her, as one past human help. As her knees doubled under her and she sank on the stool she could hear their voices, loud because of Dame Eleanor's deafness, talking by the fire, but the sense of their words could not penetrate the terror, which, like a wall of glass, enclosed her, narrowing always.

The father took hold of her chin; the wall of glass came so close as to suffocate her; she opened her mouth, gasping. Then he thrust into her mouth a great pair of pincers which rattled against her teeth. She struggled a little, but he had her tight. Pain shattered the wall of glass. She screamed, and the tooth was before her eyes, small, bloody, and now quite strange after years of closest companionship. When Father Richard loosened his grip on her jaw, as if he had given her face back to her, she covered it tenderly and tremblingly with her hands and sobbed.

"That fellow," said the good father cheerfully, "that fellow won't trouble you anymore, no, not till Doomsday."

At the words relief began to creep into her mind, but it was soon a flood of pure joy. When they came out of the cottage she saw the sunshine for the fairest that ever shone. Even Dame Eleanor's disjointed comments upon everything they bought could not fret her this morning: there was time for them on this sweet day, there was time for anything, for time stretched ahead with nothing in it which was not pleasant to do, with no fear such as that which had stood in the way as they came to Grinton. She was so happy that she could even spurn from her the thought that though today was free from fear there would come another day, when another tooth must be outed. She swung the basket recklessly.

She and Dame Eleanor were to meet Dame Bess on the bridge, but when they reached it there was no Dame Bess, and now Dame Eleanor clapped her hands together in distress. "There!" she cried. "The linen for the Lady's stockings. Gregory was fetching it from Richmond. And I've forgotten it." And now what was to be done?

No, July could not go because the prioress had been particular that Dame Eleanor must see that it was the right, fine, Flanders weave. And Dame Eleanor could not leave July on the bridge, because that would not be seemly. And they could not go both together, because Dame Bess would come and would not know where to find them. The problem seemed insoluble. "And there will be no time if we wait, for now there's but time to be back for dinner." Dame Eleanor looked toward Fremington Edge and wrung her hands together; no help was visible in that direction; she looked back over the bridge toward Grinton and her face brightened. She pushed July gently aside, and moving a few paces held out her arms wide as if to stop a runaway horse.

Master Aske, who was strolling across the bridge idly twirling in his fingers a young foxglove spike, stopped, pulled off his cap and wished her, "Good day, cousin. What's your will?"

She explained the dilemma to him, holding him firmly by the wrist, and talking a great deal and fast, with soft mumbling motions of her lips rather like a rabbit. He listened gravely but once or twice his eye caught July's and she could have sworn that there was a laugh in it.

"So cousin," the old lady concluded, "if you should stay here with this young gentlewoman till I return, all will be well."

He said he would, and nodded so that she should get his meaning.

"You will not leave her?"

He said he would not, and shook his head.

"You will stay here till I come back? You understand?"

He said he understood, and she went off, in a great hurry, but turned and came again to say that he need not stay if Dame Bess returned. "But not to leave the young gentlewoman alone."

When she had gone right away he turned his eye on July, and the laughter in it was plain to see.

"If I mistake, correct me. But I think I am to stay with you," said he.

There were quite a number of people passing one way and another over the bridge, and now a train of packhorses came along, their bells jangling. Master Aske led July to one of the angels over the buttresses of the bridge. He leaned his elbows on the parapet and looked down at the river. She looked at him.

He talked, lightly, of this and that. He was staying up at Marrick Manor. He had lost a hawk the other day in the woods. Fenland such as he knew at home he liked better for hawking than these thick woods. By and by he plucked one little glove finger from the foxglove spike and stuck it onto his forefinger.

"That," he said, poking it up to show her, "was what we did when we were little brats."

He was surprised when her hand came down and snatched it off.

"There is poison in it," she cried. "It will do you a mischief." He saw that her eyes were very round and serious, and he laughed.

"That's fiddlesticks. I've done it a thousand times."

She faltered, "There is poison in it. Anyone will tell you," and she slipped it on her own finger.

"Silly little wench," he said, but kindly. "You see, you don't believe it yourself."

Yet she did at least half believe it, and was afraid in a kind of misty way, but much more glad to be sharing the danger with him.

He was silent for a little while, and again July watched him. Now that he was neither laughing nor talking his mouth was shut very tight and hard, and his heavy brows were drawn into a straight frown. She cried suddenly, feeling as if the shadow of a cloud had fallen on her face, chilling it, "Oh sir! What's amiss?"

He started round, frowning now at her—a thin girl at her most awkward raw stage, and looking younger than her fifteen years.

She said, with her eyes on his, "I would do anything for you, Master Aske."

He flushed at that, though she did not. "What a child!" he thought, and felt suddenly warm toward her, forgetting for a moment that she was Margaret Cheyne's sister.

"That's a large offer," he said lightly, but yet he was moved, though he did not come near to guessing how amply true her words were.

She repeated, "What is amiss?" and the frown returned to his face as he looked up the dale to where the great hump of Calva drowsed in the heat.

She thought that he was not going to answer, and she had no other words to move him, but suddenly he began to speak. It was about statutes, laws, Parliament, Thomas Cromwell, the bishops, the King. In all this she did not follow him well, but when he spoke of headings and hangings, and, driving the words through his teeth, of butchering deeds that he had himself seen done, then she understood only too well and felt her face and her very heart grow cold from fear, even when he broke off short and muttered, "No need for you to know these things." But it was as if she had always known them.

After a while he turned to her again with a sharp, bitter look.

"This is treason now, by these new laws, only to speak as I have done to you."

"You will not speak so to others," she urged him, and he shook his head and turned away. To Will Wall he had spoken, because Will would betray him as soon as his own hand, and now he was speaking to this child and it did not occur to him to wonder why.

"So," he said bitterly, and shrugged, "we have now taken that oath."

She said, eagerly, "Why! Yes!" being thankful to find him disposed to talk of such a harmless, unbloodied topic as an oath. "We took it in the chapter house, each one of us. The prioress said we should, or the house would suffer."

"That was how we all took it. Priests and monks so that the church should not suffer, and I—"

"Oh!" she cried, "Oh! your hand!"

He looked down at it. His knuckles were bleeding where he had struck his fist against the coping of the bridge. He put it to his mouth and then lowered it to tell her, "It's nothing," and whipped it behind his back as he saw Dame Eleanor and Dame Bess bearing down on them, and the two priory servants carrying baskets and bundles.

That afternoon when the novice mistress set the girls their task of reading, July asked that she might read in the book called *The Revelation of Divine Love*, and when told she might, fetched it, and settled herself in very studious solitude apart from the others.

She had feared that the pages for her reading might be prescribed, but no, she was free to choose, and it did not take her long to find the place that she wanted, and to slip into it, unnoticed of any, the foxglove cup which she had taken from Master Aske's finger.

When she had done that she let out a soft breath of relief. This doing of hers was a spell or an invocation—she didn't know which. But as the poisonous foxglove had no power to harm him "so," she thought, "if I lay it on that page, among those very words, and it stays safe there, he shall be safe." Not even to herself would she own what it was against which she wished to assure him, but seeing that he was dearest, she must fear for him always the worst.

To comfort and give herself confidence she read over many times that afternoon the words in which the charm consisted, turning back again and again to where the foxglove cup, limp now and flat, lay pressed between two pages.

"See I am God," the book said—

See I am in all things. See I do all things. See I never left my hands of my works ne never shall without end: see I lead all things to the end that I ordained it to, fro without beginning, by the same might, wisdom, and love, that I made it with. How should anything be amiss?

October 1

"Get me out the King's letter. There is the key."

The archbishop dropped the key of the painted coffer on the table and went away to the window. There was little there to be seen but rain driving before the wind, the tossing branches of the trees and leaves that streamed away among the rain.

The little wainscoted room, with its books, and viol on one table and recorder on the livery cupboard, and the brightly burning fire, was much pleasanter, but it was unwillingly that Dr. Cranmer moved back to the table where his secretary had laid out the King's letter. It was dated just a fortnight ago, and this was not the first time that the archbishop's secretary had taken it out of the coffer, and afterward laid it there again, with its command not yet fulfilled.

The archbishop stooped over it, as though he must read it through in order to master it; his secretary picked up a quill and tried the nib on his nail. He kept as much of his attention on that as was necessary not to seem to watch his master, but enough of it was free to make him raise his head as the archbishop lifted his eyes from the letter.

"If," said the archbishop, "I should put it to His Grace once more how the Scripture may be so interpreted, and indeed I think truly so interpreted, indeed I do—" He lost himself and began again. "If I put it to him and show him in Scripture how the bishop's jurisdiction is by the law of God—"

He waited, but the secretary seemed now to be completely absorbed in testing the quill.

"You think I should not?" The secretary almost imperceptibly shook his head.

"There are," the archbishop admitted, "other ways of interpreting the same Scripture." He sighed. "And if our jurisdiction come neither from Scripture, nor from the bishop of Rome, as none holds now, then is Master Cromwell true to his logic when he argueth that it must come from the King, and so, by the King may be intermitted."

He drew a quick breath as though he had reached a decision, and said, "Write—'To the bishop of Winchester.'"

But after that he got no further. He stood up and began to roam round the room.

"It is strange," he said, speaking to the secretary, but looking into the fire. "It is strange and new that the bishop's visitation of their own dioceses should be inhibited, and Master Cromwell visit here and there throughout my province. It is very strange— I did not think . . ." He coughed.

"What other letters are there?" he asked.

The secretary said letters from Lord Lisle and others about the weirs in Hampshire.

"A troublesome business," says the archbishop. "Read me the letters."

When the letters about the weirs had been answered it was time for the archbishop to go to dinner. The secretary locked up the King's letter in the painted coffer and gave the key to his master.

"Tomorrow," said the archbishop, "I shall write to the bishops what is the King's command."

October 5

The nuns' priest had been back at the priory for a week. He had told the prioress, in private, that his conscience was quieted, and he rattled past the omitted words in the Office so confidently that it was plain he had well rehearsed the new Office. Rarely, before he went away, had he had anything to do with Gib Dawe, but today, meeting him by the churchyard gate, he brought Gib up to his snug room, where a fire burnt pleasantly and there was a jug of French wine in the cupboard.

The nuns' priest told him to sit down, and poured out some of the wine for each, and then began to talk about the woman Malle and her visions. He said that he wanted to know Sir Gilbert's opinion, and in the caressing way he had he patted Gib's bony forearm with his plump, smooth hand; but it seemed rather that he wished to tell Gib that he himself thought visions to be awkward, chancy things to deal with. "Marry," said he, "though she be no nun of Kent, seeing visions of Kings and Queens to bring her to the gallows, still less would I be as those unhappy priests who were hanged together with the nun," and his hand went down to his silver-plated belt and caressed the roundness under it, as if he reassured his belly against the executioner's knife and scrabbling hand. Indeed it seemed that his thoughts had gone that way, for he shuddered, and for a minute his face became quite pinched and pale.

"So," said he, "I would have naught to do with these things, but I think to warn the Lady that there is much talk of them, which, I believe, she doth not hear."

"And also," said the nuns' priest, reaching out for his wine, "what has this poor soul seen and heard but common folk and common things—neither saints nor angels, nor our Lady and her Son throned in bliss, but a young poor man, and simple shepherds? And not in church neither, but openly in the dale. Mass! It's not seemly."

He tipped up his can and drank, and Gib watched his throat working as the wine ran down; it was a thick throat and above it a plump, close-shaven jowl. Gib got up abruptly.

"Seemly?" said he, very harsh. "And what were those holy shepherds but plain, poor, homespun men such as our shepherds today? And what was the Lord himself but a carpenter's son that swinked and sweated over a bench?" He stopped, and even in his anger must laugh at the way the other's jaw had dropped at his fierceness.

"So you believe," said the little fat priest, "that these be true visions?"

Gib began to say that he did, but that was purely out of contrariness; it was long since he had put any faith in Malle's visions, and honesty pulled him up short, so that he had nothing better to say than "Tsha!" He left the nuns' priest by the fire with the wine at his elbow, and a dish of filberts, and a book of tales beside him on the bench, and went out into the wind, and into a cold driving rain that had begun to fall.

At the parsonage house the chimney was smoking and the pottage was burnt. It was a very scurvy dinner. Then Wat managed to trip and spill some of his pottage over Gib's shoe. Gib got up and beat him, and throwing him into the shed beyond the dairy, shot the bolt on him. But when he came back to the house place he could still hear Wat's whimpering, and after a bit he took his own bowl and tipped what was in it onto the fire, making a worse foul stink than ever.

After that he sat with his arms tight about his knees, staring before him at the bunches of herbs hanging from the rafters, a long string of onions, and the ox harness for the plow.

He wished he could have denounced the nuns' priest for unbelief, but himself he could not believe the visions, though not for the same reason. That talk of the young men going up to Keld, which had seemed to mean freedom, he had long put away from him. And surely, if God showed visions to any these days, it would be of threatenings of wrath and judgment. An angel with a burning sword, devils dragging rich men to hell—these he could have readily believed. But Malle, so far as he could hear, had talked only of bliss and of peace. Wat's whimpering went on and Gib shifted his shoulders as if something galled him. To be rid of it he went and fetched the book of the Scriptures and, opening at the Book of the Revelation, read of the casting down of Babylon. As a background to the mighty winds and trumpets of that Book his mother breathed hard at the pain that gnawed her belly, and sometimes groaned; occasionally Wat cried out, but at last he seemed to fall asleep.

October 8

The two ambassadors of his most Christian Majesty, Francis I of France, to the King of England, sat together at a table on which their wine stood among a litter of paper, pens, and ink. Monseigneur Antoine de Castelnau, bishop of Tarbes, had been writing with his own hand instructions for his fellow, the bailly of Troyes, who tomorrow would return to France to report to their master. The instructions lay now spread out before them, sprinkled over with fine powder of cuttlefish shell, ground small, to dry the ink. As they waited, the bishop stretched out a hand for his wine; it was in a goblet of Venice glass, and it was wine of his own country; he held it toward the candle flames till the edges grew translucent, with a glorious color. Then he lifted it to his mouth, breathed in the faint, vinous aroma, and at last drank.

"Hah!" said he pensively, "I know the vineyard where those grapes grew," and his mind saw it, and the bleached rocks of the higher hills above, while his eyes rested on the lined and bearded face of the bailly. "And you will be home in time for the vintage." He sighed, and began to talk about a new vineyard he had planted, and a garden at a small house in the hills which was very dear to him. Outside a wild wind caught the notes of the chimes from a nearby church, swinging them close and away as if they had been a shaken banner of sound. After the chimes ceased there came the sharp rattle of heavy rain upon the window, and smoke swirled out from the hearth.

The bishop recalled himself from his thoughts of France, and none too soon, for the bailly, an impatient man, was drumming his fingers on the table edge. The bishop tipped the powder back from the paper into the box, blew the last grains from the page, and gathered the other sheets together.

"As I see it," he said, "our master can do what he will with this King, so great is King Harry's need of a friend, and so many his enemies."

The bailly nodded shortly. All this was in the written instructions, but he knew the bishop too well to think that he would get off without a repetition of it, unless he avoided that by taking his leave; but the bishop's wine was good and plenty, and while this storm of rain lasted he would remain; better the bishop's prosings than to be abroad, exposed to this sacred climate of England.

"If any Prince, the Emperor or another—"

"What other?" the bailly cried scornfully.

"If there were any other. If any Prince were to take up the quarrel of the Queen Katherine and her daughter, the people love them so well they would rise."

"Hm!" said the bailly.

"Such is the opinion of noblemen, and commons; yea, and I have heard it spoken even by the King his servants. You yourself—"

"They talk," said the bailly.

"There's too much talk to take lightly. See how openly the poor folk cry out against this Queen Anne, calling her—" He hesitated, and the bailly with his curt laugh supplied a string of names which the poor folk, and others not so poor, called Queen Anne.

The bishop held up his hand. "There is also the subversion of religion. Also this terrible weather, whereby the harvest's half destroyed."

"*Mordieu!*" said the bailly. "You do not need to tell me about the weather."

"And they fear also an interruption of trade with the Emperor's countries. That, with the scarcity of bread, would be a shrewd blow, especially if our master were to refuse corn. And if the Emperor were to move war—"

"He will not," said the bailly.

The archbishop was nettled. "How do you know?" he inquired tartly. "If he does, they will rise for the old Queen and the Princess, but especially for the Princess. Be very sure you make our master understand how they still, notwithstanding all the laws made in their Parliament, count her as Princess. And especially tell him of those citizens' wives that came about her when she was brought last from that palace down the river, weeping and crying out that she was still Princess, whatever laws the men might make."

The bailly, during the pause in which the bishop took another sip of wine, turned his head to listen. There was now no sound of rain on the windows. He stood up.

"Tell him also," said the bishop, "how all, even gentlemen at court, at first believed that we came to pronounce excommunication against the King, and that they prayed for us."

The bailly had taken up the written instructions, folded them, and slipped them into the breast pocket of his doublet. Now as he buttoned himself again he said, "It is written here," and he tapped his breast.

Yet the bishop followed him to the door, and held him there with a hand on his shoulder, still telling him how all England, and the Princess Mary herself, thought of nothing but that marriage of the Princess to the Dauphin should at last be made, and so save the Princess her rights.

When the bailly had twitched his shoulder free and gone, the bishop came back to the table. He burnt all the half-written sheets that lay there, and then settled himself comfortably with a book and his wine. But now and again his mind would go back to the small house and its garden, and the vineyards round about, and above the vineyards little woods of pines, where, when the singing of the vintagers ceased, you heard the warm, dry note of the cicadas.

November 20

M. Chapuys's servant was shaving him, when his discreet Burgundian secretary knocked and came in. He remained near the door, but Chapuys could see who it was in the wall mirror, and said, "Another ten minutes, Philippe," and gave his face again to the razor.

But the secretary did not go away, and the ambassador, waving the servant off, turned to look at him. Then he saw that the sober and correct M. Philippe had his cap in his hands, and the cap was full of brown eggs.

"And have you been robbing a farmyard?" asked M. Chapuys pleasantly, but the secretary told him "No," and came nearer so that he stood between his master and the man who was shaving him. "A countrywoman is below, who brought these eggs," he said; but unseen by the servant his finger pointed at a little posy of late flowers that lay among the eggs. There were a few marigolds, tied up with some pansy leaves.

"Ah!" said the ambassador, "I'll buy them. Go and bring her in." And to the servant, "Make haste."

"She is within," Philippe said, and went and sat down by the door with the cap full of eggs, and the posy in which were marigolds for Mary and pansies for Pole, between his respectable black knees.

The servant found his master hurried and fidgety that morning. "That'll do. That'll do," he said, and caught up the towel to wipe off the last of the lather from his face. "Come, truss up these points. Now, the sanguine gown. No. I'll not stay for a doublet."

Then the ambassador and his secretary passed out into the big room that looked over Cheapside, M. Chapuys in shirt and hosen and loose gown, though he was used to dress early and always with the most exact care.

"Is she from the marchioness?" he asked as soon as the door was shut behind them. A fortnight ago the Marchioness of Exeter had sent her chaplain to tell the ambassador that the King threatened to have done at last with Queen Katherine and Princess Mary.

"She does not speak."

"Dumb?"

The secretary allowed himself the slightest smile and shake of the head.

"You said a countrywoman?"

"She has a basket, and garments convenable."

"But—?"

"Her hands are not such as brew, bake, and milk kine."

"Bring her here."

When she came in, following the secretary, Chapuys saw a small plump woman with a big white veil flapping on each side of her face, a gray homespun petticoat, a brown kirtle hitched up on one side over a stout leather belt, and strong shoes. The shoes were too big for her, and when he looked at her hands he saw that Philippe was right. She carried a basket, but even as he looked at her she held it out to him, and, from that instinctive gesture of one used to be served, he knew who she was.

"My lady!" he said, and led her to a chair, and poured out wine, and served her himself. The Burgundian secretary had gone out softly, and Chapuys knew that now he would be keeping the door.

The marchioness drank, and set the cup down, and he noted that her hand shook.

"My lord marquess would have come," she said, "but I said he must not, for he might be known."

Chapuys nodded. The marquess with his great height and long sad face was hard to disguise.

"Therefore I came myself—so that I may make you believe the danger—the danger—the danger I sent word of a fortnight ago."

"Madame, I do believe it. I promise you on God's Passion."

"I thought that perhaps when I sent that message you did not believe." She looked hard at him. "But you must make the Emperor believe."

He said, "Tell me, madame, what I shall tell him from you and my lord marquess."

She gripped her hands together at her breast and told him. The King was determined, when Parliament met again (and but for the sickness it would have been sitting now), that the Queen Katherine and her daughter should follow where Fisher and More had gone; and on the same charge, for neither had they sworn the oath.

"And he will do it. I heard him swear by God's Majesty that he'd do it, if he lost his crown in the doing. Sir," the marchioness looked up into Chapuys's attentive, serious face, "sometimes I think he is mad—or all the world is mad—or I myself."

Chapuys shook his head.

"The Queen—" he began, meaning Queen Katherine, but the marchioness mistook him, since at court "the Queen" had for so long meant Queen Anne.

"Jesu! yes!" she said. "It is Anne Boleyn that has done all this. And now works against the Princess. She hates her the more because she fears her."

"Fears her?"

"She has heard a prophecy of which she told us all, openly. There were her maids, and other ladies, not a few gentlemen, and that pretty singing fellow Smeton sitting at her feet. I did not hear how they came to talk of it, but I heard her say, 'No, by the Mass, I do not love my stepdaughter Mary. And,' says she, 'I know well that she is my death and I am hers; for so it is by the stars.' Then she laid her hand on Mark Smeton's head, toying and tugging at his curls. 'Therefore,' quod she, 'I will take good care that she shall not laugh at *me* when I am dead.' And she began to laugh."

The marchioness shivered. "She would laugh indeed if the Princess died."

"Madame," Chapuys tried to comfort himself and her, "God will preserve from harm those two good ladies."

"God," the marchioness said with bitterness, "is very patient. He did not preserve neither the bishop of Rochester nor Sir Thomas More, nor yet the brethren of the Charterhouse. It is the Emperor who must—"

"I will write," he told her eagerly, yet when she had gone he wondered whether the Emperor's patience might not exceed even that of God. The doubt did not however prevent him writing a letter which was most urgent and energetic in asking help for Queen Katherine and the Princess.

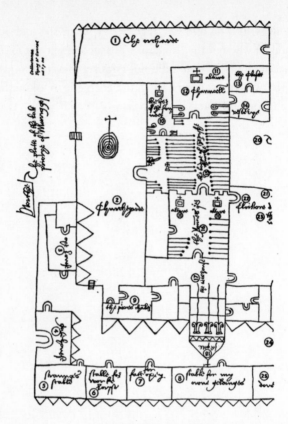

MARRICK PRIORY.

From a plan drawn up probably about fifty years after the Dissolution.
(Reproduced from Collectanea Topographica et Genealogica, 1838.)

1. The orcharde.	8. stable for my owne
2. Churchyarde.	geldinges.
3. oxe house.	9. the priores chamber.
4. gate house.	10. the quier of the
5. straungers stable.	founder.
6. table for worke horsse.	11. altare.
7. for fatt oxen.	12. Chancell.

13. the Closett.
14. vestereye.
15. the bodye of the
   paryshe churche.
16. the Nonnes quier.
17. the bell house.
18. stepell.

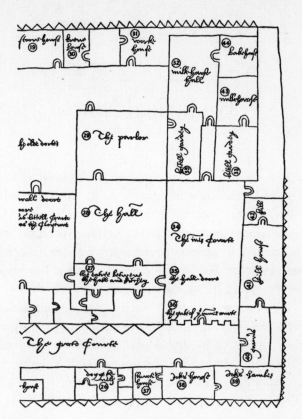

19. stoore house.
20. The olde dorter.
21. wall doore.
22. Cloistore doore.
23. This littell Courte was the Cloisture.
24. The grate Courte.
25. dove house.
26. dogge kenels.
27. the entree betwene the hall and the kitchen.
28. The hall.
29. The parlor.
30. brewe house.
31. worke house.
32. milk house hall.
33. littell gardne.
34. The inner Courte.
35. the hall doore.
36. the gate of the inner courte.
37. slawter house.
38. Joks house.
39. Joks chamber.
40. garners.
41. Still house.
42. Still.
43. milk house.
44. bake house.

Historical Note

A great many historical persons appear in this book, of whom Henry VIII, Katherine of Aragon, Anne Boleyn, Cardinal Wolsey, Thomas Cromwell, Princess Mary, Sir Thomas More, and Archbishop Cranmer are the best known. Not all, but many of the episodes in which they appear are founded upon documentary evidence. To take a few examples: much of Foxe's report to the cardinal in 1528 is drawn from the letters of the English agents in Rome; what Queen Katherine said to Montfalconnet, to the nobles and clergy in 1531, and to Mountjoy was reported to the Emperor by his ambassador; Anne Boleyn's arrival at the Tower in 1536 and her conversation with Kingston were described by Kingston to the King.

The description of Marrick nunnery is founded upon the late sixteenth century plan, reproduced on pp. 504–5, as well as upon local knowledge. The names of the prioress and her nuns are drawn from the (slightly longer) list of those pensioned at the Dissolution. Owing to delays in publication caused by the war Archbishop Lee's last visitation of the nunnery was not available for reference, but though there is little evidence for the character of the prioress, that little is interesting, and, I think, suggestive of her personality.

Much of Lord Darcy's life is known from documents; these have been used in this reconstruction, and his rather puzzling character inferred from them. On the other hand Julian Savage and Gilbert Dawe are imagined and without any historical foundation. Of Robert Aske's life before 1536 practically nothing is known except his connection with the Percys and his entrance into Gray's Inn; his association with Margaret Cheyne is entirely fictitious. Margaret herself is, however, historical, though it is doubtful if she was in fact a daughter of Buckingham. The events of her life, again with the exception of her relations with Robert Aske, are taken from contemporary documents. From these I had already supposed her character when I found my supposition confirmed by the fact that up to the early years of the nineteenth century she was still remembered in Yorkshire under the name of Madge Wildfire.

For the Pilgrimage of Grace, in which the historical theme of the book culminates, there is a mass of evidence, so that almost all the scenes connected with the rising are founded upon documents. To take some instances: Robert Aske's report to the King gives an account of his own movements during the first few days of his connection with the Lincolnshire rising. Lancaster Herald described his mission to Pontefract in a long document, much of which has been used verbatim; the Duke of Norfolk's dealings with the leaders of the pilgrimage are revealed in his own letters and in such confessions as that of Cresswell. Aske's replies to examination in the Tower throw much light both on his character and on the motives of the pilgrims, and I have made use of these, as well as of many other depositions, though unfortunately, again owing to the war, I could not, except in a very few instances, go behind the printed version to the original manuscript.

To indicate to what degree and where this book reproduces authentic history would need, however, far greater space than can be spared in a note. This is a novel, and much in it is, necessarily, imaginary. But I have been scrupulous to preserve undistorted any fact known to me, with two minor exceptions.* In broad outline the account which I have given of historical events is as correct as I have been able to make it, and there are besides, indistinguishable to the reader among the imaginary scenes and persons, many such intimate yet authentic facts as the devotion of Aske's servant to his master, the dislike of Anne Boleyn for monkeys, or the quarrel of Mr. Patchett's servant with the ostler at Cambridge. The music of the song in *Part 2* on p. 418 may be found on page 509, reproduced from the *Antiquaries' Journal*, vol. XV, 1935, p. 21.

---

*[Some information in this note may spoil *Part 2* if you have not read it.— Ed.] The name of Robert Aske's servant was Robert Wall, but the name was changed to avoid confusion. The disposition of the buildings of St. Helen's, Bishopsgate, was not that which is here described. In one important particular I have differed from other writers upon the Pilgrimage of Grace. My authority for the King's vengeance upon Robert Aske is Wriothesley's detailed account of the execution of the leaders of the pilgrimage, in which he mentions the punishment which each received, and distinguishes between the hanging of Sir Robert Constable and that of Robert Aske (Wriothesley I, 65).

Questions for Reflection and Discussion

Use the following questions as guides to deeper individual understanding of the novel or for group discussion.

1. Katherine of Aragon has just given birth to a daughter, and there is apparent peace and happiness between Katherine and her husband, King Henry VIII. What indications does the author give that all is not well in their relationship? (47; March 19, 1516)

2. How does Prescott introduce Lord Darcy? (64–73) What is Darcy's greatest regret? How comfortable will Darcy be in the ways in which power will be used in Henry's court?

3. How does Darcy react to the way Henry is beginning to use his power? (84–86; May 19, 1521)

4. How does the author show that the relationship between Henry and Katherine is now suffering? In what ways is Anne Boleyn beginning to influence Henry? (101–7; November 19, 1524)

5. How would you describe Julian "July" Savage's relationship with her family? (108–18)

6. In what ways does Christabel show that she sees her job as managing the priory and not being too concerned for the needs of others? (131–33; December 31, 1526)

7. How does Darcy hear of the growing disenchantment of Henry with Cardinal Wolsey and the growing influence of Anne Boleyn? (171–75; October 1, 1527)

8. What implications does Cardinal Wolsey see in the pope's unwillingness to grant him the power to annul Henry's marriage with Katherine? (183–87; May 3, 1528)

9. What does the conversation between Robert "Robin" Aske and his colleague begin to reveal about his character? (193–96; November 10, 1528)

10. Describe the character of Gib Dawe. How do his failings make him susceptible to the teachings of Brother Laurence? (200–2; January 4, 1529)

11. Describe Henry's reaction to seeing the wealth Cardinal Wolsey had accumulated from closing the monasteries. (224–27; October 24, 1529)

12. What are Christabel's first thoughts when she is elected Prioress of Marrick? (248–50; July 28, 1530)

13. Describe Katherine's reaction to the announcement that Henry has been proclaimed "Sole Protector and Supreme Head of the Church and Clergy of England." What are the implications for her? (262–64; February 11, 1531)

14. What is Henry's reaction to Katherine's plea for reconciliation? (280–82; July 25, 1531)

15. In what way did July's chance meeting with Robert "Robin" Aske begin to give her some hope for herself? (288–291; October 30, 1531)

16. How does Christabel deal with the stories she has been hearing about Gib Dawe? (299–303; January 8, 1532)

17. Describe the ways in which Katherine seems to be living in denial of her situation. (321–23; May 20, 1532)

18. How does Prioress Christabel show herself to be a shrewd manager of the priory's affairs? How will she spend the money? What does it say about her values? (328–33; July 15, 1532)

19. As Cromwell and Darcy ride through London, what do they hear that disturbs Cromwell? What is Darcy's reaction when he realizes who the speaker is? (349–52; May 29, 1533)

20. Describe the signs that the relationship between the King and Anne Boleyn will be troubled as they move ahead. (352–59; June 8, 1533)

21. What does the birth of Elizabeth foretell for the future of Anne Boleyn? (371–72; September 6, 1533)

22. What are signs of growing concern in Katherine's court? (410–12; January 20, 1534)

23. Describe the nature of the oath that all English people were required to take. What is Robert Aske's reaction to his own taking of the oath? (416–18; April 16, 1534)

24. Describe July's reaction on hearing the readings of Christ's suffering for sins of the world. (421–24; June 2, 1534)

25. What is the tone of Henry's ongoing relationship with Anne Boleyn? (428–30; August 20, 1534)

26. What are some of the indications that Lord Darcy may be ready to act on his concerns with Henry's policies? (435–40; September 30, 1534)

27. How does the author show the growing isolation of Anne Boleyn in Henry's court? (446–48; February 2, 1535)

28. Compare the reaction of King Henry and Robert Aske to the execution of the Carthusian monks who had refused to take the oath that Henry required. (451–53; May 4, 1535)

29. In his hearing before his peers, what does Thomas More say sealed his fate? (467–69; July 1, 1535)

30. How does Gib Dawe react to the loving message that Malle speaks about in her visions? (492–95; October 5, 1535)

About the Author

Hilda Frances Margaret Prescott was born in Latchford, Cheshire, on February 22, 1896, the daughter of an Anglican clergyman. A brilliant student, she studied modern history at Oxford University and medieval history at Manchester University, receiving master's degrees from both institutions.

Prescott taught in private schools for a time but in 1923 gave up full-time teaching for writing, though she maintained a connection with Oxford University as a tutor in history. Her first novel, *The Unhurrying Chase,* was published in 1925, followed by *The Lost Fight* in 1928 and *Son of Dust* in 1932. Each of these historical novels is set in medieval France and centers on a moral and sexual conflict in the midst of a harsh feudal world. All three novels were praised for their historical depth and their style, "a constant careful beauty which from the first page marks her work as both unusual and distinctive," as the *New Statesman* put it.

Prescott's most acclaimed work was *The Man on a Donkey,* a powerful historical novel of early Reformation England published in two volumes in 1952. Set mainly in Yorkshire, the novel is a multifaceted historical panorama of the Roman

Catholic reaction against the new religious policies of Henry VIII. *Commonweal* lauded the book as "a profoundly moving chronicle, a beautifully executed piece of literature, and a massively impressive work of power, sensitivity, and drama." Prescott also received acclaim for *Spanish Tudor: The Life of Bloody Mary,* a biography of Mary Tudor that won her the James Tait Black Memorial Prize.

While many of her historical novels are engrossing epics of romance and adventure, H. F. M. Prescott lived a quiet life for many years in Charlbury, Oxfordshire. A committed member of the Church of England, she had a great fondness for travel and the English countryside. She died in 1972.

LOYOLA CLASSICS

Catholics	Brian Moore	978-0-8294-2333-4	$12.95
Cosmas or the Love of God	Pierre de Calan	978-0-8294-2395-2	$12.95
Dear James	Jon Hassler	978-0-8294-2430-0	$12.95
The Devil's Advocate	Morris West	978-0-8294-2156-9	$12.95
Do Black Patent Leather Shoes Really Reflect Up?	John R. Powers	978-0-8294-2143-9	$12.95
The Edge of Sadness	Edwin O'Connor	978-0-8294-2123-1	$13.95
Five for Sorrow, Ten for Joy	Rumer Godden	978-0-8294-2473-7	$13.95
Helena	Evelyn Waugh	978-0-8294-2122-4	$12.95
In This House of Brede	Rumer Godden	978-0-8294-2128-6	$13.95
The Keys of the Kingdom	A. J. Cronin	978-0-8294-2334-1	$13.95
The Last Catholic in America	John R. Powers	978-0-8294-2130-9	$12.95
The Man on a Donkey, Part 1	H. F. M. Prescott	978-0-8294-2639-7	$13.95
The Man on a Donkey, Part 2	H. F. M. Prescott	978-0-8294-2731-8	$13.95
Mr. Blue	Myles Connolly	978-0-8294-2131-6	$11.95
North of Hope	Jon Hassler	978-0-8294-2357-0	$13.95
Saint Francis	Nikos Kazantzakis	978-0-8294-2129-3	$13.95
The Silver Chalice	Thomas Costain	978-0-8294-2350-1	$13.95
Son of Dust	H. F. M. Prescott	978-0-8294-2352-5	$13.95
Things As They Are	Paul Horgan	978-0-8294-2332-7	$12.95
The Unoriginal Sinner and the Ice-Cream God	John R. Powers	978-0-8294-2429-4	$12.95
Vipers' Tangle	François Mauriac	978-0-8294-2211-5	$12.95

Readers,

We'd like to hear from you! What other classic Catholic novels would you like to see in the Loyola Classics series? Please e-mail your suggestions and comments to **loyolaclassics@loyolapress.com** or mail them to:

Loyola Classics
Loyola Press
3441 N. Ashland Avenue
Chicago, IL 60657

A Special Invitation

Loyola Press invites you to become one of our Loyola Press Advisors! Join our unique online community of people willing to share with us their thoughts and ideas about Catholic life and faith. By sharing your perspective, you will help us improve our books and serve the greater Catholic community.

From time to time, registered advisors are invited to participate in online surveys and discussion groups. Most surveys will take less than ten minutes to complete. Loyola Press will recognize your time and efforts with gift certificates and prizes. Your personal information will be held in strict confidence. Your participation will be for research purposes only, and at no time will we try to sell you anything.

Please consider this opportunity to help Loyola Press improve our products and better serve you and the Catholic community. To learn more or to join, visit **www.SpiritedTalk.org** and register today.

—The Loyola Press Advisory Team